what
you
wish
for

Also by Kerry Reichs

Leaving Unknown
The Best Day of Someone Else's Life

what
you
wish
for

KERRY
REICHS

WILLIAM MORROW

An Imprint of HarperCollins*Publishers*

P.S.™ is a trademark of HarperCollins Publishers.

HarperCollins books may be purchased for educational, business, or sales promotional use. For information please write: Special Markets Department, Harper-Collins Publishers, 10 East 53rd Street, New York, NY 10022.

FIRST EDITION

Designed by Diahann Sturge

Library of Congress Cataloging-in-Publication Data has been applied for.

ISBN 978-0-06-180814-2

12 13 14 15 16 OV/RRD 10 9 8 7 6 5 4 3 2 1

For Declan Rex Reichs,
who is everything I wished for and more

Acknowledgments

This book would not exist without many families. A million thanks to my publishing family: my incomparable agents, Dorian Karchmar, Cathryn Summerhayes, Lauren Whitney, Anna DeRoy, and Tracy Fisher; and my stellar team at William Morrow, Carrie Feron, Liate Stehlik, and Tessa Woodward. Luminaries one and all.

A writer needs a family of readers, and no book of mine would be possible without Ted Robertson and Alastair Sadler. (Welcome to the world, Finn and Matilda!)

Single Mothers by Choice introduced me to a clan of remarkable women who struggle a little harder to have the family they want. I salute all single and nontraditional parents. I hope this book can in some small way break down the misperception that there is one "best" form of family.

I rely on the shared experience of my family of friends. Amanda Clark and Althea Lean gave birth to parts of this novel while hiking along the Great Wall of China. Jessica Gibson shared a different perspective. Monique Moore shared Charlie the adorable chin-wa. I learned from Dan Savage's excellent *The Kid*. I suffered for my art at the Trapeze School of New York. My team of "experts" responded to regular requests for input: Veronique, Kirsten, Emma, Page, Kristen, Karina, Kathy, Christina, Trish, Caren, Andrea, Cass, Jen, Ruth, Jane, Lisa, Wendi, Lori, Lesley, Gabi, Britlin, Missy, Hillary, Sabina,

Sabrina, Stacey, Tasha, Leslie, Michael, Monique, Sharon, Sara, Jamie, Janelle, Kimberly, Hiwa, Tricia, Tammi, Amy, Heather, Julia, Ann, Leigh, Mina, Christelle, Sandra, among others.

I'm grateful to my "extended family" for helping a single mom get it all done: Ines Rodas, Rebecca Fry, Kathryn Chinnock, Anil Zenginoglu, the Milhollin family, Matt Gavin and Holidae Hayes, Martha Whitley, Lisa Hopson, the Meridian Hill Coop, and All Souls Church of DC. Katie Worthman is the glue that holds it all together.

Last but not least, I thank my actual family. My parents, Kathy and Paul, are supportive beyond measure. Courtney, Brooks, Brendan, Emily, and Henry surround me with love, as does my boisterous extended clan in Chicago and Texas. Most of all, I'm grateful for my son, Declan, who is, simply, everything.

what
you
wish
for

Dimple Wants a Change

I have a baby shower, sort of an afternoon/
evening thing, so unfortunately I can't get
together Saturday night.

I looked at the clock and the calendar on my desk to verify
the ordinariness of everything but the e-mail, making sure I
hadn't tumbled into a parallel dimension where men scrap-
booked and women peed standing up. Nope. My new tampon
box was on the counter where I'd tossed it.

It didn't take a genius to figure this one out. A healthy adult
male such as my, apparently former, boyfriend Tom choosing
Gerber party games over sex with me was more than a scheduling conflict. Men did not do baby showers. If they did, it was
a twenty-minute drive-by under duress, fleeing at the sight of
miniature rattles on pink icing. They did *not* pass their Saturday evening rocking the all-day-all-night shower. I'd received
a thinly disguised "Dear Dimple" letter.

Yes, Dimple. It's a terrible nickname, but the alternative,
Dimples, would be intolerable, leaving me with little choice
but to become a birthday clown, forever making people inde-
finably uncomfortable. In fact, I owned a matched set of girl-
ish dents, but from babyhood, I'd responded to most situations
with a speculative half smile, lifting only one corner of my lips
as if I wasn't sure a thing merited full two-dimple approbation.
Hence Dimple, singular.

My real name is Agnis. In a misguided fit of trying to repair a fractured relationship with her mother, my own named me after hers—Agnis Dýemma Bauskenieks. No one calls me that because it's a dreadful name for a baby, a name that should only be applied from age fifty onward. Since I'm an actress, I'll never become fifty. I'll also never have the last name Bauskenieks. Everyone calls me Dimple Bledsoe.

I called my agent.

"Freya Fosse." Herself barked into the phone.

"Demoted to answering your own phone?" I teased.

"Ugh. They're having cookies for somebody's something-or-other in the break room. I fled immediately but Brooke wanted to stay." Brooke was Freya's assistant. Freya was a petite, platinum Norwegian windstorm.

"I finally heard from Tom," I said.

"And?"

I told her.

"A baby shower? Like, a hen party where a fetus is about to come out of a woman's vagina and everyone coos over onesies and talks about breast milk?"

"Irrefutable, isn't it?"

She sighed. "I'm sorry to say it but . . . *incontrovertible* comes to mind." My mind's eye saw Freya lay down her Mont Blanc and straighten her posture in her black Arne Jacobsen chair. "Dimple. Tom is a perfectly . . . *respectable* person, but . . ."

I was glad she didn't go into ex-bashing. Tom *was* a perfectly nice person who didn't deserve to be vilified for failing to have strong feelings for me.

"The important thing is . . ." It must have been a slow day at the office for Freya because this quantity of uninterrupted personal talk was unusual. We were usually on work-related topics by minute three.

"Besides . . ."

I fell into the comforting rhythm of her speech. Maybe it was weird that I called my agent about a breakup but it was either her or my hairdresser. In my line of work, an impermeable watershed separates us from "ordinary" people. Aspiring actresses should hang on to their high school pals, because once you get on the talking box, everyone secretly wants to ask you about the time you met Julia Roberts, no matter how cool they play it. We aren't different, but tabloids triumph in catching actors Just Like Us. If they thought I was just like them, seeing me pump gas wouldn't be noteworthy. Instead, my parking ticket is news.

"Besides . . ."

I took guilty pleasure in being coddled by Freya. The Just Like Us thing and the long hours isolate actors. To be fair, the immigrant in me wouldn't be a hand-holding sharer if I had a legion of sympathetic ears. Pain was something I did behind closed doors. No matter how deeply you felt your personal tragedies, they didn't count for more than a mosquito bite in the face of real suffering. Darfur. Tsunami. Holocaust. That was real. That was malaria. My little welts didn't count.

"I'm confident . . ."

The truth was, Tom's most attractive quality had been that he was age appropriate and wanted kids. I didn't think I'd miss him. I was sorry the length of time between now and the possibility of having a baby multiplied exponentially. My biological age was outpacing the range I offered on my curriculum vitae, and while Wikipedia attributed me with only thirty-six years, the California Department of Vital Records knew the number 3 no longer factored into the equation.

"Nowadays you can't really dismiss online opportunities . . ."

At that comment I toggled over to look at the website I'd bookmarked. Visiting it was becoming a regular pastime. I considered what I sought in a profile.

"I have good news." Freya switched to shoptalk. "I had an interesting telephone call from Julian Wales. He directed that extremely well-received independent film *Pull*."

I snorted. "Of course I know who Julian Wales is. *Everyone* knows who Julian Wales is."

"He's sending over a script. He has you in mind for a role."

"Me?" Freya had my full attention.

"Why *not* you?"

I twisted my rope of hair. *Because I'm old,* I thought. But that was taboo in this line of work, akin to chumming the water. On paper I was still fabulously midthirties. "He won the Oscar for Best Director last year. I'm a TV actress."

"He met you at a party, and apparently you made quite an impression."

I remembered. A Hollywood rarity at six feet four inches, eyes that had to be described as piercing despite how naff that sounded, and steel neck cords supporting a bald head. My internal sexual beast, LaMimi, had woken up and tried to take the wheel but I'd held firm. One didn't give in to a pheromone-driven libido at a business event.

"Because I'm freakishly tall and could look him in the eye without craning?" In Hollywood I made most men look like they came from the Shire. As I spoke, I navigated to Julian Wales's IMDB website. Yes. He was tall. And handsome.

"Or because he could see without craning that those enormous brown eyes of yours beg to be gently lit on the big screen."

"He wants me to play a deer?"

Freya did a controlled exhale. "Let's wait for the script and see, why don't we?"

"Of course. This is very good news." My voice was measured but my stomach lurched. A movie. A *Julian Wales* movie. It could be huge. Risky.

"It's more than 'good news.' You've been looking for the perfect vehicle to move from television back to the big screen for a long time. Getting a part in Julian Wales's follow-up to *Pull* would be like taking an express Lamborghini to the stars. Think . . . *life changing.*"

"Mm-hmm," I agreed. She was right, though to be honest, she'd been the one looking for a movie while I rested comfortably in my current role. I toggled back to the website I'd been considering before. My stomach fluttered like I'd skipped to the edge of a cliff.

"Any actress your age would kill for this chance." Freya never pulled punches. "*He* came to *us.*"

"It's quite an opportunity." I refused to get excited.

"Think capital *O* Opportunity." Freya's voice carried a grandiose arm gesture.

I split my screen so I could look at both websites.

"This could be big, Dimple," Freya said. "Big change."

Julian Wales's penetrating eyes looked back from one. The wide-eyed baby on the home page for Hope Women's Health and Fertility Clinic looked back from the other.

Yes, I thought. This could be big change indeed.

Wyatt Rides the Bus

Wyatt looked up when a brunette boarded the bus at Georgina and Seventh, not far from UCLA. The bus was not crowded, but filling up, each row hosting a single rider. Wyatt slid his courier bag to the floor. After assessing the bus, the brunette settled next to Wyatt.

There was nothing threatening about Wyatt. He was Clark Kent with greying temples. Strong jaw, kind face. The suede patches on his elbows were neither retro nor ironic. If he was sporting a purple sequin jumpsuit, he'd still be the first guy you sat next to on a bus.

Wyatt was forty-eight and no one ever argued that it simply wasn't possible. His gold-rimmed glasses framed cobalt eyes. He was neither effeminate nor macho, he neither slouched nor strutted, he neither beamed nor frowned. Everything about him was . . . grounded. Men wanted him to marry their sisters. Their sisters wanted to marry him after the first reckless romance to the brooding musician ended in divorce. It would surprise observers to know that as a high school principal, this calm man commanded the obedience of a thousand teenagers. A disciplinarian at school, after the bell Wyatt was eminently likable.

Wyatt noted with approbation that the brunette was reading Chaucer. Homework no doubt, but it was better than something about vampires. Wyatt resisted commenting on the Chaucer, as that was what creepy and/or annoying people did. If it was his daughter, or one of his students, he could comment. But not a stranger on a bus. A life of public service had taught Wyatt the importance of boundaries. Once adopted, Wyatt's beliefs were firm. Which was what had brought him to being on the bus today.

It was very inconvenient timing. Wyatt normally rode his bicycle to school. He'd grown up in Minnesota, where he'd liked his upbringing, the farm, and for that matter, his parents, all just fine. He'd even liked his college and graduate school experience in the Middle. But he never wanted to live in a cold climate again. Wyatt was made for Southern California. He wasn't a barefoot kind of guy, and he didn't care if he saw the beach, but he'd push through dirt like a sugar beet for vast blue skies and a steadily shining sun. The whisper of palm fronds and bright fuchsia bougainvillea were a bonus. Palm trees! Fuchsia! He was a long way from St. Paul.

When he'd moved west twenty-odd years ago, his mother had asked, "Don't you get tired of sunny weather all the time? Don't you miss the seasons?"

To Wyatt, "seasons" was a delusional word representing "rain," "sleet," "soggy brown leaves gunking up the gutters," and "red-knuckled windshield scraping in subzero temperatures."

"No," was his unequivocal response. "I've adapted fine. The girls have long legs and wear shorts all year."

"But *California* . . ." Though her own sister had lived in California for decades, his mother viewed it as a strange and alien place.

"I still don't like tofu," he reassured her.

Wyatt missed his commonsense, beef-eating Midwestern parents. They'd died in the way of old married couples, one following the other. At seventy-eight. Barbara had broken her hip in a fall and never been well again. During the cold winter she'd contracted pneumonia and slipped away in her sleep to rest forever under a thick, quiet blanket of snow.

Wyatt's father, Hank, himself eighty-two, had soldiered on, continuing to work the farm, but Wyatt had sensed a vacancy. Wyatt suspected Hank stuck around only for his son, loath to leave him alone in the world. Despite this, Hank had followed his wife a mere six months later. As Wyatt buried Hank next to Barbara under waving autumn grasses, he wondered if his father saw September, the advent of the academic year, as the real beginning of a new year. It had always struck Wyatt as silly to herald the big leap from one year to the next in the unchanging dark of winter. But summer to fall—bounty to harvest to dead stalks in the field—now that was change. That signaled the death of one year and the long, slow gestation of the next. Wyatt suspected that harvest had signaled to farmer Hank the beginning of a new trip around the sun, twelve long months without Barbara, and he'd elected to quietly bow out after the sugar beets were reaped.

In California, there was no fall. September meant sharpened pencils, less surfing, perhaps a closed-toe shoe. The sun shone on. While the thought of never returning to Minnesota made Wyatt feel oddly untethered, he had his cousin Eva in Los Angeles and the relentless progression of bright seventy-degree days to console himself. After visiting Los Angeles for the first time, Wyatt had wondered why people lived in St. Paul and Ann Arbor. Didn't they *know*? Riding his bicycle to work was Wyatt's celebration that he could absorb his recommended daily allowance of vitamin D through the top of his head.

But not today. Today he had an appointment after school. More vexing, today was National Leave Your Car At Home Day. While he preferred not to drive, Wyatt had no aversion to it. Driving was expedient and practical, and often, in the sprawling city, necessary. On normal errand days, he'd add his Prius to the procession of irritated commuters on Sunset Boulevard. Today, however, Wyatt felt it was imperative to set an example for what he sought from his students. Wyatt had urged everyone to go green, and bus, bike, or walk to school. Which is why, despite the inconvenience, he was riding the bus.

"Don't worry about it," Ilana had said when he'd called.

"I hate to make you pick me up." Wyatt felt he should drive the lady.

"It's, like, no problem." She sounded relieved. Wyatt wondered if he was a bad driver. He did get distracted by his truant-officer eyes, scanning roadside youth. "Um, I'll pick ya up between three and four-thirty."

That was quite a range. "What time is the appointment?"

"Um, I gotta check the *specific* time, but if I get ya, like, between three and four-thirty, we'll be fine. It's not far to where it's at."

Wyatt winced at the dangling modifier, but let it go. She was a grown woman.

"Where is it?"

"Oh, ya know. Not far." Ilana wasn't big on precision. "So did'ja put that money into my account?"

"Yes. Six thousand for the test and another five thousand for various and sundry, correct?"

"Uh-huh."

"You could have the bills sent directly to me, and I'll take care of them." Wyatt didn't like the current arrangement, but he would discuss it in person.

She snorted. "I'd worry about looking cheaper than fourth-day bread. I'll bring receipts this afternoon, for ya know, your files or whatever."

"Do you think you might be a little more specific on when you plan to get here? Since you don't have a cell phone, I won't know when precisely you'll arrive. I'd hate to make you wait." Ilana thought cell phones caused brain tumors and refused to get one.

She smacked her gum. "Gee, I dunno. Traffic, ya know." She paused. "I could go by myself." Did she sound hopeful?

"No!" Wyatt modulated his voice not to spook her. "It's no problem. I'll be out front."

He would wait. It was no big deal. He suppressed his discomfort. It had been a long time since he was on this side of the power differential.

"O-kee. See ya!" she sang and hung up.

So they were set. She'd get him after classes and they would go together.

Wyatt came back to the present when the bus stopped not far from his school.

"Yo, Mr. O!" A shaggy adolescent cruised up the sidewalk as Wyatt alighted. "My wheels didn't use gas!" He gestured to his skateboard.

Wyatt took in his student's *Haywood Jablowmi* T-shirt and suppressed a wince. Not against the rules . . . technically. "That's wonderful, Dylan. You may have positively impacted the life of a polar bear cub. Certainly a smelt, at the very least."

"Rad!" The boy looked pleased as he kicked off on his board. Wyatt mused over what an odd blend of child and adult were high school students. They tested the boundaries of authority even as they sought the approbation of their elders, shaping themselves to stand alongside them. As he ascended the school steps, a knot of freshman girls peeked at him and giggled, blushing when he waved. Students in a rainbow of offensive and rebellious clothing called out their alternative methods of travel. He praised each one.

Wyatt strolled to his office, speculating on what form of rebellion his own son or daughter would demonstrate in adolescence, smiling as he unlocked his office door. His conjecture soon would be specific. Today he and Ilana would learn whether the baby was a boy or a girl.

Maryn Makes a Call

Maryn was overwhelmed with rage. She wanted to slappity-slap happy couples on the streets. She saw pregnant women and wanted to shout that they didn't appreciate their luck. She wanted to scream at a mother berating her child. You have no idea how good you have it, Maryn's anger accused. She wanted to yell at her bookkeeper for dodging his wife's call. Don't just avoid what you don't want to deal with, Maryn wanted to warn. You'll be sorry.

It wasn't that Maryn minded being alone in the world. Her parents had died years ago. They hadn't been particularly close and she didn't feel a keen loss. She didn't hate her ex-husband, Andy, though he was the cause of her current problems. It would be like being annoyed at the lawn mower rather than the neighbor who cranked it up at six AM. She didn't have the energy to hate his new wife, Summer, though Maryn found Summer's pretense of trying to re-create her boyish husband into "Andrew" laughable. Andy was a perpetual child, lovable and biddable. Pliable and forgettable. Maryn had been busy battling breast cancer when Andy left her, but it didn't pass her notice how quickly she'd adapted to his absence, how small the gap in her life, and how easily filled. No, she didn't hate Andy.

But now, five years after her divorce, Andy was driving Maryn to impotent rage. It was a gooey black presence, and she carried it like an alien in her stomach, aware that it might burst out at any time and savage an unsuspecting victim for the million hurts she sustained each day. It could be the secret smile on a woman as she rested a hand on her swollen belly. It could be a coworker showing off pictures of the family vacation to Yellowstone. It could be twentysomethings swearing they would never be single when they were forty. Hah! She wanted to shout, You think you know? Hah! Just wait and see what life does to you.

It didn't bother Maryn to be surrounded by younger, beautiful women. Los Angeles was teeming with them, but Maryn didn't consider it worth considering. Everyone was attractive when they were nineteen. She'd been a knockout herself. She'd had her fun. The hardest part of passing through her midthirties had been coming to terms with no longer being the most attractive person in the room. She was still good looking, sure, but in a mature way. She had wrinkles. She had a belly. She had one fake breast.

At first it had been hard to watch the formation of permanent lines around her mouth, between her brows. The slackening of her skin. The transformation of her hands into her mother's hands. But, she'd accepted it. Maryn didn't believe in lying about her age or in Botox. It seemed to her that if you were a great beauty when you were young, you went one of two ways in your forties. You could fight to preserve your youthful looks at all costs, pursuing plastic surgery, collagen, eyelid lifts, tummy tucks, chemical peels, liposuction, you name it. Or you could recognize that you'd had a good run and age as beautifully as you could. Maryn knew she couldn't compete with the nineteen-year-olds anymore. Or even the twenty-nine-year-olds. But she'd age into a good-looking older woman, probably better than most.

Don't get her wrong—her face lotion retailed at $98 per wafer-thin bottle, and she'd have Philippe keep her swinging auburn tresses free of grey as long as she was ambulatory. But Maryn didn't want to wage an all-out war against age. She'd expended a lot of energy, and one breast, to beat cancer. It seemed foolish to waste emotional wealth on a battle that you simply couldn't win. Maryn didn't believe in God particularly—not that she *didn't* believe in God, to be honest, it was more that she didn't think about him (or her)—but she sort of believed that when time eroded your looks, it was because God figured you had the strength of character not to care anymore. It never occurred to Maryn to wonder what strength of character God attributed to homely children, because, as a beauty, she'd never had to. There was a confidence in that as well. Marginal self-unawareness made life a little easier. Not that life was easy right now.

No, Maryn was fine with her wrinkles and the extortion she paid to touch up her roots. It was happiness that made her rage bubble over like oobleck, sticking to everything it contacted. This morning was textbook.

"Here's that electric stapler you wanted." Maryn had stopped by Staples.

"Oh my god!" her assistant Kay shrieked. "Is this the Swingline Optima?!"

The oobleck pressed on Maryn's brain. "I don't know. The guy picked it out."

"This is, like, totally awesome. It staples seventy sheets at a time. It's, like, the gold standard of staplers!" Kay effused. "I love it, I love it!"

"Jesus, get a life Kay, it's a stapler not a pony!"

"There's a lifetime warranty." Kay's voice was tiny.

Maryn felt like she'd trod on a kitten.

"I'm sorry. That was a terrible thing to say. I have a horrific headache." She'd fled to her office, and later given Kay a Starbucks gift certificate.

Maryn's problem, and the fount of her viscous rage, was impotence. Literally and figuratively, Maryn was impotent. Treatment for cancer had rendered her infertile. This didn't preclude having a child—she was capable of carrying an implanted embryo to term. And she had the embryos. *Of course* she'd planned for this eventuality. Prior to beginning her cancer treatment, Maryn and Andy had undergone the necessary procedures to freeze fertilized eggs. At thirty-four, it had been no problem. Maryn was as proficient in egg harvesting as she was in everything else. They'd easily secured a good number of follicles in a single procedure.

Maryn had done everything correctly and there was nothing to prevent her from unfreezing an embryo and having a child. While not in Maryn's life plan, the divorce didn't make a difference. Maryn wasn't intimidated about raising a child on her own. Andy had fled at the first sign of chemo vomit, and Maryn had fought off breast cancer alone. Pregnancy would be a walk in the park by comparison. A can of corn, as Andy would say.

Maryn was secure in her job as Vice President of a company that transported horses around the world. She liked to say, "There will always be wealth and there will always be horse racing, so I'll always have a job." Maryn loved her job. She enjoyed sassing the grooms who flew with the horses. She liked to finesse her high-brow clients. She joked to friends that she'd be right with them, but first she had to FedEx a horse. Maryn used to be a joker.

Maryn had a hefty salary and vested shares in TC International. She had secure accounts with Middle Eastern breeders, Kentucky racers, and several companies that liked to transfer horse-owning executives to foreign locations, ensuring Maryn of five-figure bonuses each Christmas. She had the wherewithal for all the health care, nannies, private schools, high-end safety-tested nursery furniture, tutors, ballet lessons, and summer vacations to France a child would ever need. Maryn had everything in order except one small thing.

Maryn needed Andy's consent. One unuttered little yes

was going to blow up the works. And she was impotent to do a single thing about it.

Maryn went to her Andy Zone in preparation for the call and picked up the phone.

"Andy Knox," came his chipper Midwestern greeting. Maryn was relieved that despite his new wife's pretentions, he wasn't pretending to be an Andrew.

"Andy, it's Maryn."

"Maryn!" His voice was warm, as if it was her regular afternoon call to plan dinner. The frozen lake surrounding the vault of Maryn's memories of Andy softened to allow a hairline crack. She hardened herself.

"Andy, you haven't returned the paperwork I sent you."

"Um. Yes." Wariness crowded out warmth.

"Why not?"

"Why not? Maryn, you can't just ask me, 'Why not?' like you're asking if I can stop for bread and milk on the way home. This is a big deal."

She'd once been fond of his old-fashioned folksiness. Today she found the clichés annoying. Who bought bread and milk anymore? Bagels and nonfat creamer were more like it.

"Andy, this *was* a big deal years ago when we first decided. It was a big deal when I had to take drugs and undergo painful medical procedures. Now it's paperwork. You don't even have to leave your office."

"That's overly simplistic and you know it. We aren't negotiating who gets the sofa. We're talking about fertilized embryos, which will become children."

Seven, to be precise. Seven healthy fertilized eggs that glowed like gold nuggets in Maryn's mind, the barrier between her and childlessness.

"The reason I harvested eggs was so I could have children later. You came to terms with your concerns back then. It shouldn't be difficult to allow me to use the eggs for the very purpose that I froze them. They're my eggs."

Maryn was an expert arguer. She could talk him into or out of things so thoroughly that for weeks afterward he couldn't recall what he'd actually wanted. If she'd tried to talk him out of divorcing her, they'd be married today.

"First of all, they're not *your* eggs. They're fertilized embryos. They have *my* sperm, *my* DNA, and *my* chromosomes. Any child conceived by those eggs will be as much my child as yours."

Maryn sighed. Andy was making his bullet points. She wouldn't be able to bulldoze him. Andy's defense against her was scribbling lists of his points and refusing to agree to anything without hanging up and thinking about it. She could practically see his rounded hand.

1. *Embryos have MY DNA*

"Second, things are different now. I'm married to Summer. We plan to start a family of our own. It wouldn't be right for me to start a family with you."

2. *Summer*

"I'm not asking you to start a family with me. I'm asking you to let me start a family on my own. I don't want help and I don't want money. I don't need anything but your signature. It won't affect your life at all. Let me try, Andy."

"It's not a signature, it's a baby. You're not talking about unfreezing a TV dinner. I'd know that my child was out there, needing care and support. Being a father is a big responsibility."

3. *Responsibility*

"Don't think of it like that. You wouldn't be the father any more than a rancher is a cook. He provides the steer, but it's the chef who creates the meal. It's like the house. We bought everything together, but now you have nothing to do with it, and aren't responsible for cleaning and repair. I maintain it and pay for it by myself. You have a shiny new house. I bet you never miss the old stuff."

"A baby isn't furniture, Maryn. I can't forget all about it. What kind of father walks away from his own baby?"

"What kind of husband walks away from his wife?" It was out before she could help herself and she was shaken, unsure where it had come from. They were silent in the aftermath, like a bus had crashed through the plate-glass window of their civil facade, shocking everyone.

"Not a good one, Maryn," Andy finally said quietly. "I don't want to make the same mistake twice."

Tears really do prickle, Maryn thought.

"Andy, please," she whispered. "It's my only option." Though she tried not to think about it because it threatened her icy lake, Maryn knew Andy truly was a good person. "Please."

"I need to think about it." And he hung up.

The phone was emitting a fast busy signal when Maryn finally replaced the receiver. Still, she sat. For the first time in a long time the shiny black oobleck of her rage had abated. In its place crept a cold grey mist that blurred her vision and chilled her bones.

Andy Doesn't Live in L.A.

I need to think about it," Andy said, though every chord in his gut shrieked, *"No, no, no!"* so loudly he thought his ex-wife could hear it over the phone. He couldn't refuse Maryn outright. She'd be a wonderful mother.

As he heard her hiccup in a breath, like a tendril of hope, panic's talons dug deep.

"I have to go," he said, "I'll call you." He hung up hastily. He shouldn't have given her hope. He had no idea what to do.

Andy dragged a tired hand over his face. Maryn hadn't changed her tactics in five years apart. He stared at the points he'd scribbled on his deskpad.

1. MY sperm
2. Summer
3. Children!!!
4. NOT furniture

Andy wished it was as simple as dividing marital furniture. Was that where the expression "easy chair" came from? He wanted to promise Maryn a recliner, a leather sofa, a table made of rubies, an ivory throne complete with castle, a diamond tiara, a fur coat, and an emerald scepter. Anything that could make a woman forget what she'd lost. Anything that would let him walk away from his guilt. But of course it didn't work that way.

He was resting his forehead on his fingers when there was

a knock and his office door opened. His senior partner, Jacqueline Mann, led a man and a woman into the room. Was it four o'clock already? Andy straightened, tightening the knot of his silk tie and resisting the urge to give his hair a spit and a lick. His cowlick was likely to be standing up like a third-grader's on picture day.

"This is Andy Knox. He'll be handling your real estate settlements." Jacque was all professionalism, resisting even the slightest frown at Andy's rumpled appearance. "Andy, these are the representatives for the Cornin account."

"Pleased to meet you." Andy stuck out his hand. He ignored their looks of dismay. His youthful appearance did not inspire confidence.

Jacque did not believe in ignoring client alarm. "Of course, I'll be working closely with Andy on this part of the project," she assured them.

Andy didn't mind. It comforted him to know Jacque would be supervising. She was assured and competent. No one questioned her authority or intelligence. With her short hair and her name she even seemed like a man.

"Please, have a seat." Andy gestured expansively at the fancy leather chairs his wife had insisted upon.

As always happened, the clients warmed toward Andy, seduced by his blond-haired blue-eyed good looks. Andy had learned early on that this was the case. People liked good-looking people. Add designer office chairs and an easygoing charm and you were aces. When the pair departed, it was smiles and firm grips all around.

Jacque gave him her crisp "well done" nod as she led the clients out. Andy was pleased. He was capable at his job, but he didn't consider himself a real lawyer. Real lawyers strode confidently into courtrooms and yelled at narrow-minded judges, exposed prosecutorial misconduct, and exonerated wrongfully accused clients. Andy's job involved boring administrative work, preparing the same filings year after year. It was a great scam created by the Bar that an attorney was required at all. You didn't need a law degree for Andy's job. But he had one, which made him happy because it had made his mother so proud to say, "My son the attorney." His wife, Summer, also called him Andrew-a-Partner-at-Cayce-Lanfranco-&-Moody, as opposed to Andy, which everyone else called him. Technically, he wasn't a partner, only Of Counsel, but he never quibbled. Summer knew how to promote.

At the thought of his wife, Andy looked hurriedly at his Tag Heuer watch. Crap. He threw some files in his walnut leather briefcase and snapped the brass locks shut with an authoritative click. He always carried his briefcase because it was what lawyers did, even though he would not open it again until he was back at his desk tomorrow and removed the files. Case in hand, Burberry raincoat hung not exactly casually over his arm, revealing just enough signature plaid, Andy hurried out of his office and home to his wife, who would tell him what to do about Maryn.

As he paused for his driveway gates to admit him, Andy felt the usual twin emotions—pride that he lived in this glamorous and tantalizingly invisible Spanish Mission–style house in Santa Monica, and panic at the thought of how much he owed. Sometimes when he was waiting, tourists craned to see what important Hollywood shaker was sliding to privacy behind these gates. Andy loved that. But today there were no gawkers and the gates leered like juicy fangs of debt.

"What about that one in Brentwood?" he'd asked Summer after she'd decided this must be the house.

"Brentwood is part of Los Angeles," Summer had replied without looking up.

Times like these made Andy wonder if he wasn't very

smart. Usually he'd let it go, so no one would catch on, but this time he persisted. "We both liked the other one better." The modest ranch on Carmelina Avenue had delighted them with its pretty yard and sunny rooms.

Summer sighed and put down her pen, swiveling to face him. Her tone did little to diminish his feeling of stupidity. "Andrew. Los Angeles is the second-most-populated city in the United States, with the second-highest crime rate. It's facing a one-billion-dollar budget shortfall for this year because of the mammoth bailout needed for the city's employee pension funds. It's not somewhere I want to send my children to school, when we have children." Having children was a discussion Summer usually postponed. "Santa Monica is just better. Besides, think of your political aspirations."

"Political aspirations?" Andrew wasn't sure he would glamorize his vague attention to current events as "political aspirations."

"You've never held public office and don't have a political background. It'll be a longer ladder to reach a meaningful position in a major urban center like Los Angeles. I don't want to fuck around for years with you on the Brentwood Library Book Selection Board or the Safety Commission on Jailhouse Plumbing before we get a real leg into a position of value. Ronald Reagan went straight to Governor of California and so can you."

"What about parks and recreation?" Andy was passionate about green space. He appreciated the beach, but it wasn't the same as a wide swath of green grass for throwing a football.

"Andrew, parks and recreation in the city of Los Angeles isn't about green spaces. It's about prying Sureño gangs out of dusty barrios in Compton. Besides, whites are a minority in Los Angeles, under thirty percent of the population. In comparison, over forty-six percent of the population is Hispanic or Latino. The mayor's name is Antonio Villaraigosa, with City Council members Reyes, Cardena, Alarcón, and Huizar among others. You don't stand a chance."

While everything Summer was saying was strictly factual, it made Andy uncomfortable in ways he couldn't put his finger on. Was it racist to speak flat facts if they carried an aura unfavorable to a specific race? Or was his the oversensitivity conservatives ranted about, blinding liberals from finding solutions because they wouldn't acknowledge a politically incorrect problem? Growing up in Nebraska they didn't talk about race all that much. There'd been only one black family in Andy's town.

Summer sensed Andy's discomfort. She rose from her desk chair and moved to the sofa, patting the cushion next to her. Andy sat.

"Besides being beautiful, and close to your office," she said, "Santa Monica has the political benefit—for *you*—of being over eighty percent white. It has an older average voting-age population, and over ninety percent have a high school education, with close to fifty-five percent having a bachelor's degree or higher. That will help you run an issues-based campaign."

Summer's certainty that Andy would run a campaign, that he had *issues*, caught him a bit by surprise. He wasn't opposed to the idea of running for City Council—it sounded great. But it would never have occurred to him before. He was more likely to organize a Fantasy Football league than a political rally. Summer spewed census details; Andy was sports stats.

"Maybe you should run," Andy said. "You're smarter than me and you already know all about it."

Summer had a mind like a trap. Any piece of information that made it into her brain was stored forever. During her morning weather forecast, if she said something like, "The last time we had this much rain in Glendale was in 1972 when they got seventeen inches in four hours," she wasn't reading off the cards. She knew it.

Summer blushed, for a second not a polished on-air reporter but a girl, awkward in praise, tucking her hair behind an ear so she wasn't looking at him. "Flatterer."

"I mean it!" Andy protested. "It isn't my contributions that beat the pants off everyone at Trivial Pursuit." They'd long since stopped playing at home because her drubbings were boring for them both.

She smiled. "I appreciate your vote of confidence, but being a politician is a man's job." Summer had some old-fashioned Alabama beliefs. "If I was elected to anything other than Magnolia Queen, my daddy would think I'd stopped shaving my legs and become a lesbian. That's not how we do things down in Jasper."

Summer had grown up outside of Birmingham. Though Andy had never met her family, they still lived in Jasper, Alabama—population: fifteen thousand people, four trailer parks, and two defunct coal mines. Summer's family had come from all three. Summer didn't talk about her life before she became a weather girl for WBPT 106.9 FM radio in Birmingham. She'd eviscerated her accent so completely, most people didn't even know she was from the South.

Andy tugged her hair. "I know hanging out in Denny's was fine dining in Jasper, but I'm not sure I'm cut out for it. Politicians seem to spend more time shaking hands over Breakfast Buster Platters than anything else."

"That's not funny, Andrew Knox." She slapped his hand away, no humor in her look. "Being a politician is honorable and privileged. When Ronald Reagan came to speak at Maxwell Air Force Base in 1982, my daddy drove us all the way down to Montgomery just to stand outside the gates and wave little flags. I thought we'd come to see the king. He flew *on a*

plane in and out of Alabama *on the same day.* I was so embarrassed to be in sneakers, I drew flowers all over them with a
marker to make them look like fancy slippers." She laughed at
the recollection. "You can call me a redneck, but I still believe
there is no nobler calling than getting elected. It's American
royalty."

Andy knew if she mentioned her upbringing, it was important.

"You should be the one to run. You'd be a great queen."

"No, sir." She shook her head. "I'll be Jackie to your Ken-
nedy. A woman takes office when she's a widow stepping into
her husband's shoes. Even in the ultraliberal People's Republic
of Santa Monica this is the first time they've had two sitting
female council members, and that's only because of political
infighting over Housing Board control."

"If I have to win so you can have my seat when I die, I guess
we're moving to Santa Monica." Her happiness made her plain
face almost pretty. He squeezed her hand. "You'll be my chief
of staff."

"*Unofficial* chief of staff." Summer smiled.

"What exactly will you be unofficially chief of staffing
over?" Andy asked. "Besides green spaces?"

She shrugged. Now that his candidacy was settled in her
mind, she was more interested in getting back to the dinner
invitations on her desk. "Local concerns tend to remain static.
Homelessness and affordable housing top the list."

"Speaking of affordable housing," Andy remembered.
"That house on San Vicente is still out of our budget. Let's call
Dale and see if we can find something a little more within our
price range." He started to push off the stiff sofa.

Summer's huge eyes swung back toward him like lanterns,
pinning him in their beam. Andy froze.

"Andrew. The median home price in Santa Monica is close
to a million dollars. There's no way we can run a credible cam-

paign from a crappy bungalow east of Lincoln." For a second Andy thought he heard the bark of his ex-wife Maryn's laughter. She'd have been unable to contain herself at the argument for a million-dollar headquarters to run an affordable housing campaign.

Summer continued, oblivious. "It's imperative that we associate with the right community to facilitate your entrée into Santa Monica society. That house off San Vicente is perfect. It has a gate. I think a Baldwin lives on that block—one of the good ones. It has space for entertaining. It's *the* address."

Andy's father hadn't believed in debt. He'd drilled into Andy the importance of not being house poor. "It'll eat you alive, son," he'd warned. "Where's the point in havin' that extra bedroom if your home's your nemesis? Better git somethin' smaller and furnish it so's you can relax and enjoy it a' night."

"But, Summer—"

Summer fixed him with her stare. "Andrew, either you want something or you don't. I didn't marry you to live a half-assed life of unaccomplished goals. I married you because I thought we had the same aspirations, to own a nice home, to raise a family, and to contribute back to the community. Don't tell me I was wrong."

Andy was confused again. He did want those things. But a mansion and a City Council seat seemed to be only one, very high-end, version of those things. "We do have the same goals. We can still have—"

"You don't like the house?"

"I do. It's just—"

"Would you rather look in Malibu?"

Andy blanched at the thought of property costs in Malibu. "No, no, I like Santa Monica. But I worry . . ."

Summer changed her tactic, scooting up against Andy, and sliding an arm around him. "Baby, don't worry. You're a great provider. I know you can take care of everything. You're a prestigious law partner with a large salary, and in time, you're going to be a Santa Monica City Council member! I'm so proud of you."

Andy hesitated. Summer, as usual, was overstating things. But Andy didn't want her to think he wasn't a good provider. They hadn't been married that long, and Summer was young. He wanted to give her what she wanted.

"Besides." Summer laughed. "We have my income from the station! If we play our cards right, as your political star rises I'll be right behind you, moving up to anchor!" The gleam in Summer's eye told Andy this was no casual fantasy. She turned to face him, eyes beseeching. "A power couple needs a power house."

For a moment he glimpsed a pigtailed girl with dusty sneakers as she read magazines about a glamorous place by the ocean and vowed to get there someday. This reminder of their twelve-year age gap made him feel tender.

"How about if we go look at it again on Sunday?" He relented. "We'll see if they'll come down a bit on their asking price. It's been on the market over a month." Summer squealed and flung both arms around him. It felt good to be the hero.

As the gates closed behind his car, Andy wished he could satisfy Maryn so easily. The embryo situation was ridiculously tangled. He'd never heard of anyone having to deal with a problem like this. Whenever he tried to read the consent forms, or think about the Problem of the Eggs, his brain skittered away. It was happening now, her call shoved into his mind's junk closet by thoughts of a cold can of Miller Lite and the growl of his stomach. He wondered what Summer had prepared for dinner. Maybe she'd planned dessert, and he could wait until then to bring it up.

Dimple Reads a Script

I put down Julian Wales's script, heart beating fast, as if I was standing too close to the edge of a cliff. Freya had messengered it over, and I'd torn through it in an hour. I crossed my trailer from the bench to the desk. Three steps, but I needed space. To dull my thumping blood, I dug the current *Pulse* script from my bag. I got the irony.

Pulse is a hospital drama at the fictional Cedars Hospital in L.A., where doctors, nurses, and patients basically get it on. You know the one. I play the staff psychiatrist. My battered script was a rainbow of colors, red, green, yellow, and pink pages reflecting all the rewrites from first draft to the final version. We were almost done shooting and I knew the episode by heart. There was a lot of hype surrounding this script because it was the show's 200th episode. In an era of fickle viewers and risk-averse studios, few dramas lasted six seasons, much less nine.

"I can't believe you've hung with *Pulse* for almost a decade," Freya had said when the script came out. She gracefully placed a sliver of yellowtail sashimi in her mouth. I fumbled my chopsticks, fish flopping in soy sauce as if it was still alive.

"What do you mean?" Her tone surprised me. Role security is rare in my industry, so I counted myself successful.

"Well, darling, you used to do all edgy, independent films. It doesn't get much darker than *White Lies*. And *Cold Shoulder*? That movie was . . . *magic*. In a creepy sort of way."

"For the six people who saw it. I was twenty-five when I did

Cold Shoulder. It's fine to bare your tits when you're twenty, not forty." The cardinal rule of independent films is that the lead actress usually bares her tits.

"Thirty-six," Freya admonished me with her chopstick. "I don't understand why you don't do film anymore."

"Because it's inconsistent and it doesn't pay well. You of all people should be happy with *Pulse*. Your fifteen percent goes a lot further." A piece of eel slid from my chopstick and landed on my lap. "Freya, why do you bring me here? You know I can't manage chopsticks. We could've met at your office."

"There is no such thing as bad publicity, darling, even if you're wearing your lunch." There were always paparazzi outside Koi. "Right now you're on the market and you need to be seen. Even the great Julian Wales is not impervious to the power of magazine covers. Now don't change the subject."

"No one's asked." I answered her earlier question.

"That is not true. You've turned down four projects this year. Why did you turn down that script about living on Mars? And don't make jokes about not wanting to wear a unitard, because you have an excellent rack."

I felt the moth beating in my chest. "*Pulse* isn't the most worthy part, but it pays the mortgage. Before Dr. Roxy Page, my pilots were as short lived as the resurgence of bell-bottoms, and less compelling. I'm grateful to be on a successful show."

Freya laid down her chopsticks in perfect alignment, and faced me. "Dimple. Before your failed television pilots there was a budding film career. You have a craft that's wasted on *Pulse*. You went to TV for *Six Feet Under*, which was a clever show, but you died after five episodes. Now you're stalled on the small screen and *Pulse* is no *Six Feet Under*. You turn down so many potential roles it makes me think your confidence has eroded. "

"I . . . I . . ." I was fishier than my lunch, mouth working, nothing coming out. I collected myself. "You know I had to put my mom in a semiassisted living facility right when the radio fell in my bathtub on *Six Feet Under*. Darkly artful scripts are alluring, but the paychecks are wafer thin, and excitement turns into gut-wrenching anxiety in the wink of an eye when you can't make your mother's rent. I'm forty. I can't do that anymore."

"Thirty-six. Dimple. You cannot hide behind Roxy until she limps into a retirement home herself. When's the last time she had sex on air? You're not Roxy. You still have fire and leading-lady capability. In the wink of an eye, as you say, you could be on top. Don't let risk aversion keep you from your potential."

"Forty. I'm forty, Freya." The word rolled in my mouth like a steel marble, alien and uncomfortable.

She looked at me. "Are you having a crisis?"

I was having a crisis. "I feel old." I sighed. "Half the cast of *Pulse* takes spring break and I get discounted membership invitations from AARP."

"It's a cliché, but age is just a number, Dimple. You can manipulate it as easily as you do on your CV. The older I get the older old is." Her eyes were sympathetic.

"Not forty," I said. "Forty is when everything falls apart. Forty is that monumentally unfair age as a woman when you've run out of time. You can't coast along anymore waiting for things to happen. Forty is oh-shit-I'd-better-have-a-401K time."

"Do you think you're being a little . . . *cataclysmic*? Since when do you care about forty?"

"I don't know," I said. "Since I want to have a baby?"

She shrugged, remarkably unfazed. "Sleep on it. Either it will pass, as a hormonal spike associated with your birthday, or it won't and you'll find a nice little Haitian." She elegantly ate some salmon. Apparently, bearing a child didn't play into

Freya's worldview. "But right now, finish your fish. Put lipstick on that beautiful face. Go to work. If you think about today as the day you have to sort out the rest of your life, you'll lose your mind. If you think about what you want for dinner, it's more manageable. Look at the scripts I sent your way. Change will rejuvenate you."

"Dimple?" A knock at the door called me back to the present. "Hair and makeup is ready for you."

I popped out of my trailer like a cork. I was dying to talk to Justine. The beauty truck was a minisalon on wheels, white leather swivel stools before large bulb mirrors, countertops cluttered with all manner of tongs, curlers, straighteners, and other hair-torture devices. With the door closed, you forgot it could do sixty on the interstate.

"Good morning, gorgeous! Bring that rope to mama."

Justine, my hairdresser, was waiting with her usual wide smile. Today her hair was a blunt turquoise bob. Her soundtrack was a-ha's "Take on Me."

"Roxy's in the present today," I reminded her. The 200th episode had flashed back to how all the characters arrived at Cedars Hospital.

"I know." Justine sighed. "I'm in mourning. Your eighties looks were so much fun."

"For you." Roxy Page's backstory had involved some hair treatment that required deep-conditioning rinses and Bobby Fischer to unravel.

"You looked as fresh as the cocaine-induced love child of Sonny Crockett and Bananarama. Sit."

I slid into my chair and Justine threaded her hands through my heavy brown hair.

"Like mink," she sighed. "If I had this I'd never dye."

"We're all going to die." God, I was morbid today.

"Whatcha got?" She nodded toward the episode outline peeking out from beneath my script. Our Monday routine was to discuss new story lines. Actors were in the dark until they received the new scripts, and were often surprised to discover they were suddenly a lesbian, a serial killer, eloping, cuckolded, dead, or sometimes all of the above in a Very Special Episode.

My frown returned. Freya might have been right. "Roxy is developing an alcohol problem."

"Oh."

There weren't many awkward silences between us, but this was one.

"Arthur was an endearing drunk," Justine tried. "And they remade it!"

"Stop. I'm one step away from Aunt Sassy." I sighed.

"No, c'mon," she protested. "You're hot."

"Remember the steamy days?" In my first years on *Pulse* Roxy slept with *everyone*. "The torrid affair with the head of surgery? The seduction of the billionaire Chairman of the Board who I left tattered in a cutthroat divorce? Those were good plots." Both actors had left the show to become leading men in features.

"That was some good bed hair," Justine recalled her art. "But I liked Roxy-in-Danger best. The time you were kidnapped by that deranged patient, or the time you were exposed to a rare tropical illness."

"It was all passion and danger once." I sighed.

"You had sex with the environmentalist in Episode 904."

"Those sex scenes were as edgy as bunny slippers. We shared an ice cream sundae first. In an ice cream parlor! No wonder they're giving me a drinking problem." Justine giggled. "In the past two years, I've only done the bed boogie with well-meaning social workers and earnest cops. And *never* on camera. Where are the bodice-ripping scenes in the on-call room with tormented medical geniuses?"

We both knew the answer. Younger actresses got all the porn. My shrinking story lines centered on heartwarming psychological dramas—saving an abused child; counseling a troubled veteran; and the occasional illegal, but sympathetic, assisted suicide.

"At least you're having imaginary off-camera sex," Justine comforted. "Look at Miho."

Miho was an actress a year or two older than me. Hard to say in Hollywood years. Miho's character had been crushed by an out-of-control ambulance crashing through the ER, leaving her in a wheelchair. We expected a poignant death scene any script now.

"Miho shouldn't have slept with the supervising producer then dumped him," I said. "Do you think I need to worry, Justine?"

She reassured me with the cardinal rule of a long-running series. "You don't need to worry until they give you a child old enough to talk."

Sex, intrigue, marriage, divorce, pregnancy, murder, even the occasional return from the dead were all staples of prime-time drama. But if a pregnancy resulted in a living child who wasn't stolen from the maternity ward or given up for adoption, it was jumping the shark. If it was a precocious black kid between five and ten years old, you might as well start sending out your resume.

"Alcoholism could be fun! You can disgrace yourself at the office Christmas party and have lots of ill-chosen sex partners." Justine tried to cheer me.

"We can only hope." I wasn't optimistic. Substance abuse wasn't funny or appealing. No one wanted to watch it, and I didn't want to parody real pain. The industry was rife with addiction, and I knew its ugly face well. I hoped Roxy would recognize she had a problem after very few scenes at our Brewmeisters. Maybe the writers could throw in an affair with the rehab counselor.

"So I got this script," I ventured.

Justine perked up. "The movie about the hikers who end up in an Iranian jail?"

"I passed on that."

"You did?"

"I would've had to miss sweeps week."

"I'm surprised Clyde wouldn't write you out."

The producer had been happy to write me out, but I'd been too nervous my absence wouldn't make a difference and they'd notice.

"Was it that one about living on Mars . . ."

"It's for Julian Wales's next movie." I interrupted her recital of projects I'd turned down. The Mars pilot *had* required bodysuits, for god's sake. I have a nice figure, but no woman in her forties should wear a unitard. Period. Not to mention that it would be impossible to disguise a pregnancy. *If* I decided to get pregnant.

"What?" Justine yelped, and for a minute I thought I'd said "pregnant" out loud. "Sorry!" The curling iron yanked my hair in her excitement. She released the wave, then spun my stool to face her. "Julian Wales, for real? I can't believe you've been holding out. Everyone's buzzing about his next project. Is it a big part? In a *movie* movie?"

"It's the lead." I felt that dizzying near-the-precipice anxiety again. I took a deep breath. "It's good," I admitted. I'd been distracting myself all day from thinking about *how* good it was. Very, very good.

Justine embraced me, stool and all. "That's a-MA-zing! I'm so excited!"

"I just read the script!" I protested.

Justine gave a little hop. "Julian Wales. God, he's dreamy. Promise me I get to come visit you on set."

"Let's not get ahead of ourselves. For all I know he sent the script to every actress in Hollywood." If you got your hopes up, you ended up disappointed.

"*He* sent the script to *you*?" she squealed. "That's tantamount to offering you the part! I've read about him. He's very intense, and only considers one or two actors for big roles. He spends all this time auditioning his picks in different situations, testing how they react. It goes on for months!" Justine was making me nervous.

"Freya didn't mention that . . ."

"Then, when you're in his fold, you're, like, his go-to gal. He'll use you in all his films. Like Woody Allen and Mia Farrow." Justine was oblivious to the flaw in her analogy. I spared a sympathetic thought for Diane Keaton. "Just think of it. You can tell *Pulse* to take their alcoholism and shove it."

That caused anxiety. "I wouldn't *quit*. *Pulse* has been very good to me. . . ."

"Dimple?" A head poked into the trailer. "They're looking for First Team."

"Two secs," Justine said. She twirled me to face the mirror, using the curling iron to finish the last of my waves. "There you go. Fresh as a newborn opening your eyes for the first time. Promise me you'll give me details after you see Julian Wales."

I promised, and headed for the set.

Wyatt Waits

The back of Wyatt's neck prickled. It was a sensory reaction, like cricket hairs. An ESP that specially qualified you to be a high school teacher. A youth was Up To No Good. Wyatt couldn't tell how he knew, whether it was a hushed conversation, an imperceptible contraction of student clusters, a hasty look away, but his career had selected him because of this intuition.

Wyatt's destination would be one of four places—the boys' locker room, the girls' locker room, behind the field house, or under the bleachers. From his window, he surveyed the grassy quad that was the heart of campus. Couples ate lunch on the grass. Boys were throwing Frisbees, playing hacky sack, or kicking a soccer ball. Girls were clumped in large knots rather than sprawled in twos and threes with T-shirts rolled up for midday sun on their stomachs. Girls, then.

Wyatt's district was affluent and the students generally well behaved, but no high school was free of bullying. In his student days, it was always boys. A fist to the nose and it was done. Today, the girls were worse than the boys, and they did it insidiously, e-mailed words sliding a stiletto between the ribs of a classmate. Girls were the masters of cyberbullying. But on National Leave Your Car At Home Day, someone was bringing it to campus.

Wyatt left his office. The school was small enough that any prey would do. The perfect mark was scurrying down the hall.

"Hello, Lizzie." Wyatt pounced on the eleventh-grader.

"Oh! Hi, Mr. Ozols." She looked anxious.

"In a hurry?"

"No!" she answered too loud. Soon, then.

"Did you enjoy your visit to Duke?"

"I loved it!" She brightened. "Their gym was amazing!"

"Got time to escort me into the ladies' locker room and show me what we might do to improve things here?" Wyatt had a hunch.

A look of horror came over her face. "Um. Well. I have a lot of homework before fourth period."

As he'd thought. Girls took their fights inside.

"Perhaps after seventh period? Or tomorrow?"

"Sure, sure." She looked relieved. "I'll bring my brochures."

She practically flew toward the library, far from the gym.

Coach Davis was at lunch and the girls' locker room was deserted. Wyatt settled himself in the coach's guest chair, concealed behind the door. He gestured Steff, next to him, to silence. He'd brought her to avoid any impropriety about being in the girls' locker room. Before long they heard a shuffling of feet and a whispered "All clear." He remained out of sight.

"Where is she?"

"Chickened out."

"She's scared of you, Harper." Wyatt was unsurprised to hear Harper Dixon's name.

"I'm here." The high-pitched voice had a slight tremor. It was Tia Sanchez, a timid girl who commuted from Compton through an academic exchange program for underprivileged students. "What do you want?"

"I want to know why a skinny mongrel like you is panting after Troy Martin," Harper menaced. "I want to know why you don't take a lesson from the news and off yourself like other teenage losers."

"I'm not a loser. Troy texted me first."

"He only wants to screw you because you're an easy wet-back!" Rage frayed Harper's voice.

"He dumped you." Tia stood up to Harper. Wyatt was impressed.

"You skank! What're you even doing here? You should only come to this part of town to clean my house, and I wouldn't let you do that because I'd get lice!"

There was the distinct snick of scissors.

"What's that?" Tia's voice quavered.

"Lice removal. Let's see how Troy likes you with no hair."

"Better than he liked you." Defiant.

Harper gave a snarl as Wyatt stepped neatly between the girls, easily disarming Harper's swing. The scissors he prised from her hand would go in his pile of confiscated pocket-knives, mace, blades, nunchakus, and one staple gun.

"Good work, sir," said Steff. Wyatt nodded. One girl with scissors was easier than last month's clash between senior boys staging a vanilla version of a gang fight.

"Steff, please escort these ladies to my office." He gestured to the knot gathered around Harper and Tia. All would be sanctioned, even Tia—fighting was not allowed at school—and he had to start making calls if he wanted this situation addressed by three.

He held Harper back. "Walk with me."

They took a different path, and he said, "I was sorry to hear about your brother's death in Afghanistan. He served bravely and he will be missed."

Harper jerked as if tasered.

"It must be especially difficult that Troy has moved on during a painful time."

The girl's jaw thrust forward and her face clamped. For just two seconds, Wyatt laid a hand on her shoulder, then said, "I can't offer consolation that will diminish your pain, but I can assure you, it *will* get better."

Her lip trembled, just a hair.

"Acting out won't take away the pain, Harper, but it might take away opportunities to benefit yourself and honor your brother. We can talk more about that if you like. In the meantime, why don't you wait in the conference room next to my office so you can have some privacy. I am going to have to suspend you, but hope the time will help you clear your perspective."

Menacing only moments ago, the girl's hunched back seemed fragile. Wyatt stared after her with mixed emotions. Babies evoked images of floppy bears and fluffy blankets, but he, more than anyone, had no illusions about what happened when the training wheels came off. Children grew up and had learning disabilities and illnesses and rumspringa and pain and loss. Wyatt had never been able to do more than briefly lay a hand on slumping shoulders. He wanted more. He couldn't wait to become tangled in the complications of another life, even the messy bits.

At 2:55 PM precisely, Harper and her cohorts had been dispatched on two-week suspension, with parental assurances of severe punishment. Wyatt was anxious for the last to leave. He had no idea when Ilana would arrive, and though 4:29 PM wouldn't be out of the question, he intended to be on the drop-off bench promptly at three. He brought employee evaluations to read while he waited.

The day was all the unfun side of his job. Wyatt was about to fire one of his science teachers. Terminating Jim Lang didn't trouble Wyatt—in this circumstance of gross incompetence it was his personal pleasure. The man had failed to give a test all semester out of laziness, and nearly poisoned a study hall monitor through careless chemical storage.

What frustrated him was that in a time of severe budget shortfalls, where good teachers were laid off, Wyatt had to exhaust rigorous union-stipulated procedures to fire a dreadful one.

Particularly offensive was that, in addition to his ineptitude, Lang was having an affair with the school's Summer Program Director. Wyatt didn't mind dating among his staff—he himself had dated the college guidance counselor until she'd decided a plumber she'd met on eHarmony was better marriage material. What bothered Wyatt was that the Summer Program Director was married. Wyatt was no prude, but he held infidelity pretty low on his personal scale of evils. Or high. Whichever one was bad. Worse than men who fake-tanned, but not quite as sinister as world domination.

Wyatt found it repugnant that Lang had seduced a young and dumb girl into betraying her marriage, but that was outside of Wyatt's business. It was squarely Wyatt's business that the affair had prompted Lang to leave his lab class unattended long enough for Spencer Loveland to ignite his station. Wyatt had to act speedily to prevent Lang from torpedoing the school's No Child Left Behind scores in science or burning down the whole institution. Wyatt was forced by protocol to complete an exhaustive peer evaluation. Blessedly, the majority of Wyatt's teaching staff consisted of dedicated, clever instructors, and he was looking forward to their comments.

Jim Lang doesn't strive to go the extra mile in the classroom.

Translation: Lang sets low personal standards and consistently fails to achieve them.

Jim struggles to adequately convey the currently accepted science curriculum to students.

Translation: Lang's one-celled lab organisms would outscore him on an IQ test.

Jim Lang doesn't always grasp the nuances of the material.

Translation: If Jim were any more stupid he'd have to be watered twice a week.

Lang has been inconsistent in his shared teacher responsibilities, failing to show up for his shift as detention supervisor.

Translation: That jackass made me miss my bowling league.

Wyatt smiled as he reached the bottom of his stack. He'd saved biology teacher Linda Wei's for last. The evaluations were anonymous, of course, but he was so familiar with each teacher's style and handwriting they might as well have submitted their thoughts on monogrammed paper. Linda held nothing back.

Jim Lang is a prime candidate for natural deselection. He has delusions of adequacy as a teacher. As a scientist, he would be out of his depth in a 3mm pipette. He works well when under constant supervision and cornered like a rat in a trap. He should go far, and the sooner he starts, the better.

He wouldn't be able to include Linda's comments in the final report, but they were amusing.

"Hooligans chase you from your office, Wyatt?"

Wyatt looked up to see Linda herself, a pretty, black-haired woman in her midforties. He straightened.

"Linda! I was just reading yo—er, evaluations of Jim."

Linda cast her eyes down. "I'm afraid I was rather frank." Originally from Hong Kong, her British accent surprised first-time listeners. "But honestly, I don't know what irritates me more—his complete disregard for the education of his students, or that we have to expend all this time and money to replace him with someone who cares." She fiddled with the brooch on her knit dress. Linda was the only high school teacher Wyatt knew who dressed each day as if she was going to a corner office on Madison Avenue. It was like spying a snapdragon among weeds.

"Please don't apologize for being frank. Honesty makes evaluations useful. That's why they're anonymous."

Linda gave him a look, and Wyatt chuckled.

"Hopefully we'll resolve this mess soon. I have a stack of qualified resumés." Wyatt didn't believe in wasting time when something had to be done.

"Yo, Mr. O!" One of the Quinn brothers waved from across the quad and executed a tricky maneuver on his Rollerblades. He looked up triumphantly just as Cass Bernstein walked out of the library sporting a tight T-shirt, causing the wide-eyed freshman to skate right into the trash receptacle.

"Oh!" Linda gasped, and Wyatt half-rose. They heard the boy's faint "I'm all right . . ." and saw his feeble wave.

"Speaking of summer school . . . ," Linda grinned. Then she became serious. "What are you going to do about Amber Paley?"

Amber Paley was the married Summer Program Director. It pained Wyatt to pass her bovine gum-snapping face each day en route to his office. She made him sad.

"Nothing," said Wyatt.

"You don't think she could cause trouble?" Linda persisted. "She's got quite a chip on that resentful shoulder, and for reasons unfathomable to me, she's fond of Jim."

Wyatt sighed. "Amber's a dim girl with a history of romance paperbacks who has substituted a resolutely average eleventh-grade science teacher for the handsome hero. I hate to punish her for a personal mistake."

"I'm happy for Jim to bear the consequences." Linda smiled at Wyatt. "As long as we're nattering on the street, do you want to grab a coffee?"

Wyatt looked at his watch: 4:16 PM. Consternation settled in his chest.

"Unfortunately I can't. I'm waiting for someone." He couldn't help looking past her to the entrance. No battered blue Camry.

Linda straightened. "Right then. I'm off to flag the bus."

Of course Linda would observe his green transportation day. "Husband can't pick you up?"

"Busy today. See you tomorrow!" She hurried off, a lilac bloom weaving among the black T-shirts swarming out of detention hall.

Wyatt extricated his phone. No missed calls.

"Mr. O, as a scholar and a gentleman, I swear to you I did not place the fecal matter in Coach Lugar's backseat." Seth Ames popped up in front of Wyatt, pimples shining in the sun. "This sentence to two weeks' detention is fallacious. The musical musings of my band are suffering."

"Seth, you posted a photo of yourself engaging in exactly that crime for all the world to see on Facebook."

Seth looked crestfallen. "Dude. You're on Facebook?"

"My grandmother is on Facebook, Seth. Count yourself lucky you aren't in detention all semester. Coach Lugar had to fumigate the car."

Wyatt tried to turn his attention to the latest issue of *Education Week*, but the article on algebra readiness couldn't hold his attention. He kept peeking at his watch. He'd give it until 5:00 PM before calling her home.

At 4:58 PM he broke down. There was no answer at her home number, not even the usual machine. At 5:11 PM he let it ring thirty times.

"Something wrong with your car, Wyatt?" Paul Kelly was not going green.

"Waiting on a ride."

"I won't invite you for a beer then." He winked. "But I want the details on poker night." With a wave, the small-framed detention master headed to his car.

Minutes turned to quarter hours. All pretenses at diverting himself abandoned, Wyatt stared at every car driving close to the school entrance, most continuing on by. There was a wave of activity around 5:30 PM as athletes and coaches left the fields and headed home. Still Wyatt sat.

Wyatt rarely got drunk, but he periodically had moments that felt like being drunk. This was one of them. It *was* today that he'd spoken to Ilana? He checked the calendar on his phone. Yes, there it was. She *had* said between three and four thirty? Yes, he was certain she had. They *had* agreed to meet at the school? It went on and on, Wyatt dissecting every nuance of their conversation to see if he'd forgotten or misunderstood any element.

By five forty-five most doctors' offices were closed. It was unmistakable that Ilana wasn't coming. Wyatt was crushed, and irritated at the burning behind his eyes. Some days he swore he was pregnant too, emotions uncharacteristically at the surface. He focused on the positive. His absence didn't change the outcome. Ilana would have the full evaluation, not just sex, but also heart, brain, kidneys, stomach, and bones. There would be sonogram images. She'd tell him all about it and it would be like being there.

At 5:59 PM he accepted defeat and dialed his cousin Eva.

Eva Goes to Dinner

E va smiled fondly at her cousin as he slid into the car. It was always amusing to watch Wyatt fold his proper frame into the MINI Cooper convertible.

"Top down okay?"

"Definitely. You look pretty." He complimented her, even though she could tell something was on his mind.

Eva was the epitome of "pretty," a china doll with wide blue eyes, natural platinum hair, and delicate features. To Eva, being pretty wasn't anything to be cocky about. It was more of a relief. Life seemed harder for people who weren't pretty. Pretty wasted less time fussing and got out the door quicker. That's what mattered to Eva.

One of the things Eva liked about Wyatt was that while he never failed to give her compliments, her looks had nothing to do with his approval. To Eva, Wyatt was the kind of family that was both born and created—they were first cousins, stepping up for each other in the void of siblings. Wyatt was her emergency contact, her support system.

"Nice elbow patches. Rooting in the seventies portion of the closet today?"

"Nice skirt. Where's the rest of it?"

"You are your mother's son." Eva had thought that gingham dresses only happened in pioneer stories for girls until she'd visited her aunt in Minnesota. Her own mother, the vivid, wild-haired Cynthia, had run away from the farm to dance in L.A. when she was seventeen.

"Nice air freshener," Wyatt said. A pine-scented Chuck Norris was dangling from Eva's rearview mirror. Chuck Norris was Eva's hero. "It's like a five-dollar security system."

"If Chuck Norris has five dollars and you have five dollars, Chuck Norris has more money than you," Eva said.

"If I had a million bucks and Chuck Norris had a wooden nickel, he'd have more money than me," Wyatt said.

"What happened?"

"Ilana was supposed to pick me up for the twenty-week sonogram appointment but never showed." Worry threaded his voice.

"That woman needs to join the twenty-first century and get a cell phone." Eva hadn't taken to Ilana.

Wyatt stared distractedly out the window.

"Let's go by the doctor's office," Eva offered. "I've got time before dinner." She didn't, but Bryan would understand.

"I don't know where it is." Wyatt sighed. "You'd better take me home."

"Why don't you come to dinner with us?" Eva didn't want to leave Wyatt alone to brood. He was a brooder. "Bryan won't mind." Bryan would totally mind.

"I appreciate the offer, but you know I'm going to brood, so you might as well take me home to get on with it." Wyatt smiled at her, fatigue in his face.

"Promise you'll at least pretend to watch *Top Chef*?"

"Promise."

Eva pulled up in front of Wyatt's. "Call me tomorrow and let me know what happened," she demanded.

"There'll be some nail-biting tension about plating on time and a chef will be eliminated." Wyatt clambered inelegantly from the coupe. "Prying myself from that tin can is going to give me a heart attack someday."

"Chuck Norris will never have a heart attack. His heart isn't foolish enough to attack him." Eva waved as she pulled away.

* * *

Fifteen minutes later, Eva joined her date on the patio at Gaucho Grill.

"Sorry I'm late. Wyatt needed a ride." She grabbed a piece of calamari and ignored Bryan's disapproving look. "Mmmmm."

"How does Wyatt manage when you're not fussing over him?"

Eva ignored Bryan's tone. "He drives his car, silly. His baby mama was supposed to pick him up today, but she no-showed."

"Baby mama?"

"He's adopting."

"I didn't think Wyatt was married. What would you like to drink?" The waiter stood by.

"White Rioja, please. He isn't."

Bryan frowned. "Is he gay?"

"No. Why would you ask that?"

"I never heard of a straight guy wanting a kid on his own."

"Why should a straight guy be any different from a gay guy or a woman?"

Bryan looked uncomfortable. "I don't know. Why doesn't he get married?"

"He hasn't met the right woman."

"Isn't he fifty?"

"Almost."

"And he never found a woman?"

Eva thought Bryan was being a little holy for a single guy pushing forty. "He dated someone for ten years, but she waffled on the kid thing. Eventually she decided no kids. He wants one." Wyatt's words at the time had stayed with Eva: *I was shocked to find myself alone, then I was shocked to find how easy it was.*

"I never heard of a straight man adopting before," Bryan repeated. "It's weird."

Eva controlled her irritation. "Don't you think men have paternal urges?"

"No," Bryan said. "That's why women make the babies."

"There are lots of single dads."

"Those are their own kids. They aren't adopting strangers' kids."

"Why is adopting normal for single women or gay men, but not straight guys? You don't give men much credit."

"I don't know." Bryan looked uncomfortable. "It seems odd. Pervy."

Eva snorted. "Society sends some pretty mixed messages. We want men involved with our children, but if they're too into it, they must be perverts."

"Look at that guy in San Diego with the kid in his basement."

"You think any straight man left alone with a child not of his loins will lock them in the basement and do something terrible?"

"I—"

"Do you think all priests are pedophiles?" Eva pressed.

"Of course not. Priests who molest children are criminals."

"Did your sixth-grade math teacher want to give you special lessons? Your swim coach? Your Boy Scout troop leader?"

"No."

"But you think adult men left unattended around children want to commit lewd acts?"

"This argument is ridiculous."

"Your reaction is ridiculous. You're saying a man can only be alone with his children if he can go home after hiking or Indian Guides and fuck his wife."

"I'm not saying that at all." Bryan gave her a leer. "But after I take our kids to Indian Guides, *I'm* going to want to come home and fuck my wife."

"It'll have to be after golf with your buddies. You know I don't want kids."

"You *didn't* want kids," he corrected. "But we're in a relationship now."

"I don't *ever* want kids," Eva assured him. "Snot and mashed peas and bed-wetting. Ugh."

Bryan wasn't laughing. "You don't mean that."

"My name is Eva but I'm no Eve."

"You don't like apples?"

"I don't want to be the mother of humanity."

A furrow creased Bryan's forehead.

Eva tried to explain. "Kids change you. I was raised by a single mom and I had a wonderful childhood. She was dazzling and creative and vivid. Having kids ruined that."

"You were her kid," Bryan pointed out.

Recalling Cyn Lytton, she tried to explain. "My mother was flamboyant and crazy, like Auntie Mame. Her nickname was 'the Original Cyn,' and she named me Eva because I came from playing with the snake in the garden while naked. She didn't change for me, she popped me in her purse and took me along like a toy poodle. I don't think you could get away with her style of guardianship today."

"It must've agreed with her. She went back for another bite at that apple."

It *hadn't* agreed with her. "When she married, her husband talked her into more kids. He wasn't a bad guy, and didn't want to make her a different person, but it changed her." She didn't mention the smothering depression. "I don't want that. I like the way I am now. I love my job. I love being able to travel and eat out without permission. I like owning nice things."

"You don't decide not to have kids because you don't want to break a vase," Brian voiced disbelief.

"Being a mother means giving up some of yourself because you want something else more. If you don't, the sacrifices would be misery. I don't have an urge for children strong enough to justify the sacrifices. I'd resent it."

"That'll change when you get married," Bryan persisted.

Eva opened her mouth, but he held up a finger in an annoying way. "*All* women want kids eventually, even if they say they don't. They only pretend they don't want them in case it doesn't happen." His smile was infuriating.

Eva realized her fingers were clenching the edge of the table. She forced her grip to relax. "Bryan, I told you when we met that I didn't want kids."

"I didn't think you meant it."

Eva's blood pressure thrummed. "Why would I say something I didn't mean?"

"So you wouldn't scare me off? I thought you were waiting until the right time."

"There will be no right time."

Bryan considered her. He reached across the table to take her hand. "I could be happy with one." He smiled. "If she looked like you."

For a moment, Eva was uncertain. Then she thought of her mother.

"It's not a negotiation." She wondered what exactly she was turning down.

Bryan's face hardened. "I want kids and you want none and so it's none? That doesn't sound like much of a negotiation to me."

"You can't bargain the kid thing. It's not a summer vacation."

"All I see is someone too selfish to think of anything but herself. Travel? Nice things? Instead of having children?"

"Maybe I'm selfish, but I like myself just as I am. I have a successful career. I stay in shape. I don't want to lose that."

"You're not a natural woman."

His words shocked the breath out of her.

The waiter approached. "Are you ready to order some dinner?"

"No." Bryan stood abruptly. "I think we're done here." He looked at Eva as if he wanted to say something. Then he shook his head and walked away, leaving her gaping in her chair.

The waiter looked uncomfortable. "I'll bring the check," he finally said as Bryan disappeared.

"Wait." Eva was stunned. She had to get control of this situation. "I'll have the Lomo steak. Medium." The waiter looked surprised but nodded.

She would eat. There was nothing in her pantry and she was starving. There was nothing she could do about Bryan. What would be the point? It would only postpone the inevitable.

The waiter delivered her steak.

"Thanks," Eva said. "You know, when Bruce Banner gets mad, he turns into the Hulk. When the Hulk gets mad, he turns into Chuck Norris."

"What happens when gorgeous blondes get mad?" he asked.

"Steak for one," she answered, digging in.

Eva drove home with the top down to enjoy the warm air. It smelled like wisteria. She heard a siren and saw flashing red lights and pulled over to let an extension-ladder fire truck barrel past. It was hard to believe someone's house was on fire on such a beautiful evening. It reminded her of that morbid ladybug poem: *Ladybug! Ladybug! Fly away home. Your house is on fire. And your children all gone.*

Just another reason not to have kids.

Andy Goes to Dinner

Andy was surprised not to smell dinner when he entered the house. The kitchen was cold, and there was no sign of Summer. She'd be happy he'd gotten the Cornin assignment. He found her in her dressing room, fastening a string of pearls. He stepped behind her and took over as she held up her straw hair. She was wearing a little black dress, which meant they were going out. For the life of him, Andy couldn't recall where.

"Hurry up," Summer urged as she stepped to her scarf shelf. "You're late." Andy had stopped trying to understand why Summer deliberated among her scarves when she was only going to tie the lucky selection to the strap of her purse, but he knew better than to ask. He could tell that he was expected to remember where they were going.

"What tie should I wear?" he fished.

She eyed him. "The blue one I brought back from San Francisco."

That could mean anything.

"Will there be food?" he hazarded.

She came over, scarf in hand, and kissed his cheek. "There better be after we spent three hundred dollars a plate to attend."

It was the Herb Green fund-raiser. Herb was the current Chair—and iron fist—of the Santa Monica City Council. He faced reelection in the fall, though his incumbency was assured, and he was hosting a series of campaign fund-raisers. Every Democratic member of the City Council would be there, which was basically every member, and Summer was determined to insert Andy into this social sphere. She radiated excited energy, and he decided not to bring up the Maryn problem.

"Let's hope it's not boiled chicken." He went to get his tie.

"Silly, it's at Morton's," Summer said, and Andy's mood lifted for the first time all day at the thought of a well-cooked steak.

At the steak house they were shown to a private room. Summer coughed discreetly and Andy couldn't blame her. Pungent smoke permeated the air. The source was a bald, red-faced man with a fat cigar clenched in his teeth. Herb Green was as rotund as Boss Hogg.

Summer drew a deep breath, as if to last, and they approached.

". . . they don't even try to stop me anymore," the fat man chortled. "That's Morton's official Herb Green memorial ash-tray. I pass the ordinances, so I guess I can pass the exceptions. Exception one is a two-foot radius encircling the corpus of one Herb Green, a full smoking zone by order of the Chair of the City Council!" His gesture sprinkled ash on those unfortunate enough to be close, and his guffaw turned into rasping coughs. A woman whose ridiculously skinny arms hardly seemed up for the task of her bangles pounded him on the back.

"You tell 'em, Herb."

The councilman's shirt appeared to be strangling him, fat rolls spilling over the straining collar button. Andy was concerned the fastening would burst, striking someone in the eye.

"Chairman Green? Summer Knox. We met through Josh Myers." Summer held out her hand.

"You're the weather gal."

Andy noticed the suppressed wince. "This is my husband, Andrew." She gestured.

"Hello, hello." Herb's giant paw swallowed Andy's hand. "Glad you could come."

He started to turn away, but Summer was used to having to work harder than beautiful girls. "Delighted to be here. We moved to Santa Monica because of the excellent governance under your stewardship. In fact, we were interested in becoming involved with your campaign. Perhaps we could host a fund-raiser at our home on San Vicente."

Herb perked up. "Well, that's a fine offer. You should speak to my campaign manager here, Charming Tommy." He clapped the back of a tall, thin man wearing spectacles and a bow tie.

"Tom Sizec." The man shook hands but didn't engage, more stressed than charming. He seemed anxious to shepherd Herb among his supporters, but Tommy was no match for Summer.

Summer wooed Herb Green, and when dinner was served, Andy found himself seated next to the large man as Summer deftly deflected Charming Tommy.

From his vantage, Andy marveled over the amount of starch, steak, and wine Herb consumed. The rotund man only passed on the vegetables.

"Strictly a meat and potatoes man," Herb confided, globbing another dollop of sour cream on his mashed potatoes. "Roughage doesn't do right by me."

That was more than enough information for Andy. He found himself principally listening to talk about recent budget debates. They could have been Charlie Brown's teacher for all he understood. A young man wearing a bolo tie also wasn't saying much. He seemed to be waiting. Andy found the bolo tie surprising because the man wore a wedding ring, and neither Maryn nor Summer would have let Andy out of the house in one. Something about Jed Clampett and the eighties.

" . . . so a sliding scale of pay cuts is preferable to layoffs," concluded a corpulent man to Herb's left.

Herb grunted at the waiter for more wine. The man with the bolo tie leaped in.

"What about the Bs, Councilman Green?"

The ridiculously skinny woman rolled her eyes and the corpulent man snorted, a scornful Jack Spratt and his wife. Herb remained neutral.

"What d'you think?" Herb directed his question to Andy.

Andy panicked. What could the Bs mean? The Better Business Bureau? A pneumonic, like Buses, Bikes, and the Boardwalk? Andy didn't know. Luckily bolo tie didn't wait. His words made Andy feel like an idiot.

"I speak for the entire American Beekeeping Federation when I say the crisis of colony collapse disorder has reached critical proportions! Fifty percent of honeybee colonies in California have been killed or severely weakened."

"California honeybees are responsible for nearly half of the state's eighteen-billion-dollar agricultural industry." Charming Tommy sent Herb a look.

Herb took his cue. "Tell me more."

"One-third of the human diet is derived from honeybee-pollinated crops. Unless measures are taken to protect bees, many fruits and vegetables may disappear from the food chain. Human life would end within four years!" The earnest man was vibrating. "The City Council must stop the practice of exterminating feral bees in favor of relocating them, and lift the ban on beekeeping."

Andy thought about bees and came to the conclusion that he didn't think much about bees. They did make him think of honey, which made him think of the Santa Monica farmers' market, which reminded him of how much he loved the farmers' market and made him wonder why he didn't go more often. Then he remembered Summer bitching while they were stuck in market traffic, roasting in the car, and recalled why he didn't go more often. Andy decided to have an Issue.

As Charming Tommy placated the bee advocate and the woman turned to order coffee, Andy leaped in.

"I'll tell you my issue," he said casually, hoping he recalled the statistics. "Traffic light synchronization. Did you know that traffic jams in the most congested sections of the city could be reduced by twenty percent with a traffic-signal timing plan for the downtown area? I was reading—"

"Son, it's been great talking to you. I gotta go," Herb boomed, standing abruptly and clapping a hand on Andy's shoulder. "I feel a poop coming on. It's my personal curse that it doesn't happen as often as I'd like, and at the moment I haven't crapped since Wednesday. Unless you count shitting all over crazy Richie Gregson's plan to expand the smoking ban to inside apartment units." His bark of laugher caused another coughing spasm. Charming Tommy Sizec's anxiety became both amplified and understandable. Herb bid the table farewell. "I never poop in a public place. It's best enjoyed at home."

He lumbered off, Charming Tommy scrambling after. While most of the other diners seemed unfazed, Andy was so shocked he forgot to mourn the demise of his Issue. He didn't care for open discussions of bodily functions.

"Lord, if I couldn't poop in public restrooms I'd have to give up going out or put on sixty pounds," the impossibly skinny woman said to Andy, washing a laxative down with her coffee.

Dimple Goes to Dinner

I 'm here," I called to my mother as I dropped my scarf on the
foyer table next to the wooden frog with an amber-studded
clock in its stomach. It was a centimeter past a gallbladder.

"*Jūs esat vēlu.*" You're late.

"I know, I know. I'm sorry. Traffic."

"You cannot say that, traffic. Every day there is traffic in Los
Angeles. You must think about traffic and be on time. When I
was a young girl working we had no traffic, we had no cars. I
walk forty-five minutes to the factory. I was not late."

"I know, *Mamu.*" I kissed the top of her head, distressed by
how I had to bend to do it, my shrinking mother. "What's for
dinner?"

"Your favorite. Bratwurst and sauerkraut."

I detested sauerkraut, but once my mother gets something
into her head, it's as impregnable as the Scientology records
room. Better to choke down the kraut. The one time I'd protested, I'd left so confused that for three days I'd been persuaded I loved fermented shredded cabbage.

"*Kā bija jūsu diena?*" How was your day?

"Same, same. Always same. These eyes! I cannot see, I
cannot sew, I cannot read, your old useless mother. Good for
nothing. They call this golden age. They can keep their golden
age." Macular degeneration had stripped my mother of the enjoyment of retirement.

"I have this." I held up a cassette tape. My mother might be the only person to listen to cassettes since Y2K.

"Ay! *Paldies*. I want to know if Dr. Reyes, she tell Dr. Wade to shove it. "

The cassette was the latest *Pulse* episode in Latvian, with me performing all the parts. Audio stories helped pass the long hours, but English-language recordings went too quickly for her to understand. I taped *Pulse* and the various scripts I received in her native tongue. This week, Dr. Reyes did indeed tell Dr. Wade to shove something somewhere, but not in my G-rated adjustment. I only prayed that the Latvian church ladies didn't watch *Pulse* because their recount and my mother's would never match.

"Don't you want to know what happens to me?"

"Pffffft," she dismissed. "You I know. You save some young girl, be sensitive. Come. We eat."

I glanced at the frog, and congratulated myself on forestalling dinner to 5:17 PM. Often so eager for the big event of the day, if you didn't intervene, my mother's anxiousness to tend to the roast led to four thirty dining. I didn't complain because I couldn't imagine a life where it was evening all afternoon. It would be like Clarissa Dalloway without the flowers or the party, only the endless, ever-dropping hours you could not fill. My mother's acute brain had been cheated by her failing body.

"Next week I'll record a new movie script I got. It's called *Cora*," I said as I calculated how much sauerkraut I had to gag down to be suitably grateful.

"*Paldies, mīlas vārdi*," she thanked me again. "Is Western?" My mother loved Westerns. They were so very American.

"No. It's a film I'm considering." Strong words since I'd learned of it this morning.

"What!" She put down her fork. "*Pulse*, it's canceled? You killed?"

"Nothing like that. I've been asked to look at a part. It's the lead." I tried to suppress the excitement in my voice.

Her beady stare didn't waver. "What you thinking? You have good job!"

"This wouldn't interfere with Roxy," I assured her. "It's a movie I'd do in addition to *Pulse*."

"Is risky. They find other actress while you away. Roxy's part disappear."

"This movie could be great for me, *Mamu*. The director, Julian Wales, he won the Academy Award for best director last year. It's worth a risk."

"No." My mother pulled me down with a bump. "Risk is no getting on the boat for America because you have fungus infection on your nails from digging in dirt to make food for your family. Risk is your *vecamama*, your papa's *mamu*, having fingernails pulled off her hands with no medicine for the pains so she get her family on that boat and come to America for a better life. Why you want risk? Is crazy."

"It's not the same . . ."

"You make good money, you have nice house, you no worry. You want like before, when you live eight girls? You so skinny I see through you. You no eat, you no have car, you no have gym and hairsdo and nice things you got now."

My palms started to ache. "No." I did not want to return to my Ramen hot pot pre-Roxy days.

"You pick crazy job. I no understand why. You should be lawyer or bookkeeper, but no, you choose job with no jobs. America crazy that way. In my country we farm, we make food. We build, we make houses. Here, you make costumes and speeches. And for what? For worry all the time about the money. And when you get one job, good one, pays bills, you want to screw up?"

"No," I repeated. I did not. She was right. There were few steady jobs for B-list or below actresses, and I was D list at best.

I'd been letting red-carpet fantasies about Julian Wales carry me away. I blamed LaMimi's imagination.

Mamu waved her bony finger at me. "You good girl, *dārgais*. You need be responsible."

The idea *was* foolishness. Julian Wales wouldn't pick a TV actress to play Cora. "I was only thinking about it. I wouldn't have gotten it anyway." Thank god I hadn't said anything on set. It would have been embarrassing. "What's for dessert?"

"Orange fluff." My mother pushed back her chair. "Then you read bills for me. No can read, even with magnificent glass."

Wyatt Goes to Tea

W yatt?" came the gruff voice over the telephone. "Katherine Feely Jones here."

Katherine Feely Jones was Wyatt's adoption broker. She had three names and she used all three of them every time she identified herself, though her smoker's rasp was its own unmistakable signature.

Wyatt's heart sank. Ilana's phone had rung endlessly for two days, and he was bordering on frantic. Something terrible had happened. "Hello, Katherine," he managed around a dry mouth.

"Congrats on those Vikings. Minnesota sure kicked Oakland's butt." Katherine believed that every client interaction should commence with exactly three personal observations to strengthen the relationship. Katherine was right, but Wyatt was anxious to get to business.

"Yes."

She continued to number two unfazed. "I thought of you when I read an article on the twenty-first-century classroom and the argument for introducing elements of online social communities such as YouTube as early as kindergarten . . ."

. . . *And when I learned that Ilana and the baby were crushed into a molten ball of glass and steel by an out-of-control eighteen-wheeler*, whispered Wyatt's imagination. Normally impressed with Katherine's range of sound bites, today he had no time.

"Katherine." He interrupted. "What happened to Ilana? Is she dead?"

"Dead?" Katherine was startled. "No, not dead. But, Wyatt, there's been a hiccup. I'd like you to come in so I can explain and answer all your questions."

Wyatt was intensely relieved that Ilana had not been beheaded by a stray sheet of glass sliding off a flatbed on the 405. His relief was replaced by a host of more varied but less fatal worries. The emotional roller coaster left him queasy. "A hiccup? What does that mean?"

"My schedule is open for you today. Can you come by?"

Wyatt recognized that he wasn't going to get anything out of Katherine Feely Jones until he met with her in person. As the school principal he made similar calls to parents on a daily basis. He was a master. Katherine was his match. "I'll come directly after school," he capitulated.

"I'll have the kettle on." Katherine liked meetings to feel like fireside chats. They didn't. They felt like *American Idol* auditions, the applicant nervously wondering if his song and dance was going to win a golden ticket. Ilana had been his golden ticket, and now there was a "hiccup."

"I'll see you then." He disconnected.

The afternoon passed in a blur. Wyatt Googled Ilana Lloubina a number of different ways involving initials and the creative use of quotations, but it yielded no city morgue reports or *L.A. Times* exposés, just the usual nothing. An astonished Sammy Whitcomb, senior class hooligan, scurried out of the principal's office unable to believe his luck after he was dismissed with a vague "Don't do it again" for selling ninth-graders individual cigarettes at two bucks a pop behind the gym. After all, mused Wyatt, it was a victimless crime. It wasn't as if he'd mugged a defenseless pregnant woman, leaving her an unidentified amnesiac in a hospital ward somewhere.

"Wyatt! Welcome." Katherine ushered him into her office. Her artificial red hair was poufed into some sort of lopsided Victorian bun arrangement, and she wore a periwinkle suit that Wyatt was sure had A Name. Her lipstick showed little ravines where skin met her upper lip, creviced from years of smoking. They sat at a grouping of overstuffed love seats rather than by her desk. Wyatt felt he might bounce right off if someone plopped down next to him.

"Coffee?"

"No thanks."

"Tea?"

"Fine." Wyatt wanted to get on with it. He accepted tea he wouldn't drink.

For once Katherine dispensed with the jokes. "Wyatt, I'm afraid I have bad news."

Wyatt braced himself.

"It seems we've both been the victims of a scam. Ilana has disappeared without further notice. I visited her apartment to find it cleaned out, with no indication of her whereabouts."

This was not what Wyatt was expecting to hear. "What do you mean? Where has she gone?"

"I'm afraid I don't know. I received a call this morning from a diligent Assistant U.S. Attorney in Orlando, Florida. Ilana Lloubina, under the name Ilya Petrov, has pulled this scam before."

"Scam?" Wyatt was bewildered. "Before? What happened to the baby?"

"According to the prosecutor, Ms. Petrov became pregnant while unmarried, and was guided to consider open adoption by a church counselor. A broker matched Ms. Petrov with a wealthy Orlando family, who set up Ms. Petrov in a nice apartment, with a generous stipend and a car. It was a satisfactory arrangement all around."

"Can we call her Ilana, please?" Wyatt tried to take in Katherine's story.

"Of course. The situation may have proved a little *too* satis-factory. Ilana came from a large Russian family of little income, and found her new lifestyle infinitely preferable to sharing one bathroom with eight siblings. Ilana found a *second* family that sought open adoption and contracted with them as well. The first family paid the bills directly, and she convinced the second family to provide her with cash to pay the same bills. Quite enterprising."

"For the same baby?"

"Yes."

"Was it . . . is it . . . my baby?"

"No. Unfortunately, that pregnancy failed. Ilana suffered a late-term miscarriage, and both contracts were dissolved, with all the parties none the wiser. Ilana would have walked away a little richer, but she got greedy."

"She got pregnant again." Wyatt hated the thought that his baby was conceived as a scam. He wanted to steal the child away and protect it from hurt. He also wanted to murder Ilana with his bare hands.

"That part is unclear. Ilana was treated by a fellow Russian, a gynecologist of indeterminate accreditation. Perhaps she was pregnant, perhaps she was not. The doctor would create preg-nancy documentation and 'refer' her to adoption brokers. Ilana would pretend to understand little English, and refuse care by any non-Russian physician. As you can imagine, most parents are so desperate for a healthy candidate they won't pursue up-setting questions."

Wyatt felt shame at her words. He wracked his memory for a single recollection of pregnant behavior or a baby bump. How could he, the king of intuition, not have noticed? Then again, what would he notice? He was a guy.

"They worked this scam on a number of families, each time concluding with a miscarriage. Unfortunately for Ilana, one of their victims was a doctor who questioned the affair. He reported his suspicion to a prosecutor. The prosecutor began to dig around. Before action could be taken, Ilya Petrov dropped off the radar, and wasn't heard from until she popped up as Ilana Lloubina in L.A."

"How did they find her?"

"As it happens the prosecutor himself had adopted a child, and had a vendetta against adoption scams. He refused to let the matter go. He kept on the crooked doctor until he cracked. They arrested him a few days ago, after he solicited an undercover agent to engage in the same ploy. It appears Ilana passed on her taste for the good life." Katherine sighed. "Greed makes you stupid."

So did desire, thought Wyatt. "She's been arrested."

"Sadly, no. She must have heard about her partner and dropped out of sight. I doubt we'll see her again."

They sat in silence, the lowering sun slanting through the office windows, each contemplating his or her hands.

"Wyatt, unfortunately she's gone, along with everything you've put into it. I wasn't sure how to handle the situation, as it's never happened to me before. I reviewed our contract, and under the terms, I fulfilled my legal obligations. I exercised due diligence and reasonable care in ascertaining the validity of the applicant, and relied upon seemingly legitimate documentation of a healthy pregnancy. It's outside the scope of reasonable business practices to anticipate artful fraud, and the medical and personal verification I conducted satisfied the best practices for my industry."

"I understand." Wyatt understood that Katherine was worried about liability and profit. Wyatt wasn't thinking about that. He felt like his heart had been ripped out and shredded. He wondered if he could die from the burning in his chest. It was inconceivable to Wyatt that his baby had never existed.

"This is a blow. You've lost a lot of money. You're angry."

She didn't understand at all. Wyatt didn't want to sue or get his fee back. He wanted the baby. The baby who didn't exist.

"I want to help you. I'm going to put you at the top of the list. We will stipulate that you're present at *all* medical appointments and receive proof of pregnancy firsthand. I'll pay for a thorough background check by the investigator of my choice—"

Wyatt held up a hand. "Katherine, I've been supporting this girl for months. Your fee is not insignificant. I'm a public servant. I don't know if I can afford a second process."

They were both silent. "Wyatt, it's a lot to take in. Go home and think about it. I'm here when you want me. If you believe you have to go through the state foster care and public adoption route, I'll try to help there too."

Wyatt nodded.

"Perhaps you'll find an opportunity for a traditional approach to children . . ." She let the suggestion trail off.

"We'll see." Wyatt was tight. If he'd wanted to marry just to make a baby, he'd have done it. Wyatt had no trouble meeting women. Old fashioned, maybe, but he didn't believe in marrying for anything less than love. That, he'd not yet found.

They stood. Katherine was a tall woman, taller than average-height Wyatt by an inch in her square heels. She unnecessarily laid a hand on his arm, grasping the bicep and giving him a winsome smile.

"You're one of the most commendable clients I have, Wyatt Ozols. Don't let this sway you from your path. I'll consider my life less worthy if you don't have a child of your own one day."

"Thank you," Wyatt said. Her flirting made him uncomfortable, like running into your Sunday school teacher in a miniskirt at a bar. Her kindness didn't change anything.

As he walked out of the building he felt obvious, the hole in his heart glaring like a FRANKIE SAYS RELAX T-shirt. Passersby could look right through. He discarded the idea of calling Eva for support. He was angry. And emasculated. And stupid. He stared into the window of Sur La Table, lost and blind, not registering the enticing staged kitchen, seeing only the reflection of a sad stranger.

Maryn Goes to Lunch

Adina DeGuardi?" Maryn approached a tousled brunette with lips so plumped they looked like stacked figs, and offered her hand. "Maryn Windsor. Nice to meet you."

"Pleasure's mine, darling." Adina had a nasal Long Island twang unusual for L.A. and unusual for her deep baritone voice. Maryn checked the woman's throat for an Adam's apple, but Adina was all woman.

"I hope you haven't been waiting." Maryn was precisely on time. She never kept clients waiting.

"Not at all. I like this joint. Good people watching."

They sat on the sidewalk at Café Med in West Hollywood. Maryn had thought it would appeal. The waiter approached.

"Do you need a minute?" Maryn asked. She always ordered the Cobb salad.

"No, darling, I don't do solids. Just a coffee, black," Adina instructed the waiter.

"Cobb salad." Maryn didn't react. She wondered if the collagen made it painful to chew. "What brings you to L.A.?"

"My daughter." She pronounced it *daw-duh*. "She's started at UCLA and can't live without her pony. It's a gift from her father. She's such a daddy's girl."

"That's wonderful she can keep her horse nearby while she's in school."

"Yes, well, Serge—that's my husband—knows a guy with a lotta land. It should work out fine."

A yellow flag went up in Maryn's mind. She avoided clientele who "knew a guy."

"Oh?" She sipped her water.

"Yeah. Serge gave him something, I don't know what. But this guy and my husband, they love the ponies. Both got a herd of 'em. Always talking horses. Not me. I'll be honest, I'm afraid of 'em, giant hooves and rolling eyes. Unpredictable. But Serge and Tina, that's my girl, they love 'em."

"What does your husband do?"

"Whatever he wants!" the woman chortled, slapping her aqua miniskirt. Maryn kept a neutral expression, mentally turning down the deal. "No, really." Adina waved pink talon nails. "He owns a chain called Mario's Pizza. People line up to pay five bucks for a slice of cardboard with fat melted on it."

Maryn was reassured. Mario's Pizza was a huge chain. At least the guy wasn't into "import-export" or "garbage removal."

"And what he wants," Adina went on, "is for his little girl to be happy. That means carting this horse out to Los Angeles like she's Zsa Zsa Gabor flying first class with a masseuse." The woman belted out another laugh.

"What's the horse's name?" Maryn asked.

"Farasha. Here are the details."

Maryn looked over the file Adina handed her. Farasha was a beautiful three-year-old Arabian.

"And you'd like to fly her out when Tina starts school?"

"Tina's here now, so we wanna fly her out as soon as possible."

"I see."

"And Rico says you're the best."

"Rico?"

"Enrique Ruiz. That's Serge's guy, who's gonna board Farasha."

Maryn relaxed. Enrique Ruiz was a reputable horse fancier with a large property near the San Gabriel Mountains. He'd periodically used Maryn's services for stud or race travel, and she'd never had a problem. "Enrique is a lovely man."

"He's been real good to Serge, helping him learn the horse biz."

"Your husband has a fine eye. Farasha is a beautiful animal."

"Tina likes her." Adina shrugged and pulled a super-slim cigarette out of a silver box. Maryn opened her mouth, but Adina waved her off. "I know, I know. I used to live here. I just suck on it unlit."

"One-way travel from New York JFK to LAX is approximately eleven thousand dollars. The specific fee will depend upon final details such as the date of flight, available groom, and so forth."

"That's just for the one flight, right? 'Cause of course the little dear will have to come home for summer and Christmas and probably freaking Thanksgiving. And then back again." She waved her unlit cigarette. "Where Tina goes that horse will go."

Maryn concealed her excitement. This was a huge commission. "We're at your disposal. There are certain restrictions of course, for when a horse can't travel, but they tend to be rare, such as when the horse is pregnant, or contagious. Otherwise we work to meet your needs."

"Great." Adina lost interest now that the transaction had shifted to money. Maryn suspected bills were Serge's province.

Maryn's phone buzzed on the table between them. Andy. She frowned and ignored it.

"Who's that?"

Maryn was surprised to see Adina rapt with interest.

"It's nothing." Maryn slid the phone into her purse. "It was impolite of me to leave my phone on."

"Doll, that was 'nothing' like I'm twenty-nine and these are the boobs God gave me." Adina chuckled. "You got *the face.*"

Maryn raised an eyebrow. "The face?"

"It's a look only a man can cause. And I'm not talking about a male client."

"Hmm." Maryn remained neutral.

"So who's got your goat, honey?"

"Nothing so interesting, I'm afraid." Maryn forced a laugh.

Adina appraised her. "Who could the mysterious Andy be?" She tapped her chin theatrically and considered Maryn. "You've saved him in your contacts under only one name, so he's someone close. But it's hard to picture you troubled by a mere boyfriend. So even though you don't wear a ring, I'm going with husband."

"*Ex*-husband." Maryn capitulated to the game.

"Still letting him play in the henhouse?"

"Nothing like that. We have some . . . unresolved issues."

"Honey, with ex-husbands, there's only one way to 'resolve issues.'" Adina dug into her purse. She pulled out a crocodile wallet and fished out a card. "That's to sue their ass. Here." She handed it to Maryn. "I moved back to New York because California got a little crowded with ex-husbands for my taste. Selena Hernandez is my pit bull. You can't do better."

"Oh no, we aren't—"

"Sure, sure, doll, it's for a friend. Don't worry. Mum's the word." Adina pulled out a compact and examined herself. "The truth is, men are lazy. Selena files a piece of paper with their name in scary block letters, and they roll over and give you what you want. It's easier than dealing with you." She snapped her compact shut. "Works every time."

"Thank you." It was easier to acquiesce than explain. She could never sue Andy. He was . . . well . . . *Andy*.

"Gotta run." Adina gave her a toothy smile as she stood. "I'd say let me know how it goes, but you won't. Thanks for lunch."

She tottered off on her spike heels, leaving Maryn to signal for the check.

Eva Goes for Coffee

E va was impressed as she flipped through the script, sipping from her towering venti of caffeine. Julian Wales could very well add another statuette to his brag shelf with *Cora*. Every agent in town wanted in, none more than Eva. She worried that the juicy role might be too much for her young client, but felt the frisson of electricity she got when sinking her teeth into a challenge. Or maybe it came from being watched.

She looked up from her table at the Coffee Bean, sixth sense on alert. She spotted the man immediately. He was staring. He approached.

"Excuse me, do you live around here often?" he joked. He had impossibly green eyes, crinkly and sleepy.

"Were you just ogling my legs?"

"I was defenseless against them. You should be more careful." His hair was shaggy, but his demeanor was more sailboat captain than surfer dude.

"If I throw a stick, will you leave?"

He shook his head. "Only if it's a boomerang."

"Stalking is illegal."

"So is entrapment." He gestured toward her legs.

Eva was enjoying herself. She had time before her meeting. "Sit."

He did. "Sawyer Reynolds."

"Eva Lytton."

"I'm a two percent macchiato."

"Skim latte."

"We met once before."

"We did?" Eva would have remembered this man.

"At the Sony Christmas party. Bryan Wallace introduced us for a second before whisking you off."

"You work with Bryan?"

"We both work for the megabehemoth that is Sony, but I see him like I see the inside of a church."

Eva raised an eyebrow.

"Twice a year," he explained. "Fourth of July picnic and the Christmas party. He's in marketing. I license music. He's an idiot."

"I'm sorry?" Eva couldn't keep up.

"That guy had an opportunity to have all his dinners with you, and he blew it. Douche bag."

Eva blinked, dumbstruck. "Not *all* his dinners," she finally said.

"Well, naturally. There's book club."

"I'm not in a book club."

He looked affronted. "I meant *my* book club. I'm a sensitive guy."

"When women say they like men with something tender about them, they mean legal tender." Eva couldn't get offended by this guy.

He made a face. "I'm having an out-of-money experience right now. Great Uncle Ebenezer is determined to live forever."

"My mom used to say where there's a will, I want to be in it."

"Just not on the top line, right after 'of.' "

Eva laughed, and looked at her watch. "I have to go."

"Have dinner with me."

"Oh." Eva was quite attracted to Sawyer, but he was a stranger in a coffee shop. Wyatt would berate her for considering it.

"I'm sure it's out of character, but have dinner with me in a very public place at the time, date, and location of your choosing, and I'm paying so you don't have to dither about potential awkwardness when the check comes. Here is my card, so you can verify my gainful employment. We will arrive separately and leave separately, and call your mother from the table to ensure her you have not been serial killed."

Eva considered the seemingly non-serial-killing, non-dog-kicking, tax-paying, CNN-watching guy before her for only a second before saying, "Fine. But I'm not calling my mother. I'm calling Chuck Norris. He puts the 'laughter' in 'manslaughter.' "

The Dr. Seuss creature stared at Eva as she approached. She stared back. He had bulbous wet eyes and the tiniest face she'd ever seen. It was his feet that made him Seussian. Delicate little paws with tufts of hair that curled, like a creature from *Horton Hears a Who*. He yapped.

"Shush, Charlie," Daisy cooed, scooping him into her purse. "It's rude to complain about being kept waiting."

"Sorry," Eva apologized. "Appointment."

Daisy looked curious. "What are you getting done? Cheeks? Or lips?" She studied Eva, and nodded. "Lips."

"What? No." Eva was taken aback. "A work appointment."

Daisy grinned as she followed Eva into her office. "Sure."

"Have a seat." Eva touched her lips. "How was the press tour for *The Best Day of Someone Else's Life*?" Daisy's first romantic comedy had just been released.

Daisy shrugged. "The thread count in some of the hotels was questionable." Eva was distracted as the dog clambered out of Daisy's bag and settled on her lap. Daisy pushed him off, and he twirled into a knot on Eva's sofa cushion.

"You can never count on the Four Seasons." Irony was lost on Eva's spoiled client. "Did you look at the scripts I sent you?"

"I want *Butterfield 8*." Daisy commanded the role like a ham on rye.

"The reimaging of *Butterfield 8* is in postproduction." Reimaging was the politically correct way to avoid inflaming devotees of the original with the word "remake." "It was filmed with Camilla Belle. Last year." Eva hid her expression. "Did you read the scripts I *gave* you?"

"Fine," Daisy huffed, as if choice roles should remain open until she cast herself. "I'll do *Rainy Season*. And *Cora*."

Eva nodded. "*Rainy Season* is a good fit. I'll reach out to Penny Marshall."

"*Cora* is better. Get me *Cora*."

"Julian Wales is courting Dimple Bledsoe for the role of Cora Aldridge." Though the script had only been floating for a few days, word was, Freya Fosse's client was the front-runner. It irked Eva, but she'd focus on *Rainy Season*.

"He asked me first."

"It's not like going to prom, Daisy. He asked you to look at the script, but since then he hasn't returned my calls. If he's decided on Dimple, it's a waste of time pursuing it. You don't want the consolation prize of a supporting role, you need a lead. Let's focus on *Rainy Season* and see if Dimple gets the role before making a move. I'd give it until . . ."

Eva looked down at her desk calendar and when she looked up again it was like the horror scene when the medicine-cabinet door closes and something terrifying and close is reflected there.

"I'm not smart, but I'm not dumb either." Daisy's nose practically touched Eva's. Startled as she was, Eva couldn't help but admire her flawless complexion, minuscule pores blemish free. "I want that part and you're going to get it for me."

"Daisy, it's not that easy." Eva edged back.

"In fact, it is. If you can't get Julian Wales to return your calls, I'll find an agent who can. I expect you to get him on the phone, show up on his doorstep, or pop out of his freaking urinal if that's what it takes."

Eva didn't know what to say.

"I won't be waltzing up the Kodak Theatre red carpet for gold as often as Meryl Streep, but I'm good enough." Daisy managed to look both steely and smug. Maybe she was a better actress than Eva thought. "I'm tall. I'm blonde. I don't eat. I go to enough clubs to stay in the tabloids but not so many I get into trouble. I got the dog." She gestured at the Martian. "I can't do a concentration camp accent but I won't fall on my face playing a chick with more depth than Barbie. I remember my lines and show up on time, but not so on time they think I need them more than they need me. And I've got the ace in the hole." She returned to her seat.

"What's that?" Eva was relieved to have space.

Daisy perched with perfect posture and a cat-ate-the-canary grin. "I'm young. All I have to do is wait. Dimple Bledsoe, Jennifer Aniston, and Cameron Diaz will shoot past their youth and hurtle over the hill into obscurity. Today's 'hot competition' will wither like forgotten carrots in the crisper."

Eva pictured decaying veggies.

"And I'll be waiting," Daisy finished. "You only need a little talent if you're the hot new young thing."

She stared at Eva, delicate hands folded, serene. The creature next to her stared at Eva, wispy paws crossed.

"I thought the dog had to be a Chihuahua," was all Eva could think to say.

"Charlie's a Chinwa. It's a mix of Japanese Chin and long-haired Chihuahua. I couldn't bear the short hairs." She shuddered. "Like rats."

Charlie gave Daisy a reproachful face, then looked at Eva, as if to shrug and say, "What can you do?"

"Gotta run!" Daisy looked at her watch and popped up. "Call me when you get *Cora*." She paused, then said, "Agents have an arc too, you know. Today's hot agent is tomorrow's Riverside Community College lecturer. If one can't get the job done, there are always ten younger, hungrier ones ready to step into her shoes."

There was a flurry, then Eva was alone with a cloud of scent and the weight of her thirty-four years.

Dimple Stands Up

J ulian Wales is, shall we say . . . *unorthodox*," Freya said.

"Shall we? If we shall, what does that mean? Unorthodox like he casts unknown actors, or unorthodox like he wears a pink tutu and clown shoes to work and breathes through his left eyelid?" Freya's tendency to "forget" unpleasant facts drove me nuts.

"More like he chooses actors based on . . . *unconventional* methods."

"Unconventional, like they all stand around a script and the last one still touching it three days later gets the part, or unconventional like he consults a psychic?"

"Well, darling, I don't know *exactly*—it's my first time working with him too. The man is a mystery wrapped around an enigma who whirled into town with *Pull* and now can dance to any tune he likes. No one cares about his . . . *eccentricities*. They only want to polish the tiny gold statues he's going to bring them." I cursed Freya's fondness for words like "unconventional" and "eccentricities." I was convinced they shielded the worst. "Dimple. What difference does it make? We'll find out soon enough, won't we?"

"I don't like surprises," I said.

"You might, if the surprise was an Oscar nomination." Her rebuke was crisp. "Now call him. I have to run." Click.

I looked at the scribbled phone number of last year's Oscar winner. It was surreal that I had it. I didn't know why I was fighting Freya. I was dying to see Julian Wales. In the week since I'd gotten the *Cora* script, I'd thought of little else.

I wandered into the bathroom to check my eyebrows. I have a thing about eyebrow grooming. I can't talk on the phone if they're unkempt. I plucked a rogue hair. I continued to stare at myself.

"Hello, I'm Dimple Bledsoe."

Too Johnny Cash, and I didn't have what Johnny Cash had.

"Your future Cora Aldridge calling!"

God no. I was an actor, not the Avon lady.

"Julian, it's Dimple. We met last year?"

Way too Hollywood. "Let's do lunch, darling! Call me?" I waggled my hand like a fake phone at my reflection, and started laughing. Was I returning his call, or pledging a sorority?

I settled on "Dimple Bledsoe calling." It was a bit Miss Moneypenny, but who was cooler than Moneypenny? Flirtatious yet mocking, even James Bond had loved the MI5 maven.

"Dimple Bledsoe calling." I practiced a few variations until I had it right.

I brushed my hair, still wavy from Justine's ministrations, returned to my desk, and dialed. I tried to ignore my rising adrenaline.

"A termite walks into a bar and says, 'Is the bartender here?'" a deep voice said into the phone.

"Uh. Oh. What?" My practiced introduction fled. Had satellite signals crossed me into someone else's conversation?

"A five-dollar bill walks into a bar. Bartender says, 'Get outta here! This is a singles bar.'"

I hung up.

I must've dialed the wrong number. I compared my phone's history with the piece of paper on my desk. Shit. Had I hung up on Julian Wales? Or some deranged assistant? Panic rose. Now I had to call him back. I stroked an eyebrow. Then I got mad. Who answered a phone like that? Normal people did not do that.

"Crap," I muttered, and hit redial.

"A priest, a rabbi, and a Polack walk into a bar. The bartender says, 'What is this? Some kind of joke?'"

"Is this a phone or a radio show?"

"I suspect I'm hearing the melodious tones of Ms. Dimple Bledsoe, and she is irritated that the practiced poise with which she was prepared to charm me has been upset."

Thank god it wasn't videophone, or Julian Wales would see my mouth hanging open.

"Hello?"

"Are you wasting my time, Mr. Wales?"

"I'm enjoying Talk Like a Bar Joke Day. I don't believe in wasting time. Meet me at Johnny Cupcakes on Melrose by Crescent in thirty minutes."

"I . . . what? No . . . I can't just—"

"My instructions were to call when you had plenty of time."

"Well, yes. To *talk*. I—"

"We'll talk in person." He disconnected the phone, leaving me flummoxed. Until I realized I had thirty minutes to get to Melrose and leaped to the bathroom to throw on some makeup.

As I approached the plate-glass front of Johnny Cupcakes, I wasn't sure what I expected, but it wasn't Julian Wales chatting with an ancient birdlike woman perched on a stool. I looked for a camera crew and PAs but it was just himself. I studied him through the window. He had both hands in a green canvas army jacket that had seen better days, and rocked on the balls of his feet as he listened to a yarn the septuagenarian was spinning. When he laughed, he threw his head back and really laughed, as if opening his throat for the light to pour in. The exposed pose startled me. This anonymous guy nibbling a cupcake had as much presence as the red-carpet luminary accepting Hollywood's top honor.

He saw me, and waved me inside. Approaching Julian Wales reminded me of running up to a cow as a small child. As I got closer, the beast loomed larger, and my steps slowed. I'd heard about cows, seen photos of cows, thought I knew cows, but faced with my first live cow, I was overwhelmed. It was huge. Julian Wales was taller and broader than I remembered.

"Hello, I'm—"

" 'I have a split personality,' said Tom, being frank," he interrupted. "Let's go." He took my arm and hustled me right back outside.

"But—"

"We have to hurry. We're late."

He paused only to switch to the street side of me.

"Why did you have me come to Johnny's?"

He looked at me as if I was nuts. "I wanted a cupcake."

I didn't like dangling events, and the "shave and a haircut . . ." without the "two bits" of our encounter was needling me. People needed proper introductions. I could feel the spot between my shoulders where years of jabs reminded me that you greeted Latvian church ladies and other people with a formal shake as you looked them directly in the eyes.

"How do you feel about Starbucks? I mean, really feel?" Julian's look was inquisitive. "Or are you more of a Peet's person?"

"Stop." I pulled away, and planted my feet, hands on hips, stance solid. I didn't care if we were late.

He raised an eyebrow.

"Hello. I'm Dimple Bledsoe." Moneypenny forgotten, all Johnny Cash, I thrust a hand at him.

He chuckled. "This is really irritating you, isn't it?"

"Yes." I remained in position, arm extended. He shook solemnly.

"Julian Wales."

"I read your script and am impressed, Mr. Wales."

"Julian, I insist."

"Julian. I'm not one to self-denigrate, but I must say I'm honored and a little surprised that you're considering me for the role of Cora." I secretly feared he was going to look shocked and apologetic and say, *Cora? Oh dear, no. I'm afraid we were considering you for the role of her maiden aunt Gertrude. Bless your poor little over-the-hill heart.* I had no idea why in my imagination he talked like a Southern evangelist's wife.

He did look surprised. "Why not?"

I wouldn't give him a reason if he didn't have one. "The script doesn't make clear how old Cora is." It was neither a question nor an answer.

"Cora is old enough to have been knocked down a few times, and young enough to get back up again. She's alive enough to want something bad, and able enough to try to get it."

"That could be anything from eight to eighty."

"Exactly."

"I understand you're talking to Daisy Carmichael. She seems quite . . . *different* from me." God, I was talking like Freya.

He gave me Producer Face, a mask revealing nothing.

"Please trust that I am spending time with you in an earnest quest for the best actress for Cora. A superlative way to determine what you want is often to entertain opposites. You and Daisy have different attributes that immediately recollect different parts of Cora for me. In full disclosure, I've also spent time with Hiwa Bourne and Catherine Friel," he named two A listers, "but their many excellent qualities were not suitable for Cora. Today, I want to become acquainted with offscreen Dimple Bledsoe to explore her attributes."

He smiled and I returned it. Was he flirting? Grinning goofily at each other, it felt more like a first date than an audition.

"Feel better?"

"Yes."

"Did you hear about the guy whose whole left side was cut off? He's all right now." He looked at his watch. "Oh my. We're late." He was like the White Rabbit.

"What are we late for?" I started walking again, and again he smoothly switched so he was on my street-exposed side.

"We're going to a show." He led us to the box office at the Improv.

"Ah, Mr. Wales. We've been waiting." A man dressed in head-to-toe black escorted us through a crowded room to a table by the stage.

Julian rubbed his hands like he was plotting world domination. "I love a good improv."

I was bewildered. Keeping up with Julian Wales was like playing Whac-A-Mole. How was hanging out at a comedy club going to help him cast a part?

He turned to me. "Have you seen these guys? They're great!"

"I can't wait." I smiled. The show was called *Women Who Kill*, an all-female lineup. The waiter brought wine as the lights went down and the first comedienne took the stage.

"My preschool is having a thirtieth reunion. I don't want to go, because I've put on, like, a hundred pounds."

Julian laughed uproariously. I got nervous that I didn't laugh very hard. Was this a test, to see if I found the right parts funny? Maybe he would think I didn't have a sense of humor.

"A lady came up to me on the street and pointed to my leather jacket, saying, 'You know a cow was murdered for that jacket?' I replied in a psychotic tone, 'I didn't know there were witnesses. Now I'll have to kill you too.'"

I watched Julian for subtle muscle twitches to cue his reaction, aiming to laugh the same amount at the same jokes. But my staged laughs sounded like Simple Dimple, and the strain of peeking out of the corners of my eyes gave me a headache, so I gave up and laughed when I felt like it. The women were funny and the wine wasn't dreadful, so before long I forgot about it and enjoyed myself.

"Let's hear it for Jana, folks!" The emcee-type person called as the last comedienne left the stage. "Did everyone have a good time?" People hollered and banged beer bottles. Julian applauded, ringing claps with his large hands. "You guys want to call it a night?" The crowd booed. "You're in luck! We have a special performance, one night only. This funny lady has been a performer for longer than most actresses can count with their shoes on. She's five ten, a Scorpio, and hails from our own Venice Beach. Please put your hands together for . . . Dimple Bledsoe!"

My veins turned to ice and my vision tunneled. A spot swung to our table. Julian pounded his hands as if this was the greatest joke ever. I couldn't breathe.

Everyone was staring. I felt near hysteria. The longer I sat, the worse it got. I stood abruptly, crossing to the stage and accepting the microphone on autopilot. I blinked into the lights. Clapping petered out and silence took over.

"Hello," I said. People shifted in their chairs. Everyone was waiting to see what I would do. Julian beamed. Rage erupted inside me.

"How many directors does it take to screw in a lightbulb?" I said the first thing I could think of. "One hundred. One to do it and ninety-nine to say 'I could've done that.'"

Feeble chuckles.

"She's not very funny, is she?" A stage whisper to my left.

I took a deep breath. Then another. I thought of the routines that had come before me. I thought of comedy routines in general. They had a formula. I could do this. What had I said that made everyone laugh at Monday's read through?

"So I'm single. It's a challenge, but if love were easy, there'd be almost no music."

Chuckles.

"I thought I'd be divorced by now. At my age, if you're still single, you realize you missed the first-round draft picks. Suddenly, the guy with the pleat-front pants looks awfully cute carrying a diaper bag. I have to wait for trading season."

Definite laughter.

"I read about this study that says when women go on dates, they decide if they're gonna sleep with a guy in the first twelve seconds. Seems wrong to me. How are these women getting drunk so fast?"

I had a death grip on the mike, worried it would slip from my sweaty palms.

"I try to keep my spirits up, though, I do. You never know when you're going to round a corner and bump into Mr. You Might Do."

I strung together every one-liner and funny story I'd ever told. When it seemed like forever had passed, but the clock said ten minutes, I bailed.

"Thanks for tolerating me. Really. I've had a wonderful evening. It just wasn't this one."

I fled to the sanctuary of the side stage. Maybe I was supposed to feel triumph from getting laughs, but I didn't. I felt seasick. I was a camera actress, not a stand-up. My hands shook. I gripped them around an icy bottle, gulping the water.

"You were fantastic!" Julian bounded behind the curtain, wreathed in grins. He swept me into a hug.

LaMimi responded to being crushed against his concrete chest. That only fanned my ire. I yanked back.

"You think that was funny?"

"Hilarious." His eyes danced.

I stabbed him with a finger. "That was cruel."

"You aced it."

"I nailed my appendectomy too, but I didn't enjoy it."

"I thought you were wonderful." He placated.

"I thought you were an asshole," I said. I didn't care about *Cora*. "I don't appreciate being set up like that. I'm leaving."

"Let me drive you home," he appeased. It made me angrier that I was the only one rattled.

"No. You've driven me quite enough." I turned my back on him and stomped away. I'd have walked ten miles in five-inch Louboutins before riding with Julian Wales. Lucky thing I had my car. I didn't like him. I didn't get him. Particularly why he was smiling as I strode off.

Wyatt Goes Shopping

Wyatt was in Target and he thought he might be having a nervous breakdown. It was not a feeling he was used to.

"Can I help you?"

The clerk startled him and he clutched the Egg Genie, embarrassed to be considering an item emblazoned with AS SEEN ON TV!

"I'm fine." He hurried off, now committed to spending $14.99 for something he could do with a pot of water. Or maybe he couldn't. Maybe he'd been boiling eggs wrong all these years. Wyatt had a pretty simple bachelor's rule for cooking. He did what his mother had done. But maybe what had worked before wasn't good enough anymore. Ilana had spun the normally doubt-free Wyatt into crisis.

"You're going to be judged by a different standard," said the woman leading the Dad(s) Alone support group. "We're still a society that doesn't credit males with strong parenting urges. We're trapped in a decades-old film reel of the father dragged kicking and screaming to adulthood via the delivery room, where he is a comedy of mishaps before he holds his newborn child and falls in love with the wisdom beyond years in its wee baby eyes. It's a bunch of crap." Her anger was genuine, lips quivering under a poor choice of lipstick (he was going with Peach Daiquiri) and righteous indignation. Her hair looked as though it had been styled with a weed whacker.

Wyatt hadn't taken the time Katherine Feely Jones had encouraged him to take. He was an action man. He'd spent the three weeks since their meeting looking into less expensive adoption routes, like the state foster system. He'd stumbled across the Dad(s) Alone forum on the Web and decided to visit a meeting. He'd tried to blend into his folding chair, an unmemorable shade.

Fourteen other earnest men clutched paper cups and shifted in their uncomfortable plastic seats. No one wore name tags, so they were identifiable only by physical characteristics— Earring, Stain-on-Tie, Face Like a Hound Dog, Uncanny Resemblance to Jay Leno. Wyatt was reminded of Alcoholics Anonymous meetings he'd attended as a spectator. Former students, looking to get their lives back on track, would ask him to accompany them as they started the difficult journey to sobriety. Sometimes his presence helped and sometimes it didn't, but Wyatt had spent many nights in smoky church basements, clutching bad coffee cut with powdered creamer, feeling helpless in the face of the stories.

At Dad(s) Alone, the similarities ended at the basement. It was smoke free, and guests sipped herbal tea, yet Wyatt felt the same sense of helplessness.

"Adoption agencies may discriminate against male-parent adoptions," said Peach Daiquiri. "You have to work harder and be better. Things normal parents can get away with, you can't." She ticked them off on her fingers. "No smoking; no DUIs; no speeding tickets; no one-night stands; no porn; and I swear to god, even if you're a jockey by profession, you'd better not have whips in your barn. Spying eyeballs will twist them into something nefarious. Don't let your dog so much as think about taking a crap on someone else's yard. If it's not the adoption agency, it'll be some 'concerned citizen' looking to take you down. Don't let them. You have every bit as much of a right to raise a family as anyone else."

"What possible justification can someone have against a

loving couple providing a home for a child in need?" sputtered a ramrod-straight man with rapidly blinking eyes behind horn-rimmed glasses. "We saw a special about neglected children in Los Angeles, and immediately started the adoption process. It still took two years of jumping through hoops before we were approved to foster." There was a smattering of claps. Wyatt paid attention.

Horn Rims's outraged blinking escalated. "So there we were, like idiots, waiting for that call from the agency. Weeks went by, then months, and now almost a year. They even re-ran that special! And not so much as a single call!" He seemed ready to vibrate off the chair, a wooden soldier on a truck bed. His partner patted his back. "It's outrageous—there are thousands of kids desperate for a good home."

The circle of men nodded. Dapper, all, knit polos taut over biceps, military-short hair glinting with gel. Spacing between chairs indicated pairs—gaps between every other. Only Wyatt's chair had space on both sides.

Peach Daiquiri sighed. "There's still prejudice against men adopting. Some stems from fears of pedophilia. Some stems from prejudice against gays. And some is the traditional belief that a woman is the best caregiver for a child."

Horn Rims was not appeased. His partner, by contrast, was soft spoken. "The strange thing to us was how we came to the adoption process with a lot of joy, as a first choice. Nearly all the straight couples came from a place of pain, a last resort. It seemed to us that we were better suited for parenting, that we had less baggage."

Peach Daiquiri hesitated at the edge of the minefield. "There's no better or worse qualification to parent," she said slowly. "The decision to adopt puts everyone on equal footing in the most important qualification—wanting this blessing in your life."

Wyatt applauded her diplomatic response. He knew too many parents coming from that place of pain to pass judgment.

"Doesn't the fact that we're in committed relationships make a difference?" Earring clasped the hand of Stain-on-Tie.

"Regardless of whether stereotypes about two-dad families are true, if a birth mother, agency, social worker, or attorney believes that children shouldn't be placed in a two-dad home, you're going to face an uphill battle."

"Should we adopt daughters?" Stain-on-Tie spoke for the first time.

Peach looked doubtful. "I don't think gender specification is a good thing," she answered carefully. "The more open you are to any child, the less it looks like you have a suspect preference."

"It's ridiculous that we're having this discussion!" sputtered Horn Rims. "Single women aren't suspected of molestation if they try to adopt a boy!"

"It's true." Peach was genuinely sad. "We've come a long way, but there's still far to go."

Wyatt wondered if he looked gay. He was the only straight man in the room. And the only single man.

"How do we start?" asked a man so studiously dressed in every shade of blue the ensemble shrieked that he'd rather be wearing a flair of pink.

Peach brightened. "I have a sheet!" She handed a sheaf of light blue papers to her left. Everyone took one and passed it on.

It was cheerful and covered with little icons of yellow ducks and baby rattles, and provided no real information. It wouldn't have passed even the flimsiest of laugh tests with Wyatt's students. He could imagine their mockery: "Don't forget: Wake up! And breathe!" "Put on your pants! Don't shit in them!"

Sensing that the natives were restless, Peach rushed on. "Once you apply to adopt a child—regardless of whether it's through an agency, a broker, or directly to the court—the laws of California require a home study. That's the written report of the social worker who has met with the applicants on several occasions, both individually and together." Peach did not offer the single-applicant scenario.

"How long does it take?" Useful information had recaptured the group's attention, though Horn Rims rolled his eyes to make sure they knew he was ahead of the class. Wyatt had a flash of gladness the couple hadn't been given a child, but then felt guilty and disloyal.

"Three to six months, but public agencies may take longer. The criminal background check and verifying employment history can take time."

"Are there special considerations we, as gay couples, need to anticipate?" Blue Boy focused on the practical. Wyatt bet he was a lawyer. Then he wondered if he was supposed to speculate about people in support groups without name tags.

Peach looked at them frankly. "Take down the black-and-white framed nudes, no matter how tasteful. Throw out the dildos. Hide the Thunder from Down Under wall calendar. Serve homemade lemonade and cookies, not umbrella drinks and sashimi. Don't have a criminal record, and if you do, come clean at once. Get a Volvo, an ironing board, and a Crock-Pot. If you can dig up a doting granny and cart her over in a rocker, all the better."

Someone joked, "I'll lure Gran with my famous apple martini," amid chuckles. Wyatt had never owned any porn, but he made a mental note to throw out any Abercrombie & Fitch catalogs, and maybe that flammable-seeming blanket he'd kept from a United Airlines flight back from Hawaii.

"Look," Peach said. "I don't want to pander to stereotypes, but others will, so think of every gay joke you can imagine and dispel traces of it from your home. Be prepared for more challenges than a straight couple, but be persistent in pushing through them." She smiled. "It's an exhausting process, but worth it in the end."

Tension eased from most of the collective shoulders, and the men smiled at one another. Wyatt felt more isolated than ever.

"Here's an informational packet that can answer any remaining questions." Peach smiled at Wyatt, the fluorescent lighting making her frosted lipstick even more unsuitable. "Would you like a second one for your partner?"

"No thank you, I'm single."

Fifteen pairs of eyes swung in his direction. Wyatt was transported to the first time he'd volunteered as a student teacher. A little boy had informed Wyatt he had to "make winkle." Wyatt was guiding him to the miniature-size toilet when the teacher bellowed "STOP!" from across the room, halting all activity. Wyatt had frozen, foot dangling in midstep as the teacher raced over.

"I'm sorry," she'd pulled the child's hand from Wyatt's. "You're not allowed."

They'd disappeared into the bathroom, leaving Wyatt feeling like a pervert. She'd later apologized, explaining that it was strict school policy and not personal. But that hadn't stopped Wyatt from feeling dirty. He saw a new ugliness. Somewhere between changing diapers and hugging a high school graduate was a danger zone for children where adults harbored malice. It could come from anyone. It could come from Wyatt. In Wyatt's imagination, the Dad(s) Alone looked at him like that now. Or maybe it was relief that they at least had it easier than *someone*.

"I'm a teacher." He declined to say principal, then wondered if it sounded bad, as if he was inserting himself where children were abundant. He might as well announce that he was a priest, Boy Scout troop leader, and did parties on the side as Bobo the Clown.

Peach said, "Single male adoption *is* a challenge."

Horn Rims's partner smiled at Wyatt. "There are lots of special-needs children who desperately need placement."

You haven't been able to get one, Wyatt thought. He was starting to feel like a restaurant with too few customers. Wyatt wasn't opposed to a special-needs adoption, but he found it ironic that single parents were directed to children who required more support. Wyatt was no hero. He wanted a healthy baby, like everyone else.

"I'm hoping to adopt an infant," Wyatt said.

They all looked at him with pity, but said no more. They closed the meeting, and exited, two by two, each pair discussing their respective plans, together.

Wyatt recalled the meeting as he was having his nervous breakdown in Target. It was his first and he didn't like it. To be fair, Bed Bath & Beyond had to take half the blame. He'd been back and forth between the two stores for half an hour, staring at the selection of those pot thingys that cooked for six days. Crock-Pots. Who knew there were so many? He thought the basic $24.99 version would meet his needs, but he must be wrong because there were more of the $59.99 variety. Having never owned a Crock-Pot, Wyatt had no idea what he sought in one. He called his cousin.

"Surely you're joking?" Eva said.

"You like roast chicken," Wyatt said, as if Eva might have forgotten.

"Yes, I do. And when I want a roast chicken I go to Cha Cha Chicken. The more important fact here is that you *don't* like roast chicken."

"I like chicken."

"Wyatt, a roast chicken is the whole bird. It comes with the bones."

Wyatt didn't like food with bones in it. Who could be bothered to go to all that trouble?

Eva persisted. "Why do you want a Crock-Pot?"

"Mom used to make chicken and dumplings in a long-cooking pot. It was homey." Wyatt smelled chicken and dumplings permeating his home as the social worker showed up and caught him unexpectedly over the fire-retardant ironing board.

"Okaaay." Eva was waiting for an explanation that made sense. "And? What stress is this Crock-Pot triggering from deep within your psyche? A building teeming with high school children doesn't freak you out, whereas the mere thought has me reaching for the Xanax with one hand and my Snuggie with the other."

Wyatt hadn't told Eva about the Dad(s) Alone meeting. "It's all the *stuff,*" he tried. "I never got married, so I didn't get the stuff." The adrift feeling fluttered in his chest. "When a person has a baby, they have a baby shower and get the baby stuff. You know, strollers and cribs and onesies and blankets and toys. You need a lot of stuff for a baby. But see, they already *have* the other stuff. They got married and registered, and they got the blenders and food mixers and Cuisinarts and Crock-Pots and waffle makers. But I never did. Am I supposed to register for baby stuff *and* kitchen stuff?" Wyatt looked at the towering wall of appliances stretching skyward. "That's a lot of stuff."

"Wyatt," Eva's voice was patient, affectionate. "Why do you need a waffle maker?"

"Kids like waffles. A homey home has a waffle maker and a Crock-Pot." Wyatt recalled Peach's warning: do it twice as well and in high heels without porn.

"An average room contains 1,246 objects Chuck Norris could use to kill you with, including the room itself. Don't put more weapons in his hands."

"I'm serious."

"So am I. A waffle maker does not signify a homey home. Married people end up with a bunch of stuff they never take out of the box until they move, when they donate it to Goodwill. Waffle makers are chief among those items. If your kid wants waffles you take him to IHOP, like everybody else. You're going to be a great dad and your kid will love you, even if he doesn't taste a waffle until he's drunk at a Denny's at three AM after a freshman-year keg party and can't believe what he's been missing all these years. And then it'll be the pot talking."

Wyatt smiled, but Eva's support made the absence of a partner more keen. "Maybe I should've gotten married."

"You haven't lacked opportunity."

"Is it opportunity if they aren't the right person? Being female isn't the only requirement."

"It's a start."

"It certainly would be easier. People wouldn't think I was a pedophile." A shopper gave him the side-eye and hurried away. He hoped she wasn't a parent from his school. "I'd have a Crock-Pot and public assurance that I was a psychologically healthy human being who only enjoyed sex with consenting adult females."

"No one thinks you're a pedophile."

"And babies. All the free babies we could possibly make and no one would think we were weird." He felt the weight of all the Crock-Pots and waffle makers stacked before him. "No one would think *I* was weird, or a bad person for permanently scarring my child for life with the haunting absence of the perfect mother he never had."

"I was raised by a single mom and I turned out fine," Eva reminded him. "No one should get married just to have kids, like no one should have kids just because they're married."

Eva's voice was serious, and Wyatt thought of Cyn. "Any kid of yours is going to be the luckiest little parasite in the world."

"You don't think I need the fancy Crock-Pot? I don't want to have to buy one with more functions later when I realize the cheap one doesn't do what I want. Maybe I should get the digital model. It has LCD."

"Get the cheap one, five quarts, trust me. You can make your famous chili."

Wyatt perked up. "You can make chili in a Crock-Pot?"

"It's a slow cooker. You can make lots of things in it. You don't ever have to roast a chicken if you don't want to."

Wyatt loaded the $24.99 Crock-Pot into his cart, feeling lighter. "Want to come over Sunday for chili?"

"Absolutely. I'll dig through my for-your-consideration DVDs. We can watch family sitcoms and make a satisfying self-indulgent list of all the ways that you're more suitable to parent." As an agent, Eva got copies of television shows and movies before they were released in stores. It was a definite perk.

"You're on. Say, do you have a rice cooker? What brand do you like?"

"I'm hanging up now," said Eva, and did, leaving Wyatt alone to pile a waffle maker, rice cooker, Cuisinart, juicer, panini grill, Egg Genie, ice cream maker, meat thermometer, humidifier, and document shredder next to the Crock-Pot in his cart and head for checkout.

Maryn Goes to the Doctor

Maryn stared at the clock as she perched, uncomfortable in her paper gown, on the examining table for her fertility follow-up. She was still wearing her socks, more in hopes of keeping her feet warm than any claim to dignity. She'd given up on patient dignity years ago during her treatment for breast cancer and had seen no reason to reclaim it.

It was 1:35 PM.

Of course it was, Maryn thought. Thirty-five was the magic number. At thirty-five your fertility became a puny thing, assaulted by degrading eggs, lack of ovulation, and increased difficulty for whatever decrepit follicle managed to get out its walker and shuffle down the fallopian tubes. Your chances of miscarriage, chromosomal abnormalities, gestational diabetes, and labor problems increased. At thirty-five your body could turn into your own worst enemy, with your odds of breast cancer leaping overnight from one in fifty to one in nine, the almost middle-aged breasts that had proudly remained high and tight suddenly harboring your mortal enemy. At thirty-five the mind and body separated camps as the mind selected which parts to lop off to ensure survival of the whole. At thirty-five higher doses of chemotherapy were required to treat breast cancer. At thirty-five those higher doses of chemotherapy led to sterility.

The minute hand jumped to 1:36 and Maryn forced herself to exhale and inhale. She'd made it to thirty-six. And thirty-seven. And thirty-eight. Her thirty-ninth birthday was around the corner, and that was saying a lot.

"Sorry to keep you waiting." A plump, pleasant-looking Indian woman entered the examination room. "I'm Dr. Parmalee Singh."

"Maryn Windsor." Maryn introduced herself, though the doctor had all the details of Maryn's existence in her hands.

"A pleasure to meet you." Dr. Singh sat, crossing her legs and folding her hands over Maryn's file, as if she was settling in for an intimate chat. "What brings you to Hope Women's Health and Fertility Clinic?"

"I'd like to determine my ability to have a baby following chemotherapy treatment for breast cancer."

"Tell me about your treatment."

"I was diagnosed with stage IIb, IDC three centimeters, one node . . .

Maryn reverted to the language of cancer. It was mysterious and impenetrable to outsiders, but to those versed in the rhythms of the cancer universe it was self-identification, as recognizable as a classified ad. Maryn went from

38/YO DWF ISO SWPM GSOH for LTR

to

Dx 2008, IDC, 3cm, Stage IIb, Grade 2, ER-/PR-, HER2+, NED.

"Congratulations," said Dr. Singh. NED stood for "no evidence of disease."

"Thank you." Maryn gave the expected response though she'd had little to do with the outcome.

"Tell me about your treatment."

"I had a unilateral modified radical mastectomy of my right breast with immediate reconstruction, followed by adjuvant AC-T chemotherapy and localized radiation treatments."

"You took doxorubicin and cyclophosphamide, followed by paclitaxel?"

"If that's the same as Adriamycin, Cytoxan, and Taxol."

"It's bewildering when all the drugs have three names each, isn't it?" Dr. Singh smiled. "I keep a chart in my office and I still can't keep up. You took Herceptin throughout?"

Maryn was impressed that Dr. Singh hadn't yet consulted her notes. She nodded. "Yes, for fifty-two weeks. I was HER2 positive." Maryn's form of cancer had a mutation of growth factor receptors, stimulating cell reproduction.

"That makes for an aggressive cancer."

Her tone was respectful.

"We followed an aggressive treatment."

"You're a tough woman." Talking with Dr. Singh was a cross between a consult and therapy. Maryn was illogically soothed.

"I don't like to lose."

"Did you experience amenhorrea?" This was the heart of the matter, this odd word that was a hybrid of "amen" and "diarrhea."

"I had chemo-induced ovarian failure. My period didn't begin again until eight months after treatment."

"And you've had menstrual cycles since then?"

"Intermittently." Maryn's answer was terse. Her periods had been more sporadic than she'd hoped.

Dr. Singh finally consulted the folder in her lap. "Maryn, I'll be frank with you. At your request, the lab conducted three different tests, all of which support a conclusion of ovarian failure. First, your follicle stimulating hormone, or FSH, levels were high which means your body is struggling with the ovulation process. Second, your luteinizing hormone levels were low, indicating a problem releasing an egg from a mature follicle. Third the serum estradiol test recorded unusually low blood levels of that type of estrogen." She met Maryn's eyes. "Your age and medical history, coupled with these test results, indicate almost certain ovarian failure. It's medically unlikely, if not impossible, for you to naturally conceive or harvest viable eggs. It would be disingenuous of me to give you false hope."

Though she'd expected it, the diagnosis punched Maryn's gut. The office swam, and she fought for oxygen discreetly. She concentrated on a wall poster indicating embryonic stages. No. The emergency-exit chart. She stared hard at it, as if a terrorist plane would be upon the building in an instant. Though she couldn't help thinking, *Obliteration would be a relief.* She banished the thought. No one else was going to take care of this for her, so she had to keep it together.

During what felt like an interminable interval, but was probably moments, Dr. Singh sat quietly.

"How . . ." Her voice cracked, so Maryn stopped and cleared her throat. "How capable am I of bearing a child to term, if an egg was implanted?"

Dr. Singh looked down, and Maryn couldn't shake the feeling she was hiding a look of pity. "We'd want to run standard tests relating to iron deficiency and gestational diabetes, but assuming everything else is in order, ovarian failure doesn't indicate an inability to gestate to term." She paused. "I feel I should reiterate that I don't believe it would be possible to harvest eggs at this point. Your only option would be an egg donor."

"I have frozen eggs." Maryn experienced a twin surge of rage and hope, like a fiery yin and yang. She suppressed it. It was a precautionary measure, before the chemo."

"Fertilized?"

Maryn nodded. It wasn't necessary to share the complications with Dr. Singh at this point.

"That's a game changer." Dr. Singh smiled. "Success rates for IVF from frozen embryos is up to forty percent."

Maryn nodded, unseeing. There was a 100 percent chance of no pregnancy with no eggs.

"We can proceed once we receive the specimens. If one takes, there's no reason you shouldn't have a normal pregnancy with no return of your breast cancer."

Dr. Singh's words brought Maryn back with a thud.

"What?" Maryn was caught between two *Fantasy Island* monsters. On one side, Andy was a grotesque clown, with an evil smile and demented laugh, bobbing insanely, like a giant inflatable balloon character. On the other was cancer, a dark, evasive, scuttling creature, with sharp, pointy teeth and claws tinged in blood. Between them lay a helpless infant, tender skin exposed and vulnerable.

"Maryn," Dr. Singh recalled her attention. "There's no increased risk of recurrence due to pregnancy. I'm sorry if I presented it in a manner that seemed alarming."

"That part of my life is over," Maryn said firmly. Marriage, fertility, cancer. They were all over as irrevocably as death. It was only fair that the bad had to stay dead with the good.

"And that will almost certainly be the case. We would just want to be careful and monitor." Dr. Singh smiled at her. "You're valuable property."

Maryn's return smile was wan. She felt damaged and unnatural. Her body couldn't create life, instead breeding mutant harbingers of death.

"Let's run a basic pre-IVF panel, check your white blood cell count, do a glucose test, assess your general state of fitness, and proceed from there."

Maryn wordlessly accepted the sheet Dr. Singh handed her. Her colleagues would have been dumbstruck at her acquiescence. She slid off the exam table, hoping that donning her Manolo Blahniks and grasping her Tod handbag would help recapture her sense of self. She put one foot in front of the other out the door and down the hall, too flattened even to strategize her next approach to Andy.

She dug blindly for her keys. Her hand encountered the pointed corner of something stiff. She pulled out the card Adina had given her for Selena Hernandez. It was worn from several weeks of living in the bottom of her purse. She stood by the car, not sure where she was going, and looking at the lawyer's card for a long time.

Andy Doesn't Go to Dinner

H ey, Knoxy, isn't that a little formal for softball?" one of the lawyers in his office called out as Andy passed.

"Have to miss tonight, unfortunately." Andy paused in the doorway, still in his suit. "Little woman demands." His regret was genuine. He'd rather be playing softball than going to another political dinner.

"Dude. That's the third time this month! We're going to lose our number one ranking if our ringer keeps missing games."

"Next week," Andy called over his shoulder as he moved on.

"See ya, Andy!"

"Night, Knoxy!"

"Better see you on the field next week, slugger!"

Andy called out good nights to the secretaries and colleagues he passed. He was popular in the office.

"Andy!" A young man in jeans stopped him in the office lobby.

"How's it goin'?" He tried to remember his name.

"These are for you." The man handed him some papers.

"Thanks." Andy took them. "What case are they—"

"Andrew Knox, you've been served." The man smiled and walked away.

Andy looked around, but no one was watching. He opened the bundled papers. Not a litigator, Andy couldn't think why he'd be served.

As he scanned the first page, his blood turned to ice. It was a complaint in the matter of *Maryn A. Windsor v. Andrew B. Knox*. Maryn was suing him for custody of the frozen embryos.

"He what?" Andy heard Summer demand into the phone as he walked into the kitchen. He would have breezed past to get ready for another Herb Green fund-raiser, unready to discuss the lawsuit until he could get his thoughts organized, but Summer's voice stopped him.

"Oh god," Summer said, and thumped down into a chair. Andy froze. Did she know?

"Mmm-hmm. Mmm-hmm. Mmm-hmm. Valsalva . . . ?" Summer listened, brow furrowed. Eventually she hung up.

"What was that about?" Andy tried to mask his nervousness.

Summer met his eyes, her face a curious blend of horror and excitement. "That was Tom Sizec."

"What did Charming Tommy want?" Andy turned away, sorting through the mail stack as his pulse subsided. He did not share Summer and Tommy's hyperenthusiasm for the upcoming Herb Green event at their home but was glad it distracted Summer from his own agitation.

"Herb Green is dead."

The shock of her words drove all thoughts of Maryn from his head. "Dead?"

Summer nodded, eyes intense. "A Valsalva maneuver triggered massive cardiac arrest this afternoon. Apparently vagus nerve stimulation caused a fatal bradycardia arrhythmia."

"A . . . vassa what?" Andy wasn't taking it in. They were having dinner with Herb tonight.

Her lips quirked. "He had a heart attack trying to take a shit. No one found him until too late because he ducked home to use his own toilet before dinner."

"He died taking a poop?"

"Overstimulated by the vagus nerve."

"I never . . ." Andy felt a little faint. Scatological wasn't his thing.

"Apparently it happens all the time with older people and heart patients."

"Oh." Andy would never crap again without worrying.

"Incredible." Summer's face had an intensity that Andy didn't understand.

"Such a loss," he murmured. Andy wouldn't actually mourn Herb. He didn't know him well. But solemn observation of his passing was necessary. "I guess dinner's off. And the party."

"Andy, don't you see? It's a sign. This is a perfect opportunity for you to step in."

"Step in?" Andy was terrified Summer would suggest he volunteer to be a pallbearer or help with the funeral. He could think of a million reasons why that would be awful, ranging from a sitcomlike toppling of the casket to his personal horror of coming into contact with bodily excretions or embalming fluids.

"City Council. There's an opening no one was expecting. It's the perfect opportunity. No other candidate will be ready."

"Am I ready?"

Summer nodded, thoughts faraway. "We won't cancel the party. We'll have it anyway and announce your candidacy for the vacant City Council seat." She turned to him, radiant. "It's perfect."

"Is that what Tommy said?" Andy was uncertain.

"He will when I'm done with him." Summer was determined. "Come on." She grabbed her keys. "We're going down to headquarters now. That's where everyone is gathered and we can begin your campaign." She smiled at Andy as if he'd already won. "I'm so proud of you!"

Andy warmed in the glow, and happily followed her to the car. He completely forgot to mention the fact that he'd become a defendant in a lawsuit by his ex-wife.

Dimple Goes for a Drink

D r. Parmalee Singh's expression remained neutral as she listened.

"I'd like to know my options." I tucked a strand of hair behind my ear for the fourteenth time. It was hard to maintain dignity in a paper gown while talking to a stranger about your fertility. "Once I know the system works, I'll consider next steps."

A void had opened after I'd blown my chance with Julian Wales. I was craving . . . something. Progressing in baby steps on the motherhood thing felt good, like taking *some* action in my life.

"There are tests that can determine your fertility," Dr. Singh explained. "But it's merely a snapshot of this moment. It carries no predictors."

"Wouldn't it be nice if we knew exactly how long we had?" I was wistful. "You want to hold out as long as you can, to meet someone, but if you gamble wrong, you lose everything."

Dr. Singh didn't conjecture. "Fertility declines significantly after forty."

"You keep thinking it'll happen for you, you know, the right guy, settle down, have a family. Then suddenly you're 'after forty' wondering what happened." I was rambling. What could Dr. Singh say? She was my physician, not my shrink.

"It's a sad fact that no one is happy to see me, married or single," Dr. Singh said. "They're glad I'm here, but they never wanted to be on that table."

I agreed but didn't want to be unkind. "I'm not even sure what I'm here for."

"By the time they come to me, most single women have made up their minds, whether they know it or not," the physician offered.

That was something to consider.

"Every woman's situation is different," Dr. Singh continued. "It would be easier if we could measure fertile life with certainty, but we can't. All we can do is check your hormone levels to make sure your body isn't struggling to ovulate, and make sure your fallopian tubes and uterus look healthy."

"It's like Easter candy in September," I mused. "Most of the chocolate eggs have turned that nasty grey color. But if you unwrap enough of them, you can find one or two that are still perfect."

"You just need one," Dr. Singh reassured.

I sighed. "Isn't it funny how you spend most of your life trying not to get pregnant? One time, in college, I took so much vitamin C that my pee was neon yellow. I'd read that too much vitamin C made your uterus acidic and inhospitable. I just got dizzy and sick. All because a condom broke. Now I want to get pregnant and have no idea if I can. You wonder if all those years of the pill were even necessary. Maybe we should reeducate girls about fertility, teach them to take it less for granted."

"Technology has come a long way to enable women to become pregnant when they are best equipped to handle it and understand the consequences," Dr. Singh said.

I sighed again. "I feel like I was made to do this, but I may have to face the consequences of not having children because I waited too long."

"Let's see what we're dealing with before we jump to any conclusions." Dr. Singh snapped on rubber gloves. "Scooch down and put your legs in the stirrups."

* * *

I slipped into my seat for the new-episode read through, wondering if Roxy was in rehab yet. My head was swirling after my appointment with Dr. Singh. She'd made no bones about the difficulties of getting pregnant over forty. The kernel I clung to was, *"You just need one."* How many millions of eggs did I have, decayed or otherwise? How many millions of sperm were out there? The average guy produced a thousand sperm per second, meaning millions were swimming around the table right now. The show's male lead dispensed a billion weekly, if tabloid reports were correct. I only needed one.

I accepted a script from one of the PAs. Her name was either Laura or Lola, but I always got it wrong, so I never used it. I was flipping through it when a wave of Diorissimo perfume rolled over me. Nikki Hill slid into the adjacent seat.

I was surprised. There wasn't a lot of unscripted drama with our cast, but there was social stratification. Nikki was the Female Lead. She sat with other Leads. I was Secondary Regular. I sat with my kind—Cute Nurse, Surgeon's Wife, and Infectious Disease Specialist. We appeared in almost every show, though sometimes briefly, and rarely in an "A" story. I'd been with the cast longer than Nikki, but we didn't socialize. I sort of preferred it that way.

"Hi!" she bubbled, blond ringlets boinging.

"Hi." I was cautious. Nikki was volatile. I trod her vicissitudes carefully.

"Wonder what we'll get today!" Exactly. The day the Mauna Loa erupted started out sunny.

After pretending to read a page, Nikki paused as if struck by a thought. She actually put her Mango Passion manicured fingernail to her chin. "Oh, Dimple . . ." Maybe *Pulse* performances weren't as solid as I thought. A real surgeon wouldn't wear Mango Passion nail polish.

"I heard this crazy thing," Nikki continued.

"If you haven't heard three impossible things before lunch, it isn't Hollywood." I shrugged.

"My trainer, she trains the stylist for Daisy Carmichael, and said Daisy is in contention for the role of Cora Aldridge in Julian Wales's new movie."

The hope I denied I was harboring congealed in my stomach. I'd blown it.

"Here's the weird part." Nikki opened her eyes really wide. "My trainer said the stylist said Daisy said her main competition is . . . you." If Nikki's brow hadn't been frozen by injected parasites, it would have wrinkled..

The hope fluttered. Maybe I was still in the running despite my tantrum. It *had* only been three weeks.

"So?" She looked at me as if to share a guffaw.

I considered my replies. Nikki was desperate to trade up. It would not please her to think I was going to pass her. "My agent gave me a script," I hedged. "It's good."

Exasperation. "I know it's *good*. *Everyone* knows it's good. Are you reading for Cora Aldridge?"

Everyone knew it was good? I'd assumed the script was traveling a small circle. "Yes."

"But. But." Nikki was dumbfounded. "Cora Aldridge is bold and strong and doesn't give a shit what anyone thinks. And, you, well, you're just so . . . *likable*." Her lip curled as if the word was foul.

Irritation flared. "*Roxy* is likable," I corrected. "I've played a variety of characters." I'd never talked someone out of thinking I was likable before.

"*Ages* ago." She was perplexed.

I was about to retort when the producer rapped on the table.

"Quiet!" He started running through notes, and the room settled. I heard sniffling, and looked over to see tears on Miho's face. I flicked through my script, and sure enough, Dr. Nori Yuzuki suffered a pulmonary embolism. Miho was dead.

I was sorry. We'd worked together for six years. Only one or two faces around the table were old guards like me. The rest had "bridged up" to film or been written out, younger faces filling their seats. The interns were now the doctors.

I was relieved to find standard fare: Roxy sympathetically listened to Lead Surgeon Female bemoan star-crossed love with Lead Surgeon Male, and helped a teen boy accept a prosthetic leg with compassion and sage advice. My thoughts slid to Roxy's more exciting past. I wouldn't mind a *little* more action. We hadn't had a hostage in a while. Or . . .

"Dimple?" The producer snapped his fingers at me.

"What? I'm sorry." I blushed. "What?"

"Breast cancer awareness week." He looked at me expectantly.

Pause. I had no idea.

"I could be pregnant." I said the first thing that came to mind. All rustling in the room stopped, thumbs suspended over BlackBerrys, and eyes swung to me. I was horrified.

"I mean Roxy! *Roxy* could get pregnant."

Nikki emitted a high-pitched giggle. "Dimple, Roxy is thirty-six!" She made it sound like Roxy had a prepaid plot at Forest Lawn Memorial Park and one orthopedic shoe in it.

"I was thinking more along the lines of wearing a pink shirt." The producer's tone was dry. "How does getting pregnant support breast cancer?"

I scrambled. "Roxy could find a lump. She'd go to the clinic to get it checked and interact with patients and survivors. Maybe she could counsel someone getting a mastectomy. Then, she'd discover she was benign but pregnant, sort of a 'life-after-cancer' moment." I could see myself—*Roxy*—tenderly cradling her belly.

What was I doing? Advocating for a kid was character suicide. But a fake pregnancy sure as hell seemed like the sign I
was looking for.

"Didn't we do that in season four?" one of the newer writers piped up.

"Different. She had radiation exposure," I said.

The producer was nodding. "I like it."

"It could happen to Erika." Nikki never missed a shot at
more pages.

The producer waved her off. "It's more believable with
Roxy. She's older." Ouch. "But not the pregnancy."

"Why not?" I asked.

"Roxy isn't single-mother material," the writer chimed in.

"What do you mean?"

"She's too vanilla for a one-night stand."

Nikki smirked, as if I should concede the role of Cora Aldridge to her on the spot. LaMimi wanted to tell them all about
the time I'd screwed a stranger with a pierced dick in a pool in
Thailand, but I held our tongue.

"She slept with the visiting African dictator." I spoke for
Roxy instead.

"That was in season two." The writer banished Roxy's wild
youth to the annals of history. I wondered if Roxy was fated
to follow Miho. Substance abuse could end up in a fatal car
accident as easily as an affair with a rehab counselor. "It won't
work now," the writer continued. "She's too . . . mature. It could
be sad."

The producer clapped his hands. "Roxy gets a tumor for
breast cancer awareness, and everyone remember to wear pink
to their interviews. Moving on . . ."

"Dimple!" Lola (or Laura) intercepted me as I scooted out after
the meeting.

"Hey . . . there."

Her twitch suggested she was on to my amnesia. "We're doing a collection for Liz's baby shower. Do you want to chip in?" Liz was one of the writers who thought Roxy was too old and boring for a baby.

"Of course." I reached for my wallet automatically.

"Great!" She was very perky. "We're doing a nursery book theme. We have Beatrix Potter napkins, Curious George plates, Winnie the Pooh cookies, and a red velvet Velveteen Rabbit cake. Isn't that cute?"

"Adorable." My smile became forced. I blindly handed over a bill that was probably large from her delighted expression, then shot out the door.

"Lame, lame, lame," I chastened myself as I escaped across the lot. It was ridiculous to be upset. I didn't know what bothered me—Nikki's digs about Daisy Carmichael, the writers' comments about Roxy, or the Velveteen Rabbit cake.

In my twenties I started collecting all the bunnies children's literature had to offer: *Velveteen Rabbit,* Beatrix Potter, *Runaway Bunny, Goodnight Moon,* Winnie the Pooh's Rabbit, Alice in Wonderland's White Rabbit. Without naming the purpose of my collection, it didn't take a genius to see it in a future nursery. Now, Friends of Liz had appropriated "my" special thing. I'd felt the same way when my trainer named her daughter Iris. That had been *my* chosen name. People were stripping off bits of my future like scraps of wallpaper. The longer I waited the more dreams I handed off, like fifty-dollar contribution bills. My daughter's name, my nursery, my red velvet fucking rabbit cake.

I shook my head to pull it together. I was acting like a spoiled eight-year-old. Sadness was an earthquake in Haiti. It wasn't a pathetic woman pouting because she didn't get a bunny cake. I was fine.

I sprinted the last few yards to my car so I'd be in private when the dam broke.

* * *

"Want another?"

I looked toward the voice. Attractive. And young. A cocky James Franco. LaMimi stirred. I tamped her down. He was *really* young.

"No thanks."

"I hate to see a pretty lady look sad in a bar with no drink." He slid onto the stool next to me, then paused theatrically. "Unless you're here with someone." He knew I was alone.

"Fine." I shrugged. If Roxy was developing a drinking problem, let the research begin.

"What're you drinking?" He scooted closer and I got a whiff of woodsy aftershave. *Thailand could happen again*, LaMimi purred. What the hell, I thought. I wasn't old and boring. Julian Wales might not like me, but this guy did.

"A pickleback."

"Jameson's whiskey and pickle juice?" He laughed. "What are you, a Brooklyn hipster?"

"Too Lutheran."

"Salty. Beats baking to cure a bad day." A grin.

He knew who I was. Roxy baked when she was stressed. His reference suggested a sly joke between friends, which it wasn't, because we weren't.

"To mental health." He quoted Roxy's catch phrase. I hear it every time I go out. Strangers feel intimate with television actors, like we're old pals. I find it smug, but LaMimi gave this guy a hall pass. I angled my legs toward him.

"I'm Dimple."

"Keith." We shook. "Bad day?"

"Happy hour took its time."

"I feel sorry for people who don't drink. When they wake up, that's the best they're going to feel all day." I speculated how young he really was. Twenty-five? Twenty-nine?

"It takes only one to get me drunk," I said. "The trouble

is, I can't remember if it's the fifth or the sixth." There's an art to seduction, and it starts with suggestive words. *Drunk* suggests *drunken behavior*, which evokes *promiscuous choices*. He responded immediately.

"Bartender!" He gestured. "Five more!"

"Stop!" I batted his hand. Seduction stage two: unnecessary casual contact.

"I'm a big fan, Dr. Page." No matter how they tried to play it, even the coolest cat would eventually cave in to his need to discuss my job.

"Thanks."

"So tell me." Conspiratorial. "Did you have *anything* on in that houseboat scene?"

"The radio." I smiled over my glass.

Over our second drink (my third), Keith had me laughing. By the next, I decided he was mature for his age. When another arrived, I protested.

"I have to go." Was it really nine o'clock?

"You said that last time," Keith dismissed. "You owe me a question!"

We'd been playing a game. God, he was attractive. I nodded.

He leered. "What do you wear to bed?"

"L'eau d'Issey." I named my perfume.

It sank in. "I'd like to see that."

I didn't pause long. "Perhaps you'd better call a cab."

I woke with a terrible taste in my mouth. My brain groped. Pickle juice and whiskey. My stomach revolted and I leaped for the bathroom, but the nausea subsided, leaving me limp against the sink. I was naked and cold but I didn't care.

I pressed a washcloth to my face and it felt stupendous, but the pounding didn't abate. The face in the mirror had yesterday's mascara smeared on her cheeks, hair wild. Everything looked blurry—my eyes were puffy and my brain was throbbing. The mirror showed a wild tangle of white sheets on the bed behind me. It was empty now, but it had been very occupied last night.

I filled a water glass, gulping down cool liquid. I'd look for Advil in a minute. Right now I enjoyed having my eyes closed. Images from the night before flooded back.

Oh god. My eyes flew open.

Keith's face close to mine, my chin stinging from his end-of-day stubble, panting and grasping. "Do I need protection?" Breath stopping for a beat.

Oh god.

"No. I'm okay."

Oh god.

"What were you thinking?" I railed at the mirror. "He was young and foolish!" I was a horrible person because I took advantage of him with an answer that was neither a lie nor the truth. *I'm okay* is not the same as *I'm on birth control*. I was an insane person because I didn't know what the hell I wanted and I was playing with fire. I was an idiot because I had rolled the dice.

"I'm a fucked person because I could be pregnant," I said out loud.

Adrenaline nearly exploded my pounding head.

Ohgodohgodohgodohgodohgod.

What had I done?

When I got my period a week later, it was like an obscene phone call from nature. I didn't know if I was distressed, or perversely pleased to be singled out. I laughed. Then I cried.

My Latvian side had refused to splurge $14 on a pregnancy test on the grounds that I would know for free if I waited, but now I wondered if I'd wanted to stretch out the possibility. I sat on the toilet listening to the heavy breathing of my biological clock asking, *Do you feel lucky?* It was like stumbling across my impending death in a compact mirror. The inevitability was never absent, but was held in abeyance by hubris and daffodils and sunny days. But once in a while a startling claw slipped out of your lingerie drawer or medicine cabinet, a pebble in your shoe, a whiff of body odor, mortality, always there, always in charge.

I saw two stark images in the blood-stained Rorschach of my panties. One, I didn't know if I felt relief or sorrow. Two, I'd thought of nothing but having a baby since the night with Keith—every nibble, every sip of nonalcoholic beverage, every swipe of the mascara wand, I'd been thinking, *Baby, maybe.*

Eva Goes to Glendale

J ulian, it's Eva Lytton calling, to discuss Daisy Carmichael and *Cora*. I understand from Daisy that you surprised her with karaoke last week. Can you give me a call at your earliest convenience?"

Eva thumbed off her Bluetooth with impatience as she navigated the MINI onto the 110 freeway toward Pasadena. A month had passed on the *Cora* project. She wasn't used to having her phone calls unreturned. In fact, she wasn't used to leaving messages. People answered when Eva called.

On cue, the phone rang.

"Eva? Penny Marshall."

"Penny! What's up?"

"I went back to the studio on *Rainy Season*, and they're prepared to offer Daisy three million plus five percent net."

"Penny," Eva chastised. "Really? You know Daisy couldn't consider it for under three and a half million plus five percent gross."

"Eva, my hands are tied. It's the studio. I can't budge."

"Penny, I know the studio, and we can save ourselves the trouble of my making some calls over there if you look down at your notes. I'm betting there's a range with $3 million at the bottom, and the top somewhere around $3.8 million. We're willing to settle below that top number, if you'll work with me."

"Maybe we can meet that number, but then I can only offer three percent net."

"Net points are monkey points—with Hollywood accounting, no movie ever shows net profit. We couldn't accept anything other than gross."

"There is absolutely no way we can offer three percent gross."

"We'd settle for two percent."

"One."

"Let me check with my client." Eva was elated. This was better than she'd hoped. "But we'd expect a generous rider for Daisy's comfort requests."

Penny laughed. "Lord save me from gold faucets that run French mineral water! I can see why you're already a force in the industry. At your age I was Laverne De Fazio."

"You were a star. I'm more into behind-the-scenes action."

"Well, you're the star maker for young actresses. You know what directors want before we do." Forecasting was Eva's job, and she was uncannily good at it.

"I love my work," was all Eva said.

"We'll get along like milk and Pepsi," Penny answered. "Get back to me on that one percent."

Eva was euphoric. The deal was done. Daisy was wrong about Eva's shelf life and Julian Wales could screw himself. She was *good*.

Her good feeling lasted until she saw the Kenneth Village exit off Highway 5, and had died completely by the time she pulled into the driveway off Bruce. The tension and guilt twins settled into their usual places between her shoulder blades. Glendale gave her a rash.

Curtains twitched in the Spanish ranch house, and Eva grabbed the expensive champagne and shiny, gift-wrapped box. The front door was already opening.

"Hello, Mother." Eva kissed her cheek. "Happy birthday!"

"Eva!" Her mother's smile was placid. "Come in."

"How's your day been?" Eva asked as they settled at the kitchen table. Eva hated it and its dated glass top with an emotion disproportionate for an inanimate object. They'd never owned a kitchen table when she was growing up.

"We eat where we like," Cyn had proclaimed, throwing a batik *scarf over a packing box. "Fit for royalty."*

"Very pleasant," her mother said. "Timothy and Julia made me pancakes for breakfast, and Jim took me to lunch at the club. We're all going to Macaroni Grill for dinner, with the Bernsteins. Join us?"

Eva's heart clogged up her throat. "I can't," she managed. "Work." *When Eva was nine, Burt Reynolds had brought a chimpanzee to Cynthia's birthday party, hosted in a scarlet tent on Lee Majors's lawn.*

"All right then." Her mother's smile didn't waver. "Are you sure you wouldn't be more comfortable in the living room?"

"This is fine." Eva hated the sectional sofa and wall-to-wall carpeting more than the kitchen table. "I brought champagne!" Her pitch was too chirpy. "Let's be naughty girls and have some before supper." Suddenly she was Nora Helmer?

"How lovely of you, Eva." The smile didn't waver. "I'm so sorry that I can't." She gestured toward the prescription bottles crowding the windowsill. "Dr. Albright says no alcohol."

Eva felt queasy, as she always did, when a gesture exposed the irregular, pale scars on her mother's wrists.

"Mmmmmm, darling, this is your best yet." Cyn smiled over the *rim. "My daughter makes the best dirty martini in all of L.A.!" she shouted to the crowd.*

"I'm next, short stuff." Ryan O'Neal *winked, holding out his glass.*

"Ladies first!" Farrah Fawcett's smile was toothy as she elbowed in.

"Drinks for everyone!" Cyn *twirled, elegant hands graceful overhead, not spilling a drop from her stemmed glass.*

"No matter." Eva shrugged. "Open your gift." She pushed the gold-foil-wrapped box toward her mother.

"It's so beautiful I don't want to open it!" Cynthia concentrated on pulling the bows and slitting the tape as if it was heart surgery. Eva took deep breaths.

When Cynthia revealed the opal pendant, she said, "Eva, it's lovely," exactly the same way she said "Macaroni Grill."

"You can wear it tonight." Eva fastened the chain around her mother's neck.

"How do I look?"

"Beautiful." Eva's voice was husky.

"Just beautiful? Come, you must do better than that!" Cyn demanded as she spun before Eva in a red evening gown.

"Stunning, glorious, enchanting, divine!" With each word young Eva jumped on the bed.

"That's better! Now help me pick out a necklace. Something big and shiny!"

Eva had to stop. She was making herself ill with memories that did no good. She hated her mother doped up like she was behind a layer of glue. But the alternative was much worse.

"How are Timothy and Julia doing in school?" Eva changed the topic to her stepsiblings. She would not calculate how soon she could leave.

Eva stayed as the light faded, stayed as the twins came home and hugged her excitedly, stayed as Jim returned from work, stayed until no one would accuse her of being a bad daughter, of hating her mother.

When she left, she waved, smiling her face off as she reversed down the driveway. She controlled her speed to a Kenneth Village community-safe twenty-five miles per hour, coming to a full stop at the corner sign before turning out of sight of the family, still waving from the front step. She drove several blocks before she stopped, blindly parking and drawing ragged breaths.

The identahouses, the glass-topped coffee tables and sectional sofas, the Mr. Frostees on the corners, the cactus landscaping all closed in on her. Her past was ripped away, and she had no idea who she was. She needed something to bring herself back to Eva Lytton. She punched numbers on her phone.

"It's Julian. Leave a message."

She thumped the steering wheel. Really?

She called Sawyer. They'd seen each other often in the past few weeks.

"Hiya, hot stuff." His smile came over the line.

"I'm in Glendale. There's a Chili's, an Olive Garden, and a Red Lobster all within three blocks of my vehicle."

"I'm in disbelief."

"I've had a terrible day."

"The Valley will do that to a hardened, urban-dwelling sophisticate of the Santa Monica metropolis."

Eva didn't want banter. "My mom's bipolar."

He was quiet. "That's hard."

"I swear she was never depressed growing up, just delightfully manic. She got postpartum after the twins were born, and the depression never went away." Eva didn't care if Sawyer was scared off, if he was mentally reviewing her own actions for warning signs. "I left my fun, lively mother to start college, and when I came home she'd been replaced by a stranger."

"Did something happen today?"

"It's her birthday." Eva swallowed.

"Come over."

Eva's heart jumped. She hadn't been to Sawyer's.

"Do you have a sectional?"

"Hell no. I have a giant leather man-cave sofa, extra deep."

It took Eva an hour and a half to get to Culver City, but she was impressed nonetheless by the chicken stir-fry steaming on the candlelit table.

"Coat," he said, and she let him slip it off. "Shoes." She kicked them off herself. "Wine." He handed her a glass.

"I brought champagne." Eva held up the bottle, and suddenly she was crying.

Sawyer led her to the sofa without a word, pulling her onto his lap. He stroked her hair and let her cry. Eva couldn't stop, though she desperately wanted to. She couldn't enjoy the cry, because she thought about herself doing it, and mentally raced ahead to seeing herself afterward, talking about what a good cry that had been. If Eva was riding a bike enjoyably on a sunny day, she couldn't wait until it was over so she could have ridden a bike enjoyably on a sunny day.

"This sofa really is deep." Eva sniffed.

"I'm a lot of guy," Sawyer said. "Are you hungry now?"

Eva nodded.

"How about we have a little picnic right here and skip the dining room?"

Tears welled again. "What if I can't enjoy the picnic because I'm rushing through it so I can have enjoyed the picnic when it's over?"

Sawyer didn't act as if her question was bizarre. "People rush to dessert because they don't want to miss the dessert. You don't have to rush with me. I'm not going anywhere."

Eva eyed him through wet lashes, and sniffed. "How do I know?"

Sawyer gave a devilish grin. "Because we're going to have dessert first."

He kissed her hard, pulling her beneath him. She kissed him back fiercely, gripping his shoulders and wrapping her legs around him.

"You're so beautiful," he murmured, unbuttoning her shirt.

"I like deep couches," Eva managed, threading her fingers in his shaggy hair and pulling his mouth back to hers. Their embrace intensified.

"Is this okay?" Sawyer paused.

"Oh, yes."

Eva urged him on with her body. They contorted to shed clothes without breaking their kiss. When he entered her, Eva arched against him thrust for thrust. Sawyer feverishly kissed her neck and shoulders, murmuring "Eva . . . Eva . . ."

Yes, thought Eva, *I am*, as she gasped from his penetration, feeling herself in every nerve ending.

"Chuck Norris lost his virginity before his father did," Eva panted before Sawyer again covered her mouth with his and there was no time for talk.

Wyatt Sees a Girl About a Horse

Wyatt entered as unobtrusively as possible, given that he was not a pregnant woman. He slipped into a chair in the middle of the waiting room unobserved. It was a strategic spot. He could see everyone in the room and eavesdrop on almost any conversation. He picked up an outdated copy of *Parent* magazine, and feigned a look at the wall clock, as if he was waiting for his wife, while subtly canvassing the room. There were nine women waiting. None of them was particularly striking except for a statuesque woman with long auburn hair. For a moment Wyatt forgot himself and stared. Then he collected himself—this woman was not Deborah Tanner from Fresno.

Wyatt had been startled to return from a staff meeting earlier in the week to find a message from Katherine Feely Jones on his desk. They hadn't spoken in the weeks since Ilana's disappearance. Irrational hope had flared in his chest that it had all been a mistake. Ilana was really pregnant, and the baby would really be Wyatt's. Then he felt foolish because of his gullible heart.

"Katherine Feely Jones here," Katherine rasped into the phone.

"Katherine. It's Wyatt, returning your call."

"Wyatt! How are you?"

"Fine thanks, you?"

"Cheating the reaper. Turbulent times for public schools, I see. I was just reading about Detroit and all the closings there.

It makes sense, but I can see that it'll be hard to streamline."

"That Superintendent has quite a headache," Wyatt agreed, letting Katherine flow over him, impatient to know why she was calling.

"Martha Stewart recommends cutting a lime in half and rubbing it on your forehead as a cure for headaches. Says the throbbing will go away." That was news to Wyatt. Perhaps he needed some limes. "Personally, I'll take mine in a margarita." Katherine's guffaw sounded like a rusty weather vane.

"I'll have to give that a try."

"The margarita or the limes?" The weather vane grated again. At last, "I'll tell you why I'm calling. I have a candidate who would be a good match for you."

"What?" Wyatt was confused. Katherine didn't search for candidates free of charge.

"It's a unique situation—the reverse of your circumstances, so I immediately thought of you. The young lady in question is named Deborah Tanner. She's a twenty-year-old student at Fresno City College. She was seeing a much older boyfriend she doesn't like to talk about. My money's on married—the young and gullible are the most obstinate in their refusal to see the obvious."

"The young don't own exclusive rights to foolishness." Hadn't Wyatt been blind?

"Deborah finds herself pregnant. Boyfriend wants nothing to do with it, of course, and she doesn't want the family to know. Conservative Christians, I believe. A Fresno counseling center put her in touch with me, and I arranged a situation with a local couple. Ms. Tanner told her family she was going on a semester mission to build houses for the poor in Nicaragua, and came here."

"Where do I fit in?"

"The couple has separated, and no longer wish to adopt. The baby's up for grabs."

Wyatt imagined a fat cartoon baby bouncing on a trampoline surrounded by clamoring adults with outstretched arms.

"It'll be the standard arrangement. You'd pay Deborah's medical and dental during the pregnancy, her temporary housing expenses, and a small monthly stipend. Currently, she's living in a suitable complex off Bundy, conveniently close to both her doctor's office and the UCLA Medical Center, for $975 per month." Katherine cleared her throat. "There's the matter of my placement fee. In consideration of the fact that the wily Ms. Lloubina duped us both, I've decided to reduce my placement to half."

"That's very generous," Wyatt said. It still constituted a hefty chunk.

"Under the circumstances, I can give you a few weeks to decide," Katherine said. "But I hope we can move relatively quickly. The girl is in her second trimester, and anxious to have the matter settled."

Wyatt checked his growing excitement. "It does sound like an attractive opportunity. I'll have to take a look at my financial situation. I also want to take precautions to ensure I'm not taken advantage of a second time."

"I understand," Katherine said. "It's unfortunate that one bad seed can ruin the bushel, but so it is. I'll arrange for a meeting as soon as you're available."

"No." For a man seasoned at seeing through adolescent fabrications, Wyatt was questioning his abilities. "I want to meet without her knowing who I am."

"Wyatt, I can assure you there's no conspiracy with this girl, she—"

"I insist." Wyatt was quiet but firm.

Katherine sighed. "I'd like to accommodate your wish, but I don't feel comfortable giving you her home address."

Wyatt had the mean thought that Katherine didn't feel comfortable with him negotiating a side deal with Deborah Tanner that excluded her placement fee. He banished it. Katherine was being entirely reasonable.

"What about a doctor's office?"

"Do you really feel this is necessary? I'm happy to arrange a face-to-face meeting in our office under any premise."

"I'd strongly prefer to meet her in circumstances where she is not expecting a potential adoptee."

Katherine exhaled. "Fine. She's a patient at Hope Women's Health and Fertility Clinic, located on Laurel and Twenty-fourth. She has an appointment Thursday morning, but I don't know the exact time. I'll call her and find out exactly—"

"No!" Wyatt said. "That's fine. No need to make her suspicious."

"Wyatt." Katherine's voice softened. "I know that what happened was difficult for you. You're the victim of fraud and that makes you understandably wary. But you can trust me. I'm exercising the highest degree of care to ensure that such a dreadful thing never happens again—not to you or anyone else. I want to unite beautiful babies with desirous parents."

"Thank you, Katherine. I apologize for being . . ." Wyatt didn't know what he was being. He settled on " . . . difficult. If you'll indulge me on this I'll be happier."

Katherine grated out a chuckle. "The good news is that Ms. Tanner is as skinny as a beanpole, so you'll find a comforting visible assurance of pregnancy. I'll send her file by messenger today, and look forward to your call later in the week. I recommend you bring reading material with you—the waiting room magazine selection is dismal."

Sitting in the clinic now, Wyatt wished he had taken her advice. Deborah Tanner's file lacked a photo and he felt obvious trying to identify her without a newspaper to peek over. He didn't feel convincing reading *Fit Pregnancy*.

Four of the waiting patients appeared to be in their twenties. The first had a husband. The second was Hispanic, and
he knew from Katherine Feely Jones that Deborah Tanner was
white. That left a mousy brown-haired girl in floral cotton who
satisfied Wyatt's stereotype of "country," and a blonde in a
crisp black suit with crocodile heels. Wyatt put his money on
the first one, and contemplated how to maneuver to the adjacent chair. He'd settled on a trip to the water fountain when the
nurse called, "Ina Clark?" and the mousy brunette stood and
disappeared into the back. Wyatt barely had time to turn his
astonished eyes to the stylish blonde before she disappeared
to the call of "Laney Bishop?" He sighed and settled into his
chair. Deborah must have a later appointment.

He was amused to see the gorgeous redhead look at the
clock, gather her things, and stroll coolly through the door to
the doctors' offices. Apparently she needed no invitation.

Another wave of women entered the clinic a little before
ten. This set was promising. None brought a companion, and
all appeared to be in their twenties. One by one they checked
in and took seats. One by one they busied themselves with
books, magazines, or mobile phones. The waiting room was
silent but for the bustle of the office behind the counter.

The striking woman reemerged, but rather than leaving,
she seated herself next to Wyatt. Her skin was luminescent.
He wondered if she was an actress. She saw him looking, and
smiled, before returning to her *Wall Street Journal*. Not an actress, he decided based on the paper.

Wyatt began to feel foolish. How was he going to identify
Deborah Tanner, much less initiate anonymous contact? He
surreptitiously studied the women, trying not to make pre-
sumptions this time, but inescapably focusing on a young,
tired-looking woman in ill-fitting jeans and a sweatshirt. He
was gratified that all but one had visible baby bumps. The

other he ruled out because she would not, by anyone's descrip-
tion, be described as a "beanpole" unless it was a very sturdy
stalk one clambered in search of giants.

At ten o'clock nurses began to call names.

"Kim Linkner."

"Ann Baker."

"Barbara Zeller."

One by one the women withdrew to their appointments,
including the tired girl. None of them was Deborah Tanner.
The same thing happened at ten thirty AM. And eleven AM.
Also at eleven, the woman sitting next to him got up, and, after
giving him a curious look, again disappeared unbidden into
the treatment area.

"Have I lost my mind?" Wyatt muttered. He'd been there
since they opened and had seen a complete cross section of pregnant Los Angeles, but none of them was Deborah. Or maybe
he had. For all he knew, she'd used a fake name. After all, her
family thought she was on a church mission to Honduras. He
became frustrated. Even if she strolled in with a blinky name tag
proclaiming I AM DEBORAH TANNER he didn't have an approach.

He tried to recapture his normal Wyatt self. What would he
advise a student or colleague in a similar predicament?

He couldn't make a true character assessment from a waiting room encounter, but he could determine if she was legitimately pregnant and get a gut reading. He decided he'd stick
it out until noon, the official end of "morning." If Deborah
Tanner arrived and he verified that (1) she appeared pregnant,
and (2) she was pursuing prenatal care, he'd be satisfied with
his day's mission.

He settled in for the next wave of patients. The redhead
stepped from the treatment area, and again settled herself next
to Wyatt, rolling down her sleeve to cover a Band-Aid.

"Is your wife getting the four-hour glucose test too?" she
asked. "Or do you dig knocked-up girls?"

"What?" Her joke hit too close.

"I've seen you here all morning. I'm doing it too. It sucks. I've been stuck with a needle four times since eight o'clock."

"I thought the office opened at nine?" Wyatt was startled.

"Nope. Eight. For us working stiffs." She observed him, openly curious. "What do you do?"

"I'm a high school principal." Wyatt was distracted. He'd missed an hour of morning clinic time.

The woman's eyes widened. "Are you catching truant students?"

Wyatt's attention returned to his inquisitive companion. "No. I—" Wyatt stopped. Was it criminal to stake out a waiting room for someone? He was saved by the woman's cell phone.

"Maryn Windsor." Her voice was crisp, confident.

Wyatt searched for a convincing story that felt least like a lie.

"What? Oh god!" The distress in her voice was palpable. "How bad?" Agitation spread to every inch of her body as she listened. "Where's Dr. Williams?"

Murmuring came through the phone.

"Keep her calm and use towels to tamp any hemorrhaging. [Pause.] No. I'm most concerned about saving the mother. I'll be there as soon as I can."

She leaped to her feet. Once there she stopped, paralyzed. "I didn't bring my car," she said helplessly to Wyatt. "It'll take forever to get a cab. I'll be too late!" She became agitated, looking at Wyatt as if she had no idea what to do. She gave herself a shake and pressed some buttons on her phone.

"C'mon, c'mon . . . ," she muttered, jiggling her leg, then snapping to attention. "Yes! I'd like a taxi please, it's an emergency."

"I can take you," Wyatt surprised himself by saying. As soon as the words were out of his mouth, he decided he'd lost his mind.

"What?" The woman stared at him. She disconnected her

call. "Really? Oh, thank you so much!" Without another word, she started out the door, leaving Wyatt to follow in her wake, wondering what he'd gotten himself into.

"I'm close, on Ocean and Hart. This is a huge lifesaver. Honestly, I really appreciate it," the woman babbled. "I'm Maryn Windsor."

"Wyatt Ozols." He shook her hand as they stepped outside, and gestured toward his Subaru. "Are you going to UCLA Medical Center? St. John's?"

"What? No, near LAX." She gnawed her lip, distracted.

"LAX?" Wyatt considered. "Your place is kind of out of the way. If you like, I can drive you directly there." When she stared at him, he shrugged. "I don't mean to pry, but time seems to be of the essence."

After a split second she nodded, sun setting strands of hair on fire. "You're right. If you don't mind . . . It's such an imposition. Today of all days." She remembered. "Oh god, the clinic." She was on her phone again calling the clinic as Wyatt started the car and headed toward LAX. He avoided the 405 (always), and took a street parallel to Lincoln.

" . . . an emergency. Please process the test without the last blood draw. Hopefully there'll be sufficient data. I'm so sorry, really. I'll call Dr. Singh tomorrow." She dropped the phone and sighed. Then she managed a smile. "You navigate like I do."

"I always think you're better off on side streets as long as you keep moving."

Maryn's phone rang again. "I'm on my way," she answered. She listened. "How far along? Any blood? Mm-hmm. Mm-hmm. Heart rate? Mm-hmm." She looked at her watch. "I'll be there in fifteen minutes. Keep paging Dr. Williams."

"You're a doctor?" Wyatt asked when she hung up.

Maryn smiled. "More jack-of-all-trades with my charges. Unfortunately, I've been through this before, so I know what to do."

Wyatt marveled at her calm approach to delivering a baby. He would perish at the thought of one of his students going into labor at school.

She frowned. "What makes me crazy is that I don't take on pregnant travelers, particularly not near term. I'm strict for exactly this reason. They lied to me." The lie seemed to enrage her more than the fact that she was about to deliver a distressed baby without a doctor. Wyatt began to wonder why she didn't grab one from the clinic. He also wondered what kind of passengers booked special flights that couldn't fly pregnant and/ or lied about it. Spies? Smugglers? Saudi princes?

"Turn here." Maryn pointed to a utility entrance near LAX. It felt alarmingly like he might drive right onto a runway. Hoping a plane wouldn't land on his car, Wyatt followed Maryn's directions. After passing an array of industrial buildings, one or two with planes large and small parked by enormous "garages," they arrived at a cargo bay with TC INTERNATIONAL emblazoned on the side.

"Where are we?" Wyatt asked. It looked like an excellent place to detain a kidnap victim.

"Five minutes from LAX, at a holding facility," Maryn answered, as if that cleared up everything. "Pull in here."

Wyatt parked between an enormous SUV and a sizeable animal trailer.

"I can't thank you enough," Maryn said, turning to him. "I don't—"

"Maryn!" A man in denim coveralls and plastic gloves hurried out. There was blood on both.

Maryn hesitated, then turned to Wyatt. "Is there any way you can wait for a few minutes, just in case? I'll compensate you for your time . . ."

"Of course." Wyatt was already turning off the car. He had to see what was in the building. By the time he removed his seat belt, Maryn was hurrying through the bay doors after the man.

Wyatt squinted in the shady cargo bay after the bright sunlight. Maryn and the man disappeared down an aisle. Was this the modern reinterpretation of the second coming of Jesus, born in what appeared to be a hangar-stable near LAX? He passed a series of stalls, wondering what infections might be contracted by a baby delivered on a pile of hay. At the last stall, he peered in.

It was an understatement to say that Wyatt was startled to see the stylish and aristocratic Maryn Windsor with her arm up to the shoulder buried in a horse. Even more surreal was the one tiny horse leg protruding from the mare alongside Maryn's arm. The prone mare flailed.

"I'm sorry, Maryn." The man held the head of the mare, soothing her. "Hugeley checked her in, and you know he wouldn't know a pregnant mare from a lady holding a basketball. I came around forty-five minutes ago to find the groom mucking out the stables. Said all the straw was wet. When I checked on her, the placental sac had ruptured and some was sticking out. She's been laboring but nothing's come. I got worried and called you."

"You did the right thing, Robbie," Maryn said, face pressed to the mare's flank. Wyatt stood agape as Maryn plunged a second arm into the horse. She shook her head. "It's no good. We've got to stand her up."

The laboring mare's groan was almost human.

"It's all right, Farasha. We'll take care of you," Maryn soothed as she and Robbie urged the protesting animal to her feet. "Serge promised to give him something, huh? A foal maybe? I can't believe I didn't . . . shhh, shhh, Farasha. It's not your fault your owners are idiots. Don't you worry." She looked at Wyatt. "Can you . . . ?"

Too stupefied to do anything else, Wyatt jumped to help. It wasn't completely unfamiliar territory, having grown up on a farm, but certainly not how he'd expected to spend his day.

"That's a good girl," Maryn praised the upright Farasha, urging her to take a few steps. As she did, the little leg disappeared back inside the womb. "Good job, Farasha!" They led the heaving horse on a lap of the stable until Maryn was satisfied. Wyatt marveled anew at the size and breadth of a good horse. Farasha must have been sixteen hands high and skittish, but Maryn was fearless.

They returned to the stall and Farasha lay on her side. This time, Wyatt was unsurprised to see Maryn plunge both her arms inside the mare. After some maneuvering, two miniature legs emerged from the laboring horse. This time, the foal's nose and head appeared behind them as well.

"Can you grab these?" Maryn indicated the little hooves. "Gently. Pull down first until the head has fully emerged, then straight out."

Wyatt did as he was told, and carefully pulled on the little legs, while Maryn eased the newborn's head and torso out of the mare. The little hooves were slick and Wyatt's grip kept slipping.

"Use my jacket," Maryn instructed, so Wyatt wrapped what he suspected was a thousand-dollar suit around the slippery creature and resumed drawing the foal from his mother. When only his rear feet remained in the birth canal, Maryn called a halt. "We'll let them rest for a minute," she explained. "The umbilical cord is still delivering vital fluids to the little guy." She stroked the mare. "But you did good, lady. You're a great mama." Farasha rolled her eyes toward Maryn, calmed by her voice. "Looks like you have a beautiful little boy here. I bet he's going to be quite a stallion. Make you proud."

Maryn spoke calmly to the horse for about fifteen minutes, then backed away when the mare struggled to her feet. As Farasha stood, her foal slipped completely from her womb and the umbilical cord separated. The mare immediately licked her slick son.

"Welcome to the world, little man." Maryn looked at Wyatt, her smile breathtaking. "Quite a miracle, huh?"

"It's . . ." Wyatt was speechless. He didn't know what was more fierce—witnessing an act of birth, or this woman's determination.

Maryn's attention returned to her new brood. "Get me some diluted iodine," Maryn instructed Robbie. When he returned, Maryn treated the foal's naval, then stepped away, leaving it to Farasha's loving attention.

"We need to keep an eye on them," Maryn instructed Robbie. "The little man should try to stand and nurse within a couple of hours."

A harried man in jeans and cowboy boots rushed up to the stall. "Maryn, I'm so sorry. I had no idea you might need me."

"Neither did we." Her grim tone didn't bode well for her clients. "Thanks to your crash course in foaling, I think everything will be fine. Meet Farasha and Little Man," Maryn gestured with one goopy arm.

"That's quite a suit." Dr. Williams grinned at Maryn's mucky, wet attire, jacket crumpled on the straw.

"I'm putting it on their bill. Along with whatever veterinary services you feel are appropriate, and then some. Treat this colt like the Sultan of Brunei and spare no expense. Assholes."

"I'll stay and observe for a while."

"Me too." Maryn stroked the mare, preoccupied with cleaning her foal.

Dr. Williams smiled. "You must feel a bit like a mother yourself, delivering a four-legged son."

It was fleeting, but Wyatt detected a wince of pain stamping Maryn's face. She quickly recovered. "Lord, I couldn't afford to feed a teenage boy, much less an adolescent horse."

"What time did she deliver?" Dr. Williams examined the foal with deference to the attentive mother.

Maryn glanced at the wall clock. "About one forty-five PM."

Wyatt jumped. He'd been basking in the glow of the delivery as if he'd played a significant role, and had lost all sense of time. He had a faculty meeting at two-thirty.

"I have to go!" he announced without preamble. Three pairs of eyes turned to him, and he felt like an audience member leaping into the play. How on earth did he end up in an airport cargo bay with a bunch of strangers, giving birth to a horse? "I'm sorry. I'm late." He gestured lamely with his hands.

"Please . . ." Maryn reached toward him, looked at her mucky hands, and stopped. "I have to thank you . . ."

"No, it was my pleasure. Really. A miracle." He backed away. "You'll be all right . . . ?"

"Of course, of course. But . . ." Maryn looked distressed.

"Great. Think nothing of it. Lovely to meet you." Wyatt turned and dashed down the aisle, out the bay doors, and into the sunlight. He jumped into his car, ignoring the searing leather, and pulled away before anyone could stop him.

He'd been down the rabbit hole and craved normalcy. He had a staff meeting and he needed to wash his hands. He drove too fast. He rolled down the window to air the bizarre incident out of his head. Most of all he wanted to leave behind his frustration.

He'd seen the miracle of birth and it was breathtaking. All across America young, dumb girls were getting knocked up and having or aborting babies without a thought. Women were having sex, and women were sticking pins in condoms or lying about being on the pill, and women were ordering sperm off the Internet or inserting fertilized eggs. They were blithely making babies in a variety of ways. And no matter how desperately he wanted it, or how wonderful he'd be at it, Wyatt could never, ever, simply decide to give birth to a child. He was helpless without a willing uterus, and they were hard to find.

Andy Has a Party

A ndy descended into his sunken living room to the sound of clinking glasses and muted conversations. The fund-raiser was now an Irish wake, and his home was packed with people in cocktail attire, tuxedoed waiters passing hors d'oeuvres. Summer had been in a frenzy to plan the party in two weeks.

"Great party, Andy!" A vaguely familiar man raised his glass. Andy mentally scanned the list he'd memorized. This was a two-first-names guy, he was sure. Walker Grant or Grant Walker. An influential Democratic donor. His presence was good news.

"Glad you're here, Walker!" he guessed, gripping the man's hand. "Did you get some beef?" Once again Summer had nailed it. The carving station, though costly, was a hit.

"Delicious. Herb would have loved it."

The premise for the gathering was a tribute to Herb Green. The room was filled with Santa Monica's power players, Herb Green's political web, come to salute a lost comrade.

Tommy Sizec, at the front of the room, tinked a silver fork on a glass. He stood with Summer and Jeff Cohen, the City Council Chair. Andy hurried over. He noticed School Board President, Webb Garner, sliding that way as well. Unsurprising. Summer had pegged him as a blowhard who'd suck the spotlight out of a taco truck grand opening. Andy had to admire his newscaster hair.

Jeff spoke first. "Ladies and Gentlemen, thank you so much

for coming. It's a testament to Herb that even his absence can pull together one of the best crowds in Santa Monica. I remember . . ."

Andy kept his attentive face turned toward Jeff, but mentally reviewed his speech. He and Summer had prepared carefully.

". . . and most of all, we want to thank our hosts tonight, Summer and Andrew Knox."

Andy stepped forward as the crowd applauded. He felt good.

"Herb Green was a remarkable man," he began. "He was a lion, championing his political causes regardless of popularity and demonstrating a carnivore's fondness for red meat." The crowd chuckled. "Herb was the kind of leader . . ." Andy extolled the virtues of a man he barely knew, but kept it concise so he wouldn't lose the crowd.

". . . Herb's legacy is everywhere in Santa Monica. Nowhere is his impact more evident than this room, where the best and the brightest are gathered to honor him. I, personally, know of no better way to honor his memory than to follow the path he forged, to carry on his life's work, to keep his vision alive. That's why I'm honored and delighted tonight to announce my candidacy to fill the seat vacated by Herb Green, lion, leader, friend."

Silence followed his announcement. A maniacally smiling Summer began clapping loudly. Soon the whole room was applauding. Some looked pleased, many surprised, a few confused. Only two people looked distinctly unhappy. They were Tom Sizec and Webb Garner.

Hours later, the guests were gone and Andy was in his socks drinking beer.

"We made a killing." Summer looked up from the calculator, eyes intense. The house was quiet. "KnoxPAC is flush."

Andy felt something, a flutter, perhaps his chest puffing out just a smidge. People thought he should be on the City Council.

"For little old me?" he joked.

She waved a sheaf of checks at him. "For not having to think for themselves," she replied. "Everyone couldn't be happier that the Herb Green machine appointed its heir apparent with little fuss and less bother."

"It did?"

"Not at all. We stole it. Charming Tommy is livid. But it *looked* like the Herb Green machine gave candidate Andrew Knox its blessing, and that's what matters."

"Tommy is livid?" That didn't sound like a good thing.

"He got outplayed. Tommy was cohost and gathered all the key players together for the party. Guests assumed your candidacy was the purpose, and whipped out their checkbooks without asking questions. KnoxPAC reaped the haul from Tommy's leverage. Tommy can't protest or he'd look like an idiot."

"Why's he mad about me running?"

"He intended to back Webb Garner."

"You knew this?"

Summer raised one shoulder.

"Can't Webb run anyway?"

"Not as a Democrat."

"Why not?"

"Because he was here." Summer was practically licking the canary off her lips. "His presence was a de facto tip of the hat to you. It's genius really. We hijacked Herb's machine. Webb hasn't got a move to make," She snorted. "Unless he ran as a Republican."

"And Tommy didn't know what we planned?" Andy felt a little queasy.

"Nope. And it's too late now. Santa Monica is too small for him to splinter effectively. You should be home free."

"Can't Webb run on his own, without Tommy?"

"The important checks have been written." She thumbed the stack, and Andy knew that if banks were open twenty-four hours a day they'd have been deposited by now. "If Webb wants to get into the race, he'll have to do something drastic."

That didn't sound very good to Andy. It must have shown on his face, because Summer gave him a huge smile.

"Relax, babe. The hard part's over."

Dimple Goes to Lunch

"He wants to take you to lunch," Freya said. "He feels . . . *regretful*."

"I don't care. I'm not going." I was as petulant as a grade-schooler. And mad that he'd let me dangle for a month.

"You will care when you become the Tom Selleck of actresses, known more for turning down Indiana Jones than a career as Magnum PI. You're lucky to have a chance to redeem your diva performance." Freya had already chewed my ear off.

I wanted to whine that the Improv had been torture but I couldn't. Torture was the Superdome after Hurricane Katrina or human rights abuses in Burma.

"He makes me . . . uncomfortable." I fell into the rhythm of Freya's speech.

"Perhaps that's a good thing. You napped through last year."

"What are you talking about?"

"Dimple. Every day actresses disprove the myth that women's careers are dead at forty. You, on the other hand, are lying down like Ophelia. It's time to stop playing it safe."

"That's not—"

"Meet him at the Grill at noon." She cut off my protest. "At a minimum you'll have a delicious lunch."

Even the lure of the best club sandwich in town didn't keep my feet from dragging as I pushed open the door to the Grill. I couldn't put my finger on why Julian Wales made me edgy, but avoiding it seemed wiser than dining with it. The Keith scare had jangled me, but in truth, everything was unsettling these days. I couldn't get my feet flat on the ground.

Julian leaped up, sweeping out a chair. "I'm glad you came." He was large and vibrant. I sat. He sat.

"So," I said.

"Menu?" he said.

I studied it as if it contained the secrets of the universe.

I looked up to Julian staring at me, face open, eyes intent.

"Ready to order?" A waitress appeared.

"What's the special?" he said, eyes on mine. The waitress described something involving tilapia, but I was trapped in Julian's gaze.

"I'll take that." He didn't look away.

"Club sandwich." I managed to sound normal. Neither of us broke our gaze and the waitress faded away. Seconds passed.

"Someday we'll look back on this, chuckle nervously, and change the subject," I said.

His booming laugh drew the attention of other diners. Several whispered in recognition.

"Was it really so horrible?" He genuinely wanted to know.

I considered. "I don't mind making a fool of myself. I just like to decide when."

"Stars, they're just like us!"

"Are you mocking me?"

"Absolutely not. I'm sorry if I caused you to be miserable."

"I didn't say it was your fault. I said I was blaming you."

"My mom always said you could tell a person's real character in that split second after the waiter accidentally dumps a glass of OJ in their lap, and before their mask for public approval slips back into place. I put actors in situations out of their comfort zone to try to get that glimpse of the uncensored self. It helps me decide their mettle."

"It kind of comes off like you're an arrogant prick."

"That is *not* my intent. When I'm on a project sometimes I get so caught up making my vision a masterpiece that I have the finesse of a bull, but I don't think being a perfectionist is arrogant."

"Isn't that the definition of arrogance?"

"Between jobs I pull weeds for the old lady next door." He held up his palms. "I had a job interview once where the guy said, 'Teach me something.' Now, that's arrogant. I showed him the decapitating thumb trick, which didn't get me the job." He did the decapitating thumb trick.

"How surprising."

"You think I need new audition methods?"

"Nooooo." I thought it out. Part of me rose to the idea of his challenges. "A person's just about as big as the things that make them angry. But there are ways to do it that aren't so public."

"You'll give me another try?"

"I've got nothing to hide." Mostly true.

"That is what's so remarkable about you." The gaze was intent again.

"I'm very ordinary," I said. "Just like us."

"That you think so is another remarkable thing about you."

I didn't know what to say, so I didn't. Thankfully the food arrived.

"I have no idea what I ordered." He looked down at his bun.

"It appears to have bacon on it, so you're in the winner's circle."

"A fellow believer in the restorative powers of bacon!" He pulled a second strip from the fish club sandwich and laid it on my plate. "Am I forgiven?"

"You are now." I crunched the bacon. "Tell me about the craziest things you've made actors do."

"And spoil the surprise?"

The conversation flowed smoothly, and I was surprised by how quickly two hours passed.

"Do you want dessert?" Julian asked.

"Did you see the size of that sandwich? Not to mention the bonus bacon."

"Coffee?"

I declined. He settled up with the waiter but didn't move. We sat, Julian's easy attitude gone. Directors were so moody.

"Well," I prompted as he fidgeted. "That was lovely—"

"We're not done," he said, cutting me off. "I'm treating you to a pedicure."

"Oh, that's not—"

"Yes, it is." Curt.

Oh boy. Getting a pedicure with Julian Wales sounded as much fun as a date arranged by your maiden aunt's minister.

"As long as you don't make me tap-dance for the patrons," I acquiesced.

At the door, Julian's charm resurfaced as he stopped to thank the octogenarian hostess and ask her where she was from.

Outside, he intercepted my look. "I love little old ladies. They're a director's dream—they've lived long enough to be survivors and have stories to tell. They'll also club you with a rolling pin if you deserve it. They all should have someone to pull their weeds and listen."

My brain fired up an image of Julian snacking on *piragi* as my mother spun tales of old Latvia. I erased it. Julian steered me down the street, not to the spa at Barneys but to a hole-in-the-wall nail salon. A flock of Vietnamese birds, twittering among themselves, led us to vibrating loungers. Watching Julian slip off his loafers and roll up his pants sent them into a wave of giggles, but Julian was somber.

I immersed my feet in bubbling water, while Julian stood

like a flood refugee, fat jeans' rolls at his knees. My first thought was that he had sexy shins. My second was that I was a moron for finding shins sexy. His feet were two pieces of uncooked haggis, soft and white. I'd once Googled "men's feet" to help me with a drawing class and stumbled upon an underworld of toe sex I'd never imagined. I didn't get it. Nothing about men's feet was sexy. They were long and bony, with toes like alien suction cups. Julian's feet made me want to put his socks back on.

"I don't like people touching my feet." Julian's voice was strangled as he clambered awkwardly into his chair. He looked like a forest animal that smelled fire.

"Makes it hard to get a pedicure," I quipped.

"I don't get pedicures." His high pitch was unnerving. "It's like claustrophobia. I hate tight, closed spaces too."

"Well, okay then." I pulled my dripping feet out of the basin. Directors were odd ducks.

He held up a hand. "I expect a lot from my team, but I'm equally hard on myself. If I'm going to ask you to jump on-stage, out of your comfort zone, it's only fair to hold myself to the same standards. More important, you need to know it. Today, we are getting pedicures."

He visibly steeled himself, and I might have thought I was being conned—who hated pedicures?—but his fear-of-flying grip on the armrest, and gritted expression, more matched a dentist's office than a nail salon.

"You really don't like it?" I asked.

"It feels like having bugs under my skin," he ground out. He swung his head to me. "I wouldn't do this for just anyone." Eyes locked. Again, that slippage between business and date. I resisted an urge to squeeze his hand. LaMimi resisted a different urge.

He faced forward and I stared at his profile, unsure of what to do. It didn't seem appropriate to flick through a copy of *Us Weekly* after his pronouncement, but staring at him was a bit off too. When the girl touched his foot, he jumped a mile, causing me to jump as well.

"Yow! What's that?" He pointed at her tiny nippers as if they were a mutant torture device.

"It's a cuticle trimmer," I said. He practically arched out of his seat when she touched his toes with it. She looked at me, and not knowing what to do, I nodded. She went back to work. Julian went back to clutching his armrests. I was oblivious to my own pedicure.

"Razor?" she asked him.

"Is she serious?" He swiveled wild eyes at me. "She wants to razor my foot??"

"It's elective," I assured him.

"Do you do it?"

"Yes."

"Do it." He gave a sharp nod.

I bit my lip to keep from laughing. You'd think she was going to saw off his leg with a rusty steak knife.

He leveled a finger at me. "I have no problem jumping onstage in front of twenty thousand people and cracking jokes."

I stopped laughing. Fear of flying, fear of spiders, we all had something. I couldn't say I would have done what he was doing for me. Lord knows I was keeping quiet about my lightning phobia so he didn't goad me into a field with a kite during the next storm. Latvians keep private private.

We were silent except for the protesting pleather every time the girl adjusted her hold and he strangled the chair.

"I heard Spielberg and Hanks are teaming up again," I said. He didn't say anything.

"What did you think about *Hangover VII*?" I tried again.

The girl spoke to Julian. "You wanna extra massage? Ten dolla' ten minute."

"We'll skip the massage." He'd broken into a sweat. Something happened in the middle of me.

"I hate lightning," I said. "It freaks me out. Terrifies me, really."

He faced me.

"It was the worst when I had braces. I was convinced the metal would draw electrical death."

He raised an eyebrow. I misread it. "I only had them on the bottom." I was defensive. I knew I had a snaggletooth.

"Perfection is bland. Your smile is unique." He paused. "Dazzling."

I was flustered, but he seemed distracted from the pedicure, so I kept going. "I'd sit in the middle of my room not touching anything but an old bicycle tire I'd dragged in because I'd heard rubber tires diffused electricity."

His fingers relaxed a little. "Brontophobia."

"That sounds like a dinosaur."

"Fear of lightning. Did it get better with age?"

"Mmm." I was noncommittal. The answer was emphatically *no*.

Julian's legs twitched reflexively at each touch of the nail file, but he seemed engaged in our conversation.

"I don't like tight collars. Can't stand turtlenecks."

"World-famous director inspired to profession because he didn't have to wear a tie," I teased.

"Fringe benefit. Except for the bazillion times I have to put on a tuxedo. Hollywood likes nothing if not awarding itself."

"I'll cry crocodile tears when you're forced to accept another gold statue."

"Just for that, I believe you're obliged to be my date to the Directors Guild of America Awards Ceremony."

My heart thudded. "You can't ask me to that!"

His eyes gleamed. "It appears I just did."

"Finish," the girl announced, looking relieved. I looked away. Was he serious?

Julian looked down. "Where's the polish?"

"You wanna polish?" The girl looked surprised.

"Yeah, I want polish! If I'm doing this, I'm going all the way." He turned to me. "What color do you get?"

"Anything but blue. Toes shouldn't be blue."

"Blue it is, then," he said to the girl. "The bluer the better."

The girl went in search of blue nail polish.

"So," he said.

"So," I said, suddenly shy. I studied my gleaming toes as if they held the mysteries of the universe I hadn't found in the menu.

"I hope we're done soon because I have to go home and see how many hits your Improv video got on YouTube."

I looked up in horror. Julian grinned.

"Kidding! All I want is a drink. How long do I have to wait before I can put my socks back on?"

Eva Has an Exam

Y ou want me to what?" Eva demanded.

"Come with me to the clinic."

"This is a joke, right? You know you're crazy." It wasn't a question.

Unusually for him, Wyatt didn't respond to the anxiety underlining Eva's remark. "Eva, please. It's been two weeks and Katherine's pressuring me to decide. Today's my last chance to meet Deborah Tanner. Her appointment's at nine. Yours isn't until ten thirty."

"I don't *have* an appointment." Her voice rose.

"You won't keep it, just be my cover. We'll leave as soon as I've met Deborah. Please, Eva. The last time I went by myself I was kidnapped by an insane horsewoman."

Eva had her doubts about the I-pulled-a-baby-out-of-a-horse story, it was so farfetched. She wondered if Wyatt was cracking under the stress.

"Wyatt, if this plan was a paint color, it'd be called Every Shade Of Wrong."

He knew he had her. "I'll pick you up at eight."

So Eva found herself checking in for an imaginary appointment at Hope Women's Health and Fertility Clinic, surrounded by pregnant women, feeling fraudulent.

"You're over an hour early." The clerk's Sharpie-drawn eyebrows shot up under bangs that failed to move with her forehead.

"I'll wait," Eva muttered.

"Have a seat and fill out these forms," the clerk instructed, bemused by people who had hours to waste.

Eva could only imagine what the exquisitely drawn brows would do when she canceled after waiting for an hour. She didn't really mind this caper. She needed a break from spinning her wheels on Daisy and *Cora*. Wyatt would drop everything if she asked for help. Plus, she was curious about Deborah.

"How far along are you?" Wyatt's voice startled Eva, until she realized he was speaking to the pale blonde in the seat next to him.

The girl looked surprised, as if Wyatt had violated an unwritten waiting room taboo.

"Oh. Uh. Three months?" Her answer was hesitant.

"We just moved here from Fresno." He gestured to Eva, looking expectant. Eva smiled encouragingly. The girl looked baffled.

"Oh. Uh. That's nice."

Wyatt was stumped.

Eva decided to help. "Do you know what you're having?"

"Lisa Johnson?" a nurse called.

"That's me." The girl looked relieved. "Um. Have a nice day!" She scuttled off.

Wyatt looked crushed. Eva squeezed his shoulder. "She'll show."

Her iPhone buzzed and Eva was annoyed to see a rambling e-mail from Daisy Carmichael. Eva wondered if she had the discipline to address the girl from her mobile device. Talking to Daisy usually required a piping-hot latte, a Zen state of mind, and knowing that a delicious Rice Krispies treat was but an elevator ride away.

"I'm Deborah Tanner."

Eva heard a soft voice speak to the receptionist, and felt Wyatt come to attention. A slim girl with feathery brown hair stood at the counter. She conferred with the clerk, then turned.

She looked like a snake that had swallowed a basketball. Eva smiled pleasantly. Deborah hesitated before taking a seat two down from Wyatt.

Eva was going to suggest Wyatt fake a trip to the water fountain when a nurse interrupted her.

"Eva Lytton?"

There was a long silence and no one moved. The nurse, the clerk, and everyone in the waiting room seemed to be looking right at her but Eva was immobilized.

"Eva Lytton?" the nurse repeated. The clerk *was* looking right at her.

"Wyatt," Eva hissed.

Wyatt, eyes drawn to Deborah, ignored her. Eva stood in slow motion, drawing out her movements as she collected her bag and phone, waiting to be saved. Wyatt did nothing. She bent toward him, pretending to gather her jacket, and hissed, "There is no theory of evolution. Just a list of animals Chuck Norris allows to live. You're off the list." Then she pasted on a smile and followed the nurse, who informed her how lucky she was there'd been a cancellation and they could squeeze her in early.

After she'd peed in a cup, had her blood pressure and weight cataloged, and been chastised by the nurse for her blank forms, Eva was left alone in the exam room to wait for the doctor. She penned information on the forms and wondered what she was going to say. For sure, it wouldn't hurt to get an exam. It had been two years? Maybe more. Her favorite nurse practitioner called in her birth control prescription, so Eva was lax about checkups. Her heart leaped. Maybe she'd find out she was infertile.

Eva would find this a relief. Fibroids, a hormone deficiency, endometriosis, ovarian failure, lazy-ass uterus smoking cigarettes behind the gym. She'd take anything. It seemed to Eva that if nature prevented you from having children through no fault of your own, you were a sympathetic figure, whereas her choice not to was "unnatural." Women didn't have to justify their desire to have children: why did she have to defend her lack of desire? Eva had been certain since the summer after freshman year when she took the bus across town to get her tubes tied. The doctor had refused.

"I'm adult enough to become a mother but not adult enough to have my tubes tied?" Eva had protested.

"You'll thank me someday." The doctor had said, sending her off with the number of a gynecologist and a prescription for birth control.

Eva did not thank him, and her resolve had not changed. Over time, she'd come to believe God gave you the body that suited your temperament. Until she'd accidentally gotten pregnant. Termination presented neither a complex moral or physical question for Eva. The hardship had been that she'd conceived at all.

Occasionally she felt guilt. Not for her choice, but because she had something that should belong to someone else. Women who dearly wanted babies were denied happiness by their fallible bodies. Her fertility was Frodo's ring—a precious burden. She'd be thrilled if it was lost. Perhaps God had relented in the intervening years, and brought her body in line with her will.

"Ms. Lytton? Dr. Parmalee Singh." An Indian woman shook Eva's hand. "I understand congratulations are in order?"

Eva was going to kill Wyatt.

"I bought some teak patio furniture at a significant markdown." She smiled brightly. "But I'm not pregnant." She handed Dr. Singh her forms.

"My apologies. The chart appears to be in error. What can I do for you?"

Eva kept her bright look, hoping this doctor did more than deliver babies. "I'd like to assess my fertility."

"Certainly." Dr. Singh glanced at Eva's documents. "When was your last period?"

Eva panicked. She hadn't thought of that. "I've just started," she confessed.

"Excellent. We can run some tests today." The doctor smiled and looked Eva in the eye, intending comfort. "At your age, barring unusual circumstances that don't seem indicated by your medical history, I'm sure we'll find you in perfect physical health."

Eva smiled back, fervently hoping she was wrong.

Wyatt Gets the Girl

". . . the Science Fair Committee asked to see you, and the American Democracy Initiative meeting has been rescheduled to Tuesday—I already updated your calendar. Don't forget you have to attend the upcoming School Board meeting, Gwen Eilbert is waiting to see you, and these are your messages." His administrative assistant, Steff, handed him a sheaf of pink message slips.

"What does the Science Fair Committee want?" Wyatt flipped through his messages.

"To see if you'll lift some of the restrictions on explosive materials now that Mr. Lang has been fired. They feel it's a safer environment. There's a proposal on your policies stack."

Wyatt snorted. "Not likely. Where is it?"

Steff looked up. "Right on top . . . oh." She looked confused. "Did you move your stacks around?"

"No. Though things look shifted."

"Here it is. Amber left some folders for you. Maybe she moved stuff."

"What does Gwen Eilbert want?"

"To be somewhere else."

He raised his eyes to Steff.

"I don't want to spoil it for you." She grinned. "But Mr. Kelly knows obscenity when he sees it. Here are the ACT testing forms, and you need to sign these."

Wyatt wished he could ignore the two messages from Katherine Feely Jones. The answer he had to give her was not the one he wanted.

He realized Steff was holding forms out for him.

"Sorry. What?"

"These are for you to read." She handed him some white sheets. "And you need to sign these." She handed him some yellow transfer forms.

"What is it?"

"Linny Pope is going to the evening program."

Wyatt sighed and took the forms. "Leave them with me."

"And Gwen?"

"She can sit and think profane thoughts a moment longer."

Wyatt felt heavy as he looked at Linny Pope's forms. Linny was a pretty, competent sophomore whose bright smile and bouncy bob evoked a grown-up Girl Scout. A Girl Scout who gave her cookies away for free because she was sixteen and pregnant. She was dropping out to attend an evening program for pregnant students.

Wyatt rubbed his tired eyes and wondered if a lime could really cure a headache. His fingers were itching to dial Linny Pope's house, to ask her what she was going to do with the baby. She might keep it, but she might give it up. The infant was so tantalizingly available he could see her perfectly—clean white socks and shiny white patent-leather Mary Janes, chestnut hair held back by a pink headband, listening seriously at age six as Wyatt explained the importance of birth control before they left for her first co-ed birthday party.

He took a pen and signed away his fantasy child, as he did about two or three times a year. It was torture to have the inside track on a pool of highly desirable future adoptions and not be able to partake. The impropriety, however, was irrefutable. Any School Board in the country would rightly eviscerate him.

What next? Buying six-packs for the cheerleaders so they'd get drunk and pregnant? Before you knew it, Wyatt would be a black market child trafficker.

He put the completed forms in his outbox, then called Katherine.

Wyatt hung up with a heavy heart. Deborah Tanner had been perfect—soft spoken, demure, honest face, and an obvious bump. His hand twitched remembering her surprised reaction to a little kick in her belly. You didn't fake that. But Katherine had quoted him $15,000 he didn't have. He still had savings, but after the adoption there'd be nannies and bottles and diapers and crib sheets and all manner of brightly colored Made in China plastic things that alarmed Wyatt thinking about them. He made a note to call about getting into the public foster system, banishing Horn Rims's outrage from his mind.

Wyatt opened his door. "Ms. Eilbert," he called. "Will you join me?"

Wyatt didn't know the student well, but he knew her type. She was a hefty, angry girl, prevented by bulk and acne from having the high school experience she wanted. Her anger channeled into rebellion.

"Gwen, you've been sent to see me because of your provocative attire. What do you have to say about that?"

The sullen sophomore shifted her heavy frame and adopted a defiant stance. "I have a constitutional right to express myself."

"While it's true that public school students possess a range of free-expression rights under the First Amendment, those rights are by no means boundless. Officials, such as myself, can prohibit students from wearing shirts with profane messages such as you are wearing."

They both looked down at Gwen's T-shirt, emblazoned with the hot pink script: I HAVE THE PUSSY SO I MAKE THE RULES.

"None of the words on this shirt are swear words," Gwen persisted.

"I see your point. However, the collective impression is, by most standards, profane. I must prohibit you from wearing it on school property."

Gwen smirked. "You can't stop me from thinking it."

Wyatt was immensely irritated by this stupid girl and her pussy power.

"I'm also going to require that you attend three detention periods and write me a term paper on the Supreme Court case *Bethel School District v. Fraser*'s impact on free speech."

Gwen's jaw dropped, and Wyatt felt slightly ashamed. His eyes fell to her heaving T-shirt and he didn't anymore. If she wanted to be a rebel, she should learn something about meaningful expression, not inflammatory garbage.

"That will be all," he dismissed. He followed as she trudged out of his reception area.

"Don't you think that was a little harsh?" Steff asked. Wyatt reminded himself to close his office door when disciplining students.

He didn't answer. His anger was not directed at the girl, but she was the vehicle that had flung the sentiment in his face. If Gwen wanted to flaunt her pussy power, fine. He had power too.

Wyatt felt eyes boring into the back of his head and turned to see Amber Paley staring at him. It was unsettling to see something like hate on her face.

He retreated to his office before he could call Gwen back and apologize. He aimlessly moved papers, desperate for the day's end. He wanted to be away from students and to be drinking. Steff shot him a sympathetic glance when she entered, laying the mail on his desk and exiting without a word. He pulled the stack to him, starting with the slim white envelope on top.

Two minutes later he was still staring at the contents he'd pulled from the envelope. One was a note of beautiful script that read:

The DiGuardi family wishes to thank you for your services in assisting Farasha in the delivery of her champion foal Biscuit.

The other, more official-looking instrument, read:

Pay to the Order of Wyatt Ozols $15,000.00.

Without allowing himself time to think, Wyatt picked up the phone and dialed Katherine Feely Jones.

Dimple Drives

Have you ever heard of someone afraid of a pedicure?" I'd been mulling over our lunch for days.

"Every time the local news does a special on fungal infections. Why are you answering my question with a question?" Freya steepled her fingers, framed by the black leather wing of her chair.

"Did I?"

"Twice."

I didn't know how to describe my lunch with Julian. It felt like a betrayal to share. "He's nice."

Freya did her signature controlled exhale.

"Dimple. Your attitude is . . . *bewildering*. Do you want this role?"

I was startled. "Of course I do."

"I couldn't tell."

"It's not up to me!" I protested.

"The measure of achievement isn't whether you have a challenging problem to deal with, but whether it's the same problem you had last year."

"What would you like me to do?" I didn't see how I could sway Julian's decision.

"Care," Freya ordered. "Show me, show Julian, that you want this. Put some life into it, for god's sake."

Eyes on the floor, I said, "I don't want to be disappointed."

She waited for me to look up, and held my eyes. "What's the worst that could happen?"

I didn't answer.

"Whatever it is," she said, "it too shall pass. Probably sooner than it should."

Freya's words stayed with me out of her office, past the effervescent receptionist in tangerine hoop earrings, down the elevator, and across the parking lot. I got to my car so preoccupied, I forgot to tug down my Pucci mini and seared a dermal layer of thigh on the hot leather seat.

"It's out of my hands," I explained to yesterday's Starbucks cup. "Julian makes the decisions," I protested to my Regina Spektor CD. "What can I do?" I asked my lip balm. "Honestly!" I complained to my water bottle.

"Fine," I said to them all, turning the key. "But you're going overboard."

Twenty minutes and a pair of jeans later I walked into my favorite shop in the Marina.

"Hey, Larry!" I called to the proprietor.

"Dimple! My god, it's been, what, a year? More?"

"Too long." I kissed his cheek, avoiding the grease stain.

His face lit up. "Are you a customer today?"

"You betcha," I said. He clapped with glee.

"You want the Fat Boy?" He named my usual.

"Not this time. I need something special, for two."

By the time I got to Wales Productions, I was less sure of myself. I smoothed my hair, but it was an unwinnable battle. I looked as frazzled as I felt. Could this even work?

"Can't fail unless you try." I gave myself a pep talk and opened the door.

Production offices aren't as formal as people think. The entrance of Wales Productions opened right onto a large room filled with several desks. The closest was empty, and occupants of the other two were on the phone. I walked past, toward where the great director was likely to sit. Eyes followed me, but no one objected. Confidence goes a long way in casual L.A.

I caught Julian's voice, and steered my steps that way. He was in a large office, door open, on the phone. His personal assistant, seated at a desk outside, was also on the phone. I wondered if they were all on the phone with each other.

This assistant did try to stop me, waving while not breaking his parade of "uh-huhs" into the mouthpiece, but I didn't pause until I stood on Julian's office threshold.

Arriving unexpected allowed me to study Julian in a different way. He was extremely attractive, especially if you liked bald, which I did. He had sharp cheekbones and clear, lively eyes. He was ruddy with health and everything masculine. I couldn't define the thing that made the difference between one man and another, but Julian was very, very male.

"Excuse me?" The assistant covered his receiver now, and raised an eyebrow.

I ignored him, focused on the man at his desk. He looked up. His face registered and his body shifted toward me, though his conversation didn't miss a beat.

". . . I'd rather use local light guys. It's snobbery to think only L.A. people can do it well, and locals know their own sunshine best."

"You can't just . . ." The assistant was in my ear, but Julian waved him off. I didn't move.

"Okay . . . Okay . . . No, I want Ted for that . . . Fine . . . Let me know." He hung up, and gave me his full attention. I waited.

"Well," he said. "You're a vision. You look . . . like you arrived in a hurry."

I smoothed my hair. "I wanted to see a great director at work. But I came here instead."

He waited.

"The thing about Cora," I said, "is that she didn't wait for Jonas to do the asking."

"She didn't," he agreed, eyes alight.

"So I've decided to audition you."

"When she told me I was average, she was just being mean," he said.

"It won't be a hot air balloon or zip-lining," I cautioned. "Just an ordinary lunch at one of my favorite places."

"Let me find my keys." He stood, lean in his blue jeans.

"That won't be necessary." I smiled. I spotted a leather jacket, and pointed. "Bring that."

Outside, Julian scanned the small lot for an unfamiliar car, but there wasn't one. Only the gleaming black beast of the Ducati Multistrada 1200 motorcyle. I normally rented a basic Harley for my motorcycle fix, but today I'd splashed out.

He appraised me. "That would explain the hair."

"You have an unfair advantage." I tossed him a helmet.

I had no idea if he'd ridden a bike before, and I didn't ask. I climbed on and waited for him to settle in behind me.

"All set?" I asked.

I sensed rather than saw him nod. The bike throttled to life, and we roared off toward the Pacific Coast Highway going north.

Bent low over the bike, pavement blurring beneath us, my bravado faded. Did it seem stuntlike and juvenile? Would he see this as a come-hither from a casting couch 'ho? What was I going to say when we got there? Doubt was taking root when Julian shifted his body to fit perfectly against mine, and other thoughts crowded in. His arms and chest were taut. Even through my leather jacket, I felt heat. As if he could sense my thoughts, his arms tightened around my waist.

Shit, I thought. I can't have the hots for the director.

LaMimi said, *Shut the hell up for once and enjoy the ride.*

If my hair was bad when I got to Julian's, it was unrecoverable when I pulled off my helmet at Neptune's Net.

"How was it?" I was sizzling with energy.

"One minute I wanted to buy a motorbike, the next I didn't. It's a vicious cycle," he replied.

We threaded our way through a clump of bikers straight from Casting 101, leather chaps and all. Neptune's Net was my favorite dive spot in L.A. It was chaotic and crazy, you fought for parking and a picnic table, but the fresh seafood and stunning ocean view couldn't be beat.

"Fried or not fried?" I asked Julian.

"Not."

I steered us toward the nonfried counter.

"You know your biker bar," Julian observed.

"I love dive bars. I dated this guy who didn't have any money, but he was a gentleman and always paid the bill. We went to places he could afford. I've shot pool and butchered karaoke in the seediest places in town, and loved it. I detest stinginess, so I loved his attitude. And dive bars pour a mean drink."

"What happened?"

"I drank 'em."

"To the guy," he persisted.

It was too personal to share "He didn't want kids" with Julian. "He moved to the Valley," I said.

It was our turn at the counter, and we ordered a bunch of crabs, clams, and shrimp, with corn on the cob and cold beer. I squeaked when I saw the basket of Saran-wrapped oatmeal cookies, and grabbed one. "This looks homemade."

Julian was laughing. "You're like a kid."

"Oatmeal cookies are a measure of quality," I said. "The Oatmeal Cookie Mean standard. I compare oatmeal cookies worldwide."

"And the best?"

"My *vecamama's*, of course. My grandmother's cookies

would cure amputation. But in a pinch any oatmeal cookie with milk will turn your day around."

I couldn't read his expression. "What?"

He grinned. "You're . . . enjoyable."

"Anything's enjoyable with cold beer on a sunny day at Neptune's Net."

I saw a picnic table open up and elbowed in there. It was prime real estate, ocean view. Julian brought the food.

"How about you? Got a food barometer?"

"Onion soup. The best I ever had was in a little Czech Republic town called Český Krumlov."

"I love Český Krumlov! I went after college and it's one of my best travel memories. I could've spent weeks wandering the cobblestones, sipping *pivo* in the old-town square, and floating on the river."

"Me too!" Julian lit up.

"Egon Schiele's my favorite artist, so I loved that piece of it, walking where he'd walked and painted."

"He was driven out of town after two years because the townsfolk were angry about the nude portraits of their teenage daughters in compromising poses."

"They certainly aren't short on anatomical detail." I remembered the drawings. "I liked his self-portraits best."

"Good art has to have a certain narcissism to it."

"I don't know." I considered. "I agree that to be confident, you have to have a degree of selfishness. But I don't like it when the artist interrupts my experience with his stamp. Like when you see a movie and every scene shouts, 'Look at my insights into these neurotic characters, aren't I prescient?' It takes me out of the experience."

"Isn't that a way of presenting unique suffering?"

"Is suffering unique? I don't care about you caring about you. To have value, it has to have selflessness."

"Does something have to be universal to be art?"

"No. But selflessness makes me like it more."

"Teenage girls in compromising poses makes me like it more," Julian said. I threw a clam shell at him.

We sat companionably peeling shrimp and looking across the Pacific Coast Highway at the ocean. At least I thought we were sitting companionably until Julian said, "We can't ignore the dodo in the bathtub forever. We have to talk."

His tone was sober, and my heart plummeted. He'd chosen Daisy. I kicked myself for waiting so long to show him any spunk, and for being so dense I didn't accept the reality of his recent silence.

"The demure Ms. Bledsoe-I-need-to-formally-shake-your-hand tore a new lane in the PCH with a two-wheeled monster of a motorbike, me clinging to her back like a baby lemur. Care to explain, lanesplitter?"

A laugh of relief burst from me. "Oh, the bike?"

"Oh, this old thing?" he mimicked, falsetto, to an imaginary companion.

"It takes a lot of wind to move this hair." I shrugged. "I'm not completely predictable."

"No." His gaze was intent. "You're not."

"How's *Cora* coming along?" I changed the subject to the real elephant in the room.

"Some days good, some days not so good. It's a truth that your creation will never match the vision in your mind. It's hard to accept falling short, but you'll go crazy if you don't."

"It's a wonderful project."

"I'm close to this one."

I hesitated. "I did wonder . . ."

He looked interested.

"When Cora reconciles with Jonas, the arc of her relationship with her sister fades away. It's almost as if by embracing her lover at sunset she's completely fulfilled as a person."

Julian studied me. "You find that troubling."

"Yes. I mean, resolving her emotional relationship with Jonas is important, but she had so much more going on, and it disappears unresolved. Like all she needed was the man. What happened to the rest of her life?"

"It's hard to encompass a life in two hours onscreen," Julian said, but his eyes had a faraway look. They came back to me. "It really came across that Jonas was all that she needed to be happy?"

"Sort of."

"What would you do?"

I hesitated. This was Julian's baby. "I'm an actress, not a director."

"You're a woman."

He waited.

"Maybe you don't end with the sunset clutch. You leave it anticipated. Like, instead, Cora exposes her sister and frees herself from that relationship, and when she walks out the door you know she's *going* to Jonas, but the focus is on her."

"People like romantic resolution onscreen," Julian pointed out.

"See, that's why you're the director."

He had the faraway look in his eyes again. I watched the gulls swoop in for discarded French fries and the occasional clam strip. Bikers left, surfers came. Time passed. People eyed our empty beers and the table.

I said, "How about after impressing everyone with her diction at the ball, Cora decides to swim the English Channel to prove herself, and when she gets out in Dover, Jonas beats his romantic rival Mr. Darcy in a fistfight, they rob a bank together, and canter off into the sunset on a pair of camels toward Gretna Green."

He laughed. "If I'm ignoring you, it's your fault for stimulating my brain."

"How's the cookie?"

"Like velour sweatpants in my mouth." His phone rang. "Excuse me," he apologized.

"Uh-huh . . . Uh-huh . . . Already?" He looked at his watch. "Is she there? . . . I need to . . . yes. Tell her an hour. Okay . . . Right . . . No, that's more important . . . Would you set it up? . . . I'll be there."

He hung up. "I hate to say it, but I've got to go. I've got some things to do before a production meeting at five."

I felt like a jealous girlfriend, wondering about the call. "Let's get you back, then."

"He reminded her that the speed limit was sixty, but she couldn't understand—he was talking a mile a minute."

I gave him a come-hither smile. "Don't you trust me?" I tried not to layer it with meaning.

"How about you let me try my hand at the wheel?" he asked as we walked to the bike.

The thought of clinging to his hips terrified me, and not because I might fall off the bike. When I wrapped my legs around something, I liked to be in control.

"Larry would kill me," I hedged. "Hop on."

His expression suggested he knew my thoughts but he let it pass. "Okey doke. I'm a firm believer in recycling."

Maryn Takes a Call

"Maryn Windsor." Maryn grabbed her phone before the second ring. Work was failing to distract her from her irritation, but she remained hopeful. She'd stacked a pile of invoices on top of Andy's countersuit. Selena Hernandez was on the case, and Maryn would proceed with her life. Thinking about her imperiled eggs made her nauseous.

"Maryn, Webb Garner here."

Maryn sought name recognition and found none. Was he a client? A referral?

"Hello." She waited.

"How are you today?" The voice was jovial.

Impatient, thought Maryn. "Fine," said Maryn.

"I bet you'd be a sight better if that ex-husband of yours wasn't so ungodly."

Maryn's breath disappeared.

"I'm sorry?" she managed. Who *was* this guy?

"Maryn, I'm here to help."

Maryn was too freaked out to chuckle at the cliché. Was *"Trust me, I'm a lawyer"* next?

"It's reprehensible what Andrew Knox is doing. Your eggs are living human embryos and destroying them is nothing short of murder."

"Oh," was all Maryn could manage.

"We cannot let his depravity go unchecked, nor can we tolerate him in a leadership position in this community. We need to speak for your eggs' right to life and against Andrew Knox."

"Mr. Garner, why are you calling me?"

"I'm the President of the Santa Monica/Malibu Unified School Board and a candidate in opposition to Mr. Knox for City Council. I believe in the sanctity of human life, and want to protect frozen embryos such as yours so they can realize their ultimate purpose."

The rabbit-hole feeling Maryn had experienced days earlier when she'd seen Andy—sorry, *Andrew*—on the news announcing his campaign for City Council returned. She'd been stupefied. *Andy* was running for office? She was embroiled in the fight of her life, and he had bandwidth available to give speeches and spout off about affordable housing for the needy? *Maryn* was the needy one. Maryn knew without a doubt it was Summer's doing, but she'd been furious with Andy nonetheless. She was even more pissed now with this jackass on the phone invading her personal life.

"How exactly did you come by this private knowledge?" She'd only just filed.

"Court documents are public record. I was researching my opponent, and discovered the wrong he seeks to do. I intend to expose him, and right that wrong."

"I appreciate your concern; however, my issue is one for the courts."

"It pains me to think of you struggling alone to protect your motherly rights in a soulless legal system. We need to humanize your story—and expose Andrew Knox. I can offer public support, and strong relationships with local judges. In return, I'd be thrilled to have you stand beside me on my campaign. Together we can defeat Andrew Knox."

"I appreciate your offer"—Maryn chose her words carefully—"but I must decline. This is a private matter."

"Protecting unborn children is a matter for all Christians." Maryn thought she detected the sound of shuffling paper. "It says in Proverbs 31:8-9, 'Speak up for those who have no voice, for the justice of all who are dispossessed. Speak up, judge righteously, and defend the cause of the oppressed and needy.' "

"I assure you, I'm not needy."

"Andrew Knox is threatening to kill innocent babies. They need our protection."

"They're hardly babies." Maryn was running out of patience. She didn't like being manipulated. "They're cryogenically frozen embryos."

"God said, 'Before I formed you in the womb, I knew *you.*' Jeremiah 1:5." She definitely heard paper. Was he reading from notes? "A pre-embryo is a human being from that unique moment of conception when sperm and egg come together to create life."

"There's the 'unique' moment when the egg implants in the uterus. Or the 'unique' moment when the child is born. Or the unique moment I decided that hot fries at three AM was a good idea," Maryn countered. "Just because something only happens once doesn't make it the cradle of life."

"Surely you agree that those eggs are your children?"

For a moment, Maryn saw the seven nuggets, their golden glow flickering, as if the shadow of Andy the Destroyer passed over them, and her rage bubbled. She took deep breaths. Her Spidey sense told her the man on the phone was worse.

"What I think doesn't matter, except to me."

"There's right and there's wrong. Right is protecting unborn children."

"Science doesn't support your position. An embryo isn't viable without a woman's body to sustain it. There's no guarantee any of them would result in a child."

"How could you not see them as children?" He was trying to read her.

"Do I get a tax break?"

"What?"

"If pre-embryos are children, I should get a tax advantage

for all seven of them. If they're nonviable, will a death certificate be issued? If I miscarry, do I face manslaughter charges?"
Maryn was going too far, but this guy pushed her buttons.

"Of course not," Webb blustered.

"I'm a high risk for miscarriage," Maryn kept on. "I don't
want to be liable for negligently placing the eggs in danger.
I'd be a serial killer! My doctor would be arrested for reckless
endangerment."

"You're confusing the issue . . . ," Webb stumbled.

Maryn's voice hardened. "Eggs are not humans. They don't
get constitutional rights because they can't use them."

If Maryn thought of the embryos as children, she'd go
insane. She was already a mess thinking of them as vulnerable cells. She'd cuddle them every day if she could. She had to
resist naming them, like chicks on a farm, in case they ended
up chicken dinner.

"Unborn babies are the most vulnerable elements of our society. Their lives depend on our voice. It's God's wish."

"Not my voice." Maryn wasn't buying Garner's Christian
motives. "I'm on the other side. You can't decide the constitutional status of an embryo, or anyone, based on faith. Where
reasonable minds differ, laws must be objective."

"I see." Webb Garner sounded nonplussed. He'd been expecting a different reaction. Maryn didn't ease his discomfort,
and the silence stretched.

He tried a different tack. "If you don't agree with me on the
whys, you disagree with Andrew Knox. You're suing him."

"The issue between Andy and I is a private matter that
has nothing to do with the theological question of when life
begins."

"I see that I've misjudged you, Ms. Windsor." A hardness
had crept into his voice. "I won't waste any more of your time."
He hung up.

Maryn was startled by the speed of his disconnection. Her

adrenaline tsunami receded, and she was left shaky and uncertain. She dialed Selena Hernandez.

"Maryn, how are you?" her attorney answered promptly.

"Troubled." Maryn described her call from Webb Garner.

"Your concern is legitimate," Selena said. Maryn appreciated that her lawyer skipped outrage and got right to the
matter.

"I never thought this was about pro-life or pro-choice."
Maryn was anxious. "I thought this was a marital property
dispute." Maryn had rushed Selena when they'd filed the
Complaint, dismissing explanations for later. She should have
listened.

"Without taking a position on its correctness, frozen
embryo case law is a straightforward application of Supreme
Court abortion decisions," Selena said. "The thrust of *Roe v.
Wade* is that the mother's right to privacy and control over her
body overcomes any contrary right possessed by a nonviable
fetus. Frozen embryo cases hold that the objecting donor's—in
this case, Andy's—right *not* to procreate is an equal privacy
right. Given the outcome, the right not to procreate outweighs
the contrary right of the other parent."

"So Andy's right to destroy the eggs is stronger than my
right to use them?" Maryn's chest fluttered as the tarry oobleck
approached her golden nuggets.

"There are factual considerations in every case, but it basically comes down to two issues. First, the rights of the parent
versus the rights of the embryo. Second, the rights of one donor
parent versus the other donor parent. As long as the Supreme
Court upholds *Roe v. Wade*, state courts will find that the parent's right to choose defeats the embryo's right to exist. That
means Andy could terminate the embryos, just like you could
terminate an undesired pregnancy."

"You're saying that to win my case, I'd be undermining *Roe
v. Wade*?" Maryn was upset.

"Nothing's so simple. When there's a dispute between the competing privacy interests of donors, and no written agreement exists, courts will weigh the interests of the parties."

"Divorce agreements didn't make the to-do list back then." Bitterness wormed into Maryn's voice. She didn't dwell on Andy's hospital-bed departure from their marriage. They'd barely spoken through the bloodless divorce. Andy had given Maryn everything, like the proverbial $20 taxi fare on the bed stand, in order to exit as quickly and cleanly as possible. Preoccupied with her illness, rights to use the embryos never occurred to her. To be honest, even after he walked out, Maryn wouldn't have thought Andy capable of such harm.

"So what happens without any agreement?"

"The court sees the 'right of procreational autonomy' as composed of two equal parts—the right to procreate and the right to avoid procreation. They'll consider the positions of the parties, the significance of their interests, and the relative burdens. I must be honest, the court defers to the right against the 'burden of unwanted parenthood.'"

"Meaning Andy."

"Don't rule yourself out. Every right has limits when it abuts another's rights. Without being crass, the fact that you're a cancer survivor, and infertile, makes you a sympathetic plaintiff. Plus you don't want his money."

"I feel like my private life is about to become a circus. Damn this stupid election!"

Selena was silent for several beats. "I'm concerned about this politician's call," she admitted. "Your case is one of first impression in this district, and with Andy running for office, rife with political fodder. If conservative groups jumped on it, they could make a public campaign of your personal matter. It would distort the facts and make a real mess, never mind the unwanted attention to you."

"Isn't the Republic of Santa Monica the most liberal enclave in the country?" Maryn asked.

Selena laughed. "Maybe next to Oberlin College." She named her alma mater. "Santa Monica has a small but fervent right to life community. They are educated and articulate, and would be delighted to discover a vehicle for their cause. My concern is that if they seize on this issue, they can garner significant funds from more powerful out-of-state groups with the same agenda. The Mormon Church of Utah supplied much of the funding to support California's Proposition 8's ban on gay marriage."

"Surely it won't come to that," Maryn dismissed. "That was media madness. I'm nowhere near that important."

"Don't underestimate the emotions this case could stir up." Selena's tone was troubled. "On the legal case, we'll wait for the court. On this Webb Garner thing, I'm going to make a few calls."

Maryn thanked Selena for her time and hung up. The office was silent and closed but she didn't move. She stared at the phone. She stared at the framed picture of her horse Jethro. It seemed surreal to her that she was in the exact same spot, everything completely unchanged, as when she got the call from Webb Garner, yet her whole world felt tipped on its axis.

Wyatt Goes to Lunch

When the tall girl emerged from the building, it startled Wyatt to realize it was Deborah. Despite her rounded belly, Deborah's shoulders were thin and angular, like a coat hanger. She looked barely out of high school. If not for the baby, she might be giggling on a bedazzled cell phone about the Jonas Brothers, but that wasn't her life now.

She slid into the car without a word. Wyatt handed her a smoothie.

At the clinic, they were called in promptly.

"Deborah? I'm Dr. Singh. I'm stepping in for Dr. Osmun today. So you're," Dr. Singh glanced at the chart, "thirty weeks?"

Deborah nodded.

"Shall we have a listen for the heartbeat?" Dr. Singh pulled out her portable heart monitor. An observing alien would have thought it was an instrument of pain. Mothers cried, grateful for the respite from anxiety they could not shake throughout a process completely within and entirely out of their control. Wyatt blinked rapidly every time.

"Sure." Deborah hitched up the paper gown to expose flowered pink panties. Wyatt always felt awkward, but Deborah didn't seem to care.

Dr. Singh rolled the wand across the girl's abdomen until a steady "woouw, woouw, woouw" filled the room.

"Congratulations," Dr. Singh said.

Deborah showed signs of life. "It's so strong."

Dr. Singh nodded. "Nature's been doing this for thousands of years."

They listened together awhile, the restful possibility of the heartbeat lowering everyone's blood pressure.

"That's a healthy heart." Dr. Singh put the monitor away and wiped Deborah's abdomen. "Your urine and blood tests look fine too. Have you got any questions?"

Deborah shook her head and looked at Wyatt. He didn't.

Dr. Singh glanced at the latest sonogram clipped to her file. "This little . . ." She paused. "Do you know the gender?"

"No," Deborah said. Wyatt remained silent. It was her choice.

"Would you like to know?"

The girl looked at Wyatt. "Would you like that?"

"Very much," Wyatt said.

"It's a girl." Dr. Singh smiled.

"A girl," Wyatt repeated. The word tasted like daffodils, butterflies, and rainbow sherbet. "A girl."

"Okay," was all Deborah said.

"You have a lot of sonograms for a healthy woman your age." Dr. Singh indicated the file. "Is there a reason we have you coming in so often?"

Deborah shook her head no. "It makes Wyatt feel better."

"Nervous Nelly," Wyatt pointed to his chest in self-deprecation.

"I don't mind, so long as the women in the waiting room don't eat me," Deborah said.

"Eat you?" The doctor seemed surprised.

"The ones that aren't pregnant practically drool when they stare at my stomach."

"Not everyone"—Dr. Singh paused, then—"becomes pregnant as easily as you." It would be wrong to call the girl lucky.

"Yeah, I know. It's nice that I won't have to worry when I want kids."

"*When* you want kids?" The doctor was confused.

"I don't want it, but it seemed wrong to destroy it," Deborah said, in the tone you would say, *It was wrong to throw away a perfectly good purse because it didn't match my shoes.* "Wyatt's adopting. I don't belong here."

"Of course you do," Wyatt protested. God forbid the child should get a notion to birth her baby in the dirty Jacuzzi of a hippie colony without medical attention.

"I'm nineteen for chrissakes! I want to be a reporter, and travel the world. I want to wear a belted trench coat like Audrey Hepburn and go to Africa to cover a revolution. You can't meet a secret source with a crying baby. My mom would kill me if she knew."

It was an odd combination, the womanly swollen belly with the fanciful dreams. Pregnancy didn't care what you wanted or if you were an adult.

"I'm not like you, Wyatt," Deborah continued. "You have money. So do those women out there. People with money can fix their problems. My family's different. I know I'll probably never get to Africa. But having a baby would make it certain."

It was the first time Deborah had shared her thoughts. It didn't make Wyatt feel great, but she wasn't wrong.

"Health isn't for sale, but you're rich with it," Dr. Singh diffused the awkwardness. "Keep taking prenatal vitamins and come back in two weeks."

In the waiting room, Wyatt said, "Why don't you sit while I take care of the bill?"

"I think I'll walk." She sacrificed additional time in Wyatt's presence. "I need the fresh air."

He was about to protest, to tempt her with a healthy protein-packed lunch, then reminded himself she was an adult.

"I have a School Board meeting next time. Would it be okay

if my cousin Eva drove you to your appointment?" She nodded. "All right then. Call me if you need anything."

She paused. "I wasn't trying to be mean about the money thing." She surprised him. "It is what it is. I think you'll be a good dad."

There was the awkward moment where Wyatt didn't know whether he should hug her. Wyatt was not a hugger, and it appeared that Deborah wasn't either, but for that one procreative time. They didn't. She left with a wave.

Waiting to pay, Wyatt was contemplating the importance of returning to school versus a Hot Sopressata sandwich from Bay Cities Italian Deli when he saw Maryn Windsor emerge from the consultation area.

How many awkward moments could there be in one day, he thought. He could not ignore his benefactor.

"Ms. Windsor?"

She looked up in surprise.

"Wyatt Ozols," he reminded.

A smile cracked the fatigue on her face. "My hero!"

"Chauffeur, please," he demurred. "I did nothing but grow pallid. Your check was exceptionally generous."

"We couldn't have done it without you." She didn't seem to find it odd that she kept encountering him alone at an obstetrician's office. "Say, are you free for lunch? I'm dying for a salami sub from Bay Cities."

"Sure," Wyatt said, because he was.

They beat the lunch crowd, and shortly were sitting outside with sandwiches. Wyatt felt the sunshine like a gloved hand on the top of his head.

"I hope you don't mind if I gnaw," said Maryn. "It's impossible to eat the Godmother like a lady. How far along are you?"

"Oh, I'm not pregnant." Wyatt concentrated on not getting spicy sauce on his shirt. When he looked up, Maryn's eyes were merry. He blushed. "Of course I'm not. I'm adopting. I accompany Deborah to her appointments. Want to see the sonogram?" He never got tired of the grainy windscreens of the baby's face.

"Not married?" She handed the sonogram back quickly.

"No."

"You're the first single guy I've heard of trying to adopt."

"That seems to be going around," he said.

"Even husbands don't come to every appointment. Are you sweet on the girl?"

"I just pay the bills."

"Honey, that's half the marriages in this town."

"I like to keep an eye on things," he said. "I'm not very trusting."

"Really?"

"I supervise high-schoolers." He smiled.

"What are you keeping an eye on? Smoking? Eating Carl's Jr. Double Western Bacon Cheeseburgers? Playing Lady Gaga to the baby? Or did your last pregnant girl run off with her gynecologist?"

"Something like that." She looked taken aback. "Adoption fraud," he elaborated.

"I'm so sorry." Maryn's distress was genuine. "I shouldn't make jokes. People go through such horrors trying to have a baby."

" 'A man blames the woman who fools him in the same way he blames the door he walks into in the dark.' "

"Twain?"

"H. L. Mencken."

" 'A common mistake that people make when trying to design something completely foolproof is to underestimate the ingenuity of complete fools.' "

"Wilde?" Wyatt was enjoying himself.

"Douglas Adams."

"I'm glad I ran into you. Thanks are overdue. I couldn't

have afforded the adoption without you." The words weren't big enough.

Maryn blinked rapidly, and put down her sandwich.

"What is it?" Wyatt was alarmed.

Her eyes were full of tears. "That makes me happy."

"All evidence to the contrary." Wyatt hated her distress.

"It's extraordinary that something done without thought could so completely change a person's life." She sniffled. "I was just sticking it to the DeGuardis."

"I'm dependent on a horse! I shall name the child Farasha."

"I'm dependent on a horse's ass." She dabbed her eyes.

But you have the pussy, you make the rules, Wyatt thought.

"My husband," she started. Stopped. "*Ex-husband* and I froze embryos during our marriage. We had no idea we'd split up. I had breast cancer and we were thinking about the checklist. Freeze Your Embryos was there between Write a Will and Pack an Overnight Bag. He took a girly mag, I took a Carnation Instant Breakfast drink, and we did our thing."

Wyatt listened.

"Maybe if we'd been thinking more clearly, we'd have noticed the missing sentence. But we didn't, so now I want to use the embryos, but he won't consent."

"I'm sorry," Wyatt said. They *were* alike.

"It's my last chance." Maryn's voice was low.

"What's his hesitation?"

"His wife, I suspect." She wrapped her hands around her Diet Coke like it was a hot chocolate at a ski lodge. "The women in Andy's life tend to make the decisions."

"Have you asked him?"

"We can't communicate anymore."

"Sometimes the person you once loved the most can turn you into the ugliest version of yourself," Wyatt said.

"There's nothing more wretched than lying next to someone in bed and being lonelier than you've ever been. I could no

more touch a shoulder inches away than I could swirl sand on
the floor of the Mariana Trench."

Wyatt was comfortable with Maryn's confidences.

"Relationships are like the sun," he said. "Nothing feels so
good, but if you're careless, the pain is scorching." Wyatt had
been badly burned, but he blamed his own inattention.

"I'm not holy. I'm suing him for the embryos." It was wrong
to Wyatt that a woman who could pull a foal out of a horse
while wearing stilettos should have such stark pain in her
eyes. "I don't understand how he could . . ." She didn't finish.

"Lots of stuff makes no sense," Wyatt agreed.

"*Horrible* people have babies . . ."

"*Criminals* have babies . . ."

They spoke in unison.

"We're alike"—Maryn shook her head— "when you'd think
we have nothing in common."

"I would have envied you walking down the street."

"You'd have been wrong."

"I used to get enraged," Wyatt said. "Drug addicts have
babies, murderers have babies, fifteen-year-olds have babies,
people who've had babies taken away from them have babies.
I resented how easy it was for women, like an inalienable biological right."

"I used to think like that. The loss of autonomy was a shock.
Years ago I only had to open my legs to have a baby, now the
courts are calling the shots and I have to open my home, my
bank accounts, my criminal record, and my skull to prove that
I should be able to implant my own eggs."

"Does the lawsuit make you feel better?" Wyatt asked.

"If I win. I don't care about Andy's feelings. Haven't you
ever seen a mama grizzly when a rattlesnake gets too close to
her petri dish? I want those eggs."

"What are your odds?"

"Not great. The law hasn't caught up to science. We don't

even know whether I'm seeking custody or ownership—I'm blazing a trail through this weird hybrid of family and property law."

"You're brave," Wyatt said.

"I don't feel brave. I'm systematically shaking the tree."

" 'If the world were only one of God's jokes, would you work any less to make it a good joke instead of a bad one?' "

"Sounds like *Doonesbury*."

"George Bernard Shaw."

" 'We're fools whether we dance or not, so we might as well dance.' "

"Emma Goldman?"

"Japanese proverb."

"Do you have a quote about the fools who were beaten to death with salami subs because they ignored the shank eyes they were getting from customers for dawdling on prime table real estate?" Wyatt eyed the circling vultures. A few looked ready to hop forward and peck at them.

"I don't really care."

"You *are* brave."

Maryn laughed. "But I do have a one o'clock."

A Chinese grandmother who'd garrote you for the last cannoli was in the chair before Maryn had fully stood.

"I really enjoyed lunch." Wyatt fell into step. "Perhaps we could meet again." He felt connected to this woman, who, like him, had to fight every step of the way.

She brightened. "Same time next week? We can annoy people at the French Market with a leisurely lunch at the best table."

Andy Thinks

After he divorced Maryn, Andy realized he didn't like being single. He'd assumed he'd savor the freedom like the men in movies, dissuading friends from the altar with clever one-liners. But he'd hated it. He'd married Summer as soon as possible. People thought Summer had ended his marriage. It wasn't true, but Andy didn't correct them. The truth was worse.

Summer wasn't beautiful, but she was bright and funny and strong. Andy was genuinely easygoing and preferred someone else to do planning. He brought looks and charm. He sought a decision maker. Drive and beauty didn't always go together, and he preferred initiative.

Maryn had been a rare case of both. From the moment his mother had laid eyes on Maryn at the Central Valley thorough-bred auction, Caroline had pronounced her an excellent piece of flesh. His mother had grown up on a farm, and stock and breeding were paramount. Andy never questioned her advice. When it came to people, his mother was rarely wrong. A year later Caroline was on the first plane to help him buy a ring.

Andy never wondered why Maryn had married him. All he knew was that she'd been radiant that first day they met in Ojai, radiant when he'd proposed at his law school graduation, radiant when they'd said their vows on a lawn overlooking the sea. Even sweaty from a ride and smelling like horse, Maryn glowed.

It'd been a shock when Maryn calmly told him over dinner

one night that she had breast cancer. He hadn't understood at first.

"You don't smoke."

"It's unrelated." Maryn had been patient, taking his hand across the table.

"You work out all the time." He was bewildered. "You're completely healthy."

"Cancer chooses randomly."

"Canc—" He couldn't finish the word. This wasn't happening.

"There was an abnormal area on my mammogram. The doctor did a biopsy. I didn't tell you because I thought it was nothing. It turns out I have stage two . . ." Maryn's words washed over Andy as she explained things in a calm, steady voice. She was holding both his hands, as if she was trying to quell rising panic, like one of her horses. Words like "lump" and "chemotherapy" and "estrogen receptor" flowed around him, but he couldn't take it in. He wanted to call his mother, but she had died after a too-short battle with pulmonary fibrosis. He didn't know what to do.

" . . . with treatment there's every reason to be optimistic."

Maryn didn't look sick. Her hair was its lustrous red, her eyes clear, her breasts firm and attractive under her T-shirt. It must be a mistake.

"Andy, it's going to be okay." Her tone was borderline pleading.

Andy realized he hadn't said a word since his wife had told him she'd been diagnosed with cancer. "God, Maryn, are you okay?" He turned his hands to grasp hers, offering instead of taking comfort.

She looked down. "It's been a shock. But I'll beat this and we'll do everything we talked about. The cottage in Tuscany, Christmas in Nebraska, kids . . ."

"Kids." Andy squeezed hard. They had started trying.

"I'm not pregnant." Her gaze dropped again. "They recommend that we fertilize and freeze some eggs. Just in case."

"Of course." Andy was quick to agree, but he wanted to shudder at the image of a laboratory baby. In his mind it was a grotesque mutation, like science class mole rats floating in jars of formaldehyde. But it wouldn't come to that. Maryn was vibrant and healthy and she'd be fine.

That's the way Andy had described it to his dad. "I'm confident everything's going to be fine. I really feel good about the treatment schedule."

"Son, no one gives a shit how you feel. Maryn's gonna have to put up a fight and your job is to think about her and her only. Your feelings and thoughts don't count for beans until she's better."

His father's words shocked Andy. He missed his mother. Caroline had never expected Andy to be more than he was. She understood his limitations. He needed her to tell him what to do. Without her he had spun and spun, until he'd spun completely away.

"I wish I knew what to do," said Andy. He and Summer were discussing the lawsuit.

"We know what to do," Summer said. "We're going to countersue to have the eggs destroyed."

"What?" He was aghast. "That seems harsh."

"What else are you going to do? No sons of ours are going to have some half brother we don't know," Summer said.

It alarmed Andy that Summer presumed his progeny would be boys. Though he'd been a quintessential boy—Homecoming King, wide receiver at the University of Nebraska, fraternity social chair—the idea of sons intimidated Andy. He'd prefer a little girl with pink bows and a ruffled skirt who he could bounce on his knee and soothe reassuringly as he walked next to her, on a miniature pony. The little girl, maybe called Deli-lah, would have strawberry blond hair like Summer.

"Maybe we should talk about that," he said. "Having kids."

These thoughts soothed him. The lawsuit from Maryn unsettled him. He'd prefer to think about teaching Delilah to swim or ride a bike.

"Not while we're in the middle of a campaign and fighting a lawsuit." Summer was firm. "Not until you're elected and I'm out of the weather center and on to an anchor desk. We have things to do first."

"I don't think I want to countersue."

"You can't give in to her, Andrew."

"It isn't a competition, Summer."

"She made it one when she sued you."

He thought about Maryn—calm, composed Maryn—driven to begging. She hadn't begged him to stay when he told her he was leaving her, hadn't begged him not to be his worst. But she'd begged him for this. Now she was suing him, which made him wonder if this wasn't really, now, his worst.

"I should talk to her."

"She's made it pretty clear she doesn't want to talk any-more. She doesn't care about your wishes and she's willing to air your dirty laundry in court during an election to do it. We need to beat her at her own game."

"Don't push me, Summer," he warned. "Maryn isn't out to get me and it isn't a game. She's trying to do something we agreed to during our marriage, and she filed suit before I started running for office."

"It's been five weeks since you got served and there's prob-ably some deadline for filing a countersuit. Don't Andy this situation."

"Don't use my name as a verb," he snapped. It was the first time Summer had stepped into his dealings with Maryn, and

Andy didn't like it. "This decision won't be based on what's easiest for you, and wearing pearls while you stab someone doesn't make it okay."

Her face was stricken but Andy didn't care. Maybe he wanted to make this decision for himself. He needed to make a list. He needed to figure out what his wishes were.

What amazed Andy was how nothing happened after he filed his Answer and Counter Complaint. The earth's rotation didn't screech to a halt, hurling everyone from the planet. Alarms didn't sound, God didn't smite, the clerk didn't even stop chewing her gum as she time-stamped the filing and gave him his copy. He felt foolish for clearing his afternoon calendar.

Andy had rationalized the filing because it bought him time to think. It got Summer off his back and it didn't harm Maryn. Even if he won, he could change his mind. The eggs wouldn't self-destruct when the gavel came down.

"Do you want kids?"

He and Maryn were ambling hand in hand down the beach. The wind blew her hair out like a veil and the sun painted it crimson.

"A football team?" He grinned.

"Pick another sport." She elbowed him.

"Basketball?"

"How about tennis?"

"Only if it's doubles."

"You're on."

They hadn't been in a hurry. They'd assumed the right time would present itself and they'd make a baby. He'd be partner, she'd be company president, they'd have an au pair with a charming accent.

"I'm going to name my firstborn son Magnus," Andy said, watching the World's Strongest Man Contest on television.

"No," she said. "Kids will tape condoms to his locker at school. The therapy will be too expensive."

"That's Magnum," he corrected.

"They're high school kids. They won't care."

"They're not very nice ones."

"What can you do?" She shrugged. *"Too much Red Bull and not enough Ritalin."*

"Fine. I'll name him Conan."

"Mm-mm." She shook her head. *"The Barbarian."*

"These bullies are delinquents."

"High school's a tough place."

"How about Bruno?"

"How about Stuart?"

"Rhymes with fart."

"No it doesn't!"

"High school taunting is an inexact science."

"Fine. Then Percy."

"What?" Andy nearly fell out of his chair. *"You're not going to dress our kid like Little Lord Fauntleroy are you?"*

When he realized she was teasing, it devolved from there, each suggesting names more absurd than the last. Their talk was silly, complacent. There wasn't any serious discussion until his mom was dying.

"Maryn's a good girl." His mom coughed, and wiped the sputum with a delicate hankie. Andy hid a shudder.

Andy grasped her parchment hand in terror of its frailty.

"A good woman's like a house, son. If you build a strong foundation, it'll shelter you forever. But if you neglect it, it falls apart. You're going to need looking after when I'm gone and Maryn's a good one to do it."

"Hush, Mama. You're not going anywhere."

"Andy, I won't be here next Christmas, so you have to listen to me. You take care of that girl. Promise me."

"I promise."

"And you make babies soon."

"You'll bounce them on your knee," he assured her.

"I won't and you know it, but promise me you won't wait long. You need a family and Maryn was made to be a mother. I see it in her eyes. Promise me."

"I promise."

Andy shook his head to scatter the memory. It wasn't his fault they hadn't had a baby. He hadn't neglected Maryn. They'd been fine until she got sick. His mom would understand that things were different now. Summer was his wife. If not now, he'd have his family with her someday.

He decided the lingering ominous feeling lodged in his gut was hunger not guilt, so he called Summer to meet him for an early dinner at Piccolo.

Dimple Thinks

S orry I'm late." I dropped into the hair chair. "Breakfast with my mom."

Justine attacked my hair. "Did you bring the goods?"

I handed over a Ziploc full of savory *bulcinas*.

"I love her." Justine's hair had turned from turquoise to magenta overnight, and she had bangs.

"That makes one of us."

"Uh-oh. What happened?"

I made an irritable gesture. "We argued about this new role . . ."

Justine squealed. "With Julian Wales?"

"No. *Cora* is the slowest casting process of all time. I'm going to evolve down to four toes before it's over." It had been ten days since our jaunt up the PCH, and I hadn't heard from Julian. TMZ had photos of him coming out of a West Los Angeles martial arts studio with Daisy Carmichael, though. I hoped he'd made her try to break a cement block with her forehead. "A different one."

The morning had not gone well.

"Why you play with your *pankūkas*?" my mother scolded over her skillet. "Is good. You eat."

I visited for breakfast when I had late set calls. I studied her, trying to be objective. She was thin like a bird, and getting smaller each year. Her movements were nimble, despite failing eyesight, gnarled hands manipulating crepe pancakes around cheese and cinnamon with a spatula. I tried to picture myself making *pankūkas* for my child but couldn't. I saw myself as a mother, but I didn't see myself like my mother. I needed her support, though.

"*Mamu*, you need grandkids to gobble up these *pankūkas*." I'd never asked if she was anxious for grandchildren, but I assumed all mothers were.

"Oh, Agnis, we wish, your father and I, for you to find a nice Latvian boy and have a family. But such is life. You can't make it like you want. I say good-bye to my country in 1944 and never see my grandmother again. What can you do?" She shrugged and turned off the flame.

"I'm thinking about having a baby." There. I'd said it.

I was looking at her back as she stood by the stove. She didn't respond.

"*Mamu?*"

"I hear you."

"What do you think?"

"I don't know why you ask. You no care how I think. You do what you do."

I sighed. "I do care."

She turned to face me, arms crossed, mouth set. "What you think, Agnis? You think this like movie? Life is hard. You can't just change rules and have this and have this and things always work out. You have to follow some"—she gestured at the air—"order."

"I'm forty, now, *Mamu*. I don't think I can wait to get married. I want to have kids before it's too late."

"You want, you want." She flung her hands up. "Everything not about 'you want.' Life was hard for your father and me. When you was born we have nothing. We work all the time. Lots of time I'm so tired I want to cry, but you keep going because you have baby to take care and that's life."

"I'll be able to take care of a baby. I have a good job."

"I thought you thinking about this movie? I thought you had big plans for career. Academy Award guy this, and fancy movie that."

"You said doing the movie was crazy."

"Not so crazy as having baby! Babies not fun and games. Babies is hard work. When I was baby, it was war, the Russians occupy, I have no diapers. Your *vecamama*, she use tablecloth. In the camps for people with no country, we have nothing. One family next to ours, little girl same age as me, she get sick and she died. They no even have a coffin. They bury her in blanket."

"I don't see what that has to do with anything." I was irritated.

"Life was not easy for us. Things get taken away. Things happen. I lost your father too soon. But this is the life. Why you make so hard for you?"

She blinked tears as she looked at me, and my irritation was snuffed as I saw the terror behind her eyes.

"So what's the story?" Justine brought me back to the present.

"Hmm? Oh, it's about a woman turning forty and having a kid on her own, through a fertility clinic."

"Interesting." Justine sounded bored. She'd been married since she was seventeen. "Lifetime Channel?"

"Something like that."

"Not as interesting as *Cora*."

"I think it would speak to a lot of women, you know, that moment when you give up on your fantasies about marriage and happily ever after and realize you have to go it alone if you want kids." I hoped my tone wasn't unnatural.

"Sounds sad. Who wants to have kids alone?"

"Isn't having kids alone less sad than being with the wrong person?"

"For who?"

"Think of it this way—if something happened to Big Mike, if he died or left, you'd see a way through. You could have a life with someone else. But your kids are irreplaceable."

"I hate it when you come straight from your mother's."

"If you had to choose, you'd choose the kids, right?"

"Do you know something about Big Mike that you're not telling me?"

"No." I slumped in my chair. What did I know about marriage anyway?

"Sit up," Justine commanded. I sat up.

"These are the things you think about when you don't have a Big Mike," I tried again. "Everyone assumes they'll get married. Even when it takes a while, you think *eventually* . . . All of a sudden, you're forty, and no one is as surprised as you are that you're still single."

"The key to finding a soul mate is to grow up, quit whining, and do something about your hair. You'll meet somebody."

"But will it be in time?" I stared at my face in the mirror, as if viewing myself as a stranger would help me see more clearly. "At what age do you face down the moment when you realize your life isn't going to turn out like you planned?" I had an inkling.

She stuck the pins into a twist of hair. "Most moms will tell you the fantasy is that a husband helps. Big Mike is a great guy, but I raised those kids. I doubt he could find the peanut butter if Angelina Jolie strolled up to the house and asked him to spread it on her nude body."

"Is a single parent enough for a kid?"

"If not, there's a million kids in trouble. Sometimes I envy my neighbor, Naomi. She's a single mom and doesn't seem to resent it at all. Like you don't miss what you never had. I spent a lot of motherhood being pissed off at Big Mike for not helping more. She's tired, sure, but I was tired *and* resentful. She gets to call all the shots too, and no one argues with her."

"Your mom helps out, doesn't she?" I was still rattled by my mom's reaction.

"My folks love my kids for three hours at a time, when they're shiny and charming. They aren't there at four in the morning when Luther has thrown up all over his sheets and I haven't done laundry in two weeks. I put down newspapers. Don't call social services."

"They'd be astonished that someone still reads newspapers."

Justine paused in her work. "The thing about having kids is, we're all gonna mess up. Our parents messed us up, we'll mess up our kids, nobody's going to do it perfect. You focus on getting the big stuff right, and try to enjoy the little bastards when you can."

She was right. I couldn't let my mom get to me. I was letting too many people get under my skin lately. As if on cue, a text message popped up on my phone.

```
Seven days without a pun makes one weak. Call
me.
```

It was from Julian. My stomach flipped. I typed back.

```
A good pun is its own reword.
```

Justine's grin split her face. "Enough about kids. Let's talk about Julian Wales."

"No." I put my phone away. "Are we done?"

"You look as fresh as a page from the buy one get one free clearance section of a Russian brides' catalog." Roxy was scheduled to have a rough day. "You're not going to call him?" She'd readsdropped my text, and was not to be diverted.

"There's no privacy on set for a personal call."

"You mean a work call." She grinned.

"Of course." I had no idea anymore.

"You're still toting *Cora* everywhere."

The script peeking from my bag was more battered than an onion ring. Next to it were equally dog-eared cryobank donor profiles.

I had the eerie sensation of time passing but not moving at all. I was exactly where I'd been two months ago. What the hell did I want?

Eva Sees Something, Maybe

S o." Eva tapped the steering wheel.

Deborah looked out the window.

Eva felt awkward. Deborah was such a lump of a girl.

She turned the radio up. "Do you like Justin Bieber?" She looked young enough.

The girl shrugged moth-wing shoulders. She was such a thin vessel.

"I got to see him in concert." "Got" was a strong word. Eva, feeling ancient, had been deafened by the tween "Beliebers," but she'd signed twelve-year-old sensation Madelynn Jeter. It shocked Eva that most of her clients were born in the 1990s. She peeked sideways. Deborah had been born in the 1990s, and now the baby was having a baby.

"Thought of any baby names?"

Deborah's gaze swung her way. "Why would I do that?"

Eva could have kicked herself. "Right. I'm sure Wyatt has that covered."

"Where is Wyatt?"

Eva knew it was irrational to feel stung. "He has a School Board meeting," she reminded Deborah.

"Oh."

They passed the rest of the ride in silence. It was a relief to park the car. Deborah had barely checked in when they called her name. They both stood.

"Would you like me to go in with you?" Eva offered.

She was relieved when Deborah shook her head no. She pulled out her iPhone as soon as Deborah disappeared. She'd needed to check her e-mail but hadn't wanted to seem rude to the girl.

Eva didn't know what to do about the Daisy situation. It had been over two months since she'd gotten the *Cora* script, but Julian Wales refused to return her calls. She needed to put enough pressure on Wales to get Daisy the part, but not so much that Eva compromised their working relationship. She also had to consider Freya Fosse, Dimple Bledsoe's agent. She was a force to be reckoned with—though the grapevine suggested Julian wasn't returning Freya's calls either.

Eva was reading the last e-mail she'd exchanged with Julian Wales when a text popped up from Sawyer.

> So there's this movie I want to see, and my mom said I couldn't go by myself.

She smiled. She typed.

> I'm sorry, I don't do porn.

She didn't wait long for a reply.

> The hell you don't. Last night ruined me forever. You are Mozart where everyone else is like awkward elevator music.

Eva blushed. She had no idea what to reply. Another text popped up.

> Oh, sorry. Did I send that to Eva??? Ooooops . . .

She typed.

```
Don't make me sic Chuck Norris on you. Chuck
Norris doesn't go hunting because hunting has
a possibility of failure. Chuck Norris goes
killing.
```

Sawyer replied.

```
Chuck Norris never "gets laid," rather laid
"gets Chuck."
```

I'm smitten, thought Eva. Last night had been perfect. He'd cooked for them, and they'd "watched a movie," though Eva couldn't tell you what it was about. It had been hard to leave.

"Stay," Sawyer had begged, arms wrapped around her. They were stretched out on the deep couch, his brown hair falling into sleepy eyes.

"I can't." It was tempting.

"I make good eggs."

She waited for the "fertilized" joke but it didn't come. He was really offering to make her eggs for breakfast. Her heart cooed.

"I have to go," she said anyway.

"Eventually, yes. But seeing as you're completely housebroken, there's no rush."

"Now." She untangled herself. "I have to catch a cab. After midnight cabs evaporate around here."

He tugged her back. "Be a sporting woman. Give the cabs a head start."

She bent down to kiss him. "While it turns out deep couches agree with me, I have an early appointment."

"False. No actor gets up before noon."

It was too complicated to explain about Wyatt's baby mama. She also didn't want any conversation about kids.

"Think how nice it will be to see me again if you've had more time to miss me." She slid her feet into her shoes.

"Friday?"

"Really?" That would be the third time this week.

"Who's got two thumbs and wants to see you this weekend?" He made fists and pointed at himself. "This guy."

She couldn't hide her goofy grin. "Friday, then."

A ping brought Eva's attention back to her iPhone. Her anticipation of a flirty text from Sawyer was disappointed.

```
Cora = Daisy yet???? Had to do karate class for
Julian this week. WTF????
```

Eva was irritated by Daisy's message. In fact, she was irritated with the whole Daisy situation. It used to be that producers and directors would screen suitable talent and award the role to the best actress. Now, a studio might be looking to cross-promote another picture. A niece might be involved. A director might be swayed by a persuasive agent. A male lead might be five eight. A sex tape could be released. An agent couldn't rely on talent anymore. As much as Eva resented it, her job was shifting toward marketing, and she had to aggressively pitch for roles. Clients were demanding it, even when the role was a stretch. There used to be loyalty in Hollywood, but not anymore. If an actor didn't get a part she wanted, she'd change her agent as easily as her hairstyle. If Julian Wales was seriously considering Dimple Bledsoe for the part, Eva had to slide in there like a knife.

She considered what she knew about the other actress. It wasn't much. Dimple had gotten rave reviews for some independent films a decade ago. There was no reason to dismiss her acting chops merely because she was on television. Eva wasn't rookie enough to believe that just because she was smart, the other person was stupid. In the current economy, even A-list actors moved fluidly between television and film.

What was striking to Eva was that Julian was courting two actresses from different ends of the spectrum. It wasn't so much the spread in years. There was a decade between them, maybe, and makeup and lighting could fix that. It was more that Daisy was emerging on the scene as Dimple was fading. Eva wondered what that meant.

```
Working on it.
```

She typed back to Daisy.

"Is this seat taken?" A voice asked.

"No, sorry." Eva pulled her jacket off the chair.

"It's packed today." The brunette dropped into the seat.

"They're giving away free pickles and peanut butter," Eva said.

The woman gave Eva her full face as she giggled.

Eva was stunned. Sitting next to her was Dimple Bledsoe. She thought she'd conjured her up, until a whiff of delicious perfume persuaded her that there really was a woman sitting next her.

Her second thought was that she understood why Julian Wales was talking to her. She was beautiful, but not in a conventional way. Her face wasn't perfect, and she had a crooked tooth, but she emanated warmth, richness. She was the kind of person you were drawn to. If she was aging at all, she was doing it damn well.

A third thought took over. The waiting room was filled with fecund women, abdomens rounded from gently to mind-bogglingly. Dimple was as slim as a willow. What was she doing here?

Eva realized she was staring. "Eva." She held out her hand.

"Dimple." They shook.

Eva wasn't worried that Dimple would know who she was. Agents weren't like the talent they represented. Anonymity was a job qualification, and they moved behind the scenes.

"You're on *Pulse*, right?" She had to be sure. "I love that show."

"Yes, I am. I'm glad you like it."

Eva's brain was racing. Was Dimple Bledsoe pregnant? That would be a game changer. She held herself back from asking. First, she swore by the cardinal rule that you never, *ever* asked a woman if she was pregnant unless you actually saw the baby emerging. Second, to pry here, in this waiting room, felt like a violation of sacred space. Eva was an interloper among this tribe of childbearers.

Eva couldn't jump to conclusions. Hope Clinic offered all kinds of women's care. Dimple could be getting her annual exam, picking up birth control, meeting a doctor friend for lunch, researching a role. She peeked. No ring.

She couldn't stop thinking about it, though.

"Do you like working in television?" Some questions Eva could ask.

"It's great, but since DVR you know that at any moment, out there, somewhere, your face is frozen on pause in an unflattering grimace." She made a goofy face and Eva liked her for it. "Are you in the business?"

"I thought about acting for a quick second." Eva dodged the question. "But then remembered I don't have talent."

"My mother wanted me to be a lawyer. I told her I had to follow my destiny. After I graduated, I called and asked to borrow five hundred dollars. She said 'Why don't you act like you've got five hundred dollars?'"

"Tough love."

Dimple was distracted, staring over Eva's shoulder. Eva turned to see a platinum blonde in magenta lipstick chewing gum like a piston engine.

"Is she an actress?" Eva didn't know the girl, and Eva knew everyone.

"What? No." Dimple refocused on Eva. "Sorry. It's the gum chewing. Speaking of mothers . . . I'm incapable. My mom drilled into me that chewing gum in public looked like a cow." She looked at the girl again. "She was right." The chewing was particularly enthusiastic.

Eva couldn't agree more. "Mine called herself the Original Cyn, and said the second sin was allowing yourself to be unkempt in public. That meant chewing gum, going out without makeup, or a stain on your clothes. I can't run out for cat litter without sparkly earrings."

"Your mother was the Original Cyn?" Dimple looked surprised. Perhaps she was older than Eva thought. Twenty years ago, Cynthia Lytton had been a socialite of the first order, hostess to the A list, maker of introductions, inspirer of designers, heartbreaker of the heartbreakers. She'd been vibrant and larger than life and could show the Kardashians and Hiltons how things were done downtown. "Her parties were legendary."

Eva nodded. "I used to serve champagne to Jack Nicholson in a tutu. I mean, *I* wore the tutu, not Jack Nicholson. Dustin Hoffman came to my tenth birthday party dressed as Tootsie and Bo Derek braided my hair."

"What happened to her?"

She died, Eva thought.

"She got married and had kids," Eva said. "Now she's queen of homework and orthodontists."

"That doesn't sound appealing." Dimple laughed, looking at all the future homework monitors around the room. Eva's

Spidey sense tingled. Was Dimple going to reveal something?

Instead Dimple said, "I guess it's hard for women to have a career and children."

"Doesn't that make the real enemy children?"

Dimple shrugged. "Your kids can't write you out. In my line of work, women have a shelf life, and around my age you begin to feel the footprint in your butt."

Eva was uncomfortably aware that her own spiked Ferragamo was about to find the small of Dimple's back.

"Why do we let them do that?" Eva asked out of the other side of her face.

"Good question," Dimple said. "The men get to play heroes, run government, and sit on the Supreme Court until they're ninety. Women expire at forty-five."

"It's a good thing we do just as much in half the time," Eva said.

"If they cast the movie of my life right now, they'd pick an actress half my age. I'd be the kooky aunt or the Queen of England."

"The Queen of England has an enviable collection of hats."

"Better to hide the wrinkles. Maybe your mom had it right. You finish your first life in your forties, leaving before waning, then you have a whole other one, something completely different."

Eva couldn't agree with that, but Dimple didn't know what she was talking about. Or maybe Dimple was talking about herself. Was she leaving *Pulse* for *Cora*? Or leaving *Pulse* to raise kids in the Valley?

Before she could ask more, a voice called, "Ms. Bledsoe?"

"That's me," said Dimple. "Nice to meet you, Eva." She gathered her things and followed the technician's pink scrubs through a doorway different from the one through which Deborah had passed.

As she watched her go, Eva knew three things. One, she liked Dimple Bledsoe.

Two, she had been through that doorway once, and had met that technician, a woman named Cindy. That doorway led to the technical rooms, and Cindy was not a doctor, she was an ultrasound specialist. As far as Eva knew, the only reason to get a sonogram was because you were pregnant, or trying to become pregnant.

The third thing was that Eva now had personal information about another person that she was not entitled to know. Information that could benefit Eva directly. And she had no idea what to do with it.

Dimple Weighs Her Options

I checked my watch as I left Hope Clinic. I had time for either Vinyasa yoga class or a massage. A woman waddled past me to her car, surely pregnant with nine thousand babies. Her leg descended from knee to sneaker like a mast, completely lacking in ankle. I decided on the yoga.

I arrived uncharacteristically early and settled my mat back left, close but not too close to the wall so my flank was not exposed to crowding. I settled into a resting lotus and breathed. My brain was a jumble.

"Well, look at that." The ultrasound technician had pointed at something indistinguishable on the monitor. It was grey modern art. She could actually see something in it.

"What?" Some alarm.

"You have a follicle ready to drop right now. There on your right."

"I do?"

"Yep." She removed the wand and pulled her gloves off with a snap. "Everything looks great. You're the picture of reproductive health."

And with that she'd dumped the whole dilemma in my lap. There was no impediment to having a baby other than what was going on in my headspace. I breathed deeply trying to stop my racing thoughts.

The class filled up slowly, mats quietly unfurled, students

inhaling, thumbs to index fingers. The instructor, tensile and tan, like quality leather, fiddled with an iPod until soundscapes filled the studio.

"Welcome," she said. *"Namaste."*

"Namaste," we repeated.

"I'm glad to see you all today." She folded herself like a sailing knot. "I'd like to start with pranayama, or breathing. As we breathe, set your intention and dedicate your practice."

Her voice was hypnotic, and I inhaled deeply, letting the air fill my lungs and enervate my body, focusing on posture. Everyone was breathing and coming to self when the banging door shredded the tranquility. I tried to remain meditative, but the latecomer was like a newlywed's car, clattering cans in her wake. She slapped her mat next to mine, then clacked to kick off heels and drop a purse the size of an overnight bag. She settled cross-legged with a huff, and I looked into the face of Daisy Carmichael.

"Oh!" I said.

"You!" she said. Several people craned to look.

"Me," I agreed, wondering why I was the "you," not Daisy.

"What are you doing here?"

That seemed rather obvious. "Vinyasa."

"Right." We stared at each other. She looked amazing, an expensive leotard revealing not an ounce of fat, hair perfectly tumbling from its clasp. I was wearing my ex-boyfriend's Coast Guard T-shirt and leggings from Target.

"Are you still going after *Cora*? I swear Julian spends every free minute torturing me with bizarre auditions. But he hasn't mentioned you." She had huge eyes.

"The role hasn't been cast yet," I whispered, uncomfortable disturbing the class. And uncomfortable that I hadn't seen Julian since our ride. Apparently Daisy had.

"Let's practice our sun salutations." The instructor's voice held rebuke, which almost never happened with yoga instructors. Daisy was unperturbed.

"Isn't *Cora* a bit of a reach for you?"

"That's quite rude." Whispering diluted my censure.

"Movies are different from TV," she persisted.

"You learned that from one?" was my un-yogic reply.

"One this decade." She bit back.

"Ladies, please." The reprimand was open this time. Daisy shut up, and we launched into a whole new level of competition.

"Let's go into tree pose. When you feel muscle exhaustion, release into a sun salutation."

We assumed the standing pose. Within moments, my thighs were burning. Two women to my left swanned through sun salutation. Daisy was as steady as a rock. After another minute, four more people dropped. Sweat was pouring down my face. Daisy was unaffected. Before long, we were the only two in tree pose. I was on the point of expiring but refused to budge.

I could have kissed the instructor on the mouth when she said, "All right, ladies, go ahead and move through your sun salutation."

And so it went. Bird of paradise. Revolved half-moon pose. One-legged pigeon. I began to loathe the phrase "For those who want more of a challenge . . ."

Daisy's posing was perfect. I was going to need an orthopedist to correct the damage I was doing. Ten lifetimes passed before my eyes as I held contorted poses, but I went toe-to-toe with Daisy.

We were doing compass, a complicated twist with one leg straight in the air, when a memory penetrated my pain.

You've got a follicle ready to drop right now.

I had a mental image of a little teardrop with a face, clinging desperately to the lip of my ovary, dangling over a long, barren drop. Felix the follicle, hanging on for dear life as I twisted and wrenched my body.

I eased my twist. Daisy snorted. I loathed her.

"Let's move on to inversions."

I panicked. What would inversions do to little Felix? Daisy uncurled into a flawless forearm stand. Shit. I settled for a shoulder stand. Hang on, little guy.

The class would never end. Daisy made it look effortless and I was in agony.

Finally, it was almost over. Most students were resting but I was locked in the downward dog of my life, refusing my trembling arms any mercy next to Daisy's textbook silhouette, when I saw her bag move a few inches. Was that really the new and unobtainable Birkin? And had it just repositioned itself?

I nearly cried with relief when the instructor said, "Child's pose. *Everyone.*"

I wilted into the resting pose trying not to pant audibly. I was hallucinating.

After too short an interval, the instructor said, "Come to a seated position. Before savasana, let's review our intention and keep our minds clear."

My mind was the opposite of clear. How the hell did Daisy get an $11,000 handbag that Eva Longoria couldn't get her hands on?

As if knowing I was thinking about it, the bag moved again. And yipped.

"Shut it, Charlie!" Daisy snapped.

I blinked. There was a dog zipped up in the duffle? I opened my mouth, then closed it. What would I say?

Daisy caught my look. "It's not like you can leave them in the car. Some busybody will call the cops."

"*Savasana,*" the instructor scolded.

"I'm out." Daisy stood. "Can't waste time lying around. I'm meeting Julian." She threw me a tight smile. "It's been a treat." She gathered her mat, bag (which gave a muffled yip), and about seven other things too many for exercise class before clattering out, strident against the meditation period.

I didn't believe she was meeting Julian, but it didn't ease my anxiety. She was incredibly beautiful. If she could act, I was in trouble. I detested her.

Freya would've admired my welling intense need to beat Daisy. Forget Felix, clinging to life, I'd get this part. His would be a short and tragic existence, but there'd be another.

I stopped by Whole Foods after class to grab dinner. I headed for the prepared foods section, which I dubbed the Salad-and-So-What's-Your-Name bar. Singles filled plastic tubs with prepared savories and checked out fellow grazers over the sneeze guard. I came to a dead stop. Daisy Carmichael's back was to me as she scooped lettuce into a container. Seriously? Satisfaction that she wasn't meeting Julian was overpowered by irritation. I checked out the contents of her tub. Four leaves of romaine and a radish. Of course. As she moved down the buffet, I detected a slight limp. Ha.

I'd go to Noma and get sushi. I froze, though, watching Daisy. I was struck by a memory of myself at her age, doing exactly the same thing. Had I really been getting Whole Foods takeout for ten years?

Seized with panic, I though of Felix the follicle. Did I want to be here in ten more? I hurried from the store. I'd go to my mother's for dinner.

It might have been aching muscles, it might have been unconscious, but I moved carefully even in my haste, trying not to jiggle too much.

Wyatt Meets a Bully

Wyatt was not happy to be summoned to Webb Garner's office. Webb was President of the Santa Monica/ Malibu Unified School District Board by miracle of the fact that very few people paid attention to School Board elections. He rode into office on a wave of lawn signs.

Linda popped her head around his office door.

"Lunch?"

"I have a meeting with Webb Garner."

"Bring plenty to read." Her tone was amused. Among Garner's many unappealing qualities was a tendency to make people wait. "What does he want?"

"Perhaps he wants to revise the curriculum to substitute abstinence instruction for sex education. He seems to have, overnight, embraced the right fringe."

"It was rather sudden, wasn't it? I never knew he was so conservative until he started campaigning for City Council."

Wyatt suspected Garner's values were tied to ambitions for higher office. "Let's hope he hasn't embraced Intelligent Design.

"I think he's still smarting from your dispatch of his newer-than-new-math curriculum proposal."

It was another reason Wyatt dreaded the meeting. The men got along like time and beauty, neither doing service for the other.

"His need to read his name in the papers costs me time, blood pressure medication, and microscopes. The Board has to burn valuable resources defeating Garner's attention-seeking proposals instead of keeping our classrooms equipped." Wyatt shoved reports into his bag with excessive vigor.

"Surely the Board knows this."

"He has an exhaustive grasp of arcane rule making, and uses procedure to ransom support from other Board members." No one could stall a meaningful initiative over something trivial like Webb Garner.

Wyatt hefted his satchel and checked his watch. "Raincheck?"

Linda stood, a daisy, tall and slim in cream knit, though she had dark circles under her eyes. "Good luck."

Wyatt paused. "Linda . . ." She seemed troubled, but she slipped away efficiently. He vowed to follow up when he returned.

Wyatt arrived at Garner's office on time. It went against his nature to be late, even though he was assured of cooling his heels.

"I'll let Mr. Garner know you're here, Dr. Ozols. You can step though there." Garner's receptionist gestured to an antechamber connecting her domain to Garner's office. Wyatt settled into an uncomfortable-looking tapestry chair underneath an oil print of hunting dogs.

The secretary gathered her things and left for lunch, but Wyatt couldn't concentrate on his reports. Part of Garner's set piece was his open office door so visitors could appreciate the man's important dealings. Wyatt couldn't see the president, but his ranting carried. Wyatt was startled by the language.

"Tommy, that woman was a total fucking cunt. I have a mind to . . . what?" Pause. "Hell no! She was making fun of me . . . tax breaks for fertilized . . . What? No!"

Silence.

"Well, I don't give two shits about her issues, or how sympathetic you think she is, she's trouble. Donnie over at Fragile Voices is ready to pop a load over this one, so I say we go with it and . . ."

Pause.

"Fuck yeah it'll be a circus! The bigger the better. Teach that shrew a lesson."

Uncomfortable, Wyatt wondered if he should go for a walk.

"I can guarantee that bitch won't lift a finger for Knox either, which is fine with me. I want them both to go down."

There was a loud bang.

"Screw the locals—we make this *big*. Let's get the evangelicals, the Southern Baptists, the Mormons, Westboro Baptist Church, Operation Rescue. I want Fred Phelps on her fucking lawn . . ."

More silence.

"Yes, I know the focus is Knox. We'll expose them *both* as unfit, which is why the decision needs to be given to the state. The nationals can pay for it. It's their issue, I just want Knox taken out. *And* that frigid bitch. What?" Pause. "Shit *I* don't care. I'm not freezing my progeny."

Long pause, then a lower tone.

"Look, kid, elections are your thing, and this is my thing. You get me the right media. Leave discrediting Knox to me. It's not like I'm making this shit up. Mr. Clean-cut Midwestern fucked the chicken all by himself and put Excalibur right in my hands. I'm bringing useful information to the public."

Pause.

"Well, hell, I don't give a shit if it passes, but controversy's good for the coffers. The religious right will give away their life savings and send their kids to school in paper shoes to get their issues on the ballot. I'm happy to take their money. This could be bigger than Prop 8. If we get national attention . . ."

Garner stopped and listened. "Fair point. We'll start local and see how it spins while we control it. We can decide if we want to blow it up bigger."

Chuckle.

"Sure, son, but there's always Congress."

The phone rattled into its cradle and footsteps approached the door. Wyatt gathered his things, disturbed by what he'd overheard.

Instead of opening wide, the office door snicked closed.

Wyatt was astonished. Garner had no compunction about airing his unsavory laundry to the world. What merited a *closed* door?

Two minutes later the door was thrown open.

"Ozols." Webb Garner gripped his hand. "Come in." He ushered Wyatt into an office soured with cigarette smoke. "Sit."

Wyatt sat. Garner folded his hands. He was generically good looking, a game show host with rapey eyes.

"How're things at PS 57?"

"Well." Wyatt was guarded.

Garner flicked through a file on his desk. "I see Jim Lang was terminated."

"The proper procedures were observed." Wyatt relaxed. "The documentation is thorough."

"Simmer down, son. I didn't say it wasn't." The 'son' was a ridiculous device. Wyatt was several years older than Garner. "Turns out Jim's a volunteer on my campaign. He's concerned with the decline of Christian values in our schools."

"That's ironic considering he was bending his married co-worker over the copier."

"You refer to Ms. Paley. She too figures in here. They approached me with concerns about you."

"They certainly couldn't have a personal agenda where I'm concerned."

"I'm sure it's a misunderstanding."

"Indubitably."

"Mr. Lang and Ms. Paley are prepared to publicly testify that you seek inappropriate contact with minor children."

It was every educator's worst fear. Wyatt refused to panic. His record was impeccable. He was popular with parents. They were bluffing.

"Have Mr. Lang and Ms. Paley considered that his termination and her probation for an extramarital affair on school property might tarnish their credibility?"

"They said you'd retaliate with rumors. Their ministers are prepared to speak to their character. According to your file, Lang was terminated for merit, not moral turpitude."

Wyatt felt a net tighten.

"You can't seriously support their fabrication?"

"I want to do the right thing at all costs. I ask myself, what would Jesus do?"

Give you better lines, Wyatt thought. "Of course we can't be guided by religious tenets on issues concerning the Santa Monica/Malibu Unified School District, as that would be a blatant violation of the constitutional separation of church and state." Wyatt let his temper get the better of him. "Setting that aside, when would Jesus, or any other person of conscience, believe that telling a lie was the right thing to do? This is a rather elaborate, and risky, approach to revenge by Lang." Wyatt was surprised by Garner. He thought him a more seasoned strategist. "My reputation is unassailable."

"A single lie can destroy a reputation of integrity," Garner paraphrased.

"I believe the speaker meant the teller of a lie would destroy his reputation, not the subject of one."

"You seem confident that you're above reproach." Garner pretended to look down at a file, drawing out a pause. When he looked back up, his eyes gleamed, dirty.

"Dr. Ozols, are you currently negotiating to buy an infant child?"

Wyatt went cold.

"Not so righteous now?" Garner looked smug. "According to my information, you've paid an unlicensed broker over twenty-five thousand dollars to get you a baby girl."

"No."

"No?" Garner said with exaggerated confusion.

"I didn't specify gender." Wyatt stayed cool.

"Swing both ways, do you?" Garner's grin was nauseating.

"Fuck you, Garner. What do you want?"

"I want to hear you say you're buying a baby girl."

"This isn't Thailand. I'm adopting a baby, like a hundred thousand other Americans every year."

"Most of those folks use regulated adoption agencies. You're paying one Katherine Feely Jones, an unlicensed individual, to sweet-talk a pregnant girl into giving you her baby."

Wyatt had a flash recollection of his disordered office. Amber Paley.

"Katherine Feely Jones is a reputable private adoption broker. The process is conducted with total transparency, the parties negotiate fair terms, a state-supervised home study is conducted, and documents are filed with the court."

"Heidi Fleiss was reputable in her profession as well. Isn't it true Mrs. Jones is arranging your adoption because most agencies have a strict policy against giving children to single men?"

"She prefers Feely Jones."

"You've been shelling out a fair amount for several months to remove Miss Deborah Tanner from the bosom of her family in Fresno and tuck her away here in an apartment near you. What makes Miss Tanner so lucky? Is it that baby girl?"

Wyatt didn't answer. He hoped this odious man wouldn't cause trouble with Deborah's family.

"I have to ask myself, why does an unmarried man want a little girl to himself? Seems odd to me."

"My adoption is completely aboveboard."

"You keep saying that. You also paid another young woman and rented another apartment hereabouts for six months. This Ilana Lloubina was not pregnant. She got too old for you, so you're shopping for someone younger now? Much younger?"

Garner wasn't interested in answers, so Wyatt refused to defend himself. The urge to punch Garner in the face was overwhelming.

"There's nothing illegal in my actions."

"Adult man and a baby girl. It's against God's law."

"Then let God arrest me."

"I have to protect the citizenry of Santa Monica."

"You have no more interest in protecting the citizenry of Santa Monica than you have collecting Hello Kitty memorabilia. You don't believe this crap."

Garner pointed a manicured finger at Wyatt. "What I think doesn't mean shit. I care about what voters think. I'm running for City Council guns blazing, and I won't put weapons in the competition's arsenal. As principal of PS 57, you work under my supervision. Whether I think you fondle little girl vagina doesn't matter because someone will, especially if Amber Paley looks sad at the camera and tells them to. I refuse to get tainted by that mess because some bleeding-heart liberal wants to feel the joys of motherhood. You'll drop this adoption, there'll be nothing to speculate about, and we'll all be happy."

"You cannot dictate my private, legal actions." Wyatt felt the walls closing in.

"Ozols, let me be clear how very little I think about you at all. But I'm not going to lose this election because one of my most active and recognized principals is exposed as a pervert under my supervising nose. You'll call off the adoption or I'll fire you myself before Knox's people get wind of it."

"You could expose Paley and Lang as the adulterous scam artists that they are, and publicly support your principal for providing a good home to a needy child as a shining example of pro-life Christian values in action." It was as likely as a Charlie Sheen sainthood, but Wyatt was desperate.

"It doesn't work that way, son."

"How does it work? You trump up false witness against anyone who opposes you? I go along with your agenda or get smeared out of town?"

Garner looked at Wyatt in surprise. "You *do* get it. That's exactly how it works." He bared his teeth. "Of course, I can't control what Mr. Lang and Ms. Paley say, but I'd wager if they weren't troubled by the well-being of an innocent child, they'd be willing to hold their tongues. Drop the adoption and it'll all go away."

Wyatt was enraged and impotent at the same time. Maybe Garner wanted to keep his nose clean during the election or maybe he wanted to get back at Wyatt. Wyatt loved his job too much to risk it. He'd seen honest men eviscerated by a phone number on a matchbook, never mind a public smear campaign. His dad used to say, *A reputation once broken may possibly be repaired, but the world will always keep their eyes on the spot where the crack was.* The adoption could be twisted into a guillotine. Even if he won, his child would be surrounded by whispers and side eyes. How long until she feared him herself?

"No one likes a pervert, son," Garner prompted him.

"Jim Lang will not be rehired. Amber Paley must be transferred to another school." Wyatt would not harbor poison.

"I believe there's an opening at PS 41."

"You've given me a lot to think about." Wyatt despised himself for his words. "I'll need time to look into this matter."

"I'll bet you do," the tan man said. "Now if you'll excuse me, I have to give a speech to two hundred folks in half an hour."

Wyatt concentrated on keeping his hands loose as he put one foot in front of the other so he didn't strangle Garner's smug head right off his pencil neck. He concentrated on finding his keys and sliding one into the car door. He secured his seat belt. Bound securely, he exhaled without fear that his rage would lead to a rash act. He sat, unsure of where to go next. Thoughts were swirling in his head like winged insects at a porch light, but one buzzed to the top.

What drove a man who loved a stage, even when he was the villain, the liar, the blackmailer, the crook, to seek privacy long enough for a single phone call? Wyatt's cricket hairs were on alert, as if he was about to make a trip behind the Field House.

Watching the news later, Wyatt wasn't surprised to see Webb Garner gesticulating in front of a crowd of agitators. He was relieved it had nothing to do with him. He was astonished that it had everything to do with his new friend Maryn.

Andy Speaks

I t seemed karma was not a vengeful warrior. Andy didn't get hit by a bus or attacked by a rabid bald eagle all week after filing the countersuit against Maryn. Not, Andy reminded himself, that he had done anything meriting reprisal. The only mildly interesting deviation from normal was this morning's protest outside Andy's office. There were some Social Security Administration offices in his building, so it wasn't unheard of to find angry Tea Partiers agitating against taxes. Andy kept his head down.

"Candidate Knox, do you have a comment?" Someone shoved a mike in his face. He was startled but plowed through the lobby doors. He wasn't going to connect himself to anti-establishment protesters. He was relieved when the elevator doors slid closed behind him and a paralegal.

"Irresponsible of the media to give voice to factions on the fringe." Andy had taken to speaking in sound bites.

The girl didn't say anything, but Andy sensed recrimination. Perhaps she had been raised on a compound. She wasn't wearing a linen bonnet or anything, so how could he know?

When the doors opened, the girl hurried off and huddled with the receptionist. Andy strolled to his office. He almost ran into his softball co-captain.

"Hey, Jonesy! Looking forward to tonight!"

The man looked uncomfortable. "You're playing?"

"Why wouldn't I?" Andy was confused. "Scared I'll burn through your mitt with my line drive?"

The lawyer shrugged. Andy continued down a hall as quiet as heavy snow. His secretary averted her eyes. She probably wanted to call her sister to talk about *The Bachelor.* He shut his office door, wondering why everyone was being weird.

His cell phone rang. Summer. He felt guilty when he ignored it, but on the move-a-potted-plant-to-hide-the-wine-you-spilled-on–the-neighbor's-rug level rather than the oh-god-I-ran-over-your-cat level.

He tossed his briefcase on the couch. He hadn't bothered to put anything in it last night. From the outside, an empty brief-case looked the same as one full of gold.

His office phone rang. "Andy Knox."

"Why didn't you answer your cell?" Shit.

"Sorry, honey. I must've left it in my coat pocket."

"Turn on the TV."

"What?"

"Andrew! Turn on the TV, NOW!"

Andy pointed the remote at the small television on his bookshelf. The screen popped to life, splashing a BREAKING NEWS banner across a reporter in a throng.

"Is that my office? I saw them on the way in. It's no danger, pigeon," he reassured her. "The TV makes it look bigger than it is."

"Shut up and listen."

". . . if it wasn't bad enough that the sanctity of life is perverted by creating it in a petri dish, Andrew Knox wants to destroy the very life he created."

Andy's blood curdled.

"His lawsuit is an abomination against God. Fragile Voices be-lieves it's our duty to ensure that these frozen embryos realize their ul-timate purpose—life—while sharing the hope of a child with a loving, married, Christian couple. Proposition 11, will give Santa Monica an opportunity to value human life even at the smallest stages."

The camera focused on a reporter with a grave expression

and inoffensive brooch. *"The Proposition 11 ballot initiative referenced by Fragile Voices leader Donnie Brownlow would give frozen embryos in the city of Santa Monica the legal right to adoption in accordance with the laws of California, and treat human embryos identical to a child. This little-publicized initiative languished on the ballot before local attorney Andrew Knox's lawsuit provided supporters with the platform they needed."*

Andy couldn't swallow.

"While Proposition 11 is not the first proposal of its kind, it certainly goes the furthest. Georgia recently became the first state in the nation to pass a law allowing embryo adoption, but that Act's language does not specifically define an embryo as a person. More than a dozen states are considering similar laws. None, however, has such a large target as Andrew Knox. His opponent, School Board President Webb Garner, had this to say."

The camera cut to footage of Webb Garner leaving City Hall. Andy knew Webb had no reason to be at City Hall unless he was paying a traffic ticket. The staged shot told him better than a signature who was responsible for pinning the crosshairs on his dirty laundry.

"The Lord commands us in Proverbs 31:8 to 'Speak up for those who cannot speak for themselves; ensure justice for those who are perishing.'" Webb looked directly into the camera as he delivered his campaign bullet. *"If Andrew Knox would destroy his own offspring, what would he do to his constituents? The only thing Knox can be trusted to do is show us the error of our current system. As Councilman, I'll return to a government that looks after your family."* A numb Andy could only admire how Garner radiated earnestness with a squint.

The scene cut to Andy, head down, muscling through the crowd. *"Knox declined to give a comment."* The camera returned to the reporter. *"Back to you, Daphne."*

The screen dissolved to some hamsters listening to iPods but Andy stared, unseeing.

"Andrew." He'd forgotten Summer.

"I'm here."

"You need to respond immediately."

"Respond?" Andy was terrified. "I can't." Garner was a pro. Andy was a schoolboy knocking over vases with his hockey stick.

"You must. Write this down."

"Summer, I don't think—"

"Andrew. Get a pen."

He got a pen.

"I'm a churchgoing man and I've read the Bible," Summer dictated. "Webb Garner and Proposition 11 are blasphemous. The Bible connects life with breath, and God gives life when he causes a newborn baby to breathe. To equate frozen cells with life is a transparent manipulation of Santa Monica voters for personal gain."

Summer spoke slowly so Andy could write it down.

"How'd you come up with this?"

"A website. Keep writing. Moreover, the women of Santa Monica have a constitutional right to privacy . . ."

When Summer was finished, she instructed, "Straighten your tie and comb your hair in the mirror. You don't want to look like a third-grader who just rolled out of bed. Get down there now."

She hung up, and Andy reluctantly got to his feet. There was a knock at his office door, and Jacque Mann entered.

"May I have a word?" She sat without waiting. Andy sat as well. "Quite a furor downstairs."

"I'm so sorry," Andy apologized, though he wanted it least of all.

"You're not responsible for the actions of others," she reassured him. There was a pause. "It's troubling to have the firm name connected to a controversial matter, however. Proposition 11 is certain to inflame."

Andy didn't know what to say.

"Cayce, Lanfranco and Moody's main concern is our clients. As you know, important firm client Cornin values being perceived as a Christian-oriented company. They're just one example. We'd hate to jeopardize any firm relationship with the perception of a position on a controversial religious and moral issue."

"I go to church."

"Andy, no one doubts that you're a good man. Your religious character is not in question, and the firm has no position on what you do outside these walls. As long as it's legal." She smiled. "I expect Summer will want you to make a statement to the press, and you should speak freely. Cayce, Lanfranco and Moody does not muzzle its employees."

Andy knew there had to be a "but."

"We're faced with a question of first impressions here, and the partners don't know how to manage any more than you do." She continued, "We think it's laudable that you're running for City Council, and unfortunate that the corollary to the campaign is a character attack."

She folded her hands, gaze kind. "While we respect your rights outside the office, we must protect the firm. Until this blows over, I'm taking you off the Cornin case. It's a high-profile matter and we can't risk it being sullied by association."

"But I didn't do anything wrong." Andy protested the unfairness.

"A lie can travel halfway around the world while the truth is putting on its shoes," Jacque said.

Andy was crushed. He'd liked the Cornin case. A lot better than going to Denny's to shake hands with people bitching about street cleaning.

"I'm curious, Why are you running for this office?" Jacque asked.

Andy suspected she knew.

"I believe in public service." He delivered his rote answer. She waited.

"I want to make Santa Monica as close to a perfect place to raise our kids as I can. We need to address transportation and homeless issues." He floundered in campaign speak. "I want more green spaces."

Her smile widened. "That last one, at least, sounds like the Andy I know. Today must've been a rude awakening for a boy from Nebraska looking to make Santa Monica a greener place."

She was teasing him, but he clung to the sympathy.

"It's horrible. My poor wife." He realized what he'd said. "I mean, my ex-wife." What was he saying now? "I mean, both," he concluded miserably.

"I'm very fond of you, Andy." Jacque's eyes were warm. "If you win, a sitting council member will be a feather in the cap of the firm. I just wonder if you know what you're getting into."

"I don't." It burst out of him.

She laughed. "Who could? Today's circus is unfortunate, and it's only going to get worse. Yet it goes hand in hand with a life in public office. Is that what you want?"

No way, thought Andy. "I'm prepared for the downsides," said Andy.

"Best of luck to you, then." Jacque stood and left Andy alone with her thoughts.

His cell phone rang.

"Why am I not seeing you on the news?" Summer cracked the whip.

"Ease up. Jacque came to see me."

"Andrew, you cannot let this settle into the minds of the voters, and that news crew won't wait around all day. GET MOVING."

Andy didn't know how he did it, cameras edging close to his face like predatory aliens. He delivered his statement, hesitating only once.

"I believe in family, and my wife, Summer, and I hope to have children soon." His notes read, *As a family man, I cannot condone my ex-wife using science to sully our understanding of family and raise a child of mine in a fatherless household.*

He looked into the expectant cameras. "I stand for family and for honesty." He skipped to the end. "I will serve the people of Santa Monica with courage, unlike my opponent, who hides behind deceit." He forced himself to smile and look relaxed as he ignored questions and sauntered back into the lobby with a confident wave. His hair formed a cowlick where he'd forgotten to comb it. The urge to run was overwhelming.

Maryn Doesn't Speak

Maryn had lost her virginity in college to *Led Zeppelin IV* and a box of Franzia Pink Zinfandel. She'd later learned the trusted knight she'd chosen for initiation was nicknamed "the de-virginator," and she'd vowed never to be duped again.

Andy thought his mother had picked her, but the truth was, Maryn had picked him. She'd been at the horse auction in Ojai when she'd seen him race around the car to help his mother out of the passenger side. She'd decided that he was the one, and staged herself against the rail, sure of being approached.

"You fly horses? Like Pegasus?" he'd asked. He'd been in law school, and boyishly handsome.

"Like you," Maryn answered. She gestured toward the horses in the exercise pen. "You might've shared a plane with one of these ladies on your flight here."

"Do they pay for extra leg room?"

"Lots of passenger planes hold transport stalls in the back, and passengers up front. Occasionally we get a sports car back there too."

"Does it get all trash talky over who has more horsepower?" Andy teased.

"My horses would win." Maryn was all confidence.

"And horses like equine weekend retreats in Ojai for the art galleries, spas, and natural beauty?" He worked hard to charm her.

"Only if they get the bridle suite. The rest of the time, I'm in

L.A." She'd ascertained that he attended USC. "There are only three places the USDA will allow you to import horses—New York, Los Angeles, and Miami."

They went for a drink and she sat with her body angled in his direction, leaning in to hear his stories. One drink turned into three, which turned into love, which turned into a marriage. Maryn *had* loved Andy. The fact that they divorced didn't change the Andy who lived in Maryn's mind. He'd always be a Peter Pan.

She found it surreal, therefore, to be watching the man she married dominating the six o'clock news, quoting a Bible he didn't read while discussing his intention of destroying the embryos they'd made together.

The phone rang. She lifted the receiver a centimeter then dropped it back in the cradle.

The phone had been going berserk over the Proposition 11 thing. When she'd first seen the news report, she'd thought a geyser of blood would burst through the top of her skull and her eyeballs would pop out and roll under the table. Once her hysteria subsided, an unnatural calm had settled in, like the death of the wind right before a tornado.

Her first call was to Selena.

"Right now, Prop 11 has no legal import," Selena said.

"But," prompted Maryn.

"It could affect your case," the lawyer conceded, "if it passes. Andy would be prevented from destroying the embryos."

"I'd have to have seven children or give the embryos away?

"Unfortunately, it doesn't mean you'd be entitled to *use* the embryos. Just that Andy couldn't destroy them."

It made Maryn's head hurt thinking about it.

After the news broke, she'd been surprised to find a reporter on her lawn. After a week, there were several. Maryn had a hard time wrapping her head around the fact that her private business was news. When she thought about it, it made

her angry, so she stopped thinking about it to avoid saying
something rash. She hurried by them without so much as a
"No comment."

She tried to convince herself it had nothing to do with
her. It was a political initiative unrelated to any individual.
But she couldn't relax. The tornado was just a whisper away.
When she saw Webb Garner's face on TV, or message slips
from Andy, the winds started picking up and she had to take
deep breaths to stay calm and bring six mares over from
Cambridge, England.

Maryn was a rational person, but she couldn't think ra-
tionally about Prop 11. She worried that if her mind explored
her feelings, it would discover a sinkhole of guilt and fear
that would swallow her. A part of her was awed by Andy's
audacity, quoting the Bible and fighting back at these people.
As un-Maryn-like as it was, she just couldn't. She'd put all her
reserves into one fight, and there were none left for this one.
She told herself it would be fine, cooler heads would prevail,
it would not pass. Then, she picked up the phone and called
Amanda Clark, in Cambridge, to see about the six mares.

Dimple Learns to Fly

Julian was standing on the pier, bent listening to the spitting image of Estelle Getty. I was sure he'd gotten better looking in the three weeks since I'd seen him. When he caught sight of me, he spread his arms wide, wind flapping his canvas army jacket. His companion patted his arm and shuffled off.

"A grasshopper walks into a bar. The barman says, 'We've got a drink named after you.' The grasshopper says, 'You've got a drink named Dimple?'"

I was ready. "Two hydrogen atoms walk into a bar. One says, 'I've lost my electron.' The other says, 'Are you sure?' The first replies, 'I'm positive.'"

He beamed.

"I'm glad you could come." His call had been more request than command, but it didn't matter. After the Daisy yoga-off, I would have walked barefoot, uphill (both ways) in ten feet of snow to get there.

"I was free." My mother could get new drapes next weekend.

"Come." His paw enveloped my hand as his other arm swept wide, encompassing the pier. "Isn't this great?!" He pulled me along.

I wasn't sure. It was an overcast, grey day, and the pier was swarming with children in matching T-shirts. Keeping up with Julian had me scrambling, and the uneven boardwalk required concentration. Early rain had left everything slick. "I thought only tourists and funnel cake addicts came to the pier."

He grasped my shoulders. He was a touchy guy, but I wasn't minding. LaMimi purred.

"Dimple Bledsoe, have you ever wanted to fly?"

I was suspicious. "As in 'A fly walks into a bar'?"

"As in 'through the air with the greatest of ease.'" He turned me around and I was facing the entrance of the Trapeze School of Santa Monica. Fifty feet overhead, a woman clung to a bar, swinging out over the grey, choppy ocean, a human eclipse against the sun breaking through the clouds. She soared among a jumble of ropes and platforms and nets, pumping her body faster along its pendulum before rolling forward and down onto a net far, far below.

"Oh no. I don't want to die."

"Too late. You've been stabbed by a deranged clown, electrocuted by a radio in the bathtub, poisoned by a jealous lover, and ravaged by Lymphangioleiomyomatosis." He ticked off on his fingers. "And died beautifully every time, I might add. You've lived through a shooting spree at close range, exposure to Ebola, emergency brain surgery in a janitor's closet, attempted strangulation by a crackers patient, a chase by a tiger that somehow ended up in an L.A. hospital, and mean looks from a jealous coworker. Your survival skills are impeccable and I have great hope you'll make it to the end of today."

I stared. "You saw the deranged clown thing?"

"I saw everything."

"I had to pay the rent."

"Even future Meryl Streeps start out in horror."

"Did she?"

"No. But she would have if she had to pay the rent."

I frowned at him.

"She did *Mamma Mia*." Appeasing.

"Not funny."

"*River Wild*?"

"What on earth makes you think I'm going to go up on that

thing?" I stared at the girl clambering up the platform ladder. It was a long ladder.

"You did the deranged clown movie. You'll do anything." His eyes were laughing as he tugged me under the sign. I looked skyward, all too aware that he was holding my hand.

His charm doesn't matter, I chided myself. I opened my mouth to tell him where to put his trapeze when I remembered Daisy's smug face. Julian Wales was all too comfortable and it was easy to forget this was an audition, no matter how bizarre.

"Technically, this is still public," I said.

Julian smiled like a winner. "I have blue toenails."

"I'm Monty. I'll be your instructor today." If Satan had a helper he'd look like the elf who popped up at my elbow. He was actually elbow height, and square like a cement block, with red curly hair and shoulder-to-wrist tattoos. A carrot-haired cage fighter. "Ready to fly?"

"Yes," Julian said, in unison with my, "Not really."

"Let's get you suited up." Monty's enthusiastic clap emitted a cloud of chalk. He grabbed my waist, leaving two white prints on my black Lycra hips. "I'd say you're a small."

"May I ask your qualifications?" Anxiety was making me bitchy.

"Two jumper cables walk into a bar. The bartender says, 'Hey, you two. Don't start anything,' " Julian said.

"I went to the California College of Clownology then worked Cirque de Soleil in Vegas until it seemed like a good idea to move away from the baccarat tables." The demonic cherub cinched a safety belt on me tight enough to crack a rib.

"That's a little . . . ," I gasped.

"It's supposed to be tight. If you could sign this waiver." Monty shoved a clipboard under my nose.

"Where's your belt?" I asked Julian.

"I'm going to watch." Julian popped a piece of Big Red in his mouth.

"What??"

His joviality evaporated. "That sounded pervy, but it isn't." Julian was serious. "You know I'm not here to laugh at you, or tell stories later at the bar. I respect you, respect any fears you may confront doing this, and respect your privacy." He met my eyes. "You can trust me, Dimple."

I was struggling for a reply when my Monty smacked my ass.

"Let's hit it!"

I shoved my face in Monty's so fast I don't remember moving. "Listen, you evil sprite, if you touch my ass, waist, or a single strand of my arm hair again without asking permission first, I'll use my dad's dull fishing knife that hasn't been sharpened since 1982 to saw off both your hands and turn them into an educational tool for today's youth on the importance of politeness."

Then I smoothed my yoga pants, because I'm a lady, and began climbing the platform ladder. When he recovered, Monty clambered after me like a monkey.

On the platform, we had a little lesson. It was hard to pay attention so high above ground, but I absorbed the basics.

"When I say 'Hup!' you move," Monty instructed. "Hup one for jump off the platform, hup two for swing your knees over the bar, hup three for drop your hands and swing from your knees, hup four for hands back up, hup five for legs down, and hup six, drop into the net. You can drop sitting or flat on your back, but make sure you land on your butt, not feet down."

"People really do all that on their first lesson?"

"Every day and twice on Sunday. The main thing is timing. If you move on my command, gravity will work with you. If you anticipate me, or go late, you're fighting gravity and it'll be a lot harder."

He unclipped my belt from the stationary line and hooked me to the trapeze safety line. I inched to the edge of the platform.

"Remember, I'll be holding you, so lean your weight forward. I won't let go until you're ready. When I say 'Hup!,' do a small hop off the platform." He gripped my belt and encouraged me to the edge of the platform.

"One small hop for Dimple, one giant lawsuit for Dimple's estate," I said.

"Remember the position?"

"Casually lean my face into space a hundred feet aboveground with my butt sticking out?"

"Exactly." My sarcasm was lost on him. "Shoulders back."

I precariously held the bar, suspended over the net far below in an awkward tree pose. Monty said, "Hup!" and I was out. It happened in a blink. Each time he shouted, I flung my legs and hands as commanded. There wasn't time to be scared before I was hanging from my knees, arms wafting free. In less than a minute I was bouncing on my butt in the net.

Another redheaded instructor, female this time, helped me roll-flip off the net to the ground ten feet below. Maybe red hair was a requirement for professional trapeze artists. Raggedy Ann and Andy.

"Was that really your first time?" she asked.

"Yes!" I was exhilarated.

She looked impressed. I was ready to dye my hair and join the circus. I hurried back to the ladder, sneaking a quick glance at Julian smiling on the sidelines, totally full of myself. "Great job!" Monty smiled when I reached the top. He didn't look at all demonic. "Ready to go again?"

"Let's do it!" I chalked my hands and grabbed the bar. I set my position. This time I was more prepared. The first time had been too fast to think.

"Hup!"

I hopped off the platform, thinking about how soon Monty would give the command for legs up. When he did, I was ready. I swung my knees toward my abdomen to get them over the bar, but I couldn't. I put every ounce of core strength behind it but my body couldn't manage. The window passed, and I swung back to center, dangling, impotent, from the bar. There was nothing to do but drop to the net.

What the hell? I didn't wait for Raggedy Ann to help me flip down to the ground, and almost overrotated onto my butt in my haste. Was my core strength so puny I couldn't swing my legs up twice? I didn't look at Julian as I hurried past.

At the top of the platform, Monty said, "You started early and were fighting gravity. That's why it was so hard."

I nodded, intent. I hadn't felt fear the first time, but now my adrenaline was pounding.

"Wait for my command."

I focused my attention on Monty's commands but I was worried that Julian was watching, and I was worried about what would happen if my arms got tired and I fell off, and I was worried about messing up again, and I was worried about starting too early. I refused to mess up. At his "Hup!" I swung out.

"Hup!"

I struggled mightily to raise my legs. Every fiber of my being strained.

I couldn't do it. I dangled there, frustrated and pissed, then dropped into the net. I hated Julian Wales. All of Santa Monica could see me failing. How was this relevant to acting?

"You anticipated me again," Monty said. He looked like a gargoyle.

"I'm too weak." I worried. "Maybe I can't do it. Maybe my stomach muscles don't have what it takes." My adrenaline was getting worse each time. I was fluttery and anxious. I was having a stroke.

"You can do it. My grandmother can do it." I didn't doubt that. His grandmother was Satan's mother and could do any damn thing she wanted. "Let gravity work for you, not against you. Let's try again."

The third time I was dangling uselessly, Monty said, "Let's do a backflip dismount. Swing your legs forward, back, forward on my command, and then let go and flip."

Again, I was surprised by how fast the commands came.

"Forward, back, forward, flip!" Monty shouted.

I executed a flawless backflip into the net.

"Was that your first time doing *that*?" Raggedy Ann asked. "You looked like a pro."

I wasn't flattered. The backflip was a consolation prize for losers who couldn't get their legs up.

"Can you show me what I'm doing wrong?" I hated needing help, but I wasn't getting better. The whole pier was surely pointing and laughing.

"Have you ever jumped right when an elevator drops, so you feel like you're falling? It's the same. When you swing out, there's a moment at the apex of the arc when you're suspended and gravity helps lift your legs over the bar because your momentum is upward and the bar's is downward. That's when you have to hit it."

"You're sure it's not because I don't have the stomach muscles?" Doubt gnawed. Maybe I was the one person in the world who couldn't do it.

"I'm sure."

I walked slowly to the ladder this time and chalked my hands. I sneaked a glance at Julian. His expression was open and bright.

"Ready?" Monty said at the top.

I nodded, trying not to let defeat take over. Just follow his commands.

"Hup!"

And it was perfect. I closed my eyes and blocked out everything but the sounds. When the "Hup!" came, my legs slid smoothly over the bar. I struggled a little to bring my arms back up to the bar after dangling from my knees, but not too much. It was a perfect routine, including the backflip dismount.

When I rolled off the net, Raggedy Ann was effusive. I headed for the platform.

Monty was surprised to see me pop up the ladder.

"Got one more in you?"

I was exhausted and my lady parts were crushed from the belt, never to yield children now, but I nodded. I needed to make last time not an anomaly.

I completed the routine a second, then a third time, before I was too spent to continue. I brushed the chalk off my leggings and T-shirt as well as I could (black was not the best choice) and slipped on my white button-down before joining Julian. I didn't sit, afraid I wouldn't be able to stand again. He smiled without saying anything, and I thanked the redheads as he paid.

"Forget fear. Worry about addiction." Monty's parting words had been the school's slogan. I doubted I'd get addicted, but I was feeling all-powerful.

We walked past clamoring kids in blue T-shirts, to the quiet of a few fishermen at the end of the pier. "Watch the lines." He guided me away from the men casting along the edges. We walked toward a deserted section and leaned on the rail over choppy water.

"As it turns out," I said casually, not looking at him, "I don't have a natural aptitude for trapeze."

That was a little false modesty.

"Hmmm," he said.

"What was the purpose of that? It has nothing to do with Cora Aldridge."

He faced me. "In two hours, you became Cora Aldridge." His look was intense. "It blew me away. You had triumph, defeat, demoralization, determination, doggedness, and victory in succession." He laughed. "You were so mad and frustrated after that second run, but you kept going. It killed you to ask for help, but you did it. It was like seeing Cora walk off the page. I've never felt so close to meeting her in person."

"But I didn't do it right." It was the kind of praise an actress craves from a director.

"Did you think I hadn't tried this myself? I did the same thing—thought myself right out of a natural ability. I wanted to see how you'd handle it."

I put my hands on my hips. "You *knew* I'd mess up?"

"I had a hunch." His eyes sparkled.

"That's . . . that's . . . *cruel.*"

He guffawed. "So I've heard from you before. You wouldn't think it was cruel if you hadn't made mistakes."

He had me there.

"Dimple, you can't control everything. Life isn't orderly and people don't answer the phone the way you expect or always let you drive the bike. Existing is hard. I don't want an orator to perfectly deliver my precious words. I want a woman who can reach through the screen and grip the audience with what it's like to be drop-kicked by life and keep going. Cora doesn't clutch her pearls, she has true grit." He paused. "And so do you. Watching you today was like seeing a Hank Williams song."

His praise spiked my adrenaline more than the trapeze. My veins were buzzing, which may be why I did what happened next.

It was a flash, but on the grey day, it stood out. I saw the fisherman cast, his line sailing backward just as a child ran underneath.

"Stop!" I may have knocked a man down in my haste, but I acted without thinking. I threw myself at the child, wrapping my body around her like a cocoon as a sharp stab dug into my shoulder. My cry of pain blended with the gulls, then noise erupted everywhere.

A flash mob surrounded us, shouting. I was conscious of the girl crying, and throbbing pain. I stayed where I was, encircling her, until hands lifted me off.

"Hannah!" A crying woman snatched the girl once I was peeled from her. People rushed me, clamoring.

"Give her space!" Julian commanded, a tinge of anxiety in his tone.

"She saved that girl!"

"I think she's hurt . . ."

"Thank you so much!" A stout man pumped my arm, and I couldn't suppress a cry of pain. I backed away to protect my wound, but people were everywhere.

"The hook would've hit that girl for sure."

"He threw a long cast, I saw it!"

"I'm sorry, I'm sorry," a young fisherman kept repeating. "I didn't see her."

My shoulder hurt terribly.

"Lemme take a look." A grizzled fisherman reached for me.

"Don't touch that!" Julian bellowed. Everyone quieted. "For the love of god, give her space!"

Everyone stepped back.

"I'm okay," I said. "It doesn't hu . . . ahhh!" Jostling exposed my lie.

Julian jumped like he'd been hit with a fishhook. "Are you okay? Christ, you're bleeding a lot."

A red stain was spreading across my white shirt. I refused to look, but I was pretty sure there was a fishhook embedded in my shoulder. "Is she okay?" I asked the girl's mother.

"She's fine, just scared." The mother held the crying girl. "I can't thank you enough. If it wasn't for you . . . and you're hurt . . . " Tears spilled down her cheeks.

"Anyone would have done it. It's barely a scratch." I shrugged, then winced.

"That's it, people. Clear out," Julian ordered. "The child is fine. There's nothing to see." He pointed to the young fisher-man. "You. Cut that line. And *gently*. He turned to me. "What do you think this is, an action movie? You could've been seri-ously hurt! We need to get you to the emergency room." He shielded me as he led me off the pier.

"What? No . . . ," I protested. "I'm not going to the emer-gency room."

Julian looked at me as if I was insane. "Are you insane? You have a fishhook in your shoulder."

"The emergency room is for emergencies," I said. A person didn't go to the emergency room when they could walk.

"Fishhook. Embedded," he repeated. "If that doesn't consti-tute an emergency, what does?"

"Well, you know." I was uncomfortable. "Being shot. Being stabbed. Bleeding out the eyes. Two broken legs. Ebola."

"You've been stabbed by a fishhook!" His volume spiked.

I winced. "Sorry. I didn't grow up running to the emer-gency room. My dad walked all day once with a rusty nail embedded in his heel because he couldn't miss a day at work. That's sort of how I was raised."

Julian shot me a look of disbelief. "Well, you're going now. Consider it a decadent day at the spa."

I giggled and he looked incredulous. "Unbelievable. Have you ever been to the ER?"

"Only when I got bit by a mamba," I said. "I had my brain surgery in the janitor's closet."

"Very funny."

"Did you hear about the Buddhist who refused novocaine during a root canal? His goal was transcend dental medica-tion." I giggled again. Maybe I was delirious.

"Does it hurt if we move faster?"

Several hours later, leaning forward on the gurney didn't feel so funny. I was exhausted.

Julian was hovering over the physician, getting in his way.
"How are you doing?"

"The cartoon birds are circling," I groaned.

"We're done here." The physician stepped back.

"How many stitches?" I wondered if I'd have to call a plastic
surgeon. Julian and the doctor exchanged a look that suggested
I'd asked my question before. Painkillers made me woozy.

"We used glue," the physician said. "You'll barely see the
mark. You were smart not to remove the hook yourself. Here's
a prescription for the pain. See your doctor in a week to make
sure everything is healing."

Julian helped me into my ruined shirt.

"Please let me take you out to dinner," he said. "I feel responsible."

"No," I answered, distracted by my sore ribs. On top of the
trauma to my shoulder, my muscles were stiff from the trapeze.

I registered Julian's hurt face. "I'm sorry, that was abrupt.
I'm having dinner with my mother." I had to change. A bloody
shirt would expose me to maternal inquisition, not sympathy—a glued cut was sissy stuff. My mother had lain next to
her bicycle in a field while bombs went off around her when
she was nine.

He looked relieved.

"At least let me drive you home."

I nodded and followed him to his car. I hesitated when he
pulled out his keys. In my daze, I hadn't noticed it on the way
to the hospital. I'd ridden in some ridiculous directors' cars
before—low-slung things that looked like props from *Tron*—
but nothing like this.

"This is your car?"

He looked surprised. "Why?"

I didn't hear the expected creak when I opened the dented
door; it rolled smoothly on well-oiled hinges. "Is it . . . safe?"

Julian looked offended. "Of course it's safe. My dad impressed on me the importance of two things—if you maintain a car well it'll serve you forever, and you can fit more cars in the driveway if they're from the eighties." He patted the hood of the GEO Prizm. "This hot mama was my first."

"I think it's older than I am."

"According to your résumé, maybe." Julian winked. I slid into the hatchback without another word.

At my house, I hesitated. Energy still thrummed under my exhaustion. Julian had extracted more from me in one day at the pier than a decade of *Pulse*. I didn't want to part.

"You were amazing today." He held my eyes.

I fumbled for words. "You too. I mean, I did things today that I wouldn't have done if you hadn't been directing me, so to speak."

"I don't know that I brought anything to the equation."

"You knew exactly what you were doing, getting me on the trapeze."

"That would be false modesty, contributing to a narrative arc that is satisfying rather than accurate." Julian said. "And by no means would I orchestrate anything that would leave you pierced by a fishhook."

"But you did," I insisted. "You made me come *alive*." I felt fatuous. It was time to go. "Do you need to schedule a reading for *Cora*?"

He hesitated, then said, "Yes. Yes, that's what I need."

"Great." I got out and leaned into the window. "Gotta go. I need a drink before dinner with my mother."

He smiled. "A baby seal walks into a bar. 'What can I get you?' asks the bartender. 'Anything but a Canadian Club,' says the seal."

Andy Doesn't Clean a Beach

It had rained, which made for a less than ideal day. The water was metallic, the sky leaden.

"Overcast skies make for better photos." Summer remained optimistic. Andy wasn't sure. When it rained in Southern California, Los Angelenos abandoned their cars, canceled dinner plans, and stayed home. He'd rather be watching the Nebraska Huskers play on TV than working Coastal Cleanup Day.

Summer's enthusiasm was undampened. "You're going to get your campaign poster out of this!" She literally rubbed her hands together. "And we can undermine some of that embryo-killing bullshit from Webb."

Andy and Summer were working with a group called Heal the Bay, Heal the Body. Summer had managed to secure Andy the position of Site Captain for the choice Santa Monica Pier location. Andy would speak a few kick-off words, then groups would disperse to pick cigarette butts and candy wrappers off the beach. The participants were children with cancer, muscular dystrophy, cystic fibrosis, and multiple sclerosis. Summer viewed this pairing as the key to a landslide election.

"Picking up trash is solid. Helping sick kids is better. Helping sick kids pick up trash is gold! This is your money shot!"

Andy was pretty sure the "money shot" referred to a specific moment in porn films, but his discomfort with the comparison was overshadowed by his anxiety over spending the day with sick kids. He didn't have a good poker face when meeting unnaturally adult gazes staring from washed-out little faces. Since Webb had labeled Andy a heartless baby killer, he was particularly sensitive. Andy would never terminate a baby because of disability. But his aversion to illness now seemed suspect, hinting at a malevolent streak. Maybe Webb saw something Andy didn't.

Summer had insisted they arrive early. "It's important to identify a kid to stand with you. Someone visibly sympathetic, but cute."

"Visibly sympathetic" was politically correct for obviously ill. Andy didn't know why his reaction was so strong. He hadn't been exposed in childhood to anyone suffering from a lingering ailment. His family had been as healthy as oxen until his mom got sick, and she'd had the courtesy to keep her illness brief before dying. Andy was just afraid of sick people, and that was that.

Andy had deteriorated faster than Maryn when she was diagnosed with breast cancer. The vomit, the cracked lips, the hospital smell of urine. He'd lost ten pounds and developed the shakes whenever he had to accompany his wife to appointments. He detested meeting other patients. The hospital gave him palpitations.

As if she heard his thoughts, Summer mused, "It's too bad Maryn's such a bitch. It would be strong if she stood by you as a breast cancer survivor." Summer used words like "strong" now that she was spending time with the campaign boys.

To Summer's credit, Andy didn't talk about Maryn's illness, so Summer didn't know. Even so, it was delusional to think his ex-wife would take a break from suing him to stand by his side with a Miss America wave. To Maryn's credit, she'd never called Andy a fucking bastard for leaving her with cancer. She'd never told anyone he'd fled eight years of marriage after a few months of illness. She'd never said anything at all. So neither had Andy. He'd put it behind him and moved forward, so he never had to recall the look on Maryn's face when he'd told her.

They stood uncomfortably on the dock, Summer's over-dressed state drawing the eyes of tourists. She rubbed her forearms to keep warm, and Andy slipped an arm around her shoulder. Volunteers began to arrive, huddled in groups of three. A perky organizer with the requisite clipboard bubbled about the day's schedule.

When she walked away, Andy asked Summer, "Do you think she really believes three hours of picking up litter will make a difference?"

Summer was thoughtful. "The fact that a bunch of people gave up their Saturday to pick up trash makes you hope there'll be a difference."

Andy was doubtful. What could one man do? Forget healing the bay—how was collecting litter going to heal cystic fibrosis?

"If the city doesn't spend money on those expensive drainage filters, every cigarette on Main Street will end up in the bay." His discouragement was overwhelming, and the day hadn't started.

"That's why we need you on the City Council," Summer said. "Here they come."

A noisy gaggle of children approached. Most walking, two in motorized chairs. They wore helmets and head scarves, some had awkward proportions, but they all had enormous smiles. Their adult buddies were tested to keep them orderly. Summer moved toward them with a smile. Andy began to sweat.

Summer moved fluidly, despite impractical Prada heels, crouching to meet eyes, accepting hugs. Andy knew she was shopping for their photo op, but admired the ease with which she mingled. Her enjoyment seemed genuine. Andy touched the children carefully, afraid to break them. If they knew his cheer was forced, they forgave him. The ill were more charitable. And in this case, bubbling over with excitement.

"Will we see a dolphin?" a girl with watery eyes asked Andy.

"Maybe." He grinned. "If they aren't busy picking up clam shells that lazy mermaids threw on the ocean floor even though a coral trash bin was *right there*."

"If I find money can I keep it?" demanded a boy in a motorized chair that outsized him by three.

"Only if you spend it on ice cream and comic books," Andy answered.

The organizer arrived, and the kids clamored for blue Coastal Cleanup Day T-shirts. Andy edged away from the chaos to where the buildings gave way to the anglers. Few tourists ventured into the province of the fishermen.

Andy was hypnotized by the whipping lines, glinting silver flashes against the sullen sky. A cherub of a four-year-old girl was chasing around the feet of a knot of adults. Andy was happy to see a rosy, healthy child. The clustered adults were clad in fanny packs, Bermuda shorts, and sneakers. They debated over a map, not paying attention to the girl racing in wider and wider circles. Andy was as mesmerized by her exuberant activity as he had been by the casting lines. She dashed after a seagull, running perilously close to the fishermen, who didn't notice. She paused to examine fish heads and guts in a pail. Andy wanted to pull her away from the fish guts. Her parents were oblivious.

There were about ten people at the end of the pier other than fishermen, but only Andy appeared aware of the girl. A seagull drew her attention from the entrails, and Andy was relieved. Shrieking with giggles, she chased the bird. Andy watched in slow motion as the child ran behind a line of anglers as one drew his reel to cast. Andy's brain blinked twice before he comprehended. The lethal silver line soared toward the girl. He had to do something to protect her, to shield her skin and eyes, but he couldn't move. He was frozen, watching disaster gallop his way, helpless to stop it.

He was hit hard in the back. The sky and the pier tumbled as his hands and knees hit the boards, and his head reeled from contact with the boardwalk. Someone shouted, "Stop!" and he thought he heard a woman cry before the pier erupted into a cacophony of noise.

He pulled himself to his hands and knees. People were rushing past, surrounding a woman with long brown hair. She was crouched on the ground, encircling the child. The girl was crying, her family was screaming, the fishermen were shouting. It was utter chaos.

"Andy?" Summer reached him. "My god, what happened? Are you okay?" In her concern, she'd forgotten to call him Andrew.

Andy got to his feet. His ears were ringing. A tall, bald man was trying to calm the flash mob that had grown around the woman and child.

"Space!" the bald man bellowed. He had presence. Everyone quieted. Several stepped back, and Andy could see the red stain spreading across the woman's white shirt. He felt nauseous.

"I'm okay," the woman assured everyone. "It doesn't hu . . . ahhh!" She cried out involuntarily as someone bumped her. The bald man jumped, but she waved him off. "Is she okay?" The brunette addressed the girl's mother.

"She's fine, just scared." The mother held the crying girl. "I can't thank you enough. If it wasn't for you . . . and you're hurt . . . " Tears spilled down her cheeks.

"Anyone would have done it. This is barely a scratch." The brunette shrugged, then winced.

Andy almost winced himself. Anyone but him. He'd been frozen, while this woman had leaped into action and protected the child. She'd knocked him out of the way without a thought, sensing his uselessness.

"That's it, people. Clear out," the bald man ordered. "The

child is fine. There's nothing to see." In a softer voice, "We need to get you to the emergency room."

"What? No . . ." Their voices faded as the man led the woman away.

"Andy?" Summer was still at his side, looking concerned.

"I'm fine." He was gruff. "What happened?"

"I'm not sure. One of the fishermen threw a wild cast and hit someone, I think. It's not serious. Did you fall?"

"Someone knocked me over." He dismissed.

"We should go." Summer looked anxious. "We're supposed to begin at eleven thirty." She brushed off Andy's khakis. "You don't look any the worse for wear."

Andy was surprised that he looked the same. He felt diminished.

They walked back to the Pier Restoration Corporation office, where about sixty people were milling around. The kids in oversize T-shirts, grins, and eyes too big for their heads clustered together. Summer headed toward them.

"Andrew, this is Victoria." She smiled at a frail girl with a bandanna knotted around her head. "She's a very brave little girl with leukemia."

"Hi there." Andy forced a smile and took the girl's tiny hand. "Would you like to be my partner today?"

"Sure." The girl grinned.

"C'mon." Andy jerked his head toward the office steps where a mike was set up. "Let's put these lazy bums to work." She giggled and followed him. He wondered who would knock him down and save her if an out of control car barreled toward them.

Summer maneuvered them into a picturesque threesome. They smiled and clapped as the head of Coastal Cleanup Day welcomed guests.

Andy was the closer. He robotically delivered words on the importance of giving back, and his goals for City Council environmental projects. He smiled slipping his arm around Victoria, but he was sweating. He heard screams coming from the Ferris wheel, and panicked that the top chair would plummet to the earth. He felt the pier sway and wondered if the weathered boards would split, upending sick children into the cold, grey chop. The cart vendor dropped dough for funnel cake, and Andy saw hot oil spewing into the faces of waiting customers. All within his reach, and Andy impotent to stop it. In a flash he understood Maryn's rage when she'd screamed that she was impotent.

After he married, Maryn had told him what to do. Even after she was diagnosed, she shepherded him through the egg-fertilization process, the drafting of their wills, and her medical power of attorney, her treatment decisions. Then she'd begun chemotherapy, and she'd stopped.

Andy had been on his own as he listened to Maryn wretch, helpless. He hadn't known what to say when she came to him, a ghost against the clump of red hair she held, wanting to know if she should shave her head. When her blood cell count confined her to the hospital, perilously vulnerable to infection, she'd needed help deciding whether to change her treatment. Andy had failed her every time.

"I don't know," he said. "What do the doctors think?"

She was propped up on the bed, skin like an oyster, shiny with sweat and as pale as liquid. Her wig was jarring, its robust red macabre against her hollow face. She wore it for him.

"Obviously they think we need to do something or they wouldn't have suggested it." She was peevish.

"I . . . I'm sorry . . . ." Andy floundered. Hurt and confusion etched Maryn's face. He tugged his collar, feeling overheated. "I'll get some air and think about it."

"You just got here." Her tone wasn't accusatory. Andy suspected she knew before Andy did.

Andy heard his father's voice and knew he had failed. Utterly and completely. And he couldn't take it.

"Maryn, I'm not this guy." He sat on the edge of her bed and took her hand. He couldn't meet her eyes. "You need me to be strong and I'm falling apart. You're counting on me and I'm not giving you shit. I wish I was different, but I'm not. I can't do this. Staying is only going to make it worse."

He braved a glance. Her face was shocked. She pulled her hand from his.

"You're leaving me?" Disbelief.

Unbidden, a rush of relief swept him, as intoxicating as a sip of cool champagne.

"No," he protested.

"You're leaving me." This time it wasn't a question.

Andy stared at her the way he'd once stared at a hairless sphinx kitten. The Maryn he'd married had no connection to this ravaged shell.

He'd gotten to his feet without realizing it. He looked at the creature on the bed, searching for something. Her eyes burned into him, but he was curiously detached.

"Go," Maryn said. Exhaustion carved into her face.

"Maryn . . ." He willed her to understand. A lifetime free from this disease . . .

Without breaking eye contact, Maryn pulled off her wig.

"You're already gone," she said.

Andy waited a second, two. Shoulders slumped, he walked out the door, closing it as gently as he could. He only wished he could have shut out her haunted look as easily.

"Andrew!" Summer hissed. Silence had fallen. He was at the podium on the Santa Monica Pier. People were staring.

"So let's get to work!" Andy wrapped up with false cheer, raising Victoria's hand as much as her height would allow.

Summer beamed and clapped, and the event organizer gave a thumbs-up. The boisterous crowd broke into teams and began dispersing. Andy wished he was at home.

The group decided that the motor-chair kids would cover the paved beach path, the younger kids would do the playground, and the older ones could venture down the beach with their buddies until they tired. Andy elected to go with the last group, hoping they'd be the most independent. He wondered if he was legitimately ill, he was so sweaty.

"Why should we trust you?" asked a skinny black boy with sloping shoulders.

"What?" Andy was aghast.

The boy looked confused. "I'm thirsty," he repeated.

"Oh, of course." Andy handed him a bottle of water from his pack. Then he panicked. Were these kids allowed to have water? Maryn could only have ice chips, though she'd begged and begged the nurse for a cool drink.

"Are you okay, mister?" the boy asked.

"I'm fine." Andy struggled for a joke. "But if you drink that, make sure to use the bathroom before you go. You don't want to have to dig a hole in the sand. We'd all watch."

"No way, man." The boy giggled, and walked jerkily into the office.

Andy thought about the woman on the pier pushing him to the ground, to get on with the necessary business of saving a child. He tried to shake the memory of Maryn seeking something from him, something he couldn't give. Why didn't he naturally do the right thing? Was his genetic makeup lacking some humanity chip that other people had? He would've taken a fishhook, done anything, for a pain exchange where he could take Maryn's. He wasn't sure where he'd gone wrong or what to do about it.

They set off in a gawky procession down the pier. Summer

in the middle, holding hands, and smiling like the Good Witch
Glinda. Andy hung behind. Summer jerked her head for him
to join them but Andy shook her off.

"I'm the sweeper," he called. "To make sure no one gets left
behind." Summer frowned. Shepherding strays didn't yield
photo ops. He didn't care. The pier for him had become fraught
with danger. He was desperate to keep these kids safe, though
he felt puny against the threats.

As they were passing the entrance to Pacific Park, a boy
about eight years old dashed out of the amusement area and
raced down the pier, arms out, doing "the airplane." Pedestrians
dodged him, but no one paid particular attention. The people
most likely to be the boy's parents seemed to be far down the
pier, dealing with a crying child. The boy zoomed perilously
close to the edge. The déjà vu was uncomfortable. Was God
testing him? The boy stumbled on the uneven boards, but kept
going, unchecked. He steered his airplane toward a seagull
perched on a piling. Andy leaped to grab the boy's shoulders,
arresting his momentum.

"Whoa, whoa there, champ." Andy's grin was almost ma-
niacal.

The boy's mouth dropped open in shock, freckles stark
against his skin. He was wearing a cape with a giant P on a
shield.

Andy crouched down. "You have to be careful on these
boards, Super P. You could trip and end up in the drink."

The boy kicked Andy in the shin, hard.

"Oof!" Andy recoiled, releasing the boy. The boy kicked
him again, square in the nuts. Andy fell on his ass, nearly biting
through his lip to suppress a howl, fighting the urge to go fetal.
Blood throbbed in every cell as intense pain shot through him.

"Help! This man touched me! Pervert alert!" the demon
yelled. People stopped and stared. Andy's group straggled to
a halt.

"Wait," Andy croaked, reaching a hand toward the boy, the other cradling his privates.

"Keep your hands off me, homo!" the boy snarled. "Pervert molester! Queer!"

Andy was stunned at his language. Did a kid his age even know what a homosexual was? He realized people were staring and yanked his hand from his throbbing balls.

"What the hell's going on here?" puffed a red-faced man.

"That homo grabbed me!" The kid pointed at Andy. "He *touched* me! I yelled just like you said, Dad."

The ham-fisted man turned toward Andy. "Are you bothering my boy?"

"Andrew?" Summer hurried as fast as her heels would let her. She looked shocked to find him on the ground for the second time. "What's going on?"

"I was afraid he'd fall in . . . he was running so close to the edge . . . ," Andy trailed off. It sounded lame. He looked up at the man. "I didn't mean to hurt anyone."

Behind Summer, the pale, fragile Heal the Bay, Heal the Body children stared. He felt their collective doubt. "I'm sorry. I'm so sorry." Tears welled in his eyes.

"Andrew!" Summer hissed. "Get up."

But Andy couldn't move. It wasn't his tender genitals. He stared at the caped boy, his beefy father, the waifish children, but didn't see any of them. He saw a woman as pale as her sheets, the remains of her red hair shocking against her colorless skin. He saw blood spreading across another woman's white shirt. He was breaking open but there was no good red blood inside him. There was nothing but nothing.

"I'm sorry. I'm so sorry." He repeated the mantra endlessly, rocking on the boardwalk, feeling the morning's rain seep through his pants, cold against his skin.

Maryn Puts Her Feet Up

Maryn unconsciously smoothed her hair when she saw him. Andy looked like a kid bouncing in his chair.

"What do you want, Andy?" Maryn slid across from him. Seeing that he'd ordered her usual root beer evoked twin emotions of irritation and nostalgia. She went with irritation. "I have a busy day."

"Thanks for meeting me." His face was open, happy. Was he emotionally retarded? They were suing each other. "I took the liberty of ordering you a Cobb salad because I know you're squeezing me in. You look great!" he said.

She pointed to her temple. "Squint lines from busyness at work." She pointed to her cheeks. "Deep grooves from clenching my jaw in anxiety." She pointed to her eyes. "Shadows from lack of sleep due to stress."

He pointed to his face. "On TV every morning above a banner reading EVIL VILLAIN."

A reluctant smile escaped her. "I didn't think you were a born politician, but you are relentlessly cheerful."

"It only took someone else telling me I'd dreamed of it my whole life to get me started." He grinned.

"How can you be so relaxed? I'm suing you, the conservatives are baying for your blood, and your wife is terrifying."

"Don't forget being called a pervert on the pier last week! With everything this crazy, there's something calming in the fact that only I have the power to make things worse."

Her panic spiked so fast Maryn saw stars. What was he going to do?

"Andy . . ."

"Maryn, I give you consent to use the eggs."

". . . please don't . . . I . . . what?" It took a second to sink in.

He handed her a familiar document. It was creased and bore what looked like a smear of cream cheese, but it was signed. It had a Post-it note attached that read:

1. *Maryn is not my enemy.*
2. *I want her to be happy.*
3. *If you can't change something you don't like, change the way you think about it.*
4. *It's the right thing to do.*

"You'll make a wonderful mother."

Maryn didn't know what to say. She took the consent document with a shaking hand. "Thank you, Andy." She couldn't help it. She started to cry.

"Don't do that! I'm trying to make you happy here!"

"Sorry." She wiped her face with a tissue. "What made you change your mind?"

"Time to think."

She gave him a look.

"I'm a Midwestern guy! I don't talk about my feelings."

She waited.

Andy got serious. "I've made mistakes. Sometimes the accumulated weight of them stops me dead in the street. But for all their terribleness, they're familiar and they're mine, and I wouldn't change them."

Maryn noticed wrinkles she'd never seen before around Andy's eyes. It startled her that he looked like a man, not a boy.

"I hate disappointing people so badly that I couldn't deal with you. I don't know if ending our marriage was a mistake—I certainly wasn't there for you—but how I acted was. Because I couldn't handle the idea of disappointing you, I didn't acknowledge how selfishly I acted at all."

"And now?"

"This election's a hot mess. I caught myself watching them dissect me on the news one night, thinking, 'Ha! They don't even know the worst bits.' It shocked me that I knew there were worse bits."

He looked at her.

"The reason I didn't want you to have the eggs was because I didn't want a child to come into this world and learn what a coward I was for leaving when my wife got cancer. That's not a good enough reason."

He cleared his throat and took a sip of water.

"You don't have to keep paying for my shame."

The years fell away, the lake around her heart thawed, and Maryn recognized the Andy she'd married. She didn't say anything, just nodded. She might not be able to completely forgive, but at least she could have the good parts back.

"Oh look, my Cobb salad's here!" Maryn's peace offering was changing the subject.

"That looks fantastic." Andy accepted gratefully.

"So tell me about the campaign." Maryn forked a bite of salad. It was as if she'd never tasted lettuce before, it was so crispy and delicious.

"Oh lord. If I never see another Denny's . . ."

"We'll ask you to lie here for sixty minutes following the procedure," Dr. Singh said.

"Legs up the wall?"

"Not necessary," Dr. Singh reassured her. "These stirrups have caused more pregnancies than all the fraternities of UCLA."

"What about after?" Maryn chewed her lip. It was maddening that she didn't have a more active role in making this work.

"Limit physical activity for the remainder of the day. This doesn't require total bedrest, but extend the footrest on the La-Z-Boy and watch a movie. Tomorrow you can get back to normal activity. Avoid heavy bouncing of the uterus."

"How do you bounce a uterus?" Maryn knew she'd be lying on the sofa with her legs crossed until she had a positive pregnancy test.

"Waterskiing, horseback riding, uterus-bouncing sex."

"Since you're going to have to clear the cobwebs on your way in, I'm not worried about the uterus-bouncing sex," joked Maryn. "But just in case Ryan Reynolds tumbles from a hang glider into my living room, when will we do a pregnancy test?"

"You'll either get your period or we'll run a blood test after fourteen days. If embryo implantation has occurred, the HCG hormone will be detectable."

Maryn could eat delivery pizza for fourteen days as she lay on the couch with her legs crossed, no problem. Or maybe she'd eat Chinese and Indian. Those countries had terrific populations.

Dr. Singh patted her arm. "The human body is designed with enough sense that coughing, sneezing, and gravity will not cause the embryos to 'fall out.'"

"You can run a pregnancy test after ten days, can't you?"

Dr. Singh smiled. "We could do that."

"And can you give me a shiny purple pill that will make me pregnant?"

"We can offer some luteal-phase support. Estrogen tablets and progesterone suppositories can increase the chances of implantation.

"Give me the works."

"Have you considered how many eggs to transfer? Our goal is a singleton pregnancy. It's by far the safest."

"I get that," said Maryn. "I do. But I'm more afraid of failing

IVF than twins." In the back of her mind she thought, *If I have twins I get two for one, no more fighting. One and done. How nice.*

"Implantation rates decline with age. I recommend transferring three embryos as a reasonable balance of pregnancy success against the risk of multiples."

"Sure." *One and done.* Maryn crossed mental fingers.

"I'll insert a catheter through the cervix and deposit the fluid containing the embryos into the uterine cavity. The procedure should take between ten and twenty minutes. You may feel minimal discomfort, but no pain."

"If the catheter accidentally gouges out my eyeball and pokes through the top of my head, it'll feel like a tickle from God compared to what I went through to get here," said Maryn. "Let's roll."

"Would you like to see a picture of your embryos?"

Maryn would. Her throat was too constricted for speech. She nodded, the crinkling paper runner her answer. It looked like a grainy image of a Venn diagram on Mars. She clutched the photo above her face, staring hard at the nuggets, willing fetal heartbeats into them.

Dimple Goes Shopping

Can't you make him decide?" The situation with Julian Wales was making me a nervous wreck. "It's been months of nonsense. Four months to be exact. I've been auditioning for *Cora* longer than the City Council candidates have been running for office."

"What's your hurry?" Freya asked.

I couldn't explain my growing attraction to sperm donor number 11728 *and* Julian Wales. I said, "What he's asking is ridiculous! After the trapeze there was skydiving." The gaps had ended after the trapeze, with Julian demanding more and more of my time.

A pause. "Where you need a parachute?"

"You only need a parachute if you want to skydive twice."

"The thought of falling twelve thousand feet makes my blood freeze."

"Freya, your blood's been frozen for two decades. It's what makes you an agent. Besides, it's not the fall that kills you—it's the sudden stop at the end."

"This audition is certainly . . . *atypical*."

"It's not an audition, it's a season of *The Bachelor*. After the skydiving, there was the underwater scuba walk. I scream the same way whether I'm about to be devoured by a great white shark or if a piece of seaweed touches my foot. Then there was the bike ride from Santa Monica to Manhattan Beach."

"It sounds like you're dating," Freya said.

That was the heart of the problem. It felt like we were

dating. After go-carts, I'd forgotten it was an audition and grabbed Julian's hand. He must have forgotten too because he didn't let go.

"I like him." It slipped out. "We laugh a lot."

"Be careful," Freya cautioned. "Women fake orgasms. Men fake whole relationships. The first testicular cup was used in 1874 and the first helmet was used in 1974. You do the math. This is your career. Keep LaMimi in her cage."

On that cheery note, we hung up. I returned to the mess on my desk. Children's pictures peeked out between personal profiles, medical profiles, Keirsey tests, donor essays, and staff evaluations. The jumble represented about $1,700 worth of potential baby daddies.

I started at the top.

> At 6'6", Donor 11728 is a big man with a deep voice. This quiet giant may come across as intense, but his sense of humor shows in the twinkle in his hazel eyes. A straight-A high school student, this engineering major can fix anything with wires and is as proficient an athlete as an academic. While his first love is soccer, he enjoys rowing, handball, and cycling. Hardworking, loyal, and patient, Donor 11728's inventions will certainly leave a big footprint on the world one day.

The omniscient narrator of my life was Bob Barker. *Number 11728, come on down! You're the next contestant on* The Sperm Is Right!

The teasers were a cross between an Academy Award introduction and the penny-saver back-page personals, but the full files held a mother lode of information. I knew these strangers' thoughts, feelings, aspirations, and lessons learned from their parents. Julian was a mystery to me, but Donor 11728 thought there was a certain tragedy in the fact that we can only see and experience so much in one life.

In their essays, most wrote about helping infertile couples achieve the joys of family. Donor 00643 wrote, "Honestly, I need the money." He went into my pile. Donor 04377's message to semen recipients was, "You'll quickly realize that what I've done is the easy part." Donor 4116's advice was "simplicity." If money wasn't an issue, Donor 4251 would travel to Mars, because no one he knew had been there. Donor 12935 could complete a Rubik's cube in five minutes. Donor 50161's first memory was of a litter of puppies. "I still recall the funny names we gave them, especially Minnie, the runt. I don't know what it is about puppies, but it stayed with me." Donor 24580's funniest memory was a golf tournament where he'd played the entire eighteen holes naked, as tournament rules stipulated that naked play would allow him to take three strokes off his final score. He went on the pile too.

LaMimi purred, *If he played naked, he's got nothing to hide.* It brought me up short. I was screening like I was looking for a date, but I'd never meet these men. I'd just have their child. It was surreal.

I made piles. These were over 6'2". These had musical ability, something sorely lacking in my DNA. These had some Latvian genes. I tried creating a single pile by preference but it kept messing me up. I liked one best for humor and another for height. One had a great medical history but another had academic success. How did you compare a penguin to a typewriter and pick just one?

I was like Julian, auditioning prospects for a role I'd created. There were no objective standards to guide me. I decided to adopt his methods. Perhaps percolating over time would help me realize which was the one. I caught myself wondering what

Julian's funniest memory was and if there were puppies in his background.

My phone rang. It was himself.

"Two silkworms had a race. They ended up in a tie," he greeted my hello.

"I wondered why the baseball kept getting bigger. Then it hit me," I countered.

"I've converted you." He was tickled.

"If you can't beat them, join them," I said.

"I say, if you can't beat them, beat them, because they'll be expecting you to join them, so you'll have the element of surprise."

"What can I do for you?"

"You haven't returned my call. Are you punishing me?"

"It was more a reward for myself." More like a necessary breather. The man was too damn sexy.

"Reward yourself with a hot meal. I'll pick you up in half an hour."

"Julian, it's eight o'clock on Friday night. I'm off the clock. It isn't right to ask me to audition."

There was a pause. "I'm not," he said. "I'm asking you to dinner."

"Oh." Silence sat there. "Okay then. I'll see you in half an hour."

When Julian picked me up, I hustled him out the door so he couldn't glimpse the avalanche of rejected clothing erupting from my bedroom. I congratulated myself that I looked effortlessly casual, as if I'd lounged in my outfit all day.

"You have a . . . something." Julian pulled a dry-cleaning tag off my collar.

I decided no comment was the best comment, and we mostly drove in silence except for Julian's comments on passing cars.

"Now that's a hot vehicle." He pointed to a Ford Fiesta.

"He's clearly taken good care of it. It's probably an eighty-nine and look at the shine."

"Maybe it's a woman," I said.

"What?"

"You said 'he.' Maybe the driver's a she."

He considered. "It has an Iron Maiden bumper sticker."

"That shows a lack of judgment but not a gender-specific one."

"You don't like Iron Maiden?"

"I don't like bumper stickers. I don't want your smug DON'T BLAME ME I VOTED FOR THE OTHER GUY declarations. Have whatever opinion you want, but let me ask for it."

"You don't believe in self-expression."

"The bumper sticker mentality has seized American politics and it's unhealthy. Entire ideas are reduced to slogans. Look at Fox News."

"I prefer to Visualize Whirled Peas."

"I saw one that said: ISLAM AND THE LEFT—THEY BOTH LOVE KILLING BABIES. Whether you agree or disagree, stuck behind it on the 405, your hostility level will rise."

"I got a good laugh from one that said: COPS NEVER THINK IT'S AS FUNNY AS YOU DO."

"Bet the cops didn't. Have you ever had one?"

"Got it still. My mom put it on when I got my license."

"What does it say?"

"Guess you'll have to wait until we park." He shot me a wink.

We did, and Julian ran around to open my door as if I was emerging from a limo, not a Prizm. A chocolate Lab bounded up to Julian. I sneaked a peek at the bumper. A tattered sticker read: CLEAR THE ROAD, I AM SIXTEEN.

"Hello, boy! Got a pet human nearby?" Julian ruffled the dog's ears.

A teenager jogged up. "Sorry."

"No problem," Julian said. "Handsome dog."

As always, Julian switched to my street side, then threw an arm over my shoulder as we walked down the street.

"You should get a dog," I said, thinking of squirmy runt puppies named Minnie.

"I'm no good with dogs."

"What are you talking about? Dogs love you. They run up to you everywhere, like you've got bacon in your pockets."

"What's the difference between a dog and a fox?" Julian asked. "Five drinks."

"I had a collie growing up. My dad used to say, 'How many collies does it take to change the lightbulb? Just one, and while he's up there, he'll replace any wiring that's not up to code.'"

"This way." Julian led me to a wall covered in ivy, stuck his hand into the leaves, and knocked. A door opened in the greenery, and we passed into wonderland.

"Welcome to the Little Door, Mr. Wales." A maître d' settled us at a table for two in the corner. Vines fell from braided wood trellises around us, and the muted light slanted off the angular planes of Julian's skull. The restaurant made me feel as if I was dining on a patch of moss in a fairy tree castle in an enchanted forest. Julian's bone structure made me feel like I was in a 1920s production of *The Count of Monte Cristo*. It was ridiculously romantic.

Nervous, I returned to our last conversation. "Did you have dogs growing up?"

"I don't want to talk about dogs." Abrupt. At my chagrined look, his face softened. "I want to talk about you."

"Don't you know everything? I trained at the UCLA School of Theater and my first role was in a film no one ever heard of."

"I don't want to talk about your resumé. I want to know your off-the-clock self. What are your hopes and dreams? What's your earliest memory? What's your favorite color? What are you looking for?"

"My napkin," I said.

He handed one to me. "I'm serious. Other than a bumper-sticker-free life, what are you looking for in a person?"

I shrugged. "I want what everyone wants. Someone who knows the difference between 'your' and 'you're.' Someone who doesn't use emoticons. Someone who genuinely believes me when I tell him none of my car accidents was my fault. Someone who owns a passport and knows how to use it. He must agree with the statement: 'If God didn't mean for us to eat animals he wouldn't have made them so delicious.' He's kind, cannot have taken up the guitar as an adult, and isn't bat-shit insane. If I joined a cult I'd like to think he'd come rescue me. What about you?"

"Someone who doesn't wear high heels to the beach. Someone who doesn't scream uncontrollably during an alien invasion. Someone who drives a stick shift and isn't afraid to use it. That's not an analogy. She must agree with the statement: 'Bald is beautiful.' She's compassionate; cannot have long, round fingernails; and isn't an emotional fuckwit. If I went to outer space on Virgin Galactic, she'd come with me."

"Space helmets give me hat head, as you've seen."

"Me too."

" 'You have no hair,' she said baldly," I said.

"I dent easily. Have you ever noticed that most directors are completely bald or completely grey?"

"Have you ever noticed that you never see a hot young actor walking down the street with a woman who has a little potbelly and a bald spot?"

"You on the other hand, have hair like Rapunzel." He twisted a rope around his hand. "A man could get tangled in here."

"This is California. Blondes are like the state flower or something. I'm a poor cousin."

"Definitely not. Hairstyle is the final tip-off as to whether or not a woman knows herself."

"Or vanity's proving ground. It's terribly personal for something so changeable, isn't it? Jamie Lee Curtis used to say that people get comfortable with their features, but nobody gets comfortable with their hair. It's the great unifier."

"Life's an endless tangle of frustrations and challenges, but, eventually, you find a hairstyle you like. Mine's ascetic. Yours is magnificent."

"Mine's Justine's." His flirting made me skittery. Even LaMimi was hesitant because it didn't smell like sex. It smelled like complicated sex. I was relieved when food arrived.

"God, this is good." I tasted the cold salmon appetizer he'd ordered to share.

"I remember the first time we met, you said you liked your salmon cold."

"At the Improv?" I was confused.

"At an industry party on Benedict Canyon. We met by the food table and you were eating salmon."

His memory flustered me. I focused on the fish. "The dill is so clear it cuts through time. My dad called dill the King Sultan of the herb garden and tended that plot as if Elvis was buried there."

"Was he a farmer?"

"No." I didn't elaborate. Julian stared. I relented. "My father's family left Latvia before the second Russian occupation. In the States, he worked on the Wesley Allen assembly line, manufacturing iron beds for thirty-five years."

"Like where American Gothic sleeps?"

"I doubt many Iowa farmers slept in Wesley Allen beds. They were pretty high end. I had one my dad got cheap because of a ding. My bedroom was so small, it was all bed. I didn't realize until college how incongruous all the heavy iron curves and curlicues were in our blue-collar home. I still have it, ding and all."

"I'd like to see that."

It wasn't only me flushing when his words sank in. When was the last time I'd blushed? It didn't look normal for Julian either.

"How did he get into beds?"

"One foot at a time."

"Bumper sticker," he accused.

"My dad was twelve when the Soviets invaded the Baltics in World War II. His family was lucky enough to get out. They got to an Allied displaced people's camp in Germany. When the war ended, independent Latvia didn't exist. It was absorbed into the Soviet Republic."

"So they came here."

"It took them eight years."

"*Eight years?*"

"You needed a sponsor to get to the United States. Those were the worst times, after the war. The camps pulled up stakes, and refugees were left scrabbling to draw food from the dirt. My dad helped my grandmother turn a patch into a scrawny garden. That's when he started to love dill. It transformed a dusty potato or saltless broth, but it's sensitive, and hard to grow. I think he loved the challenge."

"How did they get to the States?"

"A man from the camp remembered them. He worked at Wesley Allen and convinced the company grateful Latvian labor was honest and cheap, so they sponsored a number of families. By that point my dad had met my mom, so she came too."

"Do you speak Latvian?"

"*Protams!* I was raised this schizophrenic hybrid of Latvian pride and American dream."

"Let me guess, Latvians don't rush to emergency rooms."

"Latvians don't complain, and don't talk about their feelings, but they work hard and love hard. My parents worked factory jobs, sometimes two each, to get me a good education. And a good bed."

"And you're grateful, but . . ."

I looked at my plate. "Growing up the daughter of hard-scrabble immigrants means that nothing that happens to you really counts as 'bad.' If I was devastated because David dumped me, that grief was compounded by guilt for presuming that my woes counted for anything compared to victims of famine or oppression. Like I wasn't grateful enough."

"Grief and gratitude are not mutually exclusive."

"True. And it's not a bad quality to keep your head down and work hard. My dad was never bitter. When a riveter punctured his hand, it was nothing compared to when my grandmother was stitched up without anesthesia after gallbladder surgery. When his wound developed an infection, he praised the medical treatment a poor immigrant could get. When his sepsis became fatal, he was grateful he'd saved his family from Soviet gulags and left us safely in America. He died without rancor. I took my mourning in equal parts loss and shame for focusing on my grief."

Julian was pensive. "I never thought about the kids of survivors. Hollywood focuses on Holocaust victims, but of course the bite marks would pass forward."

I rushed to correct him. "My folks weren't in concentration camps. Displaced-persons camps are different, for refugees. They could leave these places."

"Ah yes, the decadent refugee camps. I've seen them in Darfur and Burma. Regular Club Meds, all silken pillows and ambrosia."

"People assume concentration camp, and when you explain, they act like you've exaggerated for attention. It's embarrassing."

"So you spent your days navigating the Guess jeans–clad hallways of entitled American high school, and your nights in guilty gratitude at the immigrant table."

"Was there ever a point when you didn't see the world in cinematic clichés?"

"Not in years." He grinned. "My life has had narrative elements since I started writing. Can you experience things without thinking how you'd act them?"

"She said she didn't know, turning her head slightly to conceal her true feelings," I answered.

"Born to be in front of a camera."

"When a Nikon comes out, my grandmother summons every sorrow of her ninety-three years. Smiling for the camera is not part of the Latvian identity. It must be my American side."

"I like it," Julian said.

"I like this wine," I said. "Is there any more?"

We walked back to the car, pleasantly tipsy, under a leafy canopy offering slivered glimpses of the moon.

"Can I coax you back to my place for a drink?" he said.

"Are we going to hatch a plot to take over the world, Pinkie?" I'd seen a spread on his house in *Architectural Digest*. It looked like a flying saucer embedded in the hillside.

"What've you got against my place?"

"Nothing." I couldn't tell if he was wounded. I'd had a lot of wine. "I love the thrill of jutting precariously over the ocean."

"Come explore the archeological potential. I can show you my Japanese etchings." He slid his arm around my waist. Alarm bells sounded.

"I don't think this is a good idea."

I think it's a very good idea, purred LaMimi.

"What are you worried about?"

I wasn't telling him that. "Worrying works. Ninety percent of the things I worry about never happen."

He brushed back my hair. "Please trust me, Dimple."

"Directors and actresses should not get involved."

"This isn't about Julian the director and Dimple the actress. This is about Julian the man and Dimple the woman, and the incredible attraction between them." He moved closer. My focus was dissolving.

"Sex creates problems." Breathless.

"You're right," Julian said. "Sex is not the answer."

I was disappointed even though it was my argument.

He showed his teeth. "Sex is the question. Yes is the answer." This time I didn't object.

Maryn Takes a Test

The first time it happened, Maryn was sitting in her office when an odor spread itself like fecal cloth across her desk. She waited for the decay to pass with the air that blew it in, but it didn't. She rooted in her trash can to find the offending tuna sandwich or apple core. Nothing. She couldn't concentrate on work. She checked her shoes in case she'd tracked in manure. She ransacked every drawer for a forgotten hard-boiled egg. She searched the pockets of all her jackets.

"Oh my god! Are you okay?"

Her secretary Kay caught her facedown, sniffing the carpet.

"Do you smell that?" Maryn demanded.

"Smell what?"

The stink was stronger with the door open. Maryn charged into the outer office, following her nose to the coatrack.

"What's this?" She seized a handful of purple wool.

"My sweater." Kay looked puzzled.

"It reeks!" The smell of wet dog was overpowering.

"I don't smell anything. Maybe it caught some rain." It was drizzling.

Maryn tried to go back to work, but she couldn't shake the smell. Kay finally had to remove the cardigan to her car, but not without giving Maryn the side-eye.

The second time, she was at home, propped against the arm of the sofa, David Sedaris's latest on her knees. She smelled a garbage truck. It parked in the living room. Her nose led her to the cushion beneath her bare feet. Putrid. She'd sat in her reading pose, feet on these cushions, for countless odorless nights, but in an instant, the absorbed foot cheese shot the hedonic tone to rancid. She spent the rest of the night washing sofa cushions. When she straightened from zipping the last of the laundered covers back around the cushions, she staggered, light headed.

Conviction seized her. This was it.

She couldn't wait until morning. She threw a trench over her pajamas and dashed out. At the drugstore, she dithered. There were so many pregnancy tests. She picked a pink one that boasted RESULTS IN WORDS, so she wouldn't have to scrutinize whether something was a line or a cross. It also said RESULTS 5 DAYS SOONER. It had only been ten days since the implantation procedure.

The test said to wait until morning for best results, but she couldn't. She read the directions, held the stick pointing downward, and counted to five while she peed. She washed her hands and left the stick on the back of the toilet. She went into the kitchen to occupy herself with a snack, then panicked that the test might fall into the toilet. She brought the stick to the kitchen. She made tea, as if she was the sort of person who drank tea when she was home by herself. She wasn't, but she liked to think she could be. Those people seemed mature in a diversified stock and NPR sort of way. As she prepared the tea, Maryn peeped at the test, as if it might catch her looking and pull its skirt down over the results. After a hundred hours, five minutes passed. She examined the stick. The little clock was still flashing.

She stirred tea she had no interest in. After three more minutes, a question mark symbol appeared.

"No shit, Sherlock." The stupid stick was supposed to *answer* the question, not ask it. She reread the instruction sheet.

> A ? symbol indicates an error has occurred during test-
> ing. You should retest with another digital pregnancy
> test, carefully following all directions.

She wanted to use the other test immediately but restrained
herself. It worked best in the morning. She'd wait. She dumped
out the tea and drank a glass of water. Then another. She finished a third before taking the fourth to bed. She wondered if
this was what waterboarding felt like.

"I'm pregnant with a water baby," she told the clean stick as
she put it in the bathroom for the morning's use.

Despite herself, she fantasized about what it would feel
like to read the 'YES.' Sounding a barbaric YAWP over the
rooftops. Telling Kay she was pregnant. Blossoming round
and large. Feeling the baby kick. It took a long time to fall
asleep.

She woke at six with an urgent need to urinate. She'd never
been so excited to pee. This time, she used a cup and immersed
the absorbent tip for five seconds. She studied the packaging
while she waited. It was rather maddening. A "-No" result
meant *You may not be pregnant, or it may be too early to tell.* A
"+YES" result instructed *You may be pregnant. You must see your
doctor to confirm.* It was like a lawyer.

After three minutes, a "*?*" appeared in the window.

"Are you kidding me?" she shouted at it. "Stupid, crappy,
worthless piece of false marketing. What are you, Windows
'98?? "

Maryn was torn between writing an angry letter to the
FTC about false advertising in pregnancy tests, and running
out and buying more. She restrained herself on both fronts.
She dressed and went to work. At lunch, she bought another
test, steering wide of the pink ones, and selecting a blue box
that displayed "*Easy*" in large, reassuring letters. That night

she was so tired that sleep came immediately even though she went to bed so full of water she could have floated.

She woke at six desperate to expel the gallon of liquid she'd funneled before bed. She peed on the stick meticulously. She hovered over the stick, afraid to jostle it. Three minutes later the hourglass changed to NOT PREGNANT.

"Well, that's just wrong," said Maryn. She must not have sufficient levels of the HCG pregnancy hormone yet. She'd try again in five days.

It didn't occur to her to be disappointed, unless you counted deferred pleasure. She refused to not be pregnant. A person didn't grow super-smelling powers overnight.

The five days weren't unlike any other five days of her life, despite her conviction that she was pregnant. She was frantic at work, moving fifteen thoroughbreds through LAX for the Pacific Classic in Del Mar. On Thursday, she sipped a glass of wine with a client, feeling like she was cheating. Technically, there was no reason not to drink. But Maryn knew she was cheating. And she was exhausted. So very, very tired. Kay thought it was all those damn Pacific Classic horses. Wyatt thought maybe she was coming down with a cold. Maryn knew she was coming down with a case of the babies. She was only surprised by how fast the symptoms hit her.

The second time, Maryn went through the routine like it was nothing special. Just like brushing your teeth. She woke at five, peed on the stick. She transported it to the bedside table as if it was an armed nuclear weapon coated in powdered anthrax, coddling its sensitive inner workings. She snuggled into the covers and dozed while she waited. When she roused, she stretched her neck to look at the digital window without touching the sensitive oracle. She had her answer.

She lay back on the pillows. She didn't do anything for a moment. Didn't feel anything. Didn't yawp. Her hand rested on her flat abdomen, waiting for emotion. Then a slow smile crept over her face.

"Welcome to the world, nugget," she whispered.

Maryn may have been more active after her insemination than she'd predicted, but she seriously spent the next weeks on the couch with her legs crossed. It wasn't just her fear that something would go wrong.

"Women have been doing this for thousands of years," said Dr. Singh. "Relax. It's out of your hands. Absent extremes, nothing you do or don't do will cause you to lose this parasite."

"Parasite" was Dr. Singh's brand of humor, but sometimes Maryn thought she meant it. "Remember to eat well and take your vitamins," she would say. "The baby will take what it wants, so you must take care of yourself."

Maryn was doing her best, but the fatigue was killing her. It was pregnancy's dirty little secret. Everyone bitched about morning sickness and cankles, but no one told her she'd be drained to the bone. Maryn hadn't been sick once, but she was dying of tired. It didn't help that she went cold turkey on caffeine.

Each day, Maryn relaxed a little. It was like snatching gold coins one at a time. Four weeks felt good. Six weeks felt better. Eight was stupendous.

"I'm pregnant." Maryn kept it simple when she called Andy.

Silence. "What's the right thing to say?" Andy asked. They'd dismissed their case, though you'd never know it. No one reported it, and the furor over Proposition 11 raged on.

"Congratulations, and what did you just say because I've already forgotten," Maryn answered.

"Congratulations," said Andy. "I'm sorry—what did you just tell me? I've already forgotten."

Despite his newfound accommodation, Maryn knew she

wouldn't fully relax until after the baby was born and he signed the last legal paper giving her uncontested custody of the child.

At eleven weeks, she raced to the doctor for a chorionic villus sampling test. It was the earliest opportunity to rule out chromosomal abnormalities like Down syndrome.

"How's everything been so far?" the doctor asked. It wasn't Dr. Singh, it was a specialist.

"I'm good, just tired."

"Your energy will bounce back," he said. "When you hit the second trimester, you should feel an almost instantaneous resurgence of vigor."

Maryn didn't see an end to feeling saggy, but she nodded.

"How long has that been bothering you?" He indicated the sore on her lip.

"It's just a cold sore." She edged back.

"You have a history of breast cancer, correct?"

Maryn was disappointed that this doctor knew her medical history. She wanted the focus on her pregnancy.

"I've been in full remission for years."

"Anything else bothering you?"

"Nope. I feel great." She hid her exhaustion behind a perky smile.

He studied her lip a moment, then said, "Pregnancy throws the body into chaos. Canker sores are a common side effect of the additional hormones. But if the fatigue doesn't ease soon, have Dr. Singh run a basic blood panel and look at your white cell count. Merely a precaution." He smiled. "Today's procedure will only take a second. I'm going to take cells from the fingerlike projections on the placenta called the chorionic villis, and send them to a lab for genetic analysis, and hopefully rule out Down syndrome."

"And know the gender?"

"If you like. Do you want to wait any longer for your husband?"

She hadn't realized they'd been waiting. "Begin," was all she said. Otherwise, they'd be waiting a long time.

When the doctor called a week later, it was good news.

"Everything looks perfect. You have a healthy baby."

Maryn exhaled breath she'd been holding for twelve weeks.

"Would you like to know the gender?" he asked.

"Absolutely."

"What do you think it is?"

"A miracle," she said.

"And a girl," he said.

It wasn't physical changes that were hard on Maryn, though there were those too. For the most part her body took to pregnancy beautifully. She had no nausea or food aversions, her hair thickened, her appetite didn't change. Intellectually, it was surreal. Maryn the planner, the controller, couldn't get her head around it. She was growing a human brain from scratch, but there was no indication if you looked at her body in the mirror. Yet an infinitesimal body-snatching shift had occurred. She was a slave host to an alien.

The hard part was the emotional wilderness. Pregnancy was an unpredictable mare on an unfamiliar course, a thrilling and terrifying jump over a blind box hedge, bodies united but the horse in control.

Maryn didn't have confidantes. Because of her illness, her divorce, and her work, she'd become unmoored from her social life. It would be artificial to reconnect with friends long drifted, but she was desperate to talk.

She thought of Wyatt. She felt bonded to the quiet man, and couldn't wait to share with him. They were each pogo sticks on the verge of becoming two-legged stools. Together they could

make a sturdy table. Maryn needed the support. The baby registry terrified her. What if she registered for the wrong bottle
nipple and the child never went to college? That was the tip
of the iceberg. She had a million questions. She'd read all the
books, but she wanted someone to talk to, a compatriot with
whom to be mutually mystified assembling baby toys, to consult over rashes, or to talk about poop without sarcasm.

Wyatt would understand the soup of joy, terror, shock, and
awe she was feeling. They would gossip about scandals among
the Ocean Park playground parents, but also about secret fears
their children might be autistic. Their daughters could be best
friends. Maryn wanted a best friend too. Wyatt had a head
start in the wilderness, and even if it was the blind leading the
blind, she trusted that he could guide her through it.

Wyatt Goes Shopping, Again

Wyatt's situation with Webb Garner smarted on many levels.

The most obvious was that he didn't want to give up the baby he thought of as his. Wyatt wasn't a New Age type of man who wore open-toed sandals and cried about things. Wyatt was Minnesota farm stock and he didn't cry. He was in touch with his feelings but he was neither sensitive nor frail. Wyatt didn't wear clothes made out of hemp, and he wasn't saddened because he longed to give birth and could not. But a gaping hole was wrenched open in him at the thought that he might never run alongside a bike in his old Adidas before letting go, heart in his mouth as his child took a first wobbledy pedal.

Second, Wyatt didn't like being bullied, and he didn't like it when bullies won. He wanted to set an example for his students, even if they'd never learn of it. He also wanted to punch Webb Garner's smug face, but that was not a good example.

Underdog victories only happened in youth-oriented hockey movies. Real life high school could be a tormenting place. He needed his students to know that if they avoided the Webb Garners, memorized their French past imperfect and Pythagorean theorem, and scribbled doodles of Mr. Kelly with devil horns and a forked tongue to vent steam, they'd make it through. If his charges saw a lifetime of bullying spiraling before them, it could shatter their fledgling self-assurance that it would get better. The truth was, life got messier as you got older. Here was Wyatt, almost fifty years old and dealing with a bully. He wanted to protect his students from the fury of inequality that was adulthood as long as possible.

A tap on the door frame drew him from his reverie.

Linda was wearing a dove grey sweater dress with a circle pin, hair gathered into a knot with complicated-looking sticks. She was a powdery iris, and when Wyatt's mind slipped her into a slim vase, she looked good there.

"You seem lost in thought, and not good ones."

"I'm a terrible poker player because my hand falls into the eyes of everyone playing."

"Can I help?"

Linda soothed Wyatt. Like water pooling upward, his story seeped from him and he told her everything.

"Stop my adoption or lose my job," he concluded. "As if I'd burned a Koran, a Bible, and a copy of *Huck Finn* wrapped in the American flag on school grounds."

Linda gave Wyatt a look of limitless compassion. "I had no idea."

"That adoption was an act of unforgivable sedition?"

"That you were adopting at all."

"The secrets harbored outside these walls," he joked.

"I'm getting a divorce." She spoke quietly. It was an offering not to be fussed over, and Wyatt accepted it as such.

"So what happens?" Linda asked.

"Paley and Lang are threatening to claim I'm sexually inappropriate with students. I'm ill at the thought that anyone believes Chris Hansen waits in my bushes to catch a predator."

"No one would believe that for a second. Lang was fired for being a terrible teacher and a generally irritating person. His accusations are petty revenge. The strength of your character supports the school solar system in its orbit."

"Even the reputation of Abe Lincoln could be eradicated in

a one-hour newscast with discordant sound effects and grainy footage."

"Do you really think Garner would do that?"

"He'd step on a baby seal in a spiked boot to boost his career."

"As long as you're still here, bad hasn't won."

"There's bad, and there's the appalling silence of good. I keep my job, and live with my inaction. I'm trying to teach the kids not to jump off the Golden Gate Bridge just because everybody else is doing it, and I'm drawing the arrases over injustice to save my job."

"I might jump off the Golden Gate Bridge if everyone else was doing it, because if I was the only one left, the world would seem a very lonely place." She smiled. For a moment sunlight swept though Wyatt's clouds.

"I would do everything in my power to prevent that," Wyatt said.

Linda continued. "You're being unnecessarily hard on yourself. You can plug your finger in a crack in the dyke. You can't stave off a rogue wave with one brick. Keeping your job isn't a selfish act. The school needs you. If the other end of the rack was a public rather than a personal concern, you'd stand nose to pointy chin with Webb Garner for what you thought was right. The measure of your character is that you'd surrender your own dreams for service."

"It's the only answer, I suppose." A part of him had hoped Linda would tell him to flout the threats, keep the baby, even knowing it was an impossibility. How could he have a child with no job, worse, an unemployable reputation? Worst, a child who would grow to comprehend the whispers about her father.

"Wait out the election, then see what's what. Everything happens for a reason. I was disappointed when children didn't work out for us, but considering . . . it turns out it was best there were no kids."

"Linda, if there's anything . . ."

She shook him off. "It will just take time. I'll be as right as rain."

"You have a classroom full of kids who think you're the bee's knees," Wyatt said.

"I think you're the bee's knees," she said. They shared a momentary mind meld, and Wyatt knew her regard for him had inalterably shifted. It was not an unpleasant thought.

Wyatt went to see Katherine Feely Jones with a heavy heart. He'd put it off as long as he could, riding the brakes on ordinary acts in hopes that the divide between adoption and not-adoption could be somehow reversed. He didn't worry about Deborah. She'd shift smoothly to whichever new able-bodied adult Katherine provided, as she'd done before. They'd be good parents and the child would be fine. Only Wyatt would suffer. He worried the ache would swallow him whole.

In the anteroom to Katherine's office, Wyatt studied the pictures of smiling children. They were white, black, Asian, fair-haired, dark curled, wearing glasses, missing teeth, a cornucopia of children. The one thing they had in common was a smiling parent. The message was *Get your kids here, we've got kids of all sizes, kids for everyone.* But not, it seemed, for Wyatt. That's not my story, he thought. That's not my happy ending.

After he'd explained to Katherine, she asked him, "Will you be okay?" He appreciated that she kept it simple.

"Eventually."

She put a hand on his shoulder. "The loss of an adoption can feel like a death, Wyatt, or a miscarriage at the very least. Give yourself space to grieve."

Miscarriage didn't cover everything. How long before he stopped scrutinizing babies he passed on the street? Part of him had splintered into a future that wouldn't materialize, a phantom parenthood. He'd been confused by a movie in the nineties where every decision resulted in two realities, both alternatives fracturing in different directions, though the character followed only one. He hadn't understood how an unelected choice could live on its own. He did now.

When he left Katherine, he was adrift. He wanted to anchor in someone else's life for a time. He thought of Maryn's easy understanding, and reached for his phone.

An hour later he was at the French Market. It wasn't his favorite because the patio only got direct sun for about an hour at high noon, but Maryn loved the Mediterranean Croque.

She arrived in a scatter of haste and flurry, hair and trench coat swirling. "I'm sorry I'm late." Her cheeks were flushed, her eyes sparkling.

"There's no such thing as late when I have grade reports to review. I get more peace out of the office than in it."

They took turns ordering lunch to secure the table. Once they both had food, Maryn said, "I sense something rather dramatic going on in that brain of yours."

"I've given up on my adoption." He kept it simple. "The chair of the School Board thought it was inappropriate for an unmarried high school principal to adopt."

"Inappropriate how?"

"I'm not gay," Wyatt explained.

"Really," Maryn snorted. "Because my gaydar just put its hand on its forehead and passed the hell out all dramatic like."

Wyatt hadn't thought he could laugh, but he did. Maryn patted his hand. "If I had a sister, I'd set you up, and not because she needed new window treatments."

"God no. I'm the go-to single guy for most of my friends' wives. I'm set up all I can handle."

"How does not being gay affect your adoption?"

"Apparently, straight men only want babies to make stew, skin crème, or pornography. I ended my adoption to save my job."

"I imagine that would angry up the blood," Maryn said. "If you really wanted baby stew." She handed him a plastic knife. "Hold this for a second."

She captured a leaf of arugula escaping from her plate to create new life on her linen pants. Wyatt was a little nonplussed that Maryn was making light of what he'd shared. She shook open his newspaper, holding the page taut between them.

"Now stab it." Her voice was muffled behind the newspaper.

"What?" He was bewildered.

She peeked around the page with a little smile. "When I first lost my breast, I went to an anger therapy class. They told us to punch pillows to get rid of our anger. When we'd done that, they asked if it was satisfying. Of course it wasn't, but that was their point—a big loss goes beyond punchin' rage. It's *stabbin'* rage. They handed us pointy knives and told us to stab the pillows, as if our lost breast was there and we were eviscerating it for leaving us."

Wyatt, feeling like a fool, held the plastic knife. "Did it work?"

"I was distinctly uncomfortable."

"Sit back."

Her head disappeared and Wyatt stabbed the paper. After a few thrusts, it tore down the middle and he was looking at Maryn's face, like an unwrapped present.

"You stab like you're cutting newsprint pie." She laughed.

"I grew up a farm boy. I know pies, not serial killing."

"Feel better?"

"Did you?"

"I was the first to say, 'My goodness how cathartic that was,' because the sooner you said how cathartic it was, the sooner you could say, 'I think you've helped me as much as you can help me,' and never go back. Nothing is more profitless than going back over what interventions might have changed your current reality."

"I keep thinking that if I think hard enough, I can come up with a solution, but I can't. This guy isn't fooling around. He's never forgiven me for publicly exposing what we'll politely call 'gaps in his understanding' during a math curriculum reform debate. I doubt this is the end."

She looked thoughtful. "Is the School Board president that douche bag Webb Garner?"

Wyatt nodded.

"Now I need something to stab." Maryn made a face, but there was merriment beneath. The gaunt, pale Maryn of weeks ago was gone, replaced by this playful version.

"You seem happy." It made him happy too.

Maryn erased her mirth.

"Stop," Wyatt protested. "Don't be dour on my account. What's up?"

She fiddled with her napkin.

"What could be worse than what I told you?" he nudged.

"I'm pregnant." The pent-up words flung themselves at him as if they'd been ricocheting around her mouth looking for an exit.

"I'm sorry," she said. "I wasn't going to tell you today. I hate feeling jubilant during your loss." She looked miserable, but glowy. Her concern for him when she had such news was like being fed and in a bath at the same time.

"I can promise you," Wyatt said, "nothing could bring me more joy than this."

"Andy had a change of heart, and the implantation worked. I'm twelve weeks' pregnant." She was radiant. "I've been dying to tell you, but I was so nervous, I mean, the odds are totally against me. But it worked! It was the super smelling, that's how I knew. God, I'm glad I can finally share —I've been dying to talk." She babbled all the words no one had been there to receive.

"I thought this morning that nothing would make me happy today, but I was wrong. Maryn, this is wonderful."

"Maybe . . ." She hesitated.

"What?"

"Nothing."

"Come on."

"It's too much to ask, Wyatt."

"Out with it."

Hesitation. "Maybe you'd like to be my pregnancy buddy?"

"I'd love to." Wyatt didn't pause. "We've given birth together before. We're a good team."

"Good lord, I hope you won't have to pull her out by the forelegs!" Maryn seemed elated and relieved. Wyatt could, at least, be her village.

"I promise to drive to the hospital very, very fast and avoid the 405," Wyatt vowed. "If you promise to get an epidural so I don't have to go to any classes where we hug yoga balls and practice breathing."

Maryn shot him a look he could wield to hit a baseball. "Number one instruction on my birth plan." She glanced at her watch. "Darn. I've got to run. I'm going to Buy Buy Baby." She made a face. "Registering."

Wyatt had been to Buy Buy Baby, a cavernous store filled with mind-boggling car seat towers, a labyrinth of layettes, and a bewildering array of things for your breasts. He recalled his Target experience with alarm.

"Wait. I'm coming with you."

Dimple Tries the Casting Couch

O h my god. I slept with the director," I said out loud.

"You did not sleep with the director." Julian rolled over.

I gave him a look. He peeked under the sheet at our naked bodies.

"Okay, technically, you slept with the director, but not in the *sleep with the director* way." He paused. "At least I hope not. I hope you slept with the man you'd like to see more of." He wiggled his eyebrows. "Literally."

"Of course I did." His words thrilled me, but I had to voice my fear. "We're both Hollywood. What if we don't know our actual feelings and have fallen into a cliché?"

"I'm not Hollywood. Hollywood is a wretched hive of scum and villainy."

"Are you kidding me? Look at this place! You have the all-window house perched on a Malibu cliff like you stole it from *Charlie's Angels II*. You mentioned George Clooney using only his first name. Sleeping with actresses is part of the hot director cliché."

"I'm not that good a director."

"Be serious." I punched him.

"I am serious! With Woody Allen or Jean-Luc Godard, their actress-lover is their muse. Almost all of Allen's great work starred his lovers, and they inspired his writing. No matter what nonsense Godard is spewing, if Anna Karina is in the frame, he's expressing something true. It doesn't matter what she's doing, Godard's view of her makes it fascinating, the embodiment of some hard-to-define eternal truth. Their interaction is complex, obsessive, and alive and it punches through the screen."

"Hmm." In Godard's *A Woman Is Woman*, Karina wanted a child but her lover was unwilling so it ended.

"I don't know how they do it. I need to be detached. I've never been able to *see* someone close to me with unfettered clarity."

"I definitely didn't sleep with the director to get the part then."

We were facing each other, heads propped on elbows.

"Don't think I failed to consider that," Julian said seriously. "I honestly don't know how it will go. Intimacy changes everything, especially through the lens. It's been a barrier for me, but with you . . ." He played with my hair. "I get the feeling I'm on the verge of something great."

"Few people direct me to such excellent work," I joked to mask my apprehension. A one-night or one-month stand was a stupid way to lose a part. Professional athletes shouldn't ride motorcycles on icy roads and professional actresses shouldn't sleep with their directors.

"I'm being serious," Julian said, "You move me in ways that are new to me, both personally and professionally. I've never been motivated to the challenge of directing someone I cared about before. Intimacy with you may jolt me."

"But it may not. Godard and Karina broke up. Woody Allen and . . . everyone broke up. It's a big gamble." For me, I didn't say. "Voice mails outlast relationships between actresses and directors."

"I don't know how to say it just right, but please trust me that the decision to become involved with you was thoughtful, not a roll of the dice." He smiled. "And correct."

"Oh," was all I could say. He reached for me and we gambled again.

Julian tried to coax me over most nights. LaMimi always said yes, but I was more restrained. It was hard not to get swept away, though. After our adventures, it was nice to hang out in an ordinary way, if a house clinging to the side of a cliff was ordinary. The word "audition" faded from our lexicon, and we didn't discuss the bog between professional and personal where we lived.

One Saturday, we were slouching into his squishy sofa, Julian channel surfing and me reading *Variety*. I wanted to smuggle it out of the house and trash it because Daisy-*I'm-so-winsome*-Carmichael was all over it for signing on to *Rainy Season*, but I knew it was futile. She and her dumb little dog were everywhere.

"I don't get people's fascination with those stupid dogs." Julian startled me. *Beverly Hills Chihuahua II* was on the screen. "I'm stupefied by the decision to make this movie. Though I feel that way about most of what's at the box office."

"If you scorn my weakness for big action flicks, it might be over," I warned. "I love an asteroid, twister, tidal wave, or the End of the World with the full bombast of a percussion-heavy score."

"You'll test the limits of my tolerance."

"What about you?" I asked.

"I have no weaknesses."

"Pedicure."

"Animated children's pictures, then."

"That's not a weakness. *Up* and *Toy Story III* were nominated for Best Picture. What freezes your remote thumb on Saturday afternoons?"

"Heartwarming underdog sports movies. Precocious freckled kid a must."

"Like *The Bad News Bears*?" I teased.

"*Rudy* makes me weep and reach for the double-chocolate Milanos."

"I can't fault that."

He stopped on news coverage of people with signs, clamoring at people entering a clinic.

"This will be next week's made-for-TV movie," he predicted.

"What's that?"

"Proposition 11. Bigoted mobs braying for the erosion of women's rights and one lone soul standing against the horde, a profile in courage as she changes the tide of history with tearful impassioned speeches."

"Sounds like good Saturday afternoon fare."

"It's clichéd. Real people aren't heroes or villains. Everyone's got both. Parts of Proposition 11 aren't wrong."

"Proposition 11 is completely unreasonable," I objected.

"Lots of people are desperate for kids. If embryos are going to waste, why not let others have them?"

"You can't apply market principles to human beings."

"Ah-ha." He held up a finger. "Wouldn't your side say they weren't human beings?"

He was tripping me up. "Of course embryos aren't human beings. But they could become babies."

"Lots of those babies aren't wanted. Fragile Voices is saying that good couples would like to have them. Everybody's happy."

"Everybody isn't happy. I wouldn't want to give my embryo to strangers who would raise it to vote for someone who didn't believe in *Roe v. Wade*."

"Your problem is who's likely to get the embryo?"

"My problem is imposing one religious definition of right, especially when you're talking about something as intensely personal as children. I don't have any problem destroying embryos because I don't believe they're people. I'm intellectually capable of separating that from the fact that they could *become* people, which triggers my second objection, that you can't force me to give away what will become my biological child."

"Even if you have plenty and others have none?"

"That's like saying I have two hands and he has none, so he gets one of mine. You can't impose a body part welfare system."

"We let people donate kidneys."

"By consent. People are perfectly free to donate embryos, if they choose. The Snowflake folks have a thriving adoption business. To *mandate* adoption unacceptably erodes a woman's right to choose and chills individual freedom to explore fertility options." I was getting mad.

"It doesn't really—if you aren't comfortable with the consequences, don't make the embryos."

"That means no kids for a lot of people."

"The world is overpopulated."

"Stop being cavalier! Proposition 11 is scary." My agitation rose. I tried to get through to him. "You started to make a movie, but it didn't work out. Another movie came along, or you decided not to make any movies that year, whatever, you abandoned it. Now some other director wants to make the film but doesn't have any ideas of his own, so you're forced to give him your reels. He gets to finish the film, take credit, and show it to the world. You have no say."

He looked uncomfortable. "That's not the same."

"It pretty much is."

"Babies are different."

"Exactly. Proposition 11 will put a chill on people trying to conceive through IVF. That's wrong."

"But it will help a lot of people who can't afford IVF."

"Are you saying you're going to vote for Proposition 11?" I struggled not to scream. "It would hurt a lot of people." What if I needed IVF?

"Of course not." Thank god. "I'm not voting."

"What?"

"I don't vote in local elections."

"Julian, this isn't like electing the clerk of court. You need to vote against Proposition 11."

"It doesn't affect me." He shrugged.

It affects me.

"Isn't that what the intellectuals said when they came for the Jews?"

"There are only intellectuals and Jews in Santa Monica."

"I'm serious! This affects everyone."

"So am I. Politics isn't my thing. A small group of people control the fate of the majority, and the majority lets them. My puny acts don't make a difference."

"So you don't do anything?" I asked in disbelief.

"I make movies about puny acts that do make a difference."

"To do that you need examples."

His cell phone interrupted our unsatisfying conversation. I tried to calm down. He was playing devil's advocate. The importance of IVF to me couldn't be lost on him.

As I stewed over his attitude, his posture drew my attention. It was almost imperceptible, torso hunched slightly, angled a fraction, minute adjustments shielding the conversation from me.

"I need time," he said. The other end spoke. "No . . . No . . . No," Julian responded. "It's not that simple." He walked to the bedroom and shut the door. I knew it was about *Cora.*

"Julian, I've got to go," I called.

"Hold on," he called. He remerged, leaving the phone on the bed. "I'm sorry—it's work. You can't stay?"

I didn't think he wanted me to be persuaded. "Dinner with my mother." I refused.

He walked me to the door. "I'll call you later."

He kissed me, a long, thorough good-bye kiss, suitable for

a morning after, and stood at the door as I walked to my car, uncomfortable on multiple levels.

I woke gasping, heart racing. The green glow of the clock said 3:49 AM. I took deep breaths, trying to diffuse my fight-or-flight tension. My mind was a jumble of the darkened shapes in my predawn room and the taunting characters from my dream. I couldn't remember the details, but the fear was stark.

I slid a hand under the sheet to rest on my abdomen. "Please," I whispered into the dark. "Please don't let me have waited too long." One tear slid from the corner of my eye down to my ear. "Please."

Maryn Takes Another Test

"What's this?" Dr. Singh frowned as she palpated Maryn's one real breast.

"Nothing. I drink a lot of caffeine," Maryn said. "At least I did, before I got pregnant. I've always had lumpy breasts."

"Given your history, I want to be sure. It would be wise to get a mammogram," said Dr. Singh.

"Is that really necessary?" asked Maryn. Dr. Singh looked surprised. "Lumps are normal during pregnancy. It's probably milk ducts." This was true. Maryn didn't know why she felt sneaky.

"There's no harm in it," Dr. Singh answered.

"You can't actually say that for sure," Maryn argued. "Scientists can't be certain of the effect of even a small amount of radiation on an unborn baby."

"Early detection is an important part of breast health." Dr. Singh's reply wasn't an answer. "It's rare, but you can find breast cancer during pregnancy."

"I'd rather wait on the mammogram until there's a conclusive need. A manual exam is too imprecise to take a risk. You know what I went through to get this baby. How would I feel if I messed it up with unnecessary treatment?"

"It's your choice of course."

Maryn knew Dr. Singh disapproved. "It may be illogical, but it's my choice."

A play of emotions chased across Dr. Singh's face for an

instant, then detachment. "We can schedule you for an alternative imaging test if you don't want a mammogram right now. It's completely noninvasive, like a sonogram. But breast ultrasounds are not as effective, and can be easily confused by the natural changes in breast tissue during pregnancy."

"It would make me happier."

"Then that's what we'll do."

"The good news is, we can skip the mammogram," said Dr. Singh. "The bad news is, we need to do a biopsy."

Maryn opened her mouth but Dr. Singh held up a hand.

"Breast biopsy procedures, even modified radical mastectomy, are safe for the mother and fetus," Dr. Singh said.

"That's fine," said Maryn. "I'll schedule one for next month."

Dr. Singh considered her. "Maryn, there may be some urgency here. The ultrasound revealed a growth in your natural breast that is not normal."

"Unfortunately, I'll be at the Breeders' Cup for work. It's one of the most significant events in my profession. I'll schedule the biopsy as soon as I return."

Maryn's game strategy was clock management. If there was something to worry about, if the cancer was back, she was changing the rules. She wasn't plotting to defeat it in the war of strength. She just wanted to outwit it long enough to get to the prize. Besides, it was a lot of fuss over what would probably turn out to be pregnancy side effects anyway.

Maryn didn't want to get up. She was so very tired. She considered blowing off her appointment, luxuriating in a decadent marathon of *Tabitha's Salon Takeover* or *Real Housewives*. A thought of the nugget tied her shoes and got her out the door.

Now she was on the office couch facing Dr. Singh and Dr. Gavin, the oncologist. When she'd walked into the office and Dr. Singh stepped around her desk, urging them all to the chair and sofa grouping, Maryn knew the news was bad. Good news traveled safely across a desk. Bad news required proximity. The worse the news, the shorter the distance. Dr. Singh sat close to Maryn on the couch.

"Maryn, your biopsy was positive for a local recurrence of your breast cancer. I've asked Dr. Gavin to join us to discuss your options."

Of course she'd known what she would hear. She'd been ignoring the twinges, the fatigue, the lumpiness. She'd told herself it was the pregnancy, but not much got by Maryn's inner self, including Maryn.

"I thought the correlation between pregnancy hormones and recurrence was refuted," Maryn said, as if it mattered.

"We don't know why it came back," Dr. Singh said. "Your particular strain was HER2 positive, which put you at greater risk because of the increased amount of blood flowing through your body during pregnancy. As an older mother, all these risks increase exponentially."

"But my breast is gone," Maryn protested.

"Unfortunately, recurrence can take root where a mastectomy has occurred. It's not possible to remove a hundred percent of the breast tissue by surgery. If there is any microscopic spread through the lymph system cancer cells will seek, and during pregnancy, find, all the estrogen they need to keep them growing. In your case, there are nodules under the skin near your scar. With the pregnancy it's hard to tell what we're dealing with."

"I'm NED. Full remission. Pregnancy isn't supposed to increase the risk of occurrence." Maryn continued to argue.

Dr. Singh's eyes were sympathetic. "There's no apparent long-term increased risk of recurrence in pregnant women versus nonpregnant women. It may be a coincidence. In your case, characteristics of your cancer correlate with an increased likelihood of recurrence, independent of pregnancy."

Dr. Gavin spoke, "The immediate issue is mapping the recurrence. We need staging tests to determine if there is distant disease. Our highest concern is that it has spread into the lymph nodes."

Dr. Singh said, "Because pregnancy disguises the symptoms of breast cancer, pregnant women often have more advanced cancers at diagnosis. It's imperative that we move quickly to determine the scope. First, an MRI. Then perhaps a bone scan, chest X-ray, or PET scan."

"I'll have the MRI," Maryn said. "But not the contrast dye. It's been linked to fetal abnormalities in lab animals." It didn't matter what tests they wanted to run. They could do phrenology and leech therapy, so long as it didn't hurt the nugget, but she wouldn't budge if there was fetal risk.

"Maryn." Dr. Singh considered her words. "At this stage, the health of the fetus may be a secondary concern. It's incredibly immature, and we don't know how far your disease has advanced."

"The health of the fetus is the primary concern." Maryn did not brook any argument. "We can map, but we're not going to treat. Not until the baby is born."

The doctors exchanged a look. Dr. Gavin said, "Let's see what we're dealing with before we make any decisions."

Maryn's decision was made, but she saved the fight for another day.

She thanked them both without seeing them, and left the office. She was so tired. The thought of Sherpa slippers and hot chai propelled her through the lobby. She had to get home before the collapse.

She stepped outside and her world exploded for the second time in one day.

Dimple Helps Out

The wrist was surprisingly tiny. The woman was suspended like a jellyfish, surrounded by the flashes, whirs, and shouted questions from a paparazzi mob. She hung there, wide eyed, transfixed. I split the horde like a needle, gripped her, and popped her from the locus of the storm back into the clinic. The reporters bayed at the door, as I dragged her down a hallway, out of sight. There was a ladies' room. I flipped the lock, bolting the door against others.

The woman sagged against the basin.

"Are you all right?" Arguably, being locked in a bathroom with a stranger was more alarming than rabid reporters.

She focused on me. "You have a cut."

A welt was swelling around a smear of blood on my wrist. "It's just a scratch." I dismissed. "I'm prone to rescue wounds. Are *you* hurt?"

She shook her head no.

"This will make you feel better." I pressed a wet towel to her forehead, positioning her hand over it like arranging a life-size Barbie. "Why don't you sit?" The bathroom had a chaise catering to pregos.

I knew who she was. She was the one suing her ex-husband for custody of frozen embryos. Mary something. She nodded, but didn't move. I supported her to the lounger. I knew the shaky legs a paparazzi maelstrom brought.

"Thank you." She brushed her hair back with a trembling hand. "I don't know what's come over me."

I surprised myself by enveloping her in a tight hug. She tensed, but instinct kept me holding on. A second later she started to sob. I absorbed this stranger's surprise, pain, fear, and rage.

"I . . . wasn't . . . expecting . . . it," she heaved. "There've been . . . a few . . . on the lawn but never . . . anything like that."

"You don't have to justify being freaked out," I said. "Those vultures are horrendous."

I held her until her crying slowed. She drew deep breaths, forehead on my shoulder. Then she pulled herself up.

"I'm a hot mess." She wiped her eyes.

"A good bath and a firm hairbrush, maybe a little Nutella, and you'll be right as rain. I know."

"That?" She gestured generally, outside the restroom.

"Unfortunately. It goes with my job."

She shuddered. "I don't envy you."

"The legitimate ones aren't bad. It's the ones who get paid by the picture you have to watch out for. They attack, hoping to rattle you."

"It worked. You were heroic diving in there."

"Chicks gotta look out for each other," I dismissed. "It's a form of violence."

"It's ripping me apart, all this Proposition 11 nightmare." She nodded. "Are you doing IVF?"

I was startled. "Oh. No. Checkup." It was sort of true.

"Oh." She blew her nose. "Well, it's awful what they're doing, trying to put IVF out of reach. Can you imagine what this would mean? Not just for single women, but couples too? Not everyone is lucky enough to have kids without help."

I made a noncommittal noise.

"People would be afraid of IVF because you'd have to give

birth to, like, seven children, or give them to total strangers. Can you imagine running into a kid at In-N-Out who looked like yours? Six of them?"

It made me angry thinking about it.

"The craziest thing is that abortions would probably rise if that was the only way people could terminate frozen embryos, which is the opposite of what they want." She looked at me. "Do you have kids?"

"Not yet."

"I'm pregnant." She spoke as if Santa Monica didn't know. "My case is over. I thought that was the end of it. But I've caused this . . . *thing.* I can destroy the rest of my embryos before any laws change, but what about everyone else? How awful would it be if Prop 11 passed and it was all my fault?"

"It's not your fault. It's that Garner guy and fanatics. People won't vote for anything that extreme."

"That's what I tell myself, but what if I didn't do anything and it passed? I'd feel so guilty that I left this mess in the laps of people after me."

I was struck by the contrast of this woman to Julian.

"You're doing a lot."

"I feel puny in the face of it," was her uncanny reply.

"Puny acts can make a difference."

"Yours sure did. Thanks for saving me. I was shark bait."

"I was in the right place at the right time with the right amount of outrage."

"I was missing the outrage."

As I watched, exhaustion wiped her face like a wave.

There's a loading dock," I said. "I can show you how to slip out without being seen."

"You either like your privacy or find heavy lifting a turn on." She laughed. "You a spy?"

"No," I smiled. "An actress."

"Oh," she said. "That's harder."

I held out a hand. "Whenever you're ready."

"Dimple, what the hell?" Freya barked into the phone.

I jumped. I minimized the Single Mothers by Choice chat room, knowing it was ridiculous because Freya couldn't see through the phone. But she had scary Nordic prescience, so it never hurt to be careful.

"What did I do?"

"Rile up the religious right."

"What? Roxy's most controversial act this year has been changing lipstick."

"Not Roxy, *you*. On the news with Maryn Windsor, to be precise. What are you doing getting involved in that Proposition 11 mess?"

Uh-oh.

"Hold on." I navigated to YouTube. There I was, a determined Amazon extracting Maryn Windsor from a throng of reporters.

"Since when are you political? You've never used your name for so much as a puppy adoption, and now, of all the issues, you jump into an abortion fight?"

"It's not abortion, it's the right to use her frozen embryos. Her husband—"

"What it *is*, is a mess." Freya didn't pause this time. "The studio called and wants to know how far you're going to go with this."

Normally I'd fold. "I don't see why the studio has a right to tell me what I can do off the lot," was what came out.

"I . . ." Freya was momentarily derailed. "You want to get involved in this?" I could hear the gears whirring as she calculated how to make this benefit my career.

"I don't know." I didn't want to go too far. "I think she's

right. What they want is crazy and would hurt a lot of nice people who want children."

"I didn't know you thought at all about fertility rights." Freya wasn't trying to be unkind.

"It's sad. She can't have kids because of chemotherapy."

"She can always adopt."

"It's not the same."

"Children are children."

"Do Norwegian children come down an ice chute directly from God?"

"Odin, darling."

"Adopting puts you at the mercy of others. If you have the cash for fertility treatments, nothing stops you but science or God. Fragile Voices is trying to get in there where they don't belong."

"So you have an opinion."

"Those are only my thoughts. It's not like I took a stand or anything."

"According to Channel 9, local actress Dimple Bledsoe stood by Maryn Windsor in opposition to Proposition 11 today."

"That's nonsense. I pulled her out of the mob."

"Why?"

"It wasn't fair. She's an ordinary person going about her life."

"Darling, she filed the lawsuit. She's not an innocent victim in all this."

"Since when did everyone cosign to filleting our private lives for the public?"

"Since when don't we? We watch celebrity marriage, cheating, and divorce. We watch teen moms do homework, narcissists buy wedding dresses, and strangers give birth on handheld video cameras. People's obsession with the private lives of others keeps you in a job."

"It should be different when you're ordinary. Remember

when that family was snowbound in their car? They found the mom and kids, but the father had set out for help. We watched for days, hoping, until they found his body."

"I remember."

"CNN nailed its fortunes to that story, and rode it into the ground. It was at the gym, it was at work, it was even at Hama Sushi at dinner. That guy was the first guy I kissed in college and I couldn't escape that damn story."

"The coverage was sympathetic."

"It doesn't matter. I got to feel what it's like to be on the other side, when the story's personal but you didn't choose to be news. It's like being jabbed in the eye."

"So what are you saying, Dimple?" Freya was impatient. "Do you want to get involved in this Proposition 11 thing? If so, we need to do it properly. It's blowing up, with Fragile Voices jousting with placards against Lisa Edelstein and Sheryl Crow wielding microphones. We need to control your message."

"No." I wasn't ready for that. "I just wanted to help Maryn. She looked so small."

"Maybe getting involved isn't a bad thing. You looked alive again on the news. What were you doing at that clinic anyway?"

"Checkup." It wasn't a lie. Meeting with a social worker was a required prerequisite before insemination. I recalled the Pastor Martin Niemöller poem I'd quoted to Julian, *"Then they came for me, and there was no one left to speak out for me."*

"Maybe," I said, correcting my position. "Maybe I'll get involved. Proposition 11 is nuts."

"There's a big Prop 11/Andrew Knox fund-raising gala for Hollywood types this week. I'll get you on the list. If you want to go bigger, I'll make some calls and see what's there."

"I'll think about it." Look at what happened to Maryn.

"Dimple," Freya rebuked.

"I'm in," I said. "Sign me the uppest."

* * *

When Julian asked how my day had gone, I felt furtive. I didn't mention Maryn. Our fight about Proposition 11 had stayed with me.

"You seem distracted," he observed.

He spoke casually, but was focused intently on my face.

"I'm tired," I apologized.

"Finished?" He'd cooked linguini with clam sauce, and was clearing the plates. "I can tell you hated it." My plate was shining clean.

I said, "We don't go out much. Are we a secret?"

He was startled. "I don't know. Are we?"

My irritation dissipated. I'd been ready to accuse him, but when he bounced it back at me, I reconsidered.

"It's complicated." I took a cheap seat.

"I want to protect us both professionally," he said. "I also want to parade you everywhere."

"You do?"

His brow furrowed. "Who doesn't want the hottest chick on his arm?"

"You think I'm as hot as Estelle Getty?" I teased.

"Almost."

We were quiet.

"You're my date to the Directors Guild of America Awards Ceremony," he reminded me. "That's a coming out."

"What if I want you to be my date to something before that?"

"Willing prisoner." He held out his wrists.

I declined to mention that it was a gala for Proposition 11. The whole conversation made me anxious—going public was complicated by the ongoing *Cora* negotiations. What would exposure of our relationship do to my reputation? I didn't have the guts to ask him how to distinguish between audition and relationship. The lead in *Cora* was still dangling. I rubbed my temples.

"I can help you with that." Julian caressed my cheek.

I absolutely loved sex with Julian, but my skull was splitting. I wanted to plead *I have a headache,* but that made me want to kill myself. Instead of reaching for me, Julian turned to the refrigerator.

"I can't bake, but I wanted to give you oatmeal cookies and milk." He held out a pint of Ben and Jerry's Oatmeal Cookie Chunk ice cream.

My headache evaporated. All I could say was, "Oh."

"Let's take dessert into the den," He waggled two spoons at me. "I've been saving the *Twister* DVD for when you needed a blockbuster night."

As I followed Julian into the den, I couldn't describe my feelings, but they were intense and warm and scared the hell out of me.

Wyatt Has Nun of It

The call was so garbled it took Wyatt a moment to realize what he was hearing.

". . . mnaycouldnhuhh(sniff)dnsee(garble) . . . andthenand(sob) . . ."

"Maryn?"

"Wyatt . . ." Her wail wrapped a spiky blanket around his heart. The baby.

"Are you hurt? What's the matter?"

"I'm . . . not hurt. I'm . . . (deep breath) . . . God, I thought I was done crying. I was leaving my appointment and I was . . . *attacked.*"

"Did you call the police?" Wyatt was sweating. "Go right to the emergency room. Do you know who attacked you?" He looked for his keys.

"Not . . . that . . . kind of attack." He couldn't tell if she was laughing or crying or both. She blew her nose. "It was report-ers. Right in my face . . . showing everything . . . I couldn't breathe. I'm hiding. You have to come get me." She paused. "I couldn't breathe," she repeated, on a hiccup.

"Where are you?" Wyatt needed her to focus. He'd worry later about what her face was showing.

"The loading dock."

"I'm on my way."

Rush-hour traffic didn't do Wyatt any favors, but Maryn seemed calm when he found her perched on a filthy leveler. She slid into the passenger seat.

"Are you okay?"

She nodded. "I'm sorry I overreacted. I thought I'd pulled it together, but when I heard your voice, I lost it again. You're like a human neti pot."

"Don't be ridiculous. You had the response of a normal human being."

She rested her head, eyes closed. "I should've remembered how porous medical buildings are. It was one of the things that surprised me the most when I was sick, these warrens of hallways and exit doors and subterranean passages to loading docks. If you have balls and a reasonable sense of direction, there's no such thing as visiting hours. You can have the run of the hospital."

"Except where the babies are. Those parts are strict."

Maryn looked at him.

"What? I wouldn't steal a baby!" He faced the road. "That would *definitely* cost me my job." He was pleased to see a wan smile. "I should've gone with you. When you're ready, I want to hear what the doctor said." Wyatt cared for this woman and child as if they were his.

"Thank you, Wyatt."

"Do you want to get your car?"

She turned tired eyes toward him. "Can we get it tomorrow?"

"Of course."

After a moment, "My cancer is back."

Wyatt felt his heart freeze.

"I'll tell you all about it later," she said, head on the headrest, eyes closed. "Speaking of cancer, Webb Garner tipped off the reporters."

Wyatt gripped the steering wheel so hard his hands were bloodless. "What makes you say that?"

"My secretary said someone claiming to be from Hope Clinic called to straighten out schedule confusion. She confirmed my appointment time. After the ambush she did a reverse lookup on the caller ID and it was Garner's office. She feels terrible. He's such an asshole."

Wyatt controlled his rage and his voice. "What do you say to a nap, followed by Wyatt's special London broil?" Conversational. "Let me worry about Webb Garner."

Wyatt entered Garner's office with distinctly more glee than the last time.

"Ozols." A dismissive nod. "I don't see why we couldn't do this on the phone."

"I knew I'd enjoy seeing you." Wyatt's mood was buoyant.

"What's so all-fired important?" Garner looked at his watch. "I've got an appointment tonight, have to leave at seven o'clock sharp."

"Another speech?"

"What? Yeah. Always another campaign speech."

"It's diligent of you to whip the voters."

"What?" He squinted at Wyatt.

"Like in Congress, where the Whip gets out the vote."

Garner exhaled. "I appreciate your enthusiasm. Why are you here?"

"Thought I'd whip by for a chat."

Garner's eyes bugged. "What?"

"Should we ask the secretary to whip up some cappuccinos?"

"What the hell are you going on about? I don't have time for foolery, Ozols."

"I want you to stop bothering Maryn Windsor. She's ill." Wyatt got right to it.

"I don't know what you mean." The piggishness that crept into Garner's eyes made the bile rise in Wyatt's throat. "The crazy lady who sued Knox? Never met her."

Wyatt bent low, shoving his face into Garner's. "You will

not call her, you will not talk about her on television, you will not incite others to talk about her, and you will not alert reporters to her location. You will not speak her name out loud. You will not even think about her."

Garner got angry. "Who the hell are you to tell me what to do?"

"A friend of the lady."

"She must suck chrome off a bumper to get your dandy up to stupid like this. You know what happens to a knight on horseback coming at me with a lance? I shoot him with my Colt 45." Garner was smug. "Though I've had no contact with the woman, I'll decline your request. Now get out of my office. You're wasting my time."

"I wasn't asking. I was telling."

Garner's face went red. "No one tells Webb Garner what to do, especially a gay little cocksucker like you."

"I am rubber, you are glue, whatever you say bounces off me and sticks to you," Wyatt said. Garner looked at him like Wyatt had lost his mind. "Oh, wait." Wyatt furrowed his brow. "That's not right." He tossed a brown envelope on Garner's desk. "You're rubber."

Unsure whether to buzz security, Garner slid the eight-by-ten photographs out of the envelope. The play of emotions across his face was like a *Wild Kingdom* mash up. He lost color like an albino mole; squawked like a macaque; shifted like a sidewinder; puffed up like a bearded dragon; and, finally, snorted, a cornered wild boar pawing the ground with rage.

"What the hell kind of game are you playing, Ozols?"

"Nothing as fun as those games, I can assure you." He tapped a photo. "Though that one looks like it might smart a bit."

Garner's mouth opened, then closed, now a fish.

The trick with being invisible wasn't to smear dirt across your cheekbones or wear head-to-toe camouflage. It was to look exactly like everyone else. At a wedding, wear a little black dress and walk without hesitation to the bar. At a golf club, a sports jacket from Brooks Brothers is your costume. Loud madras pants can make you look as anonymous as a stocking over the face if you're on Nantucket. You want people to remember medium height, medium brown hair, kind of like Bob here. Wyatt had the advantage of having started out that way.

It was more difficult when you didn't know where you were going, but generic was generic. Wyatt donned dark jeans, brown shoes, black button-down, knockoff Oliver Peoples sunglasses, venti Starbucks. He *was* L.A. Man.

It wasn't particularly pleasant sitting in his car. Between clinic visits, board meetings, and outings with Maryn, Wyatt had been in his car more than he liked. The afternoon was hot and there was no breeze this far off the beach. He watched a softball game on the field next to where he was parked, but the coaching was angry and it irritated him so he had to stop. His assistant, Steff, called.

"I couldn't find that information," she said.

"Did you call his secretary?"

"I checked the School Board's online calendar; I called his secretary; I called the political reporters at the *Santa Monica Daily Press* and the *Santa Monica Mirror*; I spoke to his campaign; I spoke to the city clerk, who knows everything; I Googled. Nothing. Doughnuts. Webb Garner did not give a speech last Wednesday."

Wyatt had his Kindle, but it was hard to concentrate because he was hyperalert. A jogger, a mother picking up her softball player, a secretary leaving the School Board offices, all pulled him out of his reading.

He'd parked at four o'clock, opting to be mind-bogglingly early than risk missing it. Other men might have questioned themselves around the three-hour mark, but not Wyatt. Garner had lied and Wyatt was going to find out why. He hadn't been

overseer of a self-contained population of the world's most con-
niving and devious social elements without learning a trick or
two. When Wyatt was on his game, he felt himself equal to
outwitting Dr. No, never mind a walk-in-the-park villain like
Webb Garner.

At 7:14, Webb Garner exited the building and got into his
Honda Odyssey. Wyatt worried he'd be a clumsy tail, but
Garner kept driving, oblivious. They crawled along I-10 so
slowly they could have conversed if they'd rolled down the
windows. Garner exited at La Brea, driving north along the
eastern border of West Hollywood, passing Pink's hot dogs,
with its ever-twisting line, and the clumps of tourists stam-
peding Hollywood Boulevard to Grauman's Chinese Theatre.

Wyatt concentrated as the road became La Brea Terrace
with its gated entry. At the guardhouse, he gestured to Garner's taillights. "Same." The trick was not to overplay it. The
guard waved him through.

He followed Garner from a greater distance through a
series of twists and turns. The cloistered setting increased Wyatt's confidence that "something was up." If Garner had had a
legitimate invitation to quaff from the golden teat of a La Brea
Terrace address, he'd have blared it to the world.

The house was unlike others on the block. Most were
completely shielded by cypress, the dwelling equivalent of a
mink coat. This address had a wide cobbled drive like an Italian square, and a central fountain surrounded by eight or so
parked cars. The structure was a replica of an old rectory, but
the construction was new. It didn't look right to Wyatt somehow. It wasn't the shiny BMWs and Hummers in the Old World
setting. The whole image was conceptually askew. Like a Gre-
cian goddess in Kate Spade flip-flops.

The front door opened as Garner parked, and a robed gentleman ushered him inside. Wyatt eased into the driveway. It
could be trouble if this was one of those Skull and Bones soci-

eties, but Wyatt decided that (a) there was only one way to find out, and (b) he doubted Garner would be invited to a power-elite gathering. There'd be no Honda Odysseys in that parking lot. Wyatt's Prius would also be absent.

A suited concierge materialized to open Wyatt's car door.

"Welcome." The man swept his hand to the entrance. "Absolution awaits."

Wyatt felt a stab of panic. He hadn't considered a religious cult. He wished he'd told Eva where he was going. He appreciated the value of the buddy system.

He nodded at the attendant and approached the front door, where the robed man, a monk, awaited.

"Welcome, my son."

Wyatt nodded again, appreciating the currency of nonverbal answers.

"How can we assist your repentance and salvation this evening?"

A woman wearing a rubber nun's habit crossed behind the monk. It was shiny black, ended well above the knee, and squeaked when she walked. She had to have been born wearing it, or been poured in.

Ah.

"This is my first time seeking absolution here, Brother," Wyatt said. "Is there a shepherd to guide me? Perhaps one of your Sisters?" Wyatt wanted a woman.

"Follow me."

Another nun walked by, this one's rubber habit even shorter and squeakier, and she was wearing a World War II gas mask. When she saw Wyatt, she folded her hands in prayer, and bowed.

The "monk" led Wyatt down a richly carpeted hallway, its walls of stone decorated with a hodgepodge of religious iconography, as well as whips and other torture devices. Wyatt noticed that a few displays were empty, the contents presumably in use, and admired the building's soundproofing. They stopped at an arched doorway with an ornate iron handle, which opened to an office occupied by grey metal filing cabinets and a woman dressed in a black suit that, if Wyatt didn't know better, was Armani. There was that dissonance again, the glimpse of a jogging bra under a Renaissance costume.

"I'm Sister Heavenly Body." The woman of about fifty held out an elegant hand. She wore no jewelry or nail polish. Her hair was in a chic coil, not a single strand abandoning the effort. Her body was heavenly. "Please have a seat. What brings you to the Temple?"

"I'm looking for some redemption, Sister, and I have difficulty finding the specific kind of absolution I seek"—he gestured—"out there."

"I am sure we can help you on your quest." She handed him a folder. "Here's a little information on our services, as well as the offering we request in return."

"Are you Catholic?"

"We are no religion and every religion. We specialize in helping lost souls who seek a direct relationship with God through forgiving and accommodating women of the veil. Our Sisters can be tutored by you, as you offer them specific instruction, or they are happy to take command and be firm in leading you to your salvation. We aim to please you, and discretion is paramount. The tithes we request vary according to the demands of the service."

"I'm surprised I haven't heard of the opportunities here before."

"I assure you that we are licensed and bonded for the entertainment we provide, completely in compliance with the law. I'm very strict with my girls on personal health and hygiene. Cleanliness is next to godliness." A glint of humor in her perfectly made-up eyes. "Taking the veil is a serious decision, so I require all my girls to be at least twenty-one, with documentation."

"And what about the neighbors?"

That amused spark again. "I am the neighbors. This is my place of business. My home is next door."

Wyatt considered his options. He could continue down this alarming path in hopes of catching Garner in compromising penitence. He could skulk around outside and photograph him leaving, hoping circumstantial evidence would be sufficient. Or he could tell the truth. The risk was that once his cover was blown, he wouldn't get another bite at the communion wafer.

Wyatt had always been a fan of the truth. Sister Heavenly Body listened without expression.

"I cannot confirm the identity of any of our clientele, no matter the circumstances."

"I would testify as much in the unlikely event that my knowledge of the situation came to light. You are unassailably discreet."

"I don't get involved in politics, or make character judgments about my clients." She paused. "No matter how unpopular they are with the Sisters."

Wyatt saw the crack and went for it.

"My concern is with the well-being of an innocent victim. She's pregnant, and she has breast cancer. Her life is rotten enough without being targeted for abuse by a cruel man. It's a bonus to society at large if this villain also happens to be prevented from achieving higher public office."

"I would not judge any man for his enjoyment of my services."

"Nor I. His corruption of character comes from his use of people as capital to serve his own ends." They were speaking in the hybrid language pervading the place, tongue both modern and ancient.

Sister Heavenly Body was silent for a moment. "She has breast cancer?"

"Second time. She's refusing treatment until the baby is born. It's been incredibly tough on her."

"My mother had breast cancer." Fine lines tightened around her mouth.

They both waited.

"I'm afraid I could never violate the privacy of one of my clients." She sat back. Wyatt's heart sank. "It was very upsetting last year when one client inadvertently witnessed the private session of another client because he stumbled into an observation room without my awareness."

She looked directly at him.

"Now, would you like to engage in a session?"

"I would like that very much." He did not break her gaze. "I'll tithe in advance if you'll tell me the amount."

"Very well. If you think you can manage, I don't believe you'll need an escort to find your way. You should exit the office and go up one level. Proceed down the hallway to the room labeled Vestal Virgin. Please go directly there, and under no circumstances open any other doors or enter any other rooms. Be particularly careful not to enter the unmarked door just past the room labeled Pandora's Box."

"I'm looking forward to this experience, Sister," Wyatt said as he took out his wallet.

She laughed. "Funnily enough, so am I."

"You are a blessed vessel." Wyatt stood to leave.

Sister Heavenly Body said, "I don't know if I believe in divine retribution, but I do know karma is a bitch."

The photos turned out great.

* * *

"I didn't know you were a religious man, Webb," Wyatt said now, admiring them scattered across Garner's desk.

"You don't know who you're messing with!" Garner gritted out.

"It *is* rather hard to tell with those rubber gas masks. Nun the less . . ." Wyatt drew out the pause. "I think audiences will recognize those familiar cheeks. And your less familiar ones . . ." He dropped all joviality. "So we're going to do things my way, or KCAL Channel 9 news has a wet dream."

Garner swallowed.

"Now that," Wyatt gestured at a photo, "is one bad habit. Nun too holy, I'd say." He really was enjoying himself too much.

"I'm going to mop the floor with your face." Garner tried to sound menacing.

"You won't be able to get into the corners very well."

"Do you know who you're dealing with?" He was apoplectic.

"The worst cliché ever." Wyatt grinned. "Bar nun."

The vein on Garner's temple throbbed. "Shut your fucking mouth!"

"Nun of that foul language," Wyatt reprimanded. "Here's how it's going to be. You will never, ever contact Maryn Windsor or in any way cause her so much as a whisper of distress. You're going to withdraw from the City Council election effective immediately. As it turns out, you think Knox is a capable public servant, and you desire to spend more time with your family. However, you're going to oppose Proposition 11. Are you getting all this or do you need a pencil?"

Wyatt's stern principal's voice broke Garner. He slumped and nodded.

"Good," Wyatt continued. "For the duration of your tenure on the School Board, you'll maintain a low profile. You will not introduce proposals, curriculum changes, budget cuts, or two strangers. At the end of your term, you'll retire. Just can't get enough of that family. You will fade out of Santa Monica politics entirely, not organizing so much as a clambake. In return, my memory will fade over time. I'll forget things, and I'll misplace things. As long as you keep your end of the bargain, I'll keep mine." He winked. "The world will be nun the wiser."

Wyatt hoped he wouldn't get winged when Garner's eyeballs blew out of their sockets.

"You hate the local news," Maryn protested.

"I'm inclined to watch it tonight."

"Your headache." Maryn shrugged, and switched on the TV.

Webb Garner filled the screen. *"It is with regret yet conviction that I cede the race for City Council to Andrew Knox. After deep deliberation, I believe that I am called to remain focused on our schools. I have three children of my own, and they need me to speak for them"*—he looked directly into the camera—*"to speak for you, on the most important factor in the future of our great country. Education. I cannot in good conscience abandon the School Board at this critical time. The time isn't right for Proposition 11. We must focus on today's children, not tomorrow's. I look forward to this duty in my role as President of the Unified School Board."*

Reporters clamored with questions, surging toward him, but he waved them off, fleeing into the School Board building.

It wasn't everything Wyatt wanted, but it was enough.

"How did you know?" Maryn demanded.

"He won't bother you again." Wyatt was satisfied.

"Did you do something?"

"It turns out Garner's desire to see his name in the paper had limits."

"Don't play. Tell me what happened."

"Behind every successful man is a woman. Behind the fall of every successful man is usually another woman."

"Oh god."

"Something like that."

Eva Goes to a Party

"W elcome!"
The straw-haired woman with pale lipstick was vaguely familiar to Eva. It took a minute to place her as the weather girl.

"We're so glad you came!" She held out her hand.

I'll bet, thought Eva. There were a lot of zeros on that check.

"Eva Lytton." She shook.

"Summer Knox. My husband Andrew is the Democratic candidate for City Council."

The woman became mildly interesting to Eva, and in barbaric society she might have asked what she really thought about destroying a cancer survivor's embryos. This was polite society, however, so she said, "Glad to be here."

She *was*. A reliable source had assured her Julian Wales was attending.

"Garner may be out of the race, but Prop 11 is a live threat," Summer continued. "For every donor to Stop the Prop, a postcard is sent to Donnie Brownlow of Fragile Voices, notifying him that a donation was made in his name to support efforts to defeat Proposition 11," Summer Knox chirped.

"Wonderful." Eva started edging past.

"There are three bars," her eager hostess indicated. "Enjoy the party!"

Eva was already gone. She was here to work. She was tired of being harassed by Daisy, and the sooner she put this *Cora* deal to bed, the sooner she could focus on clients she liked.

She circled the large room. It was crowded, a muted hum of conversation, clinking glassware, and a jazz combo in the air. The crowd was upscale, with a fair smattering of celebrities and a larger dollop of reality stars seeking limelight with a side of cause. Eva recognized a number of faces, but waved and looked away, hunting intently for one she didn't yet see.

A bald head bobbed above the crowd. The man was so tall, it had to be Julian. The head was on the move. Eva started after it.

"Excuse me, pardon me." She navigated the crowd. He was outpacing her, but she wasn't worried. They were in a ballroom, where could he go?

She broke through the crowd, and spotted Julian disappearing into the foyer. She hurried across the lobby, reaching him as he slipped into the men's bathroom.

Frustrated, she stared at the closed door with the little man on it.

"Not likely." Eva would not be "popping out of a urinal" as Daisy had urged.

"Excuse me?" The man behind her eyed her curiously.

"Sorry." She stepped away from the door.

It was fine. She had all night. She might as well talk to a Disney producer she'd spotted about her new preteen talent. First, she needed a drink.

"Grey Goose and tonic," Eva ordered when she reached the bar.

The bartender nodded. "And for you?" He nodded to a woman on her right.

"Club soda and lime, please," a familiar voice answered.

Eva turned. "Dimple!"

Dimple Bledsoe looked up and smiled. "Eva?" It was there again. That radiance.

"Right in one." Eva noted Dimple's drink. "Unleaded?" Eva nodded toward the club soda.

"Is it totally dorky that I wanted a Shirley Temple but was too embarrassed to ask?" Dimple sipped. "I should've at least gotten a cherry."

Eva grinned. "I recently came out of the closet about loving hot dogs."

"Fast, cheap, and tasty. There's no shame in it. Everyone's got their Trekkie thing, an unabashed love of something decidedly nerdy."

"What's yours?"

"Broadway musicals. Love 'em. Sing 'em in the shower, in my car, in my trailer. Billy Joel too. The Billy Joel musical was my mother ship."

Eva thought for a moment. "Headbands. The *Alice in Wonderland* kind. They make my button nose look adorable. And sugar cereals. I had a date who opened my cabinets and asked if I had a kid—Cap'n Crunch, Cocoa Puffs, Fruity Pebbles, Honey Smacks, Lucky Charms. I eat the marshmallows out of the Lucky Charms because I'm a selfish bitch."

"Got kids?"

"Only my clients." It slipped out before Eva thought. She didn't want to lie to Dimple, so she changed the subject. "How's work going for you?"

"Interesting! I'm getting some really good material."

"It's good to see your current troubles aren't weighing you down."

"Troubles?" Dimple was confused.

"Drinking problem? Passing out while baking and setting your house on fire?" Eva prompted.

"Oh, *Roxy!*" Dimple seemed surprised herself to have forgotten. "Yeah, she's hoeing a rough row right now. But, you know, next week she'll save someone in rehab or cure Alzheimer's."

Eva wondered what work Dimple had been thinking about.

"Look at all this fabulous food." Dimple eyed the buffet. "I'm starving."

A peek at Dimple's abdomen was unrevealing.

"I always think I should bring my old lunch box to these events and fill it up for tomorrow. Mine was Herself the Elf." It was never appropriate to ask a person their age, but knowing their lunch box gave Eva about a four-year guesstimate. Josie and the Pussycats was hot in 1972, while Strawberry Shortcake peaked in '84. Eva was increasingly curious about how old Dimple was. "How about you?"

"Brown paper sacks." Dimple laughed. "My PBJs all got smushed by the apple."

As Dimple grazed, Eva eyed the room.

"It's quite a turnout."

"I'm thrilled. I think Prop 11 is scary. No one should control embryos but the parents."

"Are you very involved?" Eva wondered if Dimple had a personal stake in this.

"No. With the exception of that Feel Your Boobies breast cancer PSA, I haven't done anything political. Most of the time I'm so overwhelmed by all the things I want to change, I do nothing. Like if you started caring, it would crush you to death. But I met Maryn Windsor and it really affected me. If people insist on putting me in magazines, it should be for something good, not eating lunch."

Eva felt a little guilty. Maryn was Wyatt's friend and she hadn't given the issue much thought. She resolved to talk to him about it later.

"What are you going to do?"

"I'm not sure, but that's why I came. Showing up's a good start." She laughed. "Let me tell you, I'm already working for it. I had to arm-wrestle Julian here."

Eva was careful not to react. "Julian Wales?"

"Mm-hm." The actress didn't meet her eyes. "We had a dinner meeting scheduled, but I dragged him here instead."

"Is he campaigning?"

"Lord no. For Julian PSA is a professional sports affinity. He'll tell you ad nauseam that he's here under duress. He doesn't like being political offscreen."

"It's funny because his films are unafraid to be controversial."

Dimple pondered this. "I wouldn't say he's afraid to be controversial. I think he's horrified at being unoriginal. If he's going to stir the pot, it has to be his recipe. Me, I don't mind being the player, not the coach."

"I wonder what Julian's Trekkie thing would be." Eva was curious how well Dimple knew him.

She grinned. "Late-model hatchbacks."

"Is he hiding in the bathroom? I haven't seen him." Eva scanned the crowd.

"If there's an old lady in the room, he's talking to her." Dimple looked around. "See? He's over there with that woman who looks like Betty White."

Eva squinted. "That is Betty White."

Julian looked up and saw them watching. Eva tensed, but he only had eyes for Dimple. His smile was bright as he excused himself and headed their way.

Eva was trapped. Her night's mission was cornering Julian Wales, and he was coming right to her. But she couldn't discuss *Cora* in front of Dimple. It was Eva's preference, for the moment, that Dimple not realize she was Daisy Carmichael's agent.

"Is that really the time?" Eva feigned consternation. "I'm sorry, Dimple, I've got a strict policy on leaving before the speeches. I've so enjoyed our chat, but I can't stay. I hope I'll see you again soon."

"Likewise." Eva was nonplussed when Dimple gave her

a quick, warm hug. It was not unpleasant. "Shoo. That perky woman's heading for the microphone."

Eva hurried away. She'd meant what she'd said about seeing Dimple again. She liked her. She didn't, however, like Dimple's effortless familiarity with Julian. Eva stopped at the edge of the room and looked back. Julian had reached Dimple's side, and stood close, bent to catch what she was saying. He threw his head back and laughed, arm slung over her shoulder, pulling her closer as he whispered into her temple and Dimple blushed.

It didn't look like a professional acquaintance at all.

Andy Doesn't Go to a Party

The television news announcer droned while Andy flopped on the couch. He loosened his tie before cracking a can of Miller Lite. Even though Garner had withdrawn and his case with Maryn was over, the Prop 11 frenzy had a bloodsucking life of its own. He was drained from keeping up appearances at work, last night's gala, and the four or more "important dinners" Summer scheduled every week. He didn't have time to exercise, which made him cranky.

"Don't you want a Dogfish Head IPA?" Summer always tried converting him to fancy microbrewed beers.

"No."

"You look like my uncle Kenny, who drank cheap beer right from the can at the dinner table," Summer snipped.

Andy ignored her. He didn't feel like pouring his beer into a glass when he was in his living room. Summer knew how he felt, so he guessed she was in a bad mood too. Normally he'd try to make her feel better but tonight he didn't feel like it.

"*. . . a three-alarm fire at a popular Mexican eatery on Lincoln . . .*"

Andy didn't like local news. They delivered trite and irrelevant regional stories instead of actual news. He liked his daily news quotient from CNN. Summer wanted to watch KCAL Channel 9 News for Santa Monica election coverage. They watched KCAL, of course.

"We have to leave in twenty minutes for the Starlight reception. Mayor Villaraigosa will be there."

"He'll be there when we get there." Andy didn't want to go

anywhere near the Starlight reception. He didn't want to meet
the Mayor of Los Angeles. He wanted to stay home in his socks
and drink beer from the can.

"Andrew, people spend all year in agony over whether
they'll get an invite to this gala."

"... *sunny and clear tomorrow, with temperatures dropping in
the afternoon ...*"

Andy ignored her. Summer opened her mouth, then closed
it. She knew the limits of pushing when he was in this kind of
mood. She'd win, of course. But not until after this beer.

"... *and in sad news today, local businesswoman Maryn Windsor has suffered a relapse of breast cancer.*"

The beer can slipped from Andy's nerveless fingers as he
sat upright, but neither he nor Summer paid attention to it
emptying its foamy contents onto the carpet.

"*Windsor achieved notoriety suing for her right to use embryos
that were contested marital property following her divorce. Infertile
after treatment for breast cancer, Windsor petitioned for the right to
implant embryos fertilized by her ex-husband, local attorney and city
council candidate Andrew Knox. Knox countersued to have the eggs
destroyed.*"

The pretty, bland newscaster delivered the pain of his life
as coolly and remotely as if she was reporting on a shamrock
shortage.

"*The case sparked national attention, and conflict over controversial Proposition 11, which would legally prohibit the destruction
of fertilized eggs in Santa Monica and require the treatment of such
eggs as children under the custody laws of California. Windsor ulti-
mately resolved her case out of court, and became pregnant as a result
of implanting the embryos. KCAL has learned that Windsor has suffered a recurrence of her breast cancer. Her prognosis at this time is
unknown.*"

The newscaster paused, glancing at her papers. Memory
refreshed, she concluded with, "*We all wish her the best. In other*

news, one Santa Monica beauty salon has gone to the dogs. Literally, that is. Nails 'N Tails on Main Street is offering simultaneous beauty treatments for pet owners and their dogs . . ."

Andy could sense Summer staring, but he couldn't look at her. Shock radiated through his body, and his hands felt numb. It had to be a mistake. If it was true, he would know. Wouldn't he? He had to talk to Maryn. He got to his feet and shuffled to the hall, up the stairs, to the bedroom. He shut the door. He sat on the bed. One action at a time, carefully measured. He dug out his phone. She would still be at work. He dialed.

"Maryn Windsor." It startled Andy how fast her voice came on the line. Did he imagine a new tiredness there?

"It's Andy," was all he could manage.

She waited, wary. "What's up?"

"The news . . . I saw . . . the cancer . . . is it true?" His voice cracked.

"It was on the freaking news? Are you kidding me?" Maryn's voice rose six octaves, and only through familiarity could he detect the distress beneath the outrage.

"Are you really sick?" He could hear adolescent pleading in his tone, begging her to refute the story, but he couldn't help himself.

"I don't know what they said, but it is true that my doctor has detected some cancerous cells. What do you want, Andy?" Her voice was hard. Andy was confused. Why was she angry with him?

"I wanted to hear it from you. I want you to be okay." He felt helpless trying to find the right words because he didn't really know what words he wanted.

Her tone softened some, but not a lot. "The baby and I are both fine. I've met with several specialists and am considering treatment options."

Andy had forgotten all about the baby.

"Can you still have the baby?"

"There are numerous options that won't hurt her."

Her. Andy's fumbling brain absorbed the fact that the baby was a girl, but all he could think of was the smell and the sick of Maryn's previous treatments. It had seemed violent. Not anything that would leave room for a baby.

"But . . ."

"It's not really your concern, Andy." The defensive edge returned to her voice. Andy felt slapped. She was right, of course. But wasn't she wrong too? Weren't they irrevocably connected since the day they'd said their vows? Wasn't he central in everything major, even long after the divorce?

"I'll figure it out and the baby and I will both be fine. I said I would handle this completely on my own, and that remains true even under the current circumstances. You needn't concern yourself."

Andy realized where the crispness was coming from. "Maryn, I'm not trying to take over any part of your baby." Andy meant it. He wondered if it should be hard for him not to say "our" baby, but it wasn't. It didn't feel like his baby at all. "I'm only concerned about you."

She hesitated. "Thank you." Her voice was more kind. Then she sighed. "I mean it, Andy. I appreciate the call."

"I'm sorry that—well, *everything*—made you feel that I'm a threat to you, Maryn," Andy said. "Please don't think that. Whatever you decide about you and the baby, I'll support you. I just want you to get better."

"From a distance," Maryn teased.

"From a distance," Andy promised.

They were quiet.

"Will you promise to call if you need anything?" Andy asked.

"Okay," Maryn agreed after a moment.

"And keep me posted?"

"Yes."

"Thanks."

They hung up, leaving Andy wondering how the conversation had concluded with him once again thanking Maryn for taking care of things.

He stretched out on the bed, mind surprisingly empty. He probed, searching for fear, sorrow. There was a quiet tap at the door before Summer peeked in.

"Andy?" Her voice was hesitant as she edged into the room.

"I don't want to go out tonight." Andy said the first thing he thought of.

"What?" Summer was startled. "Of course not. Don't even think about it."

He didn't stir. She crawled across him, and he stretched out his arm so she could tuck her head into the crook of his shoulder as she lay beside him.

"Are you okay?" she asked.

He nodded.

They were quiet for a few minutes, when inexplicably Summer began to cry.

"Hey," Andy turned toward her. "What's that about?"

"I'm sorry," Summer sniffled. "I'm sorry. It's so sad and I know you're sad, and I wish I could feel sad, but I can't. I'm so sorry, Andy, but I didn't know her. I don't know her at all. And I want to feel bad, I really want to, because it's cancer and it sucks, but I can't! I don't feel anything!" She was crying harder now, and Andy squeezed her closer, gazing at the ceiling again.

"It's okay, pigeon," he shushed.

His own thoughts tumbled. At least Summer knew what she felt. Andy kept searching for his feelings. He didn't like the one that kept sneaking in.

Andy wasn't a religious man. He understood that original sin meant everyone was born in depravity, but he didn't believe that. How could anyone look at a baby and think that? Some evil must come from original sin, though, because how else could an uncontrollable part of him whisper terribly, *It would be nice if Maryn died*.

If Maryn died of cancer, Andy's pain would have an end. It wouldn't live down the street, raising a child, marrying someone else, walking around connected to tiny unbreakable fishhooks embedded in Andy. He could take all his pain at once, and be released from the coils of regret and guilt. He would be free.

Dimple Chooses

W hen you create, it's your job to have mind-blowing, irresponsible, condomless sex with whatever idea it is you're writing about at the time," Julian said.

"That's deep."

"Lady Gaga said it first."

We were having dinner at Julian's. I was at home in the embedded flying saucer now.

"When you act, it's sublimation and control in equal parts," I said. "You want to get into the character but not lose control of the performance."

"What do you do with the other two-thirds of your brain when you're shooting *Pulse*?" he joked.

"Are you insulting sweet Roxy?" My voice was light, but his jibe stung.

"Three things make me a drag." Julian held up three fingers. "I feel superior to anything with background music in it. I mock things I don't understand. I have disproportionate guilt about these things. I'm sorry if I was rude to Roxy. I'm slightly in envy of the popularity of *Pulse*."

"How can you not like background music?"

"Background music tells you how to feel. It's a cheap shortcut."

"If you took the background music out of *The Shining*, it would be a movie about watching Jack Nicholson type."

"All lo mein and no ice cream makes Dimple a dull girl." He stood, taking my empty plate. "Dessert in the living room?"

Julian clicked a remote and the room swelled with Debussy.

"Background music?" I was arch.

"How else can I get to the mind-blowing condomless sex?" He pulled me onto the couch. *Any damn way he wants*, I thought.

After a bit and all the buttons on my blouse, I pulled back, panting. "About that condom . . ."

"Right," he murmured. "Good idea." The only move he made was down my chest.

"Julian," I gasped.

"Hm?" His tongue was exploring my naval.

"You want to keep that belly button, don't you?"

"Ffngtmly." His response was muffled.

I fought for focus. "It disappears when I'm knocked up."

"Worst ever."

"What?" I was startled.

"What?" He looked up at me.

"What are we talking about?"

"Bad movies?" He was confused.

"Getting pregnant," I corrected. He nipped my belly and unfolded himself from the couch.

"Definitely don't want that."

I felt exposed with my nipples open to the vacant air. "Not now at least."

"You don't want kids." He looked surprised as he returned from the bathroom.

"Of course I do." I matched his surprise. "Why would you think I didn't?" An earthworm of worry squiggled within me.

"Well . . . you're an actress, and you're . . . not thirty. And you've never talked about it." He was befuddled. "I assumed you'd chosen not to."

"That's a big assumption."

"At your age, most women who want them already have them."

"I still have time." My voice was too loud. "I could have a baby tomorrow."

"Do you really want that?"

"I . . ." I floundered. I *did* want that. I also wanted *Cora*. And I wanted Julian. I wanted them all together in a tidy teenybopper dream with a pink pom-pom on top. I was sick at my own stupidity. "Don't you want kids?" The answer was obvious.

"No." He shook his head for double good measure.

I buttoned my blouse. "I see." I saw that I'd been carried away by fantasy. Julian was right about the prefabricated imagery left me by the movies of my youth. Would I have been wiser without the swell of Simple Minds cuing a happy ending?

"It would ruin your career."

"You don't know that." I was angry. "And if I decided not to have a family based on my career, I'd feel pretty stupid at forty-five when work was over and I was scrapbooking about my cat."

"I never saw this side of you before."

"This side of me? I'm not a frenzied, walking ovary, Julian. I'd consider myself averagely maternal, at best. I reject your implication that the compulsion to reproduce has lurked like a shadowy lever puller behind every decision."

"Maybe the fact that you've waited means you really don't want children? Your id is battling social programming." He was like a child, grabbing at straws.

"I'm not a movie plot, Julian. I'm a mature woman who wants to have a child before she can't." His resistance was cooling molten flow into solid decisions for me. "I was giving myself time for things to happen organically before I had to make difficult decisions."

I stood and put on my shoes.

"You're leaving?" Disbelief.

"I think so." My gut was torn.

"You're walking out on this relationship the first time we disagree?"

"This isn't a 'disagreement' and this isn't a relationship. It's some weird hybrid audition-date." I was frustrated.

"I'm giving *Cora* to Daisy." He was abrupt.

I was stunned. "There's more raw emotion resonating off that empty Chinese food carton than Daisy Carmichael."

"I can't remain objective around you. You've invaded my brain. I smell you when you're not there. You're the woman a director wants to have on his side of the lens."

"For a guy who claims he's bad at grammar, the complex architecture of your sentences makes it impossible to tell if I'm included in your future."

"How the hell do I know anymore? I thought we were look- ing at a future together, but I don't want kids."

"I do." There. I'd said it, plain and simple, strong pairing of noun and verb.

"You know why I don't want to talk about dogs?" he asked.

I was thrown by the resumption of a conversation we'd begun months ago.

"I love dogs. I've always loved dogs. When I was young I pictured a life surrounded by dogs." I was startled by the stark pain in his eyes. "My mom said I wasn't responsible enough. My goldfish floated, I accidentally stepped on my hamster, I left the cat out one night and a coyote got it. My mom said I didn't think about anything but what was on my mind at the moment. I thought weaker animals had bad luck. I was meant to be a dog owner. So I waited. As soon as I was out of college, I got the fanciest dogs I could.

"Wilder and Welles were the most beautiful German shep- herds you've ever seen. Their bloodlines were perfect, their proportions a golden mean." He was looking somewhere inside as he spoke.

"I took them everywhere. I only parted with them for three months of training camp, and I couldn't sleep, I missed them so much. I was off balance without them. God, I loved those dogs." He rubbed his hand over his eyes.

"My first movie was *Fallow*. It was a low-dollar flick—no dollar, really—about a family farm. We were shooting in Sand Canyon in August and having all this trouble because there was a record heat wave baking Los Angeles." He looked at me intensely. "I *knew* it. I knew it was hot as hell. I was dealing with the problems it was causing on location daily."

My throat closed. I didn't want to hear this story.

"On Saturday, one of my producers called. There was an issue with a vendor contract and I needed to sign a new one. I was driving home from hiking in Temescal Canyon, so I swung by the production office."

He swallowed, his story hard fought.

"I was only going to be a minute." His eyes were pleading. "Sixty seconds to sign the paper, so I cracked the windows and ran in. But there was a problem. People were calling, and there was arguing, and we were trying to solve the issue so we could film Monday . . ." He broke down. I waited as he drew jagged breaths, face buried in his hands.

"I'll never forget the moment I remembered. It felt like a second, but it had been an hour. I didn't believe the clock. I ran." His eyes moist, Julian looked past me. "I never prayed so hard in my life. I bargained with God. I'd do anything if he'd let them be okay. They'd be the most spoiled dogs on earth. I'd give all my money to shelters. I'd dedicate my life to animal protection." He swallowed. "But God doesn't coddle fools."

I couldn't look at him.

His voice was bleak. "They didn't go easy."

The mental image of shredded upholstery, protruding tongues, and smeared windows would never leave my mind. I was nauseous.

"Innocent creatures died the most horrible way imaginable, and it was my fault. I was distracted by shit I don't even remember while they roasted."

Neither of us said anything for a long time. When he spoke again his voice was flat.

"I can't forget, and I don't want to. My mother was right. All my life I've been selfish, and what happened to Wilder and Welles set me straight. I can't be responsible for anything. I'm worthless at it."

Emotions warred in me. Sorrow. Horror. Exhaustion.

"I'm sorry about your dogs." He looked broken. I didn't lay a soothing hand on his nape. I stood and picked up my sweater.

"You're leaving?" he asked in disbelief.

"Not because you killed your dogs," I said as gently as I could.

"Why?"

"Did you tell me that story to explain why you don't want children?"

"Isn't it obvious?"

I faced him. "Your dogs died and you think you ruin everything you touch."

"It's not as if I had a sudden revelation when Wilder and Welles died that I couldn't be trusted with children. The veneer popped off what was already there. I'd *always* been careless with others. Their death made me look backward and see an inattentive son, an offhand boyfriend, a cavalier friend. It didn't transform me, it exposed me."

"That's narcissistic and crazy."

My reaction was not what he expected.

"I'm truly sorry about your dogs. That must have been horrible. I'm ill hearing about it, and I can't imagine what you went through. But causing the death of your dogs doesn't expose you as deficient. Using it as a shield against future responsibility does. It's bullshit."

I started to walk out the door.

"Wait." Julian was stunned. "I'm telling you this because I care about you, about us. I want you to understand."

"Understand what? That every time something important happens you'll dodge accountability? That your house, your car, your jokes are elaborate sets? You aren't a grown-up accepting responsibility for your actions. You're a kid hiding behind a romantic story."

"You think it's romantic?" he roared. I flinched.

"I don't. I think it's awful. I'll never get those animals out of my head, and there's a liquor drink in my future so I can sleep tonight. You're courageous for telling me. But I don't think one event can permanently cauterize your emotional ability. You're choosing not to make even puny efforts."

"Women may not hit harder, but they sure hit lower." He sneered.

"What do you want me to say, Julian?"

"You live in denial. You won't go to the emergency room when there's a fishhook embedded in your skin. Do you really see yourself as Mother Hale? Are you going to hand your children a splint when they break an arm? The shiny celluloid fantasy you've built around the idea of kids won't match your life."

My skin was hot. "Are you done?"

"Guess you don't want rescuing from that cult after all."

"We're all one small adjustment from making our lives work," I said. "I intend to keep making them until I get it right."

He dropped his bravado. "Did anything I said mean something to you?" He looked lost.

"Past failures aren't going to hold me back from what I want, Julian," I said. "And that includes this one." I walked out the door.

"It's a shame." Justine was sad when I told her. Work was over and we were sitting in the salon truck. Justine was brushing my hair out of reflex. "He could have been on the receiving end of your cakes."

"That's not me," I reminded her. "That's Roxy."

I was feeling less like Roxy and more like myself than I had in years. Whatever Julian's faults, he was on to something with the extreme sports. Floundering out of my comfort zone acted like a kiln, hardening a core out of something soft. I counted our relationship as one of our extreme-sport outings.

"He's a good person, but he isn't ready to grow up. He's break dancing through his fifteen minutes, which will probably be fifteen million minutes, because he's really talented. He should enjoy himself. We want different things."

I was lying. I missed him like a puncture. But he didn't have a clue about what he wanted, and I didn't want to go backward. His dogs had moved into my head too, the images haunting, but my reaction was the opposite.

I felt something akin to relief. No more Julian, no more *Cora*. My choices were simplified. It was swinging without a net, and I had no idea if I was equipped, but I had to try. We don't leave ourselves only one option if we aren't prepared to take it. My subconscious had shown faith in my future self all along.

"I'm going to have a baby," I said.

Justine froze, brush midair. "Julian's baby?"

"Definitely not. That was the problem."

"But you're pregnant?"

"As soon as I ovulate, hopefully."

"With, um . . ." Justine's face went through six expressions as she worked it out.

"A turkey baster." I laughed. "At Hope Clinic."

"What about Roxy?" Justine was still processing.

"I don't think she's pregnant, but I predict a future of unflattering empire-waisted garments," I said.

"Are you worried they'll write you out?" Anxious.

"I hope she'll be fine, but it's more important that I live than Roxy does."

"You're going to do it alone?"

"I would have preferred a different outcome, but it didn't work out. I don't have time to wait. I'm sure of my decision."

"How long have you been planning this?"

"I've had at least twenty plans that seem ridiculous now. I'm figuring out that I don't know anything, so planning is limited to one day at a time."

"Don't you worry . . ." She hesitated.

"Ask," I commanded. "There's nothing I haven't worried about."

"That if you have a kid, you might never get married?"

"It might be easier. Dating at forty gets thorny. Women rush men to settle down and it freaks them out. I'll be the no-pressure alternative."

"You're not forty yet," Justine comforted.

"Yeah, right." I laughed.

"You could join a single parents' group."

"My whole universe will expand. I've never had a life outside work before, but having a baby will force me to invest in mommy groups and schools and the neighborhood. I'll meet more people, and maybe that'll include some guys who dig a broke down old single mom. I feel pretty good about it."

"You're fearless." Justine was awed.

"There's no such thing as fearlessness," I dismissed. "Courage is the decision that something else is more important than fear. I'm scared to have a baby on my own, but I'm more scared of not having a baby. My doctor was right—by the time I saw her I'd already decided. It just took a while to admit it."

"You don't want a kid from Africa, like Madonna?"

"If it comes to that, I'll adopt. But I'd like to try to have my own first." I looked at my hands. "My handwriting is identical to my mother's. I find that fascinating. I'd like to see what half my DNA makes."

"A mess." Justine laughed. "Kids make a mess." She squealed and threw herself on me. "I'm so excited for you! Pigtails and ribbons and curly mops."

"It could be a boy." I laughed as she smothered me.

"It's wonderful." She clasped her hands, eyes welling.

"Stop that." She was making me cry. It felt so good to share. "Now you have to help me." I spread the profiles on the counter. "These are my finalists."

"Donors? OH MY GOD LOOK AT HIS CHEEKS!" she shrieked and pointed to Donor 372.

"That's his baby picture," I explained. "It gives you an idea of what your baby might look like."

"I die."

"He's a front-runner," I agreed. "He's an engineer, got a 3.0 grade point average at Columbia. Danish/English descent but speaks French, both grandparents lived until their eighties, and no history of addiction in the family. His Keirsey report lists him as a guardian, and he gets high friendly marks under staff impressions."

"Are you for real? I don't know that much about Big Mike."

"You wouldn't believe what you can learn from a donor profile." I pointed to No. 5178. "This guy's first memory was having chicken pox and walking around his apartment naked wearing mittens so he wouldn't scratch."

"This guy says in his essay, 'Being afraid to try something can be even worse than failing at it.'" She looked up from No. 1124. "He's perfect for you!"

I nodded. "He also uses the word 'iconoclastic.' The cast of *Pulse* doesn't even know what that means."

"How are you going to decide?"

"With your help."

I tossed my dog-eared copy of *Cora* in the trash, and stacked more donor profiles across the counter. I'd made my decision.

Andy Chooses

As much as Andy detested Webb Garner, once he inexplicably withdrew from the election, Andy missed him. Garner's attacks kept Andy on his toes, required strategy, drove his message. Uncontested, the race was a meander. Speeches that had been provocative became banal. Clever rebuttals became clichéd platitudes.

No one interrogated Andy. Reporters didn't hound him. Agents for Garner didn't stalk him with cell phone cameras hoping to entrap him in exploitable sound bites. It was as if the election was over. Even the Proposition 11 furor was finally dying down. With no lawsuit or candidate to agitate around, media coverage dried up. No one cared about the uncontested campaign, and that included Andy.

Andy was left to think about the job itself, and it left him cold. He wasn't like Summer. She pored over the Council's agenda. He had to force himself to plow through minutes. She went to a reception every night. He dreaded shaking constituents' hands. She attended every public meeting. Watching public access coverage sent him into a coma. When he thought about doing it for two years, his brain shut down.

Everything else was better. Jacque had restaffed him on the Cornin account. Colleagues treated him with deference as almost-elect City Council member Knox. Maryn wasn't suing him and assured him her relapse was managed. But Andy's stomach was full of acid.

"Do we have more of these?" He shook the empty Pepto-Bismol bottle at Summer.

She frowned. "I just bought that."

"My stomach's been upset."

"Are you getting sick? You tossed all night."

Andy rubbed a tired hand over his face. It ached each morning from grinding his teeth in his sleep. "Maybe."

"We can cancel the Arts Focus reception tonight if you want. Or I can go without you."

Andy sat heavily on the end of the bed. Canceling sounded so good he couldn't deny his dread any longer. "I don't know if I'm cut out for this, pigeon."

"What do you mean?"

"City Council."

Summer looked alarmed. She sat down, putting an arm around him. "Are you nervous? I know you'll do great."

"I'm not nervous, I'm miserable. I hate the receptions and the breakfasts and the awkward public forums. I hate that the same issues get debated every year and nothing has changed in twenty. I hate that you can't do anything about a good idea without strangling it in red tape. I hate that it's all dumbed down to the lowest player. And I hate that the lowest player will probably be me. I don't want to do it."

Summer looked like a girl whose dream birthday present was about to be snatched away.

Andy tried to explain. "I'm inside out. I have no idea who I am anymore. Maryn's pregnant with my kid and I have no connection to it. They have cancer and I learned about it on the news. The religious right is out to get me. Strangers have opinions about me. I see my face on the news. A local teenager has a Web page called Hot Knox with shirtless pictures of me. It's crazy. I need normal."

"Can't you be normal and be on the City Council?" she pleaded.

Andy shook his head. "No."

Tears filled Summer's eyes. "You were in. You were as good as elected. There's not even another candidate to take your place."

"That's not true," Andy had thought this through. "Didn't your dad say a wife stepped into her husband's seat when he died? Well, I'm dying."

"Don't be funny," Summer sniffed.

"I'm not." Andy was dead serious. "You thrive on this. You know the issues. You love the politics. You want the job. You need to be on the City Council, not me."

"We can't just substitute me for you."

"Yes we can." For once, Andy knew something Summer didn't. "I looked into it. All we need to do is file a few forms with the Board of Elections and you can step into my campaign."

Summer was very still.

"You know you'd be great," Andy coaxed. "Why not?"

"You think we can do this?"

"You hijacked the election from Charming Tommy. I know we can do this." Relief hovered, waiting to rush in.

"We'd have to put off having kids," Summer said.

"We have time." Andy had no idea if they had time. It wasn't the most important thing.

Excitement began to rise on Summer's face. "Is this what you want?"

"It's what we both want." That and a burger. Suddenly he was starving.

"Okay, then." She squeezed his hand. "Let's do it."

In his mind's eye, little Delilah in her ruffled socks waved and headed into a blur of light. He wondered if he'd ever see her again.

Eva Chooses

Eva was thrilled with Daisy's tape for *Cora*. The girl had burned it up. Eva retracted her doubts. Daisy deserved this role. She dialed Julian.

"Wales Productions." Crisp.

"It's Eva Lytton calling for Julian."

There was barely a pause. "I'm sorry, Ms. Lytton, but Mr. Wales isn't in. Can I have him return your call?"

I don't know, can you? Eva's thought was waspish. So far it hadn't happened. "Of course," she murmured into the phone. She hung up frustrated. After seeing her reel, there was no doubt that Daisy could handle Cora Aldridge. Why was Julian dragging his feet?

Eva knew why. Who wouldn't rather work with Dimple? Still, Julian was bailing a sinking boat. Eva had the studio on her side. They wanted a younger actress. She had to get face-to-face with Julian to knock down the last of his resistance.

You could tell him, the thought whispered.

Eva shook her head. It wasn't necessary to play dirty. She simply had to sit down with the elusive Julian Wales and be her persuasive best. This was Eva's wheelhouse. It was maddening that she couldn't get her hands on him.

Her eye fell on the *Hollywood Reporter* with Julian smiling on the cover, and she pushed it away in disgust. Julian was being honored at the film critics awards this weekend.

She sat up. Julian was being honored at the San Diego Film

Critics Awards. He would *be* at the San Diego Film Critics
Awards. Well, so would she.

After she buzzed her assistant to make the arrangements,
Eva sat back in satisfaction, feet crossed on her desk. Julian was
attending both the breakfast and the awards ceremony, so she
had plenty of time to corner him.

Wyatt called. She felt a pang that she'd been too busy to
even listen to several voice mails he'd left her.

"Greetings!" Wyatt's return hello was moderated. "What's
wrong?"

"I lost the baby," he said.

"What?" Her feet thumped to the floor. "What happened?
Is Deborah okay?"

"Deborah's fine, and the baby's fine. Unfortunately, they're
fine with someone else. The School Board didn't think it was
in their best interests that I adopt. Even though I care for their
children every day."

"I don't understand," Eva said.

Wyatt sighed. "They made me cancel the adoption, Eva, or
they were going to fire me. They said it would look bad, and
alarm parents. It happened a while ago, I just haven't seen you.
I'm sorry to do this over the phone."

A kaleidoscope of emotions hit Eva. Deborah and Wyatt
and an anonymous blue-eyed baby swirled before her eyes,
but most of all Wyatt's unspoken grief thumped into her gut.
Without being prepared for it, Eva was sobbing.

"Eva! What's the matter?" Wyatt sounded alarmed, and
who could blame him? Eva was hijacking his bad news as if
her own world had ended.

"Eva, Eva," Wyatt tried to soothe her. "If Chuck Norris cried
like that, L.A. would be Atlantis II."

Eva couldn't talk. She gasped and struggled to explain.

"I don't want a baby but you want a baby . . . and this actress
gave up the career of a lifetime to have a baby." She choked out

incoherent half sentences. "And Sawyer . . . but my mother . . . and . . . I'm deviant . . ." She broke down again.

Wyatt let her cry awhile, then said, "Get that nonsense out of your head. It's the equivalent of saying that I'm deviant for wanting a child."

"You aren't . . . ," Eva sobbed. "But I can have a baby . . . for you . . . and I don't want to and I feel so bad . . . ," she wailed.

"What?" Wyatt was aghast. "I would never ask that of you! It never occurred to me. Eva, please." He sounded tortured, and she felt worse.

"What's wrong with me? You're such a good person and I'm selfish."

"That is absolutely untrue. Where did this come from?"

Hell if she knew. Somewhere deep. She took some breaths.

"This isn't even about me, it's about you and I'm the one crying. I'm so sorry." She wiped her eyes.

"Talk to me," Wyatt said. "Please, you're scaring me."

Eva sniffled. "You know Sawyer?"

"Yes."

"It's been going great," Eva said. "Really great. But last night, I can't even remember the context, he made one of the comments that everyone makes without thinking—'When I have a kid . . .' And I didn't say anything." She began to cry again. "I don't want to lose him, but I don't want kids. And that makes me selfish, because I *can* have a baby and so many can't and I want you to have a baby more than anything but I . . . I . . ."

"Stop this right now," Wyatt commanded. "Pull yourself together. Yes, I want a child, but I do not want one from you. With my luck, she'd have your expensive tastes."

Eva laughed and blew her nose. "If you went to jail and Chuck Norris was your prison daddy, you'd get pregnant."

"Terrifying solution. It's a blow to lose Deborah, but don't think it's the end. The only tool Garner wields is the threat of public opinion and I can play that game too. I wasn't sure a single father was the best solution for a special-needs child, but if that's my only avenue, I'll pursue it. I'd like to see the politician who would deny a special-needs child a real home."

This was a different Wyatt, a determined one.

"You sound almost devious."

"You don't spend all day with teenagers and fail to pick up a trick or two. Now as for this Sawyer foolery, the lessons of high school hold equally true. The best thing you can do is be yourself. If he doesn't appreciate you, then move on."

"I have to tell him, don't I?" She sighed.

"You don't *have* to do anything, but I think you'll feel better. You don't have leprosy. It's a life choice that many share."

"You'd be surprised by how unnatural people make you feel when they're not assuring you that you'll change your mind."

"Maybe Sawyer's tired of dating women who see him as a sperm donor."

"Maybe." Eva was doubtful. "At any rate it'll have to keep a bit longer. I'm not redredging my apparently deep-seated neuroses on the subject today." She paused. "Is Deborah okay?"

"Somewhere out there a happy couple can't believe their luck," Wyatt said. "Deborah will be fine."

"What about you?" Eva worried that each setback made Wyatt a little harder.

"I'll be fine too," Wyatt reassured her. "And Eva? If Sawyer makes the grievous error of ending things, don't sleep with a random stranger you meet at a bar."

"Wyatt," Eva protested.

"I'm quite serious. STDs itch. Sleep with his best friend or his father if you must."

Eva laughed. "Wyatt?"

"Yes?"

"Chuck Norris doesn't cry. He kicks excess water from his body through his eyes."

Eva was exhausted after her call with Wyatt. She thought about reapplying her makeup, but the damage was severe, and she had no intention of facing anyone for the rest of the day. She was canceling on Sawyer. Her eye fell on the *Hollywood Reporter* and she had an idea.

"Good news or bad news?" Sawyer answered.

"What?"

"You're calling me two hours before our date. Either we're celebrating or you're canceling."

"Chuck Norris doesn't wear a watch. He decides what time it is." Hearing his voice gave Eva second thoughts about canceling.

"You've never explained your veneration for Chuck Norris."

"What's to explain? We're soul mates. He's tough as nails. I'm tough as nails. He'd have made the world's best agent if he wasn't a marshal."

"Do you think you're that tough? Because I think you're a big softie."

Eva was affronted. "I strike fear in the hearts of Hollywood. Eva's clients get the jobs."

"Do they know you still have your childhood stuffed rabbit, you DVR every episode of *Surprise Homecoming* and bawl when their dogs see the soldiers come home, and you bought, and read, all the *Little House on the Prairie* books, as an adult?"

"You may not share any of that information," Eva said.

"Why not?"

Eva was flummoxed. "That would be bad for business."

"Would it?"

"Yes! You can't take prisoners in Hollywood."

"But you're not like that."

"I'm hard," Eva insisted, thinking of Dimple. "I do what needs to be done."

"Would it offend you if I respectfully disagreed?" Sawyer asked. "I think you're warm, and sensitive, and you pour your nurturing into me and your cousin."

"I . . ." Eva didn't know what to say. She should be mad but she felt warm instead. "I love the idea that you think I'm warm. But I'm hard too, and I'm not apologetic about it."

"Maybe Chuck Norris is your alter ego."

"I'm neither wholly soft, nor wholly ruthless," Eva said. "I'm mostly good, with enough Chuck Norris to get the job done."

"Is he amoral?"

"He's . . . unperturbed. And very black and white."

"And you?"

"Quite grey."

"But to your office, you're black and white."

"The job is the job."

"Did you capitalize 'job'? And is it hard to lead a double life?"

"Not at all." Eva didn't hesitate. "So on a scale of one to Chris Brown, exactly how angry would you be if I *was* calling to cancel?"

"For abandoning me to a Stouffer's frozen dinner? I can forgive you. I like the brownies. And I like the idea that my mostly good woman is out there banging heads and taking names."

"I have a consolation prize. How'd you like to go to San Diego this weekend?"

They pulled up to the hotel Saturday afternoon in Sawyer's Mercedes. It had been a condition of his acceptance that they didn't take Eva's MINI.

"We should have plenty of pool time before we have to get ready for dinner." Sawyer pushed his sunglasses onto his head and crinkled his astonishing green eyes.

Eva hadn't exactly told Sawyer her plan. In fact, she didn't have a plan. She hadn't been able to inveigle an invitation to the awards, so she'd booked a room at the Coronado Hotel, which was hosting the ceremony. It wasn't a large hotel and she had twenty-four hours. Julian Wales would be hers.

"Just promise we won't leave the premises." Eva smiled. "I want to sun, eat, sleep, and relax right here."

As they were checking in, Eva's eyes darted around the spacious lobby. She had timed their arrival to coincide with the end of the breakfast. If Julian walked by she could accost him and be done with it. She only needed ten minutes.

Sawyer squeezed her shoulders. "Maybe you should get a massage. You seem tense."

"I'm not tense, just terribly, terribly alert." She laughed. The lobby was dead. "Want to get tea down here while we wait for the room?"

"We have a room ready right now." The chirpy clerk thwarted Eva.

"Great," said Sawyer. "I want to change and get poolside, stat."

"When Chuck Norris jumps into a pool, he doesn't get wet, the pool gets Chuck Norris." Eva trailed him to the elevator. Maybe Julian would fancy a dip.

By eight PM Eva was officially tweaking. It'd been torture pretending to relax poolside when she was tense as a guitar string, continually scanning over the top of her *Variety* magazine for Julian Wales. She'd jolted when a bald man settled onto a lounger. A not-Julian businessman from Topeka would return home puffed up over the scrutiny he'd received from a bikinied blonde in California. When Sawyer had insisted on massaging suntan lotion onto her back in long, slow strokes, she'd been as taut as a courtroom drama, anxious she'd miss Julian while facedown. She'd sprung up the moment he'd finished, ignoring the confusion in his eyes. He was going to think

she had a urinary tract infection or a cocaine addiction based
on the number of times she'd run inside to the bathroom. Each
time she'd skulked in the lobby for as long as she could without
arousing suspicion, and still no Julian.

"Tummy trouble?" Sawyer had asked after her last absence,
and she'd stopped going.

When Sawyer declared he smelled funkier than Chewbac-
ca's underpants and it was time for a nap and a shower, he was
disappointed when she opted for a snack in the lobby instead.
She knew he'd meant *just a nap* but she had feigned obtuseness.
Business before pleasure. He smelled, anyway.

Sitting alone in the lobby, her irritation with Julian Wales
swelled. He was ruining her romantic weekend, even though
he had no clue. At seven, she'd given up long enough to hastily
get ready before returning downstairs with Sawyer. The Original Cyn would have been horrified. Eva primped more to go
to the gym.

The view from their dinner table was perfect. Sawyer was
trying his best to charm Eva, overlooking her obvious distraction.

"Is something wrong?" he asked after the waiter delivered
their appetizers.

Eva felt a kick of panic. She didn't want to convey disinter-
est she didn't feel. It was time to confess.

"I . . ."

Julian Wales emerged from the banquet corridor and
headed for the restrooms.

"I have to go to the bathroom." Eva leaped to her feet and
bolted before Sawyer could utter a sound.

She sighted on Julian's bald head like an X-wing fighter on
the Death Star. It disappeared into the men's room. Sparing but
a second, Eva barged in after him.

Julian looked up, startled, hand frozen on his belt buckle.

"Hello," he said.

"Hello," Eva said.

There was a pause. Eva thought maybe she could have waited.

"Am I in the wrong bathroom?" Julian asked, standing before the row of urinals.

"Oh my goodness, I thought it was unisex!" Eva lied. "I'm so embarrassed. But how fortuitous! I've been trying to reach you for days. I'm Eva Lytton."

He reluctantly let go of his belt buckle to shake her hand. "I know who you are, Daisy Carmichael's agent."

"I've been looking forward to talking to you about *Cora*. Daisy is quite delighted with the script, and as you saw last week, her test reel was incredible. She's a natural."

"I can see that you're anxious to discuss it." His tone was wry, and he seemed to be wavering over what to do. Eva prayed he wouldn't pee in front of her. She didn't know what she'd do if he unzipped. Instead, Julian walked to the sink and washed his hands, more out of habit than need, since she'd prevented him from his purpose there.

"I haven't made any decisions, Miss Lytton, which is why there was no point in returning your calls."

"Eva, please. I'm in the men's room. That merits a first-name basis." She was acting like a teenager around a lifeguard's chair, not a competent negotiator. "Daisy is good. What's holding you back?"

"Maybe I don't want to work with a vapid narcissist," Julian said.

"Daisy is revered by the eighteen to thirty-five female demographic, and desired by the entire male demographic." "Revered" might be a strong word, but Eva seized on the opportunity to neither acknowledge nor deny that her client was a vapid narcissist. "Her attachment to this project would draw a lower age sector to your already impressive following."

"If that was my goal I'd cast Taylor Swift."

"But Daisy has talent. She's delivered the roles she's been given. Rom-coms have been stillborn at the box office for years, but *Best Day* grossed $33 million its opening weekend, with Daisy the top-billed actor in the cast. That's more than *Notting Hill*."

"It's not about money." Julian's tone suggested he'd made this defense before. She pounced.

"It is to the studio. They love you, Julian, but they have to look at the bottom line. You have a great script and a vision, but you need financial returns or you'll learn how fast everyone can say Big Screen back to Documentary Short. Remember *The Wackness*? Exactly. Even Ben Affleck couldn't make an art house movie mainstream without hot talent. Compare *Gone Baby Gone* with *The Town*. Critics loved them both, but one had fading names and the other had rising stars. Guess which one made money?"

Julian made a frustrated gesture. "So I can have a larger audience pan the lead's performance?"

"I had reservations until I saw Daisy's sample reel. Julian, she's fantastic. She showed that with richer material she has the potential to be inspiring."

"You're telling me Daisy is a role model?"

"We both know the broken toilet my mom uses as a planter in the backyard would make a better role model than Daisy Carmichael," Eva said. "But she's the best actress for this role."

"Eva, I admire your zealous advocacy for your client. I'm not afraid to tell you the studio's on your side—they want someone young and fresh. But the decision is mine and I'm still struggling to get my hand around the shape of Cora. Some days she's old and some days she's young, and I don't know which way to jump. I can promise you, you will be either the first or the second person to know when I do." So it was down to Daisy and Dimple. "Now if you promise not to follow me,

I'm going to my room to use the bathroom unmolested." He walked out of the restroom. Eva followed.

"Julian, Dimple Bledsoe is pregnant." She changed her character with a sentence.

He froze in his tracks. When he swung around, all color had drained from his face. "What?" His reaction was more intense than she'd expected.

"I have it on good information."

"No. That's wrong." Aghast.

"Ask her." Eva wouldn't say more because she didn't know for sure. Julian's horror was testing her audacity.

"Why would you say that?"

"I believe it's true." The answer to his question was a complex tangle of Eva's duplicity, cowardice, and self-absorption, but her reply was honest. "In nine months you'll be reading on the cover of *Us Weekly* how Dimple got her pre-baby body back in just ten weeks."

"I . . ." He stared at her, speechless.

"She checked herself out of the race, Julian. Daisy should get the part."

Julian rubbed his hands over a face that had aged ten years. Eva had never felt more terrible. She had to get out of there.

"Call me after you talk to Dimple, and we'll settle this thing." She used the last of her bravado to finish. "Daisy's not a consolation prize, Julian. She's the real deal, and she'll make Cora blaze off the screen." When she walked away, she forced herself not to run.

There was no rest for the wicked. When she returned, the expression on Sawyer's face indicated that another showdown was looming.

"Welcome back." His greeting wasn't warm.

"Sawyer, I don't want kids." Eva was exhausted. Broken. She didn't have the energy to sugarcoat or avoid the issue.

For the second time in ten minutes, she'd caused all color to drain from a man's face.

"Are you . . . is that why . . . all the trips to the bathroom . . . ," Sawyer stuttered.

"No." Even miserable, Eva had to smile. "I'm not pregnant."

Relief washed over Sawyer and he slumped in his chair. "That's a mercy." He hastened to add, "Not that it would have been the worst thing in the world, but it's better when you choose." His smile made his eyes do the awesome crinkle thing.

"That's what I'm saying." Eva was near tears. "I won't choose. Ever. I don't want kids."

Sawyer was silent for a long time.

"You certainly cannonball into the heavy stuff," he said, considering her.

"There's no number low enough to score the awfulness of how I'm handling this," Eva agreed. "It's just that I really like you." She looked at him straight on. "*Really* like you. I know from experience that most men want a family, and it's hard for me to get attached if things are going to end as soon as the nesting instinct comes home to roost. So it's better that you know now."

Eva needed a drink. It occurred to her that they'd enjoy several awkward hours together on the ride back to Los Angeles. Her timing sucked.

"Okay." Sawyer shrugged, after a long pause. "Then I guess we won't have kids." He cut his steak and took a bite.

Eva was dumbfounded. "But . . ."

He looked up from his plate. "But what?"

"You said, the other night, 'When I have kids . . .'"

"I've also said when I'm a hundred, when I take flying lessons, and when I take over as coach for the Lakers, Eva. It doesn't mean that it'll happen."

"Sawyer, I won't change my mind."

"You might when you try that pasta." He pointed with his fork. "My steak is much better."

"I'm serious."

"I'm serious too." Sawyer became earnest. "Eva, it's hard enough to find the person I want to wake up to every day. People date for different reasons, but I'm putting all my chips on this mythological thing called a soul mate. It's rarer than a unicorn with a winning lottery ticket. I want it, that lover and best friend. To have that would be enough. Except maybe a dog."

"I'm not going to change my mind when I get older," she cautioned, "or when we get married, or when my best friend has a kid, or when I find the right guy. I'm not saying I don't want kids *right now*. I don't want kids *ever*."

"It would be patronizing to assume otherwise. I'm saying that to find my soul mate, I accept a life without children. The one, rather idealistic, goal is hard enough without putting complicated strings on it. A vacation home on a Greek island is an acceptable trade-off for children, and a lot less expensive."

He saw the doubt in her face and put down his fork. "Eva, I'm forty-four. I'd feel like a caricature dating a twenty-something, not to mention be bored out of my mind. I accepted long ago that having an age-appropriate relationship meant that my partner was likely past her childbearing years. As it happens, in your case it's not true, but you're not wrenching me from a desperately held desire to breed. I want a family, but I'm pretty sure you can make a family without children. Right now, I'd like to continue down this enticing path we've begun to determine whether we might be each other's family."

It occurred to Eva that she might be dealing for the first time in her life with an actual mature male, something she'd previously considered an essentially cinematic concept. Tears pricked her eyes, but this time the cause was welcome.

"I might love you," she said.

"Oh, you will." He smiled. "When you see how much that bottle of wine cost."

Eva laughed too loud, the dark mass from her chest swirling up into the room and dissolving away like smoke up a vent.

"So," Sawyer said, as he returned to his dinner. "Am I allowed to get a dog?"

Dimple Colors Outside the Lines

I'm sorry, darling," Freya said when she called to give me the official bad news.

"Don't be," I said. "I had some good times and got a free rash guard out of it."

"Frankly, I think the man is . . . *unhinged* for sentencing himself to working with Daisy Carmichael."

"Perhaps they deserve each other."

Freya didn't comment. "Onward and upward. I received something interesting last week. It's a western actually, sort of a modern—"

"Actually, there's another role I'm going for."

Pause. "Without me?" I could visualize Freya's arched Nordic brow.

I gave an exaggerated sigh. "It's a pretty amazing part, but I've been hesitating because I wasn't sure it was right for me."

"Dimple, *darling*, this is why you have an agent. Where did you get this script?"

I giggled. "I think it was given to me at puberty. It's something I've considered for a really long time."

"You've lost me." I could smell the brain smoke as Freya tried to dissect what I was saying.

"I'm going to try to have a baby, Freya."

Silence. "A . . . *real* . . . baby?"

"Is there another kind?"

"Well. That's . . ."

"Unexpected?"

"To say the least. Who's the lucky fellow?"

"Donor 1124." I'd fallen for his wry humor and disease-resistant genetic history.

There was a longer pause. "I didn't see that coming. You're sure about this . . . *adventure*?"

"Of course not." I laughed. "I'm not sure what I want to do after lunch!"

"But is it the right time? *Cora* has renewed attention to you."

"I don't think there's a 'right time,' but I think sometimes the time can be right. I don't want to wait too long, Freya. *While I still can* is my right time."

"And that's now?"

"When I was a kid I saved all the best pictures in my coloring book for when I was older and had better skills, coloring pictures I didn't like as much so I wouldn't mess up the good stuff. When I had the talent, I'd lost interest in coloring. All the best pictures stayed blank."

"You've figured out there's no crayon police?"

"That and I probably would've had a pretty good time messing outside the lines. I used to hate the expression 'without great risk there can be no great reward.' It was stupid to me. Better aim lower and be sure of 'sufficient' than aim for 'great' and miss."

"Now?"

"It's not about the reward. It's about the risk itself. You live in your tries, not your endings. I don't want to look back and think I didn't have the career I wanted, or I didn't have the family I wanted. I want to be too busy looking for a lost tennis shoe while the dog needs a walk and I've got pages to memorize but I'm going on a picnic instead."

Freya said simply, "Good for you, honey."

"I should know if I get the part in about two weeks."

We were quiet for a moment.

"I suppose I could tolerate being called Auntie Freya as long as sticky hands don't touch my Birkin."

I laughed. "Freya? Donor 1124 is Scandinavian." He was also tall and bald.

I held the phone away from my ear as she squealed.

"So that script of yours might have to wait a bit." We both knew it meant more than that.

"Forget it, honey. She was a boring character who colored inside the lines. But I can't lie to you. This poses career challenges."

"I know. No one wants to tell you that you can't have it all. But you can't have it all. Telling women that if they wait, it all works out isn't true. You have to make hard choices. I like my career, but I want a baby more."

"I think you just made my no-heart beat," said Freya.

"That's not possible," I said. "You're an agent."

Maryn Chooses

Maryn was watching way too much television. Between waiting around the hospital or lying around her house, one always seemed to be on. She used to prefer riding or playing tennis during her free time, but these days, she was too tired to do anything else. Even reading a book wore her out.

She'd avoided the local news at all costs since the Prop 11 circus had begun, but it was on when she woke from her doze. It no longer surprised her to see Andy's face, but she braced herself every time.

" . . . with regret that I withdraw from the race for City Council. After long conversations with my wife and my colleagues in the Democratic Party, I feel that my candidacy is counterproductive to the needs of the people of Santa Monica. Conservative extremists have used my personal life to distract from real issues of concern. I refuse to be used as a tool of distraction. My wife, Summer, has stood with me every step of the way, and is herself committed to the best interests of the community. Her character is unassailable and her commitment unchallenged. That is why I cede my candidacy to her, and return to life in the private sector, assured that the city will be in the most competent hands available."

Andy smiled and stepped back from the podium, sweeping his arm wide to indicate his wife. Summer gave a beauty pageant wave and addressed the microphone.

"This was a difficult decision for Andrew, but one I support. This family is committed to public service. While at this time, I'm better

*positioned to dedicate myself to public service, election of either of us
will harness the energy of both. We look forward to serving you. As a
City Council representative, the first thing I will do . . ."*

Summer launched into a campaign speech, talking about
homelessness, affordable housing, and public transportation.
Maryn thought there was something different about her. She'd
been Palin-ized. Her suit didn't have the cosmetic-salesgirl
quality of her weather-girl outfits, but it was more than spiffier
threads. Summer seemed . . . happy. She was a natural at the
podium, fired up with her speech. Maryn had never seen her
so alight. Andy stood behind her, clapping. He looked relieved.

"I think those kids are going to make it," Maryn murmured
to herself.

She heard the lock turn. She'd given Wyatt a key.

"Is it four o'clock already?" He was taking her to her appointment.

"Your chariot awaits." He came into the living room.

Maryn pointed to the screen. "Did you do that?"

"I swear, I didn't."

"Just checking." It made her happy. Andy was finally doing
something for himself.

"The nugget moved today," she told him. "At first I thought
I was having some kind of nervous attack, fluttering in my
stomach. Then I realized it was my girl." It had been transport-
ing. Every milestone was a victory snatched from the greedy
reaper. Maryn would get herself across the finish line, no
matter what, but these little victories were protein boosts in a
strenuous race.

"And how are you otherwise?"

"Bored. This morning I renamed my iPod the *Titanic,* so
when I plug it into my computer it says, 'The *Titanic* is Syncing.'"

"That's bored," Wyatt agreed. "We could go for a walk on
the beach after your appointment."

"We'll see." Maryn hadn't told him about the dizzy spells,

sudden and extreme, enveloping her in a swarm of ten thousand bees. She had a hard enough time when they happened in the kitchen. She didn't want to risk one away from home.

"I'll be in the lobby," Wyatt said as he dropped her off. This meeting was at the hospital. There'd been a shift, the oncologist Dr. Gavin taking the helm from Dr. Singh. Their news was not good.

"The cancer is widespread and aggressive, Maryn. We've tried to wait as long as possible, but I believe it's urgent you start treatment."

"What kind of treatment?"

"A similar protocol to your first illness—chemotherapy and radiation."

"And the baby?"

Dr. Singh answered, "There are interventions we can take, like sheltering the fetus during radiation and avoiding certain chemotherapy agents such as methotrexate."

"Radiation therapy is known to increase the risk of birth defects. It's only an option after I deliver," Maryn said.

"Maryn, I'm afraid it can't wait. It's imperative that we commence treatment immediately. Frequent monitoring of the baby's development will help us. Given the aggressive nature of your cancer, and the treatment needed, you should consider termination." Her eyes were sad for Maryn.

"I'm not going to," Maryn said. "I understand the consequences of my decision. However, I'm declining any treatment until the child is delivered."

Dr. Gavin hesitated. "Several recent studies have found that using certain chemotherapy drugs during the second and third trimesters does not increase the risk of birth defects. Those are not the ideal prescription for your cancer, but we can substitute until the baby is born."

"No treatment," Maryn said.

"Maryn, the fetus is only twenty-two weeks. Waiting four

months for treatment could be fatal. You can't keep a child alive if you aren't alive."

That stopped Maryn. She didn't expect to survive her cancer, but she'd be damned if the baby didn't. "How early can I deliver safely?"

"It depends on the baby. Preemie survival rates have advanced miles in recent years, but they often require lengthy stays in the NICU, and depending on how early, may lead to long-term developmental issues."

"What's a reasonable minimum goal?"

"Healthy preemies have a 90 percent survival rate after twenty-six weeks," Dr. Singh answered reluctantly. "And there's some evidence that girls are slightly more likely to survive very early premature birth. Though they'll have problems and need extensive treatment in the NICU."

"Chicks are tough," Maryn said. "Can we do anything to accelerate maturity?"

"We can treat the baby with steroids to speed up lung development."

Maryn thought. "I'll consider treatment at twenty-eight weeks. At that point, the baby could be ready."

"You'd have to be admitted."

Maryn blanched at the thought of an extended hospital stay. "Whatever it takes," she said.

It was all about the nugget.

Wyatt Signs On

Wyatt must have dozed off in the wing chair because he woke to find Maryn looking at him fondly. She was so terribly thin, her rounded belly contrasting with her pale arms, like twigs protruding from a snowman. She was twenty-six weeks today. They had celebrated with cupcakes.

"What are you thinking?" he asked.

"How funny it is that I finally found the father of my children, but he's neither the father nor mine. Who knew he'd be a friend?"

"I wouldn't say I'm the father of your children, but I make an excellent godfather," Wyatt said. "It's the bow ties."

"I want you to adopt the baby, Wyatt."

Wyatt thought a gong had been struck by his ear. "What are you talking about?"

"I want you to raise this child." She rested a hand on her belly. "She's going to need a father."

Wyatt exhaled. Of course. "Naturally, I'll be there for you both."

"Not for me, Wyatt. For her. I need you to be there because I won't."

The clanging reverberated again. *"You're* going to raise that baby."

"Maybe. But I have cancer, and I have it pretty bad. I need to know the nugget is in good hands. You're the person I want to raise my little girl when I'm gone."

"You're twenty-six weeks now. You can get treatment."

"I'm not going to do that," she said. "I want to give her more time."

"Maryn . . ." He scooted his chair to the bed.

"Wyatt, you are the most gentle, moral, and kind person I know. My daughter's entering a world where she's already been dealt a bad hand. Her father's a petri dish, and her mother's dead. I want her to know the power of redemption, of good, immediately. That's you."

Wyatt started crying. "Please stop."

She took his hand. "Don't be sad, Wyatt. I knew the risks and I chose this child. Now I choose you. With you as her dad, I know she'll get a good education, have an excellent vocabulary, most certainly be served waffles, and very probably own an impressive collection of patent-leather Mary Janes." She managed a smile. "We're both getting what we wanted."

"I don't want this."

"You don't want it this way. But I know you're going to be a great dad. If anything, I worry about you. She'll have you twisted around her wee little finger."

Wyatt couldn't answer.

Her voice was steady, if soft. "If it's okay with you, we should get married. That protects you from the School Board and speeds up the adoption. I'm going to carry her as long as possible, but it's certain she'll be premature, and we have no idea how well I'll feel, so I'd like to name you my durable and medical power of attorney and the baby's legal guardian."

Wyatt could only nod. He'd been bringing her ice cream and magazines, and she'd been researching the nuances of in utero guardianship.

"Nugget is well provided for. I've left significant assets in a trust in her name. She may be the only girl in kindergarten who really gets a pony for her birthday. I'll name you as the executor, with your consent."

She kept asking his permission, and Wyatt was falling

down the Maryn rabbit hole again and he didn't know how to stop.

"I'm sure Andy will sign consent papers, and in exchange the rest of the eggs will be destroyed. There should be no challenges. If everything with the adoption isn't finished ... *before* ... as my widower you should have no problem after." She skated over her death as if it were red tape.

Wyatt had to pull it together. "I'm humbled."

"I'm not giving you a gift, Wyatt. You're giving me one. God cheated me with a bait and switch—I thought I had everything with this baby, but he had the sneaky cancer card up his sleeve. I'm diffusing my rage with thoughts of my little girl on her first day of school, or her first kiss, or falling in love. It's a comfort to know she'll be raised the way I want her to be, that she'll be *wanted*."

"What should I tell her, about us?"

"I'll leave that to you. Once you figure out what kind of child she is, you'll know the best answer for her."

"Tell me everything you want."

"What, like give her blocks instead of Barbies? I'm not going to saddle you with a bunch of rules. Let her be herself. We've both fantasized about things we'd do with our eventual children. You want to spend a summer RVing to all the national parks, while I saw myself taking her for her first manicure on her fifth birthday. Don't burden yourself with my parent bucket list along with yours. It wouldn't make sense."

"She's going to have so much of you in her. I want her to know you."

"Teach her to ride horses. Read her my journals. I'm writing down everything I can think of, every memory, every thought, every embarrassing detail. First kiss, first prom, high school's most horrifying moments, my worst haircut . . . same thing really. My political views, my thoughts on religion, our family tree, the choices that I made, advice I'd give her. I'm going to write her some letters, for milestones in her life, if that's okay with you."

"Okay with me?" Wyatt voiced disbelief. "This is your daughter. You could instruct me to enroll her in The School for People Who Hate the Name Wyatt and I'd do it."

Maryn laughed. "I'd rather she attend an institution with a broader curriculum, but thanks. I want her to have a normal life. I don't want her haunted by a spectral dead mom who keeps interrupting her life from the grave. But I think letters might be okay . . ." A crack of anguish cut Maryn's face. Wyatt couldn't imagine the pain of visualizing the life she'd never see.

"She'll value those letters above any other gift. Even the pony."

"Make sure she knows I didn't die because of her." Maryn became intense. "Pregnancy doesn't cause cancer to recur. I got sick because it was coming back anyway. Delaying treatment didn't cause my death either. We fight so hard to avoid death, or to make ourselves inexpendable through such heroics and accomplishments that death will hesitate to take us. Like dying is the worst thing. It isn't. Not treating the cancer may have shortened my time line, but more isn't better. I was going to have a long, painful illness before succumbing with nothing to show for it, or a shorter one that resulted in her. I hoped I'd beat the odds but, I didn't die because of her. I get to live on through her."

"She'll know," Wyatt promised.

"It makes it easier knowing she'll have a loving home."

Wyatt wiped his face. "Christ. We're talking like you're dead already. We shouldn't do that."

Maryn held his eyes. "Yes, we should."

Dimple Does Enough

Dimple stared at the ringing phone for so long she almost missed the call. It wouldn't be the first she'd skipped. She sighed as she hit Answer. She had to talk to Julian sometime, it might as well be when she was tired and bitchy.

"Hello, Julian."

"Don't you think it's juvenile not to return my calls for a month?" His voice was taut.

I've been busy," I said. "And before accusing me of playing the juvenile busy card, I really have been busy."

He was silent for a moment. "I read in *Variety* that you're replacing Jennifer Connelly in *Margot's Chair.*"

"She had a scheduling conflict."

"Don't you have a scheduling conflict?"

Dimple wondered why they were having this conversation. "No. We'll shoot over winter break from *Pulse.*"

"Won't *the baby* create a scheduling conflict?" His voice rose.

Shock reverberated in my skull. Five people in the world knew my plans. Julian was not one of them.

"Were you going to tell me?" His anger burned through the phone.

My fingers were nerveless. I wanted to bury my head in downy pillows, relax every muscle, and let the phone and the voice fall away as I drifted off to sleep.

"Were you going to tell me?" Louder.

"Tell you what?" I managed. For god's sake, I'd just walked in the door.

"WERE YOU GOING TO TELL ME THAT YOU'RE PREG-NANT WITH MY BABY?" he roared.

This time I felt delirious. I swayed.

"Oh my god," I whispered.

The bellowing was replaced by startling quiet. "Oh my god," he echoed. "You weren't going to tell me."

"Where did you get that idea?" I'd never noticed that crack in the ceiling. It looked like Hitchcock's profile.

"You've avoided fifty calls. Why wouldn't you tell me?" He sounded anguished.

"Who told you I was pregnant?"

"It doesn't matter. What matters is that I'll be there for you. Whatever you need. You must know that." He was urgent.

My throat closed. "Julian . . ."

"Anything," he repeated, voice intense.

This disaster was spinning out of control. I had to pull it together. "We are not pregnant!" I yelled.

Silence. "We aren't?" Hesitant.

"No." Definitive.

Hurt. "Are you pregnant with someone else?"

"No!" I protested. "I mean. It's not like that. I don't know." It was too confusing.

"What do you mean?" His voice was hard again. "It's not horseshoes or hand grenades. You're pregnant or you're not."

"I might be pregnant, I might not be pregnant. I was insem-inated with donor sperm, which is none of your goddamned business." Anger flared. "It's insulting to insinuate that if I was pregnant with your child, I wouldn't tell you. Apparently we misread each other's characters woefully."

That part hurt the most.

"That's not true." He sounded sad. "Maybe I wanted you to

be pregnant more than I believed it. Maybe I needed so badly for you to talk to me my brain went crazy."

Something jumped in me. I suppressed it. "That contradicts every aspect of our last conversation."

"I didn't say it made sense." He paused. "I've had some time to untangle my head, Dimple." I loved hearing my name in his voice.

"So have I." I cut him off. I couldn't do this. I still wanted him, but I had to keep my head straight.

"Julian." I indulged in his name, like a toffee. "It's difficult to separate fantasy from reality, especially in our business, but our fantasy is stupendous, and our reality sucks. When we're good together, we're fantastic. I loved you." He drew in a sharp breath. "But when we're bad, it's wretched. You push hard. I give way. I want things you don't, and compromise seems to be me suppressing those things to stay with you. It's not good for me."

"You said I was good for you."

"You are, sometimes. You make me feel like the best version of myself. It's like crack cocaine. It's why I could stay together with you for a really long time."

"But."

I tried to think. "If you look up at night, you see stars, bright and shiny and memorable. If you bundle them all, the mass is iridescent, but puny compared to the rest. The stripped sky is large and dark. When you care about someone, the shiny moments steal your attention from the fact that the majority is dark."

"That's very dramatic."

"You're a good person, Julian, but it's my belief that you won't meet my needs and I'd be unhappy."

"I think you're wrong."

"I'm not willing to find out." I thought of his clear eyes,

the shape of his head. His capable hands. This was killing me. "Please don't try to dissuade me."

"I miss you."

"It will pass."

"You didn't wait long to be sure, did you?" His tone was tired.

"You said you didn't want kids. I had no reason to think you didn't mean it. I want children, badly, and didn't want a *Sophie's Choice* between that and love. It made sense to end it early, before either choice caused wrenching loss." I hadn't escaped soon enough.

"And now you're pregnant."

"Maybe."

"And a movie star."

"Hardly. They needed a quick substitute, and shooting will wrap before I begin to show. *If* I'm pregnant. Who'd have thought?"

"Me," he said.

I was quiet. "I owe you. It was probably the attention from *Cora* that brought me the part."

"You don't owe me. You deserve it. You deserve it all, Dimple."

"You can't have it all, Julian."

"Apparently you can."

"Be serious. A performance so wrenching you want to print it out in sepia, put it in a locket around your neck, and run through wheat fields with a parasol won't transform my career at this point. I'll get more invigorating projects, enjoy myself more, be invited to more parties, but offers will inexorably dwindle each year."

"Because you have a kid."

"Because I'm getting older. Pretending that's not true is naive, and it isn't just Hollywood. The sacrifices needed to work full steam ahead aren't worth it to me. I love my job, but I'm reconciled to being worse at it so I can be a mom." Knowing it at last was so relaxing I wanted to sob.

"Seems like you're giving up a lot."

Listening to the timbre of his voice, I thought, *Yes, I am*.

"You can't have it all," I repeated. "But you can have enough."

I didn't think it was possible to be more exhausted, but I didn't have an ounce of energy left when I disconnected. I walked into the living room.

"Ach. No good, you upset."

My hovering mother led me to her worn gold couch.

"I'm sorry, *Mamu*," I said. "I had to take that call."

"No worry, *mīlotā*." She fussed a blanket up over me, hand pausing briefly on my midsection. "What they say?"

For a minute I thought she meant Julian, but she meant the doctor.

"To rest. Not to do anything the rest of today. Tomorrow I can pretty much get back to normal."

"Aye, me, a *vecamama*." She smiled.

"Maybe." I smiled back.

"Dickens need something to eat. You too. I make *kāposti roll*."

I caught her hand. "You're okay with this?"

"I no know." She gave an exaggerated shrug. "My daughter, she fancy. Big movie star. Big baby. What you do?" She was teasing me.

"Big belly," I said. "*Mamu*, what changed?"

She plucked the blanket. "I scared. I see you by self with baby, and I feel scared. When I am girl, this was not done. This was no good. So, I scared for you."

I waited.

"Then, on news, there is plane crash. I feel afraid, decide no fly. Then I think of all places you no see if you no take plane. Is no way to live. God, he want you do things. To be scared, it say you no have faith in God."

"Mother Teresa said, 'I know God will not give me anything I can't handle. I just wish that he didn't trust me so much.'" I repeated my favorite quote.

"Faith means you be scared, you do anyway." She shrugged again. "I want you happy. I see you no happy. Baby make you happy, okay. Things be hard, sure, but hard no stop happy." She patted my hand. "Daughters, they make you happy."

Tears filled my eyes.

"So," she stood. "You make work. That's life."

She stopped at the doorway. "This man, it no work?"

I shook my head. "It was never about the man. I needed to find faith in myself, to *do* something."

She laughed and shook her head. "You *do* something all right."

"It doesn't feel as dramatic as I thought," I said.

"Is enough," *Mamu* said. "Is enough."

Andy Signs, Again

Summer had wanted to come.

"Have you lost your mind?" Andy flat out refused.

"I want to pay my respects . . ."

It was like tossing a cigarette at a dead Christmas tree. His anger blazed. "Bullshit. You need to stamp yourself all over me, like kudzu. Do you want to pee on my leg so the scent will remind Maryn's cancer-riddled body not to make a play for me in her last days of life?"

Summer's lip trembled and she looked so scared, Andy's hot anger faded as fast as it flared. It wasn't Summer he was mad at. He pulled her close. As soon as he touched her, she started sobbing.

"I'm sorry." He kissed the top of her head.

Summer sniffled into his chest as Andy stroked her hair.

"Do you still love her?" The words were slipped into his breast pocket. He was shocked.

"What?" He didn't want to lie, but he didn't want to upset Summer. There was no yes or no answer.

"Do you regret leaving her?" Her face flowered up, blue eyes wet.

"Yes." He stroked her cheek. Summer shriveled in shock. "She had *cancer*. I was a spoiled schoolboy and left her when she needed me the most. Of course I regret it. But it happened, and time passed. I thought I couldn't handle my wife's illness, but I had no idea about the guilt. What I left was nothing compared to what I took with me. I don't know what cancer feels like, but guilt feels like being slowly eaten from the inside. Then I met you." He tucked a straw strand behind her ear. "I met you and I kept thinking, God must be looking the other way, because I didn't deserve anything this good. I actually convinced myself I could put one over on God while he was distracted." His laugh held no humor. "All this Prop 11 shit was his smack-down reminder of who's in charge and the penalty for arrogance. The Kraken lives. But even the worst sucker gets a shot at redemption. God gave me a second chance to do right by Maryn and I won't fuck it up."

Summer was crying again, but this time it was different. He held her close, as if he could absorb some release.

"Summer, I've been a rotten failure of a husband once, and I'm not going to do it again. But I owe my first wife. She's given me every chance to hurt her and I took them all. Just once, I want to do the right thing."

"Do you know what it's like to be the second wife of a man whose first wife was perfect?" Summer whimpered.

In a way, Andy did. The Andy he'd been before he left Maryn was perfect compared to the Andy he was after. Every day he fell short. He couldn't get back through time—the web of decisions was too knotty—but he could try to get better.

"I have to do one last thing." His words were a delicate reminder that Maryn could not trouble Summer much longer. "When I get back, what do you say we blow off Chance for Life tonight and have spaghetti at Jay's?" It was a hole in the wall they both loved. "My job as ex-candidate Knox is to keep current candidate Knox from getting too wrapped up in all the noise." Summer nodded, and Andy kissed her Alabama nose before heading out the door.

"Is that all of them?" Andy had signed everything Maryn put in front of him. He grew almost gleeful with each successive page. He would have signed a last will and testament giving her everything. He would have signed an arrest warrant for Cambodian orphans. He would have signed Gandhi's death sentence. He would have signed a hundred-year contract for AT&T to be his service provider.

Maryn nodded. She looked so peaceful, Andy couldn't believe she was sick. Her demeanor had noticeably eased when he grasped the pen. She lightened with every scrawl. It made him never want to stop signing pages.

"Want any more, an autograph for posterity?" As he said it, his smile died. The reason she had hair and looked normal was because she'd refused treatment. When she'd looked like a wraith, she'd been on the road to health. She was dying now. He felt like an ass.

"No."

He slid the papers into a protective folder. When she took them, her hand shook. It wasn't a side effect of her illness. He hoped the ease with which he'd signed made her comfortable. He wished he felt more possessive of their child, but he didn't. The swell under the covers was alien to him.

"All yours then."

"She may want to know who you are."

"Absolutely anytime." Maryn seemed a little suspicious, and he thought about comparing himself to Big Brothers/Big Sisters, then he thought that might seem weird since they were talking about his own child, so he didn't.

"I appreciate that."

She was tiring, but Andy wasn't ready to leave. He settled precariously on the bed, avoiding lumps under the covers that could be parts of Maryn.

"How are you doing?" The question was stupid, but he thought it was the kind of stupid that was allowed.

"Fine." She went along. "You?"

"It's been hell."

She smiled at that. "All these starlets craving cameras. They can have them. I heard there's a bounty for a photo of my bald head. They're forgetting that I'm not getting chemo, so my hair isn't going anywhere."

"I hit one with my car last week. Or I should say, it hit me." It felt good to acknowledge a common enemy. "So, what will happen now?"

"I'll carry the baby as long as possible. The doctors are giving me steroids to develop her lungs. When she's born Wyatt will take care of her and I'll do my best to get home."

"If you want my involvement, I'm there." He repeated his offer.

"The papers . . ." Maryn gestured toward the documents, anxious.

"Maryn, I'll never invite myself in without your express request. The choice is yours or her adoptive father's. I'm only saying I'm here if you need me, or if she needs me."

"First-time frozen-embryo single parent on her deathbed," Maryn joked. "I think we'll all have to wing it."

Andy had a terrible thought that the baby might not make it, that Maryn would die first. He needed this child to live, proof of his goodness. "How far along are you?"

"Twenty-six weeks." A light crossed Maryn's face. "We've passed the cutoff point—she's old enough now that doctors will use medical intervention to save her life. At twenty-eight weeks there's a ninety percent survival rate, and good odds she won't have long-term health problems or disabilities. That's in two weeks." The way she said it made Andy wonder if that was as far as she thought she'd go.

"And this fellow of yours, he's ready for a baby?"

Maryn's face shut down a little bit. He ignored the inner voice that wondered why she saw him as such an enemy.

"I'm glad you found someone." Andy meant it. He didn't feel jealousy, just relief. "I'm happy for you, Mar." As soon as he realized what he'd said, he was back to feeling dreadful.

"It's awful, isn't it?" Maryn read the play on his face. "I'm pregnant and about to get married, but I'm dying of cancer."

He couldn't speak.

"Andy, you have an irrepressible goodness. It gets deeply banked, and sometimes you get turned around, but it doesn't go out." She was absolving him. Maybe so he wouldn't change his mind about the documents or maybe she believed it. Andy didn't care. He clung to the words.

"I want you to have this." It was time. The velvet box was familiar to her, satin worn around the corners. He set it on a lump he thought was her knee.

Maryn didn't reach for it, so it sat awkwardly between them.

"I never hated a man enough to give him diamonds back." She did her best Zsa Zsa Gabor. They both knew it wasn't true.

"It's for our daughter." He couldn't help saying "our" even though it made Maryn uncomfortable. Andy's torso strained toward Maryn, willing her to pick it up, the way his whole body played video games. "You can decide what you want to tell her, but it was her grandmother's, then it was yours. Now it's hers."

Maryn still hesitated.

"Material things aren't important, but they can be if it helps," he urged her. "Everyone should have something small that has room inside to hold their history." Sometimes, Andy got it right.

Maryn touched the box that had nestled in her silky camisoles for years, and opened it. Her former engagement ring winked at her.

"Only a diamond could still be beautiful under fluorescent hospital lights," Maryn said.

"Not true," Andy said, looking at her. Andy wondered if there was something wrong with him that he wasn't more moved by her rounded belly, his daughter. But it was her face that captivated him. His mother had been right—she was born for this. Maryn had snatched this child from cancer twice, and would deliver her safely out of its reach, the last act of a mother.

"Thank you," Maryn said.

"I'll go." Andy couldn't deny it any longer. Maryn was tiring, and her gentleman friend was pacing outside. He dawdled to the door, loath to sever this connection.

"Thank you for coming, and for agreeing." He'd noticed she tried never to mention the baby, probably to keep him from getting wobbly and changing his mind.

"Thank you for giving me a chance to not be an abominable bastard to you," Andy was surprised to say.

She gave a raspy chuckle. "Stop beating yourself up. For a smashed mechanism, this relationship made some good things." Maryn was so kind.

"I could come again . . . if you needed me." *Let's pretend*.

"I have everything I need." *There wouldn't be more time*.

At the door, he turned, tears in his eyes. "At the risk of sounding completely self-absorbed, it was hard enough to walk out of your hospital room for the last time once. Doing it twice is unbearable."

Maryn blinked hard and opened her arms. He crossed the room in three steps and buried himself in her embrace.

Face in her neck, he said, "My deathbed promise to you is that I won't look after our daughter. I'm here if she wants me, but it's your decision."

Eyes and nose shiny, Maryn whispered, "Thank you."

As slowly as he could and still be moving, Andy pulled away, touched her cheek, backed to the door, and slipped out, never breaking eye contact. He would not see her again.

In the hallway, Andy saw her man. Wyatt was his name. He looked like Mr. Chips with Superman's jaw. He looked like someone who could be trusted more than Andy. They shook.

"I think I'm a better man, if you need me," Andy said. "I warn you, though, I'm uselessly manipulated by the women in my life."

The man pumped his hand firmly. "It's good to know I won't be the only man emasculated by an infant girl."

Andy moved from the cocooned hospital interior down the stairs and along the hall toward the bright sunlight of the building doors. As he stepped outside, he had one breathless moment at the wonder that he had created a daughter, but it passed. He was Just Andy. He was happy to be Summer's pool boy with a quiet, nonambitious counsel's job. They might have kids eventually, and he could tie ribbons in little Delilah's curls. Until then, he had dinner at Jay's tonight. There was softball Thursday. Maybe he'd start a local group to create more green spaces. You never knew, his daughter might like to play there.

Eva Signs Off

Maryn and Wyatt were married by the hospital chaplain without ceremony at Maryn's bedside. Her wedding dress was a white sheet, her flowers prohibited from the cancer ward. Eva served as their witness. She'd dismissed within seconds her instinct to make the occasion festive, perhaps with rubber glove balloons or aspirin tossed in lieu of rice. Artificial gaiety would have been grotesque. The couple recited the simple vows, shared a glass of champagne, and it was done. For a honeymoon, they met with their lawyer, executing a durable power of attorney and naming Wyatt guardian of the unborn child. The marriage was the most synchronized alignment of wishes Eva had witnessed between newlyweds.

Eva felt cheated to meet Maryn like this. She would have liked this woman, would have liked more time to spend with her. She said as much to Wyatt on the drive home.

"She's lovely."

"She's remarkable."

"Lately I've had appetizers of women like Maryn or Dimple Bledsoe that are the quality ingredients I'd like in my life. Instead, I'm surrounded by deep-fried chocolate-covered pork chops like Daisy Carmichael. I wish I'd known Maryn more." Eva was wistful.

"Me too."

"Are you in love with her?" Eva didn't know if that would be better or worse.

"No. Is that funny?" He stole a glance at Eva from the road.

"I don't know."

"I care deeply about Maryn, but only as a friend. I can't tell you why, but I'm not attracted to her intimately."

"Perhaps because of a certain biology teacher?" Eva teased.

"Mmm." Wyatt was noncommittal, but his color rose. Eva dropped it. It felt profane to talk about the living and loving that might happen after Maryn was dead, and even more wicked to be thinking it while she was alive.

"It makes me feel odd," she said.

"How do you mean?"

The contrast between Eva and Maryn was stark. "I'm robust, with health and fertility, and have no desire to use the equipment. Maryn is dying because she had the desire but not the tools. God should have done a better matching job."

"You're aren't feeling guilty again, are you? Please don't do that."

"Not guilty." Eva fidgeted. "Like I'm not a natural woman." She was glad Wyatt had to keep his eyes on the road.

"That seems to be going around. Maryn didn't feel like a natural woman because she's sterile, because she had to buy her pregnancy from a lab."

"But she has a mothering instinct."

Wyatt turned into BigLots so smoothly Eva didn't notice he was doing it until he parked the car and faced her.

"Just because you don't want to birth a baby doesn't mean the adults around you don't run the constant risk of low-cholesterol meals, warm scarves, and thoughtful tokens. You lecture about losing weight and wearing seat belts and always have a Band-Aid handy. You make me key lime pie on my birthday, and chicken soup when I'm sick. If I was sick on my birthday, I'd get key lime–flavored soup."

Eva blinked back tears.

"People are conditioned to think 'within the box,' commencing, to my chagrin, in the halls of my high school. Our culture tells us a male and a female must mate for life, breed one replica of each, and domesticate a dog. Scientifically, this is illogical. While we're biologically driven to perpetuate our species, if all females bred, the human race would render itself extinct through resource exhaustion. If you give God the credit, then he has employed two methods of population control—one is physical infertility, the other, mental disinclination. You are not deviant, Eva, you are an essential part of God's plan."

Eva was crying now because Wyatt was so kind. He looked straight ahead, giving her a form of privacy.

After a pause, he said, "You can always change your mind, of course, and have children. But that would mean God would have to go to plan B and release the locusts."

Eva gave a watery laugh. "What about Maryn?"

It was his turn to chuckle. "Even God can't win an argument with Maryn. He told her she couldn't have kids. She disagreed. Maryn wins. God realizes he made a mistake and calls it a day."

"Sounds like Chuck Norris." Eva accepted his handkerchief. She was never comfortable using them because she hated giving back a cloth full of boogers, but clean, white handkerchiefs were so very Wyatt and he insisted. "Chuck Norris destroyed the periodic table because he only recognizes the element of surprise."

Eva thanked her cousin without embarrassing him by squeezing his hand as she returned the handkerchief.

"A chemist walks into a pharmacy and asks the pharmacist, 'Do you have acetylsalicylic acid?'" Wyatt said. "'You mean aspirin?' says the pharmacist. 'That's it,' says the chemist. 'I can never remember that word.'"

Eva stared out the windshield at shopping carts strewn across the parking lot like a giant toddler's abandoned matchbox cars.

"You know what makes me feel better sometimes?" she said. "Anonymizing big-box shopping warehouses. I can buy stuff I don't need to create a reward system against the disturbances of life."

"Well, would you look at that," said Wyatt, turning off the car and getting out.

Eva returned to her office, spirits lifted after fulfilling her primal gender role as gatherer. By asserting her self-worth through the purchase of bath salts, and validating her entitlement to be pampered, she felt better about her place in the universe.

"I thought you swore off shopping," her assistant said.

"Money is congealed energy. Releasing it frees life's possibilities."

"I'm glad you're in a Zen state, because Daisy's on her way in."

Eva knew. "Can you prepare two copies of form T42? I'm going to include it with her *Cora* contract."

Her assistant did a double take. "You mean a C42."

"If it looks like chicken, tastes like chicken, and feels like chicken but Chuck Norris says it's beef, then it's beef," Eva said. "I want the T42."

Eva pulled up the CuteOverload website on her computer. It was good to have photos of kittens in baskets near at hand when meeting Daisy, like laying out the morning's aspirin on the bedside table before a night out.

The actress and her little dog burst in, a chaos of static and perfume.

"Tell me, tell me, tell me, tell me!"

"I have good news about *Cora*." Eva didn't feel the magic

she normally did telling an actress she'd won the breakout part. She felt leaden.

"I did it!" Daisy gave a joyous shriek and twirled Charlie around. No thank you or acknowledgment of Eva's input. "Mine, mine, mine! I'm Cora Aldridge! I'm the *it* girl! I'm the famousest!"

Eva found Daisy's glee irritating. She'd just as soon smack the smugness out of her current client as hug her. She wished Julian Wales luck.

"Oh, Charlie! It's all coming together!" Daisy beamed at her dog. "I'm going to have my own flavor at Millions of Milkshakes and my own star on Hollywood Boulevard and my own line of shoes." She was lost for a moment in happy contemplation. Eva felt a pang of guilt over her negative thoughts when Daisy kissed Charlie on the nose. Until she continued. "Guess I don't need you anymore, runt." She looked thoughtful. "Do you suppose there's a charity auction for celebrity-owned animal friends? I could donate him."

Eva was horrified. "You can't give away Charlie!"

"Why not?" Daisy asked. "I'll be busy with rehearsals. Then there'll be the promotional tour." Her future dazzled her inner eye.

"But he's your *dog*," Eva sputtered.

A tiny wrinkle appeared between Daisy's brows. It gave Eva a satisfying glimpse of a future young actress knocking Daisy off her perch.

"I don't need props anymore. I *am* the hot new actress." She considered Eva. "You could have him."

The implication was clear.

"I have an envelope here with your contract," Eva said. "Our lawyers have reviewed it. Take a look and let me know if you want to add anything."

"Like gumdrops in my trailer?"

"Like that. We'll finish negotiating the minor items, but I

don't expect opposition to reasonable requests. You'll need to sign the final." Along with the T42 form, terminating Eva's representation.

When Daisy bustled out the door—"Got to run . . . I should be at Château Marmont when the news breaks for maximum exposure. . . ." Eva knew it would be the last time she saw her in this office. She couldn't represent a client she found repugnant.

"Everyone can be replaced," Eva muttered. "Chuck Norris was originally cast in 24, but was replaced by the producers when he saved the day in eleven minutes."

To be fair, Eva didn't know whether it was Daisy she found distasteful, or the person Eva had become while representing her. In high school, Eva had worked at a Beaches 'N Cream ice cream stand. She was alone most of the day selling cones to surfers and handling fives, tens, and twenties unsupervised. Even the honest Eva had pocketed a twenty for gas one day. It was so easy. She'd quit when she'd been tempted a second time.

With *Cora*, Eva had teetered precariously close to shady dealings. She hadn't done anything illegal, but Eva hadn't been the person she wanted to wake up with. If you didn't feel joy in getting your client the part, what was the point? Maybe Eva *was* teetering on the downslope of a relevancy razor, vulnerable to hungry young agents. But she refused to believe she couldn't do her job with standards. If she couldn't, well, there were other satisfying jobs that wouldn't require her to be a double-dealing bitch. Or leave her man watching steak cool while she stalked a director into the men's room.

The assistants were whispering that Eva had insanely cut loose a future blockbuster. Eva doubted it. Daisy was her own worst obstacle, and Eva expected word of Julian's struggle would filter back to her in a few short weeks. Eva would get the laurels of being a queenmaker without being the queen's whipping post. The check was in the bank. The clients would come. As if on cue, her phone rang. She let it roll to her assistant. She had another call to make.

She looked at the kittens piled adorably in the basket, took a deep breath, then dialed Dimple Bledsoe.

"Dimple, it's Eva Lytton calling, from the Stop the Prop gala? I got your number from Freya Fosse."

Dimple sounded surprised. "That's a first. Freya crushes direct contact with her clients like Thor's hammer. How'd you breach the Norwegian force field?"

"I'm an agent, actually."

There was a pause. "Of course, I'm quite content with Freya." Dimple sounded uncomfortable.

Eva laughed. "Anyone would be a fool to leave Freya Fosse, and more of a fool to try to steal her clients. I'm not so masochistic." She cleared her throat. "Or maybe I am. I represent Daisy Carmichael."

Silence. "Daisy is a . . . she . . . she has . . . I liked *Best Day*."

Eva would have laughed if she weren't tied up in knots.

"There's no easy way to say this, so I'm just going to come out with it. I was the one who told Julian Wales you were pregnant, and I'm calling to apologize."

The silence this time was longer. Eva realized she was holding her breath.

"Why would you do that?" Dimple sounded hurt.

That was the million-dollar question. Eva sighed. "Not because I think it's acceptable. I was under enormous pressure on *Cora* when I saw you at Hope Clinic. It burst out of me when I was talking to Julian. I immediately wished I could undo it, but we all know about Pandora's box."

"Were you spying on me?"

"Oh, god no!" Eva scrambled. "I saw you at the clinic, and then you weren't drinking, and . . ."

"And it was convenient for you."

"I can only plead temporary insanity." Truly, Daisy would make anyone crazy. "This competitive monster ate the real Eva. I've killed it, but I'm sorry to say the damage was done. I'm calling to salvage what I can."

"I don't know what you want me to say."

"I'm sure you'll have a lot to say once you've had time to think it over."

There was a pause. "I wasn't, you know."

"You weren't?" Eva felt sick.

"No."

"I didn't think I could feel worse." Eva rubbed her forehead.

"You didn't have to tell me."

"Yes, I did. Because I like you, and because I didn't like me when I betrayed your privacy. It was playing dirty. You deserved an explanation and an apology."

Dimple didn't say anything.

Eva dug for the right words. "I don't expect that apologizing makes everything okay. Confessions like this do more to relieve the guilty than appease the victim, but I really want you to know that it was a terrible, selfish mistake, and I'm deeply sorry for it. I only hope I slammed the lid on Pandora's box fast enough to save Integrity."

Dimple sighed. "I appreciate your honesty. Lord knows, I'm no paragon."

"I'd like to make it up to you."

"That's not necessary. If I didn't expect to get my toes stepped on from time to time, I'd have chosen a more nurturing environment than Hollywood, like a jellyfish-infested shark tank."

"Be a shark. Join me for a casual lunch Tuesday with my old friend Kathryn Bigelow. I should mention that she's preoccupied with casting her movie *The Hammock*, sort of a *Steel Magnolias* thing, so that topic might dominate the conversation, but hopefully it wouldn't be too boring."

Pause. "Interesting."

"I fired Daisy."

Another pause. "You did?"

"I'd like to think I learn from my mistakes. Plus, she's a brat."

"She *is* a brat." Dimple warmed. "She's not nice to her own dog."

"You have no idea." Eva looked down at the featherweight knot. He looked back with limpid eyes.

"What kind of twenty-five-year-old carries a $10,000 bag? She should still have college loans!"

"In her original rider for *Rainy Season*, she demanded that every morning her path and the set be scented in advance with Daisy fragrance from Marc Jacobs, and six bouquets of fresh daisies be placed in her trailer every day. My line-item veto downgraded her to one bunch of fresh flowers on arrival."

"Julian deserves her," Dimple sniffed. "So where's this lunch?"

"The Belvedere at the Peninsula Hotel, Tuesday at noon. You'll like Kathryn. Maybe we can all nip into the spa for a massage after."

"All right," Dimple said. "I'll join you. But no more apologizing. The *Cora* adventure is done and we don't need to speak of it again." She paused. "And that massage might need to be prenatal after all."

"I can't wait to hear about it."

"Just so long as you keep it to yourself this time," Dimple rejoined.

After she hung up, Eva felt better, if not absolved. She'd come clean, and that got her closer to the person she wanted to be if she couldn't be the person who hadn't done it at all. And she had a date with Dimple to look forward to.

She stroked the Lilliputian creature in her lap. "Looks like it's you and me, Charlie." His tiny tongue flopped out of his mouth as he looked at her expectantly. Eva considered. "How do you feel about the name Chuck?"

Eva swore the dog smiled. She smiled back, reaching for the phone again. "Guess we'll find out if Sawyer meant what he said about getting a dog."

Dimple Gets the Part

The night lit up, an instant of bright clarity, then it went dark. I froze on the couch, shriveling into as small a form as I could manage. I was torn over the television. I thought it best to turn off all appliances in a storm, but I was watching the Directors Guild of America Awards show. It was like pouring pickle juice in my eye, but I couldn't help it. I wanted to catch a glimpse of Julian. And I wanted to see if the seat next to him was empty.

The camera panned the crowd and my heart thudded. Was that Daisy Carmichael's hair? I thought of the way I'd felt with Julian, savoring his limelight, and it made me sick to think of Daisy in that role. The camera panned away, and I berated myself. I should turn this shit off.

The storm answered for me. Everything lit up then pitched to black.

There was a distant boom, then it was as silent as the grave. The power was out. My blood started thrumming. Lightning must have hit the transformer. That meant it was close. Intellectually, I knew that the bolt that killed the power wasn't now going to stroll to my house and kill me, but my pulse spiked nonetheless. I slid from the sofa to the floor and scooted to the center of the room, touching nothing. I thought I'd try some yoga, but, as always, I couldn't think of a single pose without an instructor telling me what to do. I needed a glass of wine, but that was off limits. I focused on deep breaths.

I tried not to get weepy. It happened anyway. Why was I alone? Why wasn't there someone for me, someone who would fix the lights, stop the lightning, or at a minimum, hold my hand?

"Dimple, you'd better be pregnant, because if this isn't hormones, you're pathetic." I berated myself aloud. Julian was dead wrong. I could handle myself, and be a mother too.

A flash made me cringe. Take care of myself or not, being alone was exhausting at times. During lightning storms in particular.

Thunder rolled, and I braced myself, counting. I got to seven before the strike. Seven miles away, if you believed the old wives' tale. I tried to picture what was seven miles away. All that came to mind was a smoking crater.

A knock at the door. I nearly jumped out of my skin. I sat panting and the knock came again, more forcefully. I scrambled to my feet, feeling foolish for huddling on the floor, even though no one could have seen me. I hesitated a second before grasping the brass knob, praying lightning wouldn't strike while I was touching metal. I threw open the door, letting go quickly.

Julian filled the space, bald head slick, rain soaking his tuxedo.

"It was lightning," he said simply, and shouldered his way into the room.

I remained rooted. "Aren't you supposed to be at . . . ?"

"A dumb awards show? When I could be here, helping you breathe into a paper bag?" He wiped a rivulet from his forehead. "Can I have a towel?"

"You can't just—"

Lightning struck again and my bravado ended on a squeak. Julian took two steps and pulled me tight into his arms. I let him, standing in the dark surrounded by steel bands, damp slowly soaking through my blouse. I breathed in his smell. Moments passed.

The lights flickered and came back on. The TV emitted a burst of applause. The private embrace became awkward. I stepped away, shivering in my clammy T-shirt, and held my elbows. I had no idea what to say. I turned off the TV, and we looked at each other.

"It didn't pass," he said.

"What?"

"It didn't pass. Missing you."

"Julian . . ."

"Dimple, I screwed up. You threw me a strike ball and instead of taking a deep breath and swinging, I panicked. And said some pretty shitty things."

"They'll be hard to unhear."

"Remember when we talked about that moment when the uncensored self is visible? When I look at that in myself, what I see is a selfish guy who killed his dogs. I don't mean only that, I like myself plenty. I'm as decent as anyone else. I have a good moral code. But deep down, there's this crack at the core, with that shadow.

"You're being very hard on yourself."

"I have to be hard. I have to work harder and care more to make up for it. But there's so much to care about, the poisoning of our foods with additives, the continued existence of laugh tracks, ignorance, poverty—I'm defeated before I start."

It was eerie to hear him express the sentiments I'd shared with Eva.

"I pour everything into my movies, so that I can make other people care, and redeem myself by creating this great caring army. Collectively we can care enough."

I wanted very badly to touch him, but didn't move.

"With you, I'm naked. I feel more like the guy who killed his dogs than the guy who deserves you. "

"I'm not special," I said. "I'm not particularly bad or good. Stars, they're just like us."

"You're wrong. You have an energy that makes people want to be with you. That makes people want to watch your every move on TV. That makes me think about you all day." He stepped close. "I don't want to think about you all day. I want to be with you all day."

"I want that too," I whispered. "But . . ."

"I should be more clear. I will do what it takes to be with you. What you want, I want, because what I want is to make this work." He hesitated. "If you do." The vulnerability was stark.

"I do." I was fervent. "I just don't know if it's that simple. If love is enough."

"In the movies, heroically emerging in the night to 'save' you would be a satisfyingly cinematic ending, with an orchestral crescendo telling the audience how to feel. But this is real life, and we have real issues, so it's going to take more than that. It's going to take forty-eight to seventy-two hours of lockdown hashing through this. We're going to talk it out until we can talk no more, and I'm not leaving until we're done. But, first . . ."

He bent his head and covered my mouth in a kiss that was passionate and hungry. My return kiss was starving. I clung to the cords of his neck, pressing against him as if my mind could stop buzzing if my body joined Julian's. I poured all my longing into the kiss. It went on for a long time.

When at last he pulled away, he said, "Shall we do this thing?" The hopeful look on his face made my heart ache, but I was still conflicted.

"Of course I want to try, Julian, but what if we make a worse hash of it? It could hurt more than it already does. Maybe we should cut our losses."

"I think I've changed, Dimple. I'm begging you for a chance. If I can't convince you this weekend that I'm less of a bullheaded dunce, a kiss on the forehead and I'll be gone." He cupped my face with his hands, eyes intense. "Please. Two days."

I stared at his beautiful face. Of course I was going to say yes, if for nothing more than two days together.

I nodded.

He kissed me hard, then clapped his hands. "We'll need sustenance. Do you want pizza or Chinese?"

And that's how it went. We fought for two hours, refused to speak for two hours, talked for two hours, sat in silence for two hours, fought some more, talked some more, all weekend long. After Mao's Chinese, the fights got shorter. After Abbot's Pizza, the silences were more comfortable. After Fromin's breakfast, the talk gained future tense. After Le Petit Greek, we kissed. After we slept the second time, I woke up first.

From my vantage cradled against him, I watched the light play on the planes of his face. His eyes opened, immediately alert and bright, coming right to mine. We looked at each other.

"I love you," he said.

"I love you too," I said.

He twisted my hair in his hand and inhaled its scent.

"Now that you're not going to kick me out, maybe you can help me. I've been thinking about this PSA inspired by a passionate woman. It will terrorize voters with the chilling effect of Prop 11 on women just like you. I need a worthy actress."

"You're an activist now?"

"I can't exist exclusively on the big screen."

"I though small acts were a waste of time."

"Puny is in the eye of the beholder. My PSA will be epic. Better than *Lawrence of Arabia*. More camels too."

"Why now?"

He looked in my eyes. "Someone special explained the importance of the selfless life."

"And you want kids too?" I was hesitant. It was a lot of transformation.

"Only with you."

"What if I'm pregnant?"

"I hope she has your eyes."

"You don't care if you're not the father?"

"Not in the least."

"You'd try again, if I'm not pregnant?"

"I would."

The simplicity of his answers hit me the most. I started to cry. He pulled me tight. "Dimple, please trust me. I want to buy our family pre-baked oatmeal cookies for the rest of my life. It turns out it was there all along. I only needed to figure it out."

"I like lots of raisins in them." I was sobbing now, with relief, joy, probably hormones.

"You'll be my raisin d'être," he said before possessing my mouth and body.

"You have a serious case of the *BABIES*," Dr. Singh said. "I'd say about six weeks." Her words nearly made me pee my full bladder. I was pregnant. *Pregnant*. I let the word roll around my mouth like a butterscotch candy. She turned the ultrasound monitor so Julian and I could see.

"Wow. There he is!" I pointed to the dark sac. I was astonished by how big and clear it was, the size of a quarter already.

"There *she* is," Julian corrected. "What's that?" He pointed to another dark spot on the screen.

"There *they* are," Dr. Singh corrected.

My mouth dropped open.

"Twins?" I croaked.

"Growing like a weed in your uterus."

"Twins," Julian repeated. We looked at each other. I had no idea how to react. *Pregnant. Twins.*

"You're going to have to stop buying me bunny books," I said, at last. "We need the room."

"Can we name one of them Keaton?" Julian asked.

"Anything but Agnis," I said for now, knowing that never, ever would my children be named after a director. Directors were *such* a pain in the ass.

Wyatt Finds Joy

Maryn was slipping away.

"We can't wait any longer," Dr. Singh said to Wyatt.

"It's over two months early," he protested. They couldn't come this far and lose that baby.

"Wyatt, I fear the alternative would be delivering the baby when Maryn can no longer support it."

"You mean when she's dead."

Dr. Singh nodded. "Her body is depleted. The detriment to Maryn from prolonging gestation is exponentially greater than any benefit to the child. Steroids have advanced her lung development enough that survival is likely. The baby is healthy now, but malnutrition is imminent. Maryn's body needs to conserve energy, and its ability to use food and fluids properly is decreasing."

Wyatt had never been so lost. How could he trade Maryn for the baby? The cost of this child was high.

Dr. Singh continued. "Weighing the alternatives, I believe it's best to deliver the child to the care of the NICU, and support Maryn with palliative treatment to prolong her time with the child in some comfort."

Maryn would want time with her daughter. "I'll talk to her."

Dr Singh nodded. "I'd like to do the C-section in the morning."

Wyatt slipped into Maryn's room. She was sleeping, as she often was now. He sat next to her bed.

When Maryn stirred, Wyatt allowed her time. Her changed

metabolism often left her confused. She blinked a few times, and smiled when she saw him.

"How're you doing?" He spoke quietly, which was a challenge because he wanted to shout over the howling banshees inside him.

She worked her mouth.

"Ice chips?" At her nod, he filled a cup from the pitcher. She pressed a button, and the bed angled her into a sitting position.

"Thanks," she croaked past the ice chips.

It was grotesque, the fecund health of her swollen abdomen against the wasted pallor of her frame. Her face too was swollen from the steroids. It was hard not to think of the baby as a parasite destroying its host. Wyatt had to remember the cancer was the enemy. The baby was the prize.

"Feel up for a talk?"

Maryn looked wary. "I'm only thirty weeks. I won't do anything until thirty-two weeks." She kept pushing the dates.

Wyatt looked at his hands. He thought about Dr. Singh's words.

"In chemistry, for certain potions to work, the ingredients have to be perfectly measured. A pipette too much or too little, and nothing will happen. If you get it just right, you create a miraculous reaction."

Maryn listened.

"Your energy is declining. Your body is—" He paused. "Shutting down. The baby is increasing in strength. You have intersected at the point where the elements are perfectly measured. If you deliver tomorrow, you will both come out of it with enough health and time for the miracle of overlap. If you don't, that reaction may not occur."

Maryn twisted the blanket. "What about her lungs?" she whispered.

"Dr. Singh believes the steroids have matured them sufficiently. With treatment in the NICU she should be fine. It won't be pretty at first, with feeding and breathing tubes, but it's reasonable to believe that if you take care of yourself, there would be . . . some time."

"And me?" She didn't look at him.

"Palliative care."

"And you?"

Wyatt's eyes flew to hers. "Me?"

"I don't want to leave you with a sick child."

"Oh for god's sake, Maryn! If you have to think like that, then don't leave me at all, but don't be ridiculous. The baby isn't a burden, it's a joy." Wyatt ignored his inner demon whispering, *At what cost?*

"You won't resent her, will you?" She spoke his darkest fear.

As he looked at her, the wailing inside quieted and he knew his answer. "It's hard not to feel conflicted, because I'm here with you and I don't want you to die. But when the baby is here, she'll be you. If anything, I'm going to love her too fiercely."

"I guess we're having a baby in the morning." Maryn rested her hand on her belly, looking lost, as if unsure of her existence once it was gone.

Wyatt covered her hand with his. "It'll be more real when she's here," he reassured her. A thought occurred to him. "You need to pick out a name."

"No," Maryn corrected. "You need to pick out a name."

"I'll name her after you," said Wyatt.

"No!" Maryn refused. "Don't make this girl a walking sarcophagus."

"Okay then." There was a name. It was the name that slipped to Wyatt's lips whenever he thought of the baby. "Joy. Joy Nydia."

"Joy," Maryn repeated, savoring it. "It's perfect. What does Nydia mean?"

"Nydia was a blind flower seller who saved her beloved at the cost of her own life."

Maryn frowned. "Wyatt . . ."

"That one's for me," he said. "She's saving me."

Maryn considered. "All right then." She stroked her bump. "See you tomorrow, Joy Nydia."

Wyatt helped Maryn get ready in the morning. He tucked her hair into a cap. He washed her face. He put her watch and rings in a bag. Here's what he wanted to put in the bag: his grief, and hers. His guilt. Her pain. The cold she couldn't shake. The baby's loss. The fear. The futility. The cancer. He couldn't do that, but he could walk beside the gurney all the way to the door. He could say, "I'll be waiting when you wake up." He could sit.

It was jarring when the doctor emerged fifteen minutes later to report that the procedure had gone fine. It seemed an insignificant amount of time for the culminating event of three people's existence.

"Maryn was under general anesthetic because of her weakened condition, so she'll be in recovery for several hours. The baby is healthy, if diminutive, at 3.7 pounds and 14 inches long."

"Can I see her?"

"I can take you now."

Wyatt had never seen anything so small and marvelous in his life. Watching her in the enclosed incubator, tubes invading her tiny nose, he suffered ecstasy and pain simultaneously. It left him heaving for air like an imbecile.

Dr. Singh patted him on the back.

"That monitor measures her heart and her oxygen levels. The tube down her nose is for food, the one down her throat is for oxygen. I expect that one will come out soon. The ankle band is the baby lojack to make sure she doesn't sneak off to have a smoke. She's responding well. Congratulations, Wyatt."

"And Maryn?" He tore his eyes from Joy to look at Dr. Singh.

A shadow crossed her face. "Dr. Gavin thinks she might have a month, maybe two."

Wyatt took a leave of absence from school and visited his two ladies every day. He scrubbed his hands raw for them. Eva came and brought little pink dresses for one and hand cream for the other. For Wyatt, she brought boneless chicken sandwiches.

Wyatt would go see Joy in the NICU day and night, regardless of visiting time, spending hours there during Maryn's long naps, gazing hungrily at his daughter, reading to her, letting her grasp his Goliath finger in her tiny hand. He found himself using the word "daughter" unnecessarily. Buying coffee, a call to Eva, greeting the charge nurse, were all opportunities to say it. *Daughter.*

He would bring back reports to Maryn.

On day two, "The hair on Joy! She's got a head of red curls like Annie."

On day three, "They took out the breathing tube, and she had something to say about that. She's got lungs!"

On day four, "She's chillin' like a Hilton under the sunlamp." They were treating her jaundice with phototherapy. "She's got a bright purple eye cover."

On day five, "She has a little stork bite birthmark on her elbow."

On day six, "You hang in there," he said. "She's doing great. She'll be able to come to you soon."

After a week, Maryn insisted on visiting Joy. Wyatt rolled her to the NICU in a wheelchair. No one cautioned about the risk of infection in traveling through the halls. What would be the point? Her comfort was their only concern now.

When she saw her daughter for the first time, Maryn went still. She stared. Wyatt waited.

"She's a marvel," Maryn whispered at last. "Look at that ear." Her finger traced whorls on the plastic bassinet.

"She likes to sleep with her fist by her cheek, like a miniature Rodin." Wyatt found it enchanting.

"She's flawless." Tears streamed down Maryn's face. Wyatt left her alone.

After fifteen days, Wyatt gave Joy a bath in a teeny plastic tub, and changed the tiniest diaper ever before wrapping her in blankets. He swaddled carefully because she couldn't control her own temperature. He didn't fear her fragility. If anything, he was in awe of the little mongoose. Her will was tenacious.

After twenty-one days, the feeding tube came out. They let Joy spend a few hours every day in Maryn's room. They positioned the bassinet next to her bed, and Maryn spent the time with her hand encircling a tiny wrist, withdrawing only when she feared spasms might cause her to harm the child.

The spasms came more often.

"Please take some morphine," Wyatt begged. He couldn't bear the grey waves that compressed Maryn's face. She'd refused palliative pain management.

"I only have a little time with her. I don't want to be blurry." She grimaced. "It's not that bad," she lied.

Wyatt turned to fuss with something on the windowsill. He didn't know what his hands touched, but it didn't matter. He had to hide his burning eyes from Maryn. As one became more robust, the other faded. As consumed as he was with his daughter, Wyatt's focus was Maryn first, his absorption with Joy a vehicle to bring her to Maryn.

One day, she woke when Wyatt returned from visiting Joy.

"Hi," she said.

"Hi," he smiled back.

She rested her hand on her abdomen, eyes widening. Wyatt feared she was in pain, but she laughed. "I felt the baby kick!" She looked at him excitedly.

All the blood left his body. He called Dr. Gavin, in a panic.

"You may need to prepare yourself, Wyatt," was all the man could offer.

The next day, Maryn slept all day. The nurses had to change the bed linens twice. Wyatt didn't leave that night, curling up in the corner chair.

When she woke in the morning, she demanded, "Where's Joy? Did she eat well?" It was a perfectly normal day.

Maryn herself didn't eat or drink. The hand that reached for her daughter's tiny fingers was bluish, her skin cool to the touch.

When rattling settled into the breathing that alternated between rapid and slow, Maryn talked.

"She's beautiful."

"She looks like you," Wyatt agreed.

"There's money . . ."

"Stop," Wyatt commanded.

" . . . for the funeral," Maryn persisted. "I wrote a check so it isn't . . . held in probate. And for Joy. Everything goes to you . . . both."

"You've given us the richest gift imaginable." Wyatt's eyes filled. "I wish I'd met you earlier."

"Everything . . . I've given you is Dumbo's feather. You don't . . . need it . . . to fly."

Wyatt's throat closed completely. Maryn grasped his hand. "Cancer patients talk about a phantom future . . . like amputees have a phantom limb. You see future jobs and trips and loves that . . . will never happen. I was lucky . . . in a way . . . to have it twice. Cancer freed me . . . to do the things I should've been doing all along. I did . . . what I needed to do . . . I don't see a phantom future . . . I see Joy . . . with you."

Wyatt could think of a hundred movies with gripping scenes where a beloved character was clinging to life in a precarious situation, and others encouraged them to "hang on" and "don't let go."

This wasn't that scene.

"You can trust me," was his way of saying it was okay to go.

Maryn couldn't speak or move after that day, but she was there. Wyatt sat by her bedside, quietly talking. He spoke about Joy's progress. He spoke about plans he had. He told her about the ridiculously premature pink wagon he couldn't resist. At the end, he and Joy were both there. He tucked the little bundle into the crook of Maryn's arm, and sat holding her hand.

As her rattling breath stilled, he kissed her forehead and whispered, "Check in on us, sometimes." And she was gone.

Wyatt asked a nurse to take Joy, and left the hospital. He was surprised to find it was dark outside. He walked away from the lights of the building and looked up at the stars. There were so, so many against the inky sky. It was incomprehensible that there were that many people in the world too. India had a billion. Los Angeles had four million. All those lives teeming on the planet. How could the absence of one make it seem so empty?

He sank to his knees and let the sobs come, a loosely jointed penitent wracked with grief. Every element of his body was a conduit for the pain—his back arched, tears ran from his eyes, moans raked his throat, sobs burned his lungs. He gave up to the grief and rage and unfairness until he was spent. He folded into himself and cool emptiness replaced raw bereavement. He hunched there a long time, breathing in and out.

Then he rose and brushed off his knees. He wiped his face and cleaned his glasses with a crisp white handkerchief. He straightened his shirt and tweed jacket. He looked up at the stars again, so, so many against an inky sky. It seemed impossible that just one could be enough, but he knew it could. And he went back inside the hospital to take care of his daughter.

Dimple Goes to Lunch, Again

I banged on the bathroom door as I passed.

"Hurry up, or we'll be late."

Thank god there were two bathrooms or I'd have peed in the yard. The twins loved pushing on my pillowy bladder.

Back in the kitchen, I was putting a bottle of champagne, a bottle of sparkling cider (for me), my quiche, and some of my mother's lingonberry dumplings into a basket when Julian walked in.

"How can a bald man spend so much time in the powder room?" I asked.

"Staying that way." He rubbed his freshly shaved scalp. He reached to snag a *piragi* and I smacked his hand.

"You're not in my *mamu*'s house." My mother could not have loved Julian more if he was Latvian. The fawning was ridiculous. "Are you ready?"

"You say that as if you haven't been dithering for an hour."

"Nothing fits. I hate it when things don't fit right." The twins had popped early. I was lucky there'd been no delays filming *Margot's Chair*. Another two weeks and I'd have spent every shot *behind* the chair.

"Where are we going?" He hefted the basket off the counter.

"To brunch with Eva."

"You two are as thick as thieves."

"I like her."

"I don't," he grunted.

I laughed. "You can't blame Eva for having to work with Daisy. You picked her, over some fine competition too."

"Yes, I can too blame Eva." He scowled. "It was Daisy or never pee in private again."

Daisy was a source of delight for me, and a sore subject for Julian. He was miserable working with her on *Cora*. I brought her up whenever I could. Love didn't make you pure.

"If we're going to brunch, why are we bringing the food?"

"We're going to her cousin's house. He has a three-month-old little girl, and we're celebrating her homecoming from the hospital."

"Is she sick?" Julian was concerned. "We don't want you to catch anything." Julian had taken to using "we," referring to himself and the twins. It was cute, but it made it three against one.

"She's fine. She was a preemie and had to stay in the NICU for a bit."

"Where's the mother?"

"She was the woman from the Prop 11 thing, Maryn Windsor. She died."

Julian stopped walking. He laid a hand on my belly and looked into my eyes. "I couldn't bear it," he said.

I pressed a hand to his cheek before we continued walking to the car. I always paused for the moments now.

We arrived at a neat bungalow in western Santa Monica.

"It's so homey," I said to Julian as Eva let us in, all smiles.

"God, look at you!" She gave me a squeeze. "Soon I won't be able to reach around you."

"Let's hope your arms stop shrinking."

"What's that?" demanded Julian.

A tiny thing with enormous eyes was scampering around Eva's feet.

"That's Chuck," Eva said. "This is Sawyer." She introduced

a tall, shaggy man. He lived up to his hype. I could see why Eva was hooked.

"And this is my cousin Wyatt." She introduced a steady man with a gentle smile and bags under his eyes. He was holding a pink bundle.

"I'm looking at my future and it looks worn out," I said.

"Worth every exhausting moment." Wyatt shook my hand. To Julian he said, "We've met."

"I called you for information about discipline in public schools for *Remedial Learning*," Julian remembered. "You were incredibly forthcoming. I'm in awe of your job."

"I'm in awe of twins." Wyatt laughed.

"I'm in awe of how small this town is," said Eva.

"Like a giant braid," I said. "I knew Maryn, briefly. I'm sorry for your loss."

"Thank you," Wyatt said. "She told me what you did. I think she'd be tickled that we've become acquainted."

"And this little urchin is Joy." Eva touched the bundle. "Joy, meet your future playgroup." She gestured at my belly. A tiny gnome peeked from the blankets, wide eyes dark, a tuft of red hair sticking up like Cindy Lou Who. We all cooed.

"Are those tears?" asked Eva.

"Hormones." I wiped my eyes.

"I think she was asking Julian." Sawyer was laughing.

Julian wiped his eyes too. "Thanks a lot, man."

"We're all girlie men here," Wyatt said cheerfully. "I have an apron. Now, let's eat. I made a breakfast cobbler in the Crock-Pot and I don't want it to get dry."

"Who's got two thumbs and is starving?" Sawyer asked. "This guy!"

"Is this everyone?" Eva asked Wyatt.

"Linda might come later." The man blushed. "But she said not to wait."

"Let's eat!" Eva led the way to an overladen table.

"What are you working on now, Julian?" Wyatt asked as we passed plates.

Julian frowned, and Eva giggled. "It's not funny," he said.

"No take backs," she said.

"Defeating Proposition 11 was easier than getting Daisy to focus." Julian groaned.

"All that drama, and Prop 11 limped off with but a whimper," Wyatt mused. "Once the media stopped, it shriveled up and went away."

"Are you suggesting it wasn't vanquished by one worthy PSA?" Julian said.

"He's catering to your obvious modesty," I said.

"I'm glad the election's over. The commercials were driving me crazy. How could there be so many, with only one candidate?" Sawyer said.

"I think she'll do a good job," I said. "I feel like she means what she says. With kids coming, I suddenly care about local politics."

"When are you due?" Wyatt asked.

"It's ridiculous." I rolled my eyes. "April first."

"I try not to think about it too hard," Julian said.

"Chuck Norris's calendar goes from March thirty-first to April second," said Eva. "No one fools Chuck Norris."

"Do you know what you're having?" Sawyer asked.

"A boy and a girl."

"A best friend and a boyfriend for Joy!" Eva clapped. "We can take the girls shopping!"

"Run," Wyatt warned Julian.

He took my hand. "I'm stuck to this one."

"Have you got names picked out?" Sawyer asked.

"Yes." "No." Julian and I spoke in unison. I shook my head at Eva behind his back. There was no way I was naming my son Keaton or Capra or whatever. I might compromise on Nora. Lady director names were better.

"Some days Daddy's winning, some days he isn't." Julian grimaced at Sawyer. It was remarkable how seamlessly Julian had become the father. Even I forgot the twins weren't his. Weren't *biologically* his, I corrected myself. Only a few confidants knew the truth. We'd decided to name Julian as the father and be done with it.

"We're going to Thailand for a month." Eva looked at Sawyer. "We made a pact to take off four consecutive weeks every year, and enjoy our retirement in chunks while we're still young enough to appreciate it. We're kicking off with Thailand in the spring."

"I'm enrolling her in massage school." Sawyer winked.

"You loved Thailand, didn't you, crumpet?" Julian turned to me.

"Mmm." No need to go into details.

"You must go to the Elephant Nature Park north of Chiang Mai," Julian urged. "I want to take the kids when they're old enough."

"In his mind 'born' is old enough," I teased.

"Born is something," Wyatt spoke, gaze on Joy.

"A toast," Eva said. "To babies and bucket lists! To Joy, Chuck, Thing 1 and Thing 2, and Thailand!"

"Hear, hear!" We clinked glasses, and Chuck twirled in circles, tiny tongue flopping.

"To family," Wyatt said quietly, "whatever it may look like."

"I think it looks a lot like this," Julian said, sliding an arm around my back. It fit just right.

About the author

About the book

Read on

Insights,
Interviews
& More . . .

Meet Kerry Reichs

Keith D. Arnold

KERRY REICHS, a graduate of Duke
University School of Law and Stanford
Institute of Public Policy, practiced law
in Washington, D.C. She is the author of
The Best Day of Someone Else's Life and
Leaving Unknown. ∾

Q&A with the Author

What inspired you to write What You Wish For?

I heard a story once about a man who was forty before he stopped being furious about losing his father in his youth. He explained that while he'd never say his father's death was a good thing, he'd had many opportunities and relationships that he would not otherwise have had. Still, he failed to appreciate them, always mourning the family he didn't have. He regretted wasting years in therapy and wished he'd embraced his own life.

As a single mother, I believe we do a disservice to our children by suggesting that there is an "ideal" family. Most families no longer equate to a male-female heterosexual couple having children without medical assistance. People adopt. People rely on IVF, donor eggs, and surrogates. Single parents are raising children. Same-sex couples are raising children. Biracial couples are raising children. The modern family has become an American melting pot. I hope that through my characters' stories, I can help shake loose some of the rigid judgments about what makes a family healthy. The less time kids spend mourning the phantom family, or the "real parents" they don't have, the more they can thrive in environments that may be as nurturing and loving as they are unconventional.

My characters are all alike. Each ▶

feels deviant in some way, unnatural. Yet they are unified in their certainty about family. It is only society that inflicts self-doubt. I hope that as my son grows, these strictures are loosened, and "different" families such as ours will be accepted as part of the norm.

Which character do you relate to the most?

The expected answer is Dimple, since I wrestled with the same difficult decision to become a single mother by choice. But in reality, it's Wyatt. I became pregnant while writing this book, and my locus shifted from the threat of childlessness hanging over Dimple to the anxiety Wyatt felt facing down single parenthood. His experience in Target was my experience. I agonized over my registry, convinced that if I selected the wrong bottle my child would never go to college and it would be my fault. I had to work hard to do justice to the starkness of Dimple's fear from the smugness of pregnancy. There were fears, of course, as every mother knows, but nothing like the urgent dread of being near forty and childless. It was important for me to get Dimple's feelings right, because there are legions of women out there who have otherwise completely fulfilling lives but for the pressure of their biological clocks. What was most relatable about Dimple was the fact that other than not having children, she was successful and content.

How did you come up with the idea for Proposition 11?

I'm inspired by real-life stories, but I don't draw from the front-page headlines. I draw from the stories buried on page eight. I'm fascinated by what will *become* the front-page headlines. I started writing *What You Wish For* in 2009, after reading an article about a London cancer survivor suing her ex-boyfriend for the right to use their frozen embryos. The woman lost her challenge and the story faded, but I didn't stop thinking about it.

As a lawyer, I'm fascinated by issues of medical-legal ethics. I started researching the legal status of embryos, particularly in utero adoptions, the right to use or destroy contested embryos, and the legal status of the embryo itself. What I discovered was a murky grey. Simultaneously, the Proposition 8 controversy had just ripped California in two, so I started wondering how people would make highly personal decisions about fertility under the umbrella of a similarly controversial proposition that awarded rights to embryos.

My musings were prescient, it seems. When I started writing this book, only Georgia had made page eight with an initiative such as the one I imagined. As of this writing, multiple states have hotly contested "personhood" ballot initiatives that would grant embryos the full rights of humans from the moment of ▶

conception. This type of legislation is part of the national conversation of the presidential election.

My interest goes beyond the law. As a person, I'm inspired by human behavior. I couldn't stop wondering what motivated the London woman's ex-boyfriend, and marveling how most often the ones we love have the capacity to hurt us the most. There are novels and novels to be written there, and this one just scratches the surface.

What was the most difficult part of writing this book?

Trapeze school! I took trapeze lessons to be able to write accurately about the experience. Let me tell you, it was not as fun as driving across country to research my last book, *Leaving Unknown*! I was not playing around when I described the crushing tightness of the safety harness or the futility of trying to fight gravity. I do remain convinced that for some people it is actually impossible to do those moves. I do *not* have a natural aptitude for trapeze. Stand-up comedy, on the other hand . . .

A multiple-person point of view was a departure for you. How was it different?

I often listen to music when I write, and with *What You Wish For* my soundtrack was eclectic because each character's playlist was so different. Dimple listens to Jeff Buckley, Adele, Regina Spektor,

Cathy Davey, Turin Brakes, Vampire Weekend, Maroon 5, Kings of Leon, and Carrie Underwood. Wyatt likes Belle and Sebastian, Nanci Griffith, Dr. Hook, Tom Waits, the Decembrists, and Lady Antebellum. Eva's into the National, They Promised Us Jetpacks, Arcade Fire, New Pornographers, Neutral Milk Hotel, Snow Patrol, and Pink. And Maryn liked the Sundays, Chris Isaak, Nina Simone, Tegan and Sara, the Shins, Nick Drake, Amy Winehouse, and Paula Cole. Andy just listens to whatever Summer has on.

The diversity in music was one of many things I liked about the multiple-person point of view. I enjoyed the characters being occasionally unlikeable and flawed from their own eyes. It allowed me to tackle a diverse range of highly personal stories. It was a departure from my first-person point of view in *The Best Day of Someone Else's Life* and *Leaving Unknown*. I'm not sure what I'll do next.

How does being a mom affect you as a writer?

Dimple had it right when she described being "too busy looking for a lost tennis shoe while the dog needs a walk, and I've got pages to memorize but I'm going on a picnic instead." I have three professions: writer, mother, house administrator. The only way to make it work is not to strive for perfection. I focus on the big stuff, recognizing ▶

that something will have to slide. When my son comes in for a hug or to bang on my computer keys, I stop and enjoy the moment. On a sunny day, we might walk to the zoo. Then it's a late night writing for mom to recoup the time. The focus isn't as laser, and I have to backspace over lots of zxxksflsdjkghls;dnv/fbgkl sg^nwklFH'qrgj from my "helper," but when I consider that I grew a human brain from scratch in nine months, I figure the novel will come, even with interruptions.

Considering Dimple had twins, it's hard to imagine how she won a Best Supporting Actress Academy Award for *The Hammock* while Beatrice and Milo were in their terrible twos. She had Julian, I guess. I have effective baby gates. The only flaw is the operator, who continually opens them whenever she hears "mama"! Wyatt made the smart decision when Joy was five to turn down a run for School Board President, despite the hard press from Channel 9 KCAL news anchor and City Council President Summer Knox (a very persuasive politician). He would have missed the day-to-day interaction with his students, and he would have missed too many of Joy's riding classes for administrative meetings. Joy is becoming an impressive junior horsewoman—winning her first competition at age six. She can't wait to be big enough to compete in eventing, and Wyatt doesn't want to miss a thing.

Does being a mother make me a less successful professional? Sure it does. But it's a trade I'll take. You can't really have it all, where you succeed perfectly in every category, but you can have more than enough.

What piece of advice would you give your readers?

I think an excerpt of Maryn's letter to Joy sums it up beautifully:

> I had a second chance to do everything I wanted, but that is rare. Never wait to be asked twice to dance. Dance. Laugh often. Be noisy. Hug your father. Do something every day that doesn't make rational sense. Be joyful, though you have considered all the facts. Love freely, and love those who don't deserve it. Do a selfless thing each day. Every day won't be the best day in your life, but that's okay. If someone were to tell you the world would end tomorrow, plant a tree. Most of all, don't be afraid of risk. If you open yourself to opportunities, fortuities will land on your shoulder like birds. The only thing that holds you back in life is yourself. I give you permission. Go for it. ∾

More from Kerry Reichs

FOR MORE BOOKS by Kerry Reichs
check out

THE BEST DAY OF SOMEONE ELSE'S LIFE

Despite being cursed with a boy's name, Kevin "Vi" Connelly is seriously female and a committed romantic. The affliction hit at the tender age of six when she was handed a basket of flower petals and ensnared by the "marry-tale." The thrill, the attention, the big white dress—it's the Best Day of Your Life, and it's seriously addictive. But at twenty-seven, with a closetful of pricey bridesmaid dresses she'll never wear again, a trunkful of embarrassing memories, and an empty bank account from paying for it all, the illusion of matrimony as the Answer to Everything begins to fray. As her friends' choices don't provide answers, and her family confuses her more, Vi faces off against her eminently untrustworthy boyfriend and the veracity of the BDOYL.

Eleven weddings in eighteen months would send any sane woman either over the edge or scurrying for the altar. But as reality separates from illusion, Vi learns that letting go of someone else's story to write your own may be harder than buying the myth, but just might help her make the right choices for herself.

LEAVING UNKNOWN

Sweet Lips, Tennessee . . . Toad Suck, Arkansas . . . Okay, Oklahoma . . . Truth or Consequences, New Mexico . . . Maeve Connelly's epic road trip is taking her through every colorfully named tiny town in America on her way to the far less imaginatively named Los Angeles, California. With her foulmouthed cockatiel, Oliver, her only companion, Maeve's heading way off the beaten track with little money and a load of painful baggage she wants to leave behind. But when her beloved rattletrap, "Elsie," breaks down outside Unknown, Arizona, she finds herself taking a much longer rest stop than she anticipated.

The only mechanic in the vicinity is on an indefinite walkabout, so Maeve's in for the long haul—and she'll need to find two jobs to pay for Elsie's eventual repair. But she's starting to feel strangely at home among the quirky denizens of Unknown—especially around her new bookstore owner boss—so Maeve is seriously considering saying good-bye to Hollywood for good . . . if she can keep her past troubles from coming to light.